Slaughter, Frank G.
(Frank Gill), 1908–

Doctors at risk

APR 1 8 1983

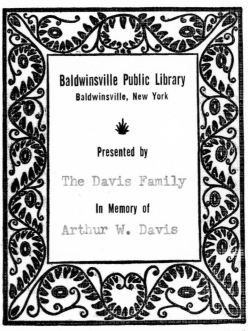

DOCTORS AT RISK

BOOKS BY FRANK G. SLAUGHTER

Doctors at Risk
Doctor's Daughters
Gospel Fever
The Passionate Rebel
Devil's Gamble
Plague Ship
Stonewall Brigade
Women in White
Convention, M.D.
Code Five
Countdown
Surgeon's Choice
The Sins of Herod
Doctors' Wives
God's Warrior
Surgeon, U.S.A.
Constantine
The Purple Quest
A Savage Place
Upon This Rock
Tomorrow's Miracle
David: Warrior and King
The Curse of Jezebel
Epidemic!
Pilgrims in Paradise
The Land and the Promise
Lorena
The Crown and the Cross

The Thorn of Arimathea
Daybreak
The Mapmaker
Sword and Scalpel
The Scarlet Cord
Flight from Natchez
The Healer
Apalachee Gold
The Song of Ruth
Storm Haven
The Galileans
East Side General
Fort Everglades
The Road to Bithynia
The Stubborn Heart
Immortal Magyar
Divine Mistress
Sangaree
Medicine for Moderns
The Golden Isle
The New Science of Surgery
In a Dark Garden
A Touch of Glory
Battle Surgeon
Air Surgeon
Spencer Brade, M.D.
That None Should Die
The Warrior

UNDER THE NAME C. V. TERRY

Buccaneer Surgeon
The Deadly Lady of Madagascar

Darien Venture
The Golden Ones

Doctors at Risk

Frank G. Slaughter

DOUBLEDAY & COMPANY, INC.
Garden City, New York   1983

The characters and situations in this
novel are fictitious. It is coincidental
if any name used—except persons in the
news, easily recognizable as such—is that
of a living person.

Library of Congress Cataloging in Publication Data

Slaughter, Frank G. (Frank Gill), 1908–
  Doctors at risk.

  I. Title.
PS3537.L38D58   1983   813'.52
ISBN *0-385-17876-X*
Library of Congress Catalog Card Number 81–43921
Copyright © 1983 by Frank G. Slaughter

CONTENTS

There are men and classes of men that stand above the common herd: the soldier, the sailor, and the shepherd not infrequently; the artist rarely; rarelier still, the clergyman; the physician almost as a rule. . . . Generosity he has, such as is possible to those who practice an art, never to those who drive a trade; discretion, tested by a thousand embarrassments; and what are more important, Herculean cheerfulness and courage.

ROBERT LOUIS STEVENSON
Dedication to *Underwoods*

Book One

Lakeview

I

The biennial meeting of the Lakeview Medical and Surgical Association was winding down to a close. *And not too soon,* Mark Harrison thought as he waited for the final speaker to end his presentation on: "More Bypass to Save Lives—Not Less."

As usual, the meeting was being held in the main auditorium of Lakeview Hospital and Medical School in Baltimore, Maryland. By courtesy of the Association—members of which had to be either alumni of the medical school or graduates of the hospital's training program of residencies and fellowships—the hospital and medical school staff were entitled to free drinks at the bar at the end of each session. When the paper finally ended, there was a concerted rush but, having taken a seat in the back row when he'd come in earlier that afternoon, Mark Harrison managed to be among the first.

As they waited for the drinks, Jim Hall gave Mark an affectionate punch on the shoulder. The two had roomed together during the four years of their medical school tenure at Lakeview. Both, too, had come up through the residency and subsequent fellowship program—though in different fields—by which the skills and knowledge of young doctors were honed to a fine edge in this most famous of American medical schools.

"These affairs get more and more like auctions every year," said Jim as they picked up their drinks and moved out of the crowd. "Had any bidders since your film presentation yesterday afternoon on testicular transplant between siblings created such a storm?"

"A couple—in the Northeast."

"Stay away from there. The most promising areas for young doctors these days are the South and Southwest—what's usually called the Sun Belt."

"I'm going to look it over, after I finish a few weeks' relaxing at Myrtle Beach. A doctor friend from Charlotte is lending me his cottage down there." Six feet two, with slightly reddish hair, even features, and a trimly cut mustache, Mark was a fine specimen of physical perfection—thanks to early morning jogs, even in the blustery Baltimore winters.

"I thought you were going to join the group that will be staffing a new Health Maintenance Organization in the North Carolina Sand Hills," said Hall.

"I was, for a while. The Veterans Administration is closing a big hospital down there and two counties were going to get together to form a regional medical center and an HMO."

"*Were* going? Why not still?"

"The congressman from that district was pretty sure he had the grant we needed to renovate the VA hospital sewed up so we could start planning the clinic," Mark explained, "until one of those Bible-pounding evangelical preachers the Republicans use to sway voters claimed the HMO would be doing wholesale abortions. That's the kiss of death in the area, so our congressman got clobbered in the last election. Now the whole project has to be put through the federal grant mill once more, so it will probably be a year or two before it can come to life again."

"Tough luck," said Jim. "You won't be left in the lurch very long, though, after that demonstration you gave of microsurgical technique in your film. In the next couple of months you're certain to find opportunities to write your own ticket."

"Right now nobody's even inviting me to dance."

"Can't Dr. Ramirez place you with one of his friends somewhere? Everybody knows you're his fair-haired boy."

The Chief of Surgery at Lakeview was one of the top surgeons in the country. He had persuaded Mark to come to Baltimore to study medicine after finishing his premedical undergraduate work at Duke—about the time Ramirez himself had moved from Duke to Lakeview to become the head of surgery in that world-famous medical school. The two had been friends all through Mark's own formative years as a surgeon.

"He offered me an assistant professorship in surgery here," said Mark. "And I suppose I could put off paying most of my debts until I'd be eligible to join the Private Diagnostic Clinic."

Operated as a group by the upper echelon of the Lakeview faculty, the PDC treated private patients on a fee-for-service basis, giving the participating doctors an opportunity to supplement their relatively meager teaching salaries.

"How long would that take?" Jim Hall asked.

"Five years minimum and the rank of associate professor but, with academic politics such a cutthroat business, it could take a lot longer."

"So you're definitely leaving Lakeview?"

"It doesn't look like I have a choice."

"The nursing service, at least, will be sorry to see you go."

"Not when you're as tired as I've been for the past six months," said Mark. "When I get to my apartment after making evening rounds, all I can do is down a couple of jolts of bourbon while my TV dinner is in the oven. Half the time I fall asleep before the television set."

"That's another thing that's worrying your friends." Jim Hall's tone was serious now. "Did you have to take on running the entire Microsurgery Department when Dr. Peters developed cancer of the prostate and had to retire suddenly?"

"Mike Peters taught me everything I know about operating under a microscope. I couldn't let the department he'd spent years building up go to pot while the faculty hunted for another microsurgeon."

"Especially when they had a highly trained one on the job," said Hall. "But they didn't show much gratitude by bringing in a hotshot from St. Louis to take Peters' place and leaving you out in the cold."

"I could still have a junior teaching position in the department—"

"When you're just as good, or maybe better, than the one they brought in?"

"That's academic politics. You've been here long enough to know how it works."

"It's still a damn poor way to reward somebody who's worked his ass off keeping the department up to scratch," said Hall. "Which reminds me, the grapevine says you've been hitting the sauce a lot lately, too."

"No more than is usual with residents and fellows," Mark protested.

"And the morning amphetamines?"

"You know how it is," Mark said with a shrug.

"I *do* know, and that worries me," said Hall. "Over the years

I've seen too many promising young doctors turn to the needle, when the combination of bourbon and amphetamines isn't enou—"

"You know me better than that," said Mark heatedly. "It's true that I've been working hard lately; drinking hard, too, I suppose. Everybody does it, but I'm nowhere near being a basket case from burnout, and I can stop the bourbon and uppers whenever I want to. Just let me get out of here and soak up the sun for a few weeks at Myrtle Beach and I'll be as good as new."

"Let's hope so." Jim Hall glanced at his watch. "I promised Mary to take her to the Association banquet tonight. Can't overlook a free meal, even if I have to pay for it by dancing."

"I'm going to cadge another jolt," said Mark. "It isn't every day that I get to drink 101-proof Wild Turkey free. See you at the banquet."

"Right. Be sure and dance with Mary tonight, will you? She gets a kick out of going even that far with the Casanova of Lakeview."

As Mark was leaving the auditorium after finishing the second drink, Dr. Aldo Ramirez called to him from the other end of the bar.

"I was going to call you when I went by my office before going home, Mark." Ramirez was silver-haired and distinguished-looking. "Wait a minute and I'll walk along with you."

"Anything wrong, sir?"

"You're going to the dinner tonight, aren't you?"

"I'm planning to."

"Unattached, I hope."

"As a matter of fact, I am."

"From what I hear, that's unusual enough to be noteworthy," said Ramirez. "Leonora and I will be sitting at the same table with Dick Barrett and his party. Dick and I were classmates here at Lakeview, but he took his surgical training at Mass. General. There's a vacant seat at the table, he tells me, and I think you would enjoy sitting with us."

"I'd like that very much, sir."

"You'll like Dick; he's a go-getter," Ramirez continued. "Has his own clinic in Gulf City and has been spectacularly successful, particularly lately. By the way, his daughter will be there, too. I'm sure you'll relish having someone in your own age bracket to talk to."

Mark could recognize a command when he heard one but didn't resent it. Ramirez had done a great deal to make his passage through medical school and the residency programs financially less burdensome by arranging substitute internships for him at Baltimore hospitals during the last two clinical years of medical school.

"We'll meet you at the hotel around seven, then," said the older surgeon.

"I'll be there." *And probably be stuck all evening with a dog,* Mark thought as he left the auditorium. *But, then the old man has been good to me, so I can't let him down.*

II

The Barretts were ten minutes late, but Mark didn't mind—once he saw the daughter. Tall, blond, and startlingly beautiful, she moved with the grace of an athlete, and her low-cut short evening dress, plus a light tan, accentuated her beauty all the more. She appeared to be about twenty-five, three years younger than Mark, and was wearing a diamond-studded wedding ring on the third finger of her right hand—a universal announcement that she'd been married but was divorced. That fact was confirmed, when her last name turned out to be Desmond.

"Please call me Claire, Dr. Harrison," she said as Mark was seating her at the table.

"I'm Mark," he told her as a waiter appeared and took the party's order for drinks: scotch and soda for the older members of the group, bourbon for Mark, and vodka and tonic for Claire.

"From your look of surprise when you first saw me, I'm sure you had decided you were being drafted into squiring a dog for the evening," she said with a smile.

"You must have ESP."

"Of a sort, where men are concerned. Most women do."

"Claire has her own advertising and public relations agency in Gulf City, Dr. Harrison," Mrs. Barrett informed him proudly from across the table. "She's very successful at everything she does."

"Except marriage," said her daughter. "I'm a great disappointment to my parents, Doctor, but I simply couldn't stand being married to a clod."

"Now, Claire," her mother protested mildly. "Abner Desmond came from an old Southern family."

"One that expected me to stay home and have babies." Claire turned to Mark. "Are you married, Doctor?"

"I've escaped so far, probably because Dr. Ramirez has kept me too busy, especially the past six months or so."

"You're a surgeon, aren't you?"

"Not just *a* surgeon," Dr. Richard Barrett interposed from the head of the table. "Dr. Harrison's film of one of his operations was shown at the morning seminar yesterday. It was the outstanding presentation of the entire program this year."

"What did you do?" Claire Desmond asked Mark.

"Well, I—" He knew he was blushing and didn't know exactly how to stop, but her father saved him.

"He transplanted a testicle from one twin to another who was born without any. The second twin's wife is already pregnant."

"Wouldn't artificial insemination have been simpler?" Claire asked.

"Perhaps," Mark conceded. "But then the baby would have lacked his father's chromosomes. With identical twins, the chromosomes are also identical."

"My recent husband would certainly have been better off with someone else's chromosomes." Claire laughed, a brittle sound that had little mirth in it. "The ones he inherited from his parents were so inbred, they'd probably have produced a monster if I'd ever let them mix with mine."

"I believe you've just formulated a new theory of heredity," Mark told her. "It will probably soon take the place of Mendel's."

"What part of the country are you from, Dr. Harrison?" Mrs. Barrett deftly turned the conversation away from her rather forthright daughter.

"I'm from North Carolina, but my ancestors fled from England two jumps ahead of Oliver Cromwell's Roundheads and settled somewhere in the Palatinate states along the Rhine," said Mark. "My paternal ancestor didn't like being German, so he came over to Virginia from Leyden and settled near Culpeper. I don't know exactly how long he stayed there, but he soon got a land grant from the Earl of Granville in the Piedmont section of North Carolina, just below the Virginia line not far from Durham. I grew up on a farm there."

"When I was about to be thrown out of Queens College in Charlotte for staying out all night, I managed to leave before the trial started and finished at East Carolina University," said Claire. "Where did you go to college, Doctor?"

"It's Mark. I took my premed at Duke."

"Finishing in three years at the head of his class," said Dr. Ramirez.

"On a football scholarship," Mark added. "If Dr. Ramirez hadn't gotten me a scholarship for the first two years at Lakeview and later arranged for me to work nights as a surgical orderly at the Baltimore City Hospital, I probably wouldn't have been able to finish medical school at all."

"Aldo tells me you can have a teaching appointment at Lakeview if you want it," said Dr. Barrett. "Have you decided what you really want as a career, Dr. Harrison?"

"I'm not sure yet, sir," Mark admitted. "I owe several insurance companies a lot of money that I borrowed on some paid-up policies to finance my tuition at college. Until a few weeks ago, I was planning to join the staff of a Health Maintenance Organization down in the Sand Hills section of North Carolina near Pinehurst. Then, unfortunately, the project ran into difficulties."

"HMOs have iffy prospects at best." Dr. Barrett's voice was disapproving. "Frankly, I'm hoping the Administration will live up to its campaign promises and do away with them altogether."

Their food came just then and the talk languished for a while. As they were finishing the main course, the music began and a few couples took to the floor.

"Would you like to dance?" Mark asked Claire.

"I'd love to."

Taking her hand, Mark led her between the tables to the dance floor. As he had expected, she was an excellent dancer.

"If you make love as well as you dance," she said while they were waiting for the music to begin again, "you deserve your reputation as the Casanova of Lakeview."

"Whatever gave you that idea?"

The music started before she could answer, and as Mark drew her close he could feel the purely physical attraction of the lithe body in the thin summer dress start to arouse in him a familiar physiological reaction.

"You really could be a Casanova." Pressing her body against his own, she leaned back to look up at him with a glint of a challenge in her eyes.

"Damn it!" he muttered. "Do you have to do that?"

"No, but I like it and so do you." She was laughing again and only pressed harder against him until in desperation he spun her away.

"If that's what you'd like," he told her savagely, "my apartment's only ten minutes away."

"Sorry." No mockery was in her tone now. "I drove four hundred miles today to get here in time for the dinner, and I'm much too tired to hold my own against a master in sexual acrobatics."

"I'll give you a rain check," he promised.

"I might just hold you to it—in Gulf City."

"Is that where I'm going?"

"Of course. It's what the evening is all about."

"You lost me somewhere."

"Right now, you're the hottest prospect at Lakeview this year and therefore a logical candidate for a place on the Barrett Clinic staff," she told him. "My father's been looking for a young surgeon to take his place in the Clinic eventually and asked Dr. Ramirez to recommend a candidate. You were first choice, so Father asked our chief surgical nurse to call a friend who's a supervisor here at Lakeview. The consensus seems to be that you're the Casanova of the nursing staff—plus several female medical students and an occasional lady faculty member."

"Why would your father check on me socially?"

"The Barrett Clinic caters to money and position, so its members automatically belong to Gulf City society—with a capital S. In fact, that's almost as important as their being skilled in their own specialty."

Mark was beginning to feel like a stallion put up for auction, but before he could speak, she continued: "Play hard to get when Father makes his first offer and haggle a little. He loves it."

"Where should I start?"

"Oh, maybe seventy-five—"

"Thousand?"

"Of course. You'll be bringing in far more than that in surgical fees the first year."

"Please go on. This is fascinating."

"When you two start dickering, come down a few thousand at a time, but don't take less than sixty-five."

"How do you know he's going to make me an offer?"

"Because he asked me to request that you meet him in the coffee shop tomorrow morning for breakfast around eight-thirty. He always does his best haggling over morning coffee."

"I still don't exactly understand why he chose me," Mark admitted.

"For the very best of reasons—the way he looks at it. He's been threatening for several years now to quit and raise blooded Arabian horses on a ranch the Clinic partners own north of Birmingham. If you come to the Barrett Clinic and pan out the way you almost certainly will, you'll be the logical candidate to take his place."

It was all very breathtaking and Mark could only wonder if he were hearing right. "I'll keep that in mind—*if* he makes the offer and *if* I decide to consider it," he parried.

"All you'll have to do is sign on the dotted line. Besides—" and here her voice took on a throaty note that made the hackles rise on the back of his neck and along his spine. "There'll be perks, perks you won't mind in the least, I assure you."

The banquet ended around ten, with music provided for those who wanted to stay on and dance. But when Mark asked Claire if she would like to stay, she shook her head.

"I'm driving up to New York in the morning," she told him.

"An advertising program is going to be staged this summer for a product I helped design—a new line of lingerie, swim-, and sleep-wear called Next-to-Nothing Intimatewear. If I can snatch the advertising contract for the Southeast away from those Madison Avenue agencies, I'll be in the driver's seat for the national campaign."

"Are you coming back this way?"

"Probably. Come to think of it, when Father makes his offer, why don't you have the Clinic pay your expenses to come down to Gulf City and take a look at the whole situation. When do you finish your fellowship?"

"June thirtieth."

"Good. I'll be driving back home the first of July and you can ride down with me if you'd like."

"Could that possibly be one of the perks you mentioned?"

"Let's call it that—for starters."

III

Dr. Richard Barrett was sitting at a table before a window in the hotel coffee shop, with a cup of coffee and the morning paper before him, when Mark arrived.

"Hope I'm not late," said Mark, taking a chair at the table. "My watch says exactly eight-thirty."

"So does mine," said Barrett. "I'm so much in the habit of operating early that I can't sleep after six-thirty, so I came on down to have a cup of coffee and read the morning paper."

The waitress came to bring Mark his coffee and they gave their orders for breakfast.

When the plates had been taken away and the coffee cups refilled, Dr. Barrett reached for a folder lying on the table.

"I guess you already surmised why I asked you to meet me this morning, Mark," he said.

"Well—Claire did put me wise."

"She's a chip off the old block," said Barrett. Then his tone became very businesslike. "Maybe you'd like a rundown on our situation in Gulf City."

"I'd appreciate it."

"About fifteen years ago, I organized a group with two men I'd become friends with during World War II. We three, plus a younger OB-GYN specialist who joined us later, formed a corporation now known as the Barrett Clinic. We mostly take our patients to Gulfside, a bang-up hospital operated by Hospitals, Inc. Our doctors are paid a set amount each month, plus a bonus at the end of every year in which we show a profit. I might add," he said on a note of pride, "that we haven't failed to show a profit since the second year of operation."

"How many men are in your group now?"

"Four, at present. My own residency at Mass. General was in general surgery, but through the years I've gradually come to handle more and more malignant conditions in the Clinic's practice. Besides Jerry Thorpe in OB-GYN, we have an excellent internist who is certified in cardiology, and an orthopedist. All of our men naturally are Board certified."

"You would appear to have covered the field pretty well," Mark observed.

"We did, until a few years ago, when your own specialty of microsurgery suddenly began to burgeon. At the moment, Gulf City has no highly trained surgeon in that field, so if you join us we'll be a long jump ahead of what's already available."

"A lot of people are doing microsurgery these days without adequate training—"

"Just another reason why the Barrett Clinic should have an expert in that field who is well suited to our class of practice."

"Class?"

"The Barrett Clinic caters to the upper levels of both society and income in the surrounding area."

"Isn't that limiting your appeal generally? Considering that most patients nowadays are covered either by Medicare, private insurance, or both."

"It has—lately," Barrett admitted. "But we're making a move in that direction, too. A few weeks from now, we expect to open a satellite Clinic in the older part of Gulf City, where many people with good incomes and plenty of complementary insurance through Blue Cross, Blue Shield, and private companies have settled in their retirement. Which means we need someone to head it who's widely experienced in all fields of surgery, besides his own specialty. And from what I've learned about your training and your ability, Mark, I might as well tell you now that you are the answer to our prayers."

"I'm flattered, sir."

"My wife and I have reached the point where we want to take it easy from now on. I'm counting on you to give the Clinic a leadership, too, that it would lack without my being there to keep things running. If you go with us, Mark, you'll not only have a chance to become one of the best-known surgeons in the Southeast but a rich one into the bargain."

"My salary as a senior fellow at Lakeview hardly lets me live and pay the interest on the loans I had to make in order to finance my medical education," Mark admitted, "so what you're suggesting is very attractive."

"If you come with us you can count on other benefits, too."

Mark couldn't help remembering the "perks" Claire had hinted at, but hardly believed Barrett was referring to them, a fact that was confirmed when the surgeon continued: "You see, we get our Clinic employees from the same corporation that operates the hospital, so for tax purposes they're not really our responsibility, as far as the retirement program of the Clinic itself is concerned," Barrett explained. "The only people on our own retirement program are the Clinic manager, the doctors making up the Clinic staff itself, plus an operative assistant, Alexa McGillivray."

"A doctor?"

"No, a nurse practitioner from Duke whose training was in surgery. Alexa's as good as any doctor in the operating room. In fact, she's much better than the GPs we occasionally have to put on as first assistants in order to pay them a fee for shuttling patients our way."

"I can understand that," Mark agreed.

"Alexa assists whoever from the Clinic is operating and also sees that our patients get top-quality care from the hospital nursing staff during the critical postoperative period." Barrett glanced at his watch. "Elaine and I are going to catch a plane for The Greenbrier in West Virginia at noon to play a little golf until after the Fourth of July. When do you finish your fellowship?"

"On June thirtieth, five days from now."

"What are you going to do when your fellowship is over?"

"Dr. Ramirez has offered me an assistant professorship in surgery here at Lakeview—"

"Under an outsider who's been brought in to take over the department you kept going when Mike Peters got his prostatic cancer?"

"Well, yes—"

"You've got too much on the ball to spend the best years of your life working up to an associate professorship, Mark—even at Lakeview. Since you're going to be free on the thirtieth of June, why don't you come down to Gulf City at our expense and look over the Barrett Clinic setup? I'm sure you're going to get other offers—"

"I've had a few."

"I could make you a firm offer now, but it wouldn't be fair to either of us for you not to have a good look at our operation before making your final decision," said Barrett. "We're prepared to bring you to Gulf City to look the situation over, but if you should decide against us, we'll certainly not hold it against you."

"That seems no more than fair," Mark agreed. "Before I put you to the expense, though, it's only fair to let you know that my salary would have to be more or less decided before I went down for the visit."

"I can assure you that we won't be niggardly. What figure did you have in mind?"

Mark took a deep breath and quoted the salary Claire had suggested—seventy-five thousand dollars a year.

"You put a high price on yourself, compared to the best you could expect at Lakeview," Richard Barrett commented. "At your age, I wasn't even making ten."

"Times have changed, sir."

"Changed a lot—but hardly that much. Nevertheless, if you impress my partners the way you impressed me when I watched your film and heard the rest of your presentation, I think I could persuade the other members of the group to go as high as fifty thousand for the first year."

"I might drop to sixty-five," Mark conceded, and felt his hopes rise when the other doctor didn't blink.

"Let's make it sixty-five thousand the first year, then—without any bonus or contribution to the retirement fund, of course. Then if we're satisfied with your work and you're satisfied with us, we'll negotiate a new contract with increasing percentages of the bonus, plus a contribution to the retirement fund every year."

"Sounds fair enough."

"What's fair enough?" It was Claire's voice, but in the give-and-take of bargaining with her father, Mark hadn't seen her cross the coffee shop to their table. Now he scrambled to pull out a chair for her.

"I thought you'd already left for New York," said Barrett.

"I overslept. Then I remembered you'd invited Mark for breakfast at eight-thirty and thought I'd have a bite with you before I leave."

She was as sleekly beautiful this morning in a green summer dress as she'd been last night. As Mark seated her, the waitress placed a cup of coffee and a plate of toast—which she had obviously ordered on her entry into the coffee shop—before her.

"Have you two made a deal yet?" she asked, biting into the toast. "I presume you didn't have breakfast together for any other reason."

"Up to your usual tricks again, eh?" Barrett gave her an affectionate tap on a lovely bare shoulder. "How much did you tell Mark to ask for last night?"

"Seventy-five for starters, expecting to settle for sixty-five. You know he'll be worth every dollar of it, too."

"The figure is sixty-five," Mark told her. "This is the first time I've ever had a woman manager, but I must say the results are more than satisfying."

"That's because I'm an expert at haggling over money. How much would you have asked, by the way, if I hadn't warned you in advance?"

"Probably twenty-five or thirty."

"That should teach you never to underestimate your own importance."

"Or the instincts of an unscrupulous woman," Barrett agreed

dryly. "Mark's coming down to Gulf City early in July to look over what we have to offer before he decides whether or not to take the job—"

"And also to give your father's partners a chance to decide whether they want me or not," Mark added.

They will and *you* will." Popping the last bit of toast into her mouth, she washed it down with coffee before pushing her plate away and rising to her feet.

"I'll be driving right through Baltimore on the way home the first of July," she told Mark. "Why don't I pick you up at your apartment about eleven? You can help me drive back."

"Sounds ideal."

"Good. We'll be in Gulf City in time for the Fourth of July binge. See you on the first."

IV

Promptly at eleven on the morning of July first, the doorbell rang in Mark Harrison's efficiency apartment in a housing unit where many of the Lakeview staff lived. He opened it to find Claire Desmond standing outside, looking like a model from *Vogue* in pale blue slacks, a matching blouse, and a bandeau of the same color holding back her shoulder-length blond hair.

"Are you packed?" she asked.

"All set. What time did you leave New York this morning?"

"About seven. I promised to get you to Gulf City in time for the Fourth of July parade and dance and I always keep my promises. Did you pack swimming trunks and a tennis racket?"

"All here. I usually drink bourbon, but I remembered that you ordered vodka and tonic at the banquet the other night, so I brought that, too."

"Good! I like a man who's observant."

While he stowed his luggage in the trunk of the Porsche, she took the right-hand seat. "It's your turn to drive," she told him.

As Mark was swinging off Route 29 at midafternoon for the entrance to I-64 leading westward across the Blue Ridge into the

Shenandoah Valley, West Virginia, Kentucky, and beyond, Claire sat up and adjusted her seat to its normal position.

"You've been making good time," she observed.

"For somebody who's not used to driving a luxury car like this," he conceded. "We need to stop for gas, so I'll let you take over there."

"Good! These service stations usually have vending machines that dispense sandwiches and coffee, so we can have a quick lunch and save time."

"Since you planned the route so far," he said, "I suppose you've already decided where we'll stop for the night."

"How would you like a romantic small motel on a hill off I-81, about a hundred miles southwest of Roanoke? The restaurant is at the foot of the hill and the view is fantastic!"

"Sounds ideal. What time will we get to Gulf City?"

"About noon, day after tomorrow. You'll like the Fourth of July parade and ball down home; it's sort of a summer Mardi Gras. Father and Mother will be flying back the morning of the fifth and he'll want to show you the Clinic and the hospital. When can you start work?"

"By the fifteenth, if your father's partners approve of me."

"They will." She gave him an oblique look that was, he thought, something of a critical appraisal before settling back in the seat. "From where I sit, it looks like you've got almost everything you need."

"Almost? What do I lack?"

"Maybe the burning desire to make money and get to the top of your profession. Without that, you'd only be another cog in the machine of a routine surgical practice."

"*You* certainly have what it takes to get ahead in *your* profession of public relations—plus the equipment you'll need to compete with men."

"To excel over men." For an instant her voice took on a hard note.

"Whatever the cost?"

"Like what?"

"Motherhood, for one."

"Oh, I expect to have a kid or two one day—when a man comes along who meets my standards."

Mark laughed. "Love has a habit of messing up the best-laid plans of men, women, and—from what I've seen in the laboratory —an occasional mouse."

"Not in my case. There's a song that sums up my creed."

"Is it *'Chacun à Son Gout'?*"

"That, too. But the one I have in mind is 'I Want What I Want When I Want It.' "

"Do you stick to that theme, too?"

"Absolutely." She glanced at a wristwatch set with diamonds. "We ought to reach that motel I told you about by six-thirty, in time for a couple of drinks before dinner."

V

The motel, Mark saw, when they left the Interstate and followed a winding road up the hill to it, was everything Claire had said it would be. Set upon the crest of a sharply sloping field of typical Shenandoah Valley bluegrass, it looked westward across a narrow valley to a towering mountain range. Also it was high enough and far enough away from the Interstate for the rumbling of a continual progression of trucks and other traffic not to be heard.

"My cousin and I will need adjoining rooms," Mark told the clerk when he registered. "She's afraid of being alone in motels."

"Of course, Doctor. I can give you two connecting rooms at the far end of the motel. It should be very quiet there."

"In case anyone asks, you're my cousin and you're afraid of motels," he told Claire as he was carrying her luggage into the end room. "But I hope we're 'kissing cousins.' "

"You *do* look ahead, don't you," she said, laughing. "We'll cross that bridge when we come to it."

Fifteen minutes later, he'd gotten a bucket of ice and poured liberal drinks. Carrying the two glasses, he knocked on the connecting door and asked, "Are you decent?"

"Not when I can help it. The door's unlocked. Come in."

She was curled up on the bed with a couple of pillows at her back watching television. When he handed her the drink, she moved over.

"What's on the news?" he asked, settling down beside her.

"The same as usual: murders, politics, and more crooks in Washington."

They watched the passage of pictures across the tube in silence while they drank. Propped as they were on pillows against the headboard, the pressure of Claire's body against Mark's stirred him, but she seemed not to notice or to be affected by his closeness. When the glasses were empty, he took them back to the other room and returned with a second round. By the time that was finished, Mark felt as though he were floating on air.

"What say we go down to dinner?" he asked. "They have the best Virginia ham in these parts."

Arm in arm, as much to steady each other as from affection, they walked down the steep curving road to the small restaurant at the foot. The ham was delicious, the rolls home-baked, the red-eye gravy a gift from the gods. Hungry after the long drive, they ate ravenously. The dessert of apple turnovers surmounted by a dollop of vanilla ice cream was beyond compare and both were panting, as much from having eaten so much as from the effort, when they reached the top of the hill.

Mark unlocked his room and let them in. "There's a James Bond movie on," he said. "Want to see it?"

"Okay, but I'm so relaxed, I'll probably go to sleep in the middle of the picture."

"If you do, I'll carry you to bed like a gentleman should."

"Promise?"

"If I can find the strength."

"You're very sweet, Mark Harrison," she said. "Much too sweet for a broad like me."

"The point is arguable," he said as he came back into his room with the two pillows they'd used from her own as props while watching television. "But since you're the only broad around, I'll have to make do."

Switching on the television, he arranged the pillows so she'd be comfortable, then placed his own as closely beside her as he could. The picture was exciting and at the half-over point Claire said, "I'm ready for some more of that vodka—watching Sean Connery is always best done when you're half floating."

By the end of the picture, they'd had three more drinks.

"Guess I'll take a shower before I turn in," said Claire. "Thanks for a lovely evening."

He had finished his own shower and was toweling himself dry with the door open when Claire's voice startled him.

"Your anatomy is certainly outstanding, darling." She was sitting on his bed with the top of the sheet lying across her pubic eminence, obviously quite naked beneath it as she raised her hands to push back the hair that fell unbound to her shoulders.

VI

Mark awoke about seven-thirty to the sound of water running in the adjoining room. The connecting doors were open and he could hear Claire humming a popular tune. With a groan, he went to the bathroom, took three aspirin from his shaving kit, and swallowed them, followed by two antacid tablets. After shaving, he stepped into the shower and turned on the cold water.

The shock of the cold shower stung him into wakefulness, if not to recovery from a massive hangover. He was pulling on a fresh sport shirt when the sound of "The Today Show" theme music startled him and he turned to see Claire standing beside the TV in his room. In brief cuffed white shorts, a snug white T-shirt, and white tennis shoes, she looked like an advertisement for AMF.

"You look like the wrath of God," she said.

"Somebody once described a hangover as having your mouth feel like the Russian Army had been marching through it barefoot. Take it from me, that was an understatement."

"Did you take some aspirin?"

"Three—plus two Maalox tablets. How can you manage to look like that after the night we had?"

"A doctor ought to know the answer to that question," she said briskly. "Wait till I open my cosmetic case. Maybe I can help you."

She disappeared into the other room and he heard the lock on the expensive matching case click open, then shut. Returning to his room, where Mark was closing his own suitcase, she handed him a tablet. "Take this. It's even better for a hangover than the hair of the dog that's so often recommended."

He recognized the pill as a particularly effective amphetamine with which he was familiar, but this dose was easily twice the strength of the one he often took to get going in the morning. Moreover, the mocking—and somehow challenging—look in her already over-brilliant eyes told him she'd already taken one herself.

"You know those things are dangerous, don't you?" he said.

"Of course. I grew up in a doctor's household where his medical bag was left on the shelf in the hall closet. Take it. You'll be surprised how soon you'll feel like a million dollars."

"The way you feel right now?"

"How else?" Claire said with a shrug. "I had mine the minute I woke up."

Tossing the tablet into his mouth, he washed it down with a half glass of water. "You'd better drive the first hundred and fifty miles at least," he told her. "You may be accustomed to these things—tolerance rises regularly with use. But the ones I've been taking are only half as strong."

"I'm planning to drive," she said. "Let's put the luggage into the car and go to breakfast before we hit the road."

By the time Mark finished packing the car, his head was clearing. More important, the queasy feeling in his stomach had disappeared. By nine o'clock, they had eaten breakfast and were winging their way southward on I-81 toward the Great Smokies. Mark was high.

They spent the second night in a charming rustic motel in northeast Alabama, where the southern tip of the Appalachian range ceased to deserve to be called mountains and became mere hills. When they were leaving the next morning, Mark swallowed the amphetamine she gave him and by the time they reached the Interstate was feeling no pain.

"Before I left New York, I called the Holiday Inn on the beach at Gulf City and made a reservation for you," Claire told him.

"You must have clout to get anybody a room on the water for July third."

"My father is the senior partner in a group of doctors who own the building and lease the franchise. I told the reservation clerk you were his guest. By the way, I won't be able to have dinner with you tonight. An engagement with a client from Montgomery was made before I left home, but I'll pick you up around noon tomorrow and show you some of the town. In the evening, we'll go to the Fourth of July dance at the Yacht Club."

Shortly after three, Claire pulled the Porsche to a stop in front of a magnificent Holiday Inn that was, Mark estimated, at least ten stories high. Like others in the phalanx of high-rise buildings dominating the waterfront as far as he could see in either direction, the inn was a gleaming white. The beach in front was dotted with colorful umbrellas, wherever there was room for them between largely seminude bathers exhibiting various degrees of tan.

"I enjoyed our trip, darling," said Claire when he lifted his suitcase and a clotheshanger from the back and came around to say good-bye. "See you tomorrow for lunch, around twelve."

"I'll manage," he said. "The rest will probably do me good."

The suite on the tenth floor atop the building to which Mark was shown by a bellman was luxuriously furnished. It consisted of a large room with a balcony, two sofa beds, and a large bath-dressing room. A basket of fruit was on the dresser, labeled COMPLIMENTS OF THE MANAGEMENT. After tipping the bellman, Mark went out on the balcony and studied the vista before him.

A line of sandbars could be seen about a mile away across a placid body of water. The sandbars were not high enough to spoil the magnificent view of the Gulf of Mexico, however. And the water inside the bar was dotted with bathers on inner tubes and colorful floats, as well as a number of small sailing craft.

Beyond the sandbar, a magnificent sportfishing boat was moving slowly along. Farther to the south, the outlines of a freighter were visible. Probably, Mark surmised, bound from New Orleans to Tampa, the nearest deepwater port farther south along the vast curving shore of the Gulf in this area. To the east and west, any further view was blocked by the wall of waterfront hotels and condominiums that make practically all Gulf cities look like duplicates of each other.

The day was hot and the humidity high so Mark decided to postpone any exploration of Gulf City until the sun was lower and the evening breeze from the water had a chance to dispel some of the humidity. Returning to the bedroom, he stretched out on one of the sofas and did not awaken until six o'clock.

He was looking for "Restaurants" in the Yellow Pages of the phone book when he happened to leaf through the section marked "Physicians and Surgeons" and remembered that a fraternity brother had come to Gulf City after finishing a residency in Pathology the year before. Nor did he have any difficulty finding the name of Patrick O'Meara, M.D. The only address listed was Gulfside Hospital, so he dialed the number on the off chance that Pat might be free for dinner, even on the eve of a holiday.

"Is Dr. Patrick O'Meara in the hospital?" Mark asked when an operator answered.

"I believe he is, sir. May I tell him who's calling?"

"Dr. Mark Harrison—from Baltimore."

Shortly, Pat O'Meara's brogue—with a South Boston Irish "a" that would have identified him anywhere—sounded in Mark's ear.

"Mark, boy! Where are you?"

"Here in Gulf City."

"What the hell brings you here?"

"I'm looking over this area as a possible location for a surgical practice. Any chance of your having dinner with me?"

"Sure. I'm Deputy County Medical Examiner, as well as pathologist and laboratory director here at Gulfside, so I had to be on call this weekend. Where are you now?"

"The Holiday Inn. Know a good Spanish restaurant?"

"Sure, the Habanera."

"How about joining me there?"

"Fine. It's only a few blocks from the hospital, so they can reach me on the beeper if I'm needed. See you at the restaurant in fifteen minutes."

"Right. I'm leaving here now."

The streets back of the waterfront were far less crowded and, Mark noted, largely devoted to business. He had no trouble finding the restaurant at the address listed in the Yellow Pages and was ushered to a table in the corner away from the noise of the bar, beside which an old man was lovingly plucking a classic Spanish guitar. Pat O'Meara came in a few minutes later and greeted Mark warmly.

"I can't get over your even considering Gulf City as a place to practice surgery," O'Meara said, when the waiter had brought them tall, frosty rum collinses and taken their orders for Spanish bean soup and *arroz con pollo,* the delectable chicken and rice dish Cubans knew how to cook better than anyone else in the world. "With Dr. Ramirez looking on you as a son and that string of papers on microsurgery you've been publishing the past few years, I expected you to stay on and one day be professor of surgery."

"I was tempted, but I had an offer in private practice I couldn't refuse."

"Here in Gulf City?"

"Yes—with the Barrett Clinic."

Pat O'Meara's lips pursed in a long whistle of admiration. "Talk about getting in on a gold mine! You're good enough for the job, but how did you happen to get it?"

"Dr. Richard Barrett and Dr. Ramirez were classmates in med school. When Barrett asked the professor to name someone, Ramirez named me."

"Dick Barrett couldn't have done better, but I thought you were headed for a teaching appointment—or that HMO plan down in the Sand Hills of North Carolina you were always talking about."

"The Carolina project is way behind schedule, if it ever develops at all," Mark explained. "I haven't given up on teaching either, but I've got a lot of debts stacked up. If I can get rid of them in a few years of private practice, I can always join the HMO if it works out or go back to Lakeview."

"You won't do either one. We all have the same idealistic convictions in medical school, but once we really get our feet in the trough, damn few of us ever manage to get out. Or want to, even though it's dog-eat-dog in the medical jungle called private practice."

"Just like the academic jungle," Mark commented. "How does it go with you down here, Pat?"

"So-so," said O'Meara, as steaming tureens of Spanish bean soup were placed before them. "I'm employed by Gulfside Hospital as pathologist, so I'm in the racket but not exactly a part of it —though the compromises I have to accept as payment for my job sometimes make me wonder."

"About what?"

"Forget it. I was just sounding off."

"I know you better than that, Pat. You've changed since you left Lakeview and I'd like to know why."

"You asked for it, but don't hold it against me if I tell you the truth about private practice in Gulf City—"

"Or Birmingham, Orlando, Miami—you name it."

"Did you mention to Dick Barrett that you're a friend of mine?" O'Meara asked.

"Yes."

"What happened?"

"He said you were a bang-up pathologist, but that you were having some problems getting along with the rest of the profession in Gulf City."

"Barrett was generous, I'll say that for him. Many of the doctors here—particularly the surgeons—think I'm a triple-plated son of a bitch for calling the shots as I see them in the Path. and Clinical Labs."

"Why? Nobody can deny what they see on slides and bacterial cultural plates."

"I came down here a year ago, full of piss and vinegar and determined to make the Pathology Department at Gulfside Hospital a small copy of Lakeview. Everything went fine, too—at first. The staff approved my starting weekly tissue conferences for the surgeons, where specimens removed at operations could be reviewed. They also okayed a monthly clinical pathological conference when the case of a particular patient who died would be reviewed—without naming the doctor in charge, of course."

"That's no more than is required for proper hospital accreditation."

"True. The trouble was, I got overzealous."

"What's wrong with that?"

"Have you met any of the Barrett Clinic group yet?"

"Only Dr. Barrett. What's wrong with them?"

"Nothing. For doctors in private practice, I'd say they're a cut above average. Their gynecologist, Jerry Thorpe, is a magician in the female pelvis. He can snake out the uterus, tubes, and ovaries, *per vaginam,* tighten up the pelvic floor fore and aft to make a forty-year-old mother of two or three as snug as the average bride these days—all in less than an hour."

"So the man's skillful. I've seen others do the same thing."

"Right. The trouble was that at my first tissue conference, I chose to present a half dozen uteri Jerry had taken out during the week and diagnosed them as being normal."

"Why would that cause trouble, if it was the truth?"

"Jerry—and the Barrett Clinic—like to preserve the illusion that his 'birthday hysterectomies' are for real pathology, instead of taking away women's worries about more children at a time when they want to be free for the things society wives like to do."

"Like having an affair?"

"That, too, if their husbands can't stand up to the fact that their wives have discovered sex can be fun without procreation. Besides, there's the excitement of having their daughters make their debuts. Down here they make a lot of that sort of thing, like the rest of the Old South."

"So what happened?"

"It was simple—and I suppose inevitable. The Barrett Clinic admits more patients to Gulfside Hospital for surgery than the rest of the doctors in town put together, so when Jerry squawked about my normal diagnoses, Dick Barrett spoke to Jack Pryor, the administrator. Jack called me in to say I should do my job as a pathologist and find more pathology. Which I do now."

"Should I ask how? Or would that embarrass you?"

"Oh, I manage to be ethical and still keep my job. Slice a uterus up enough and you'll find some tissue that looks like a fibroid, which you dutifully report as the pathologic diagnosis. It doesn't matter that the little tumor is located on the inside wall of the uterus where Jerry could never have found it on examination. Or even in the muscle of the uterus itself where nothing could discover it but a knife. Either way, the pathological diagnosis is still uterine fibroids and everybody's happy."

"What about your autopsy percentages? Hospital accrediting committees can be pretty sticky about that."

"Nonteaching hospitals don't have many postmortem examinations except on emergencies, mainly because the private physicians don't really want to see them. As Deputy County Medical Examiner, though, I naturally order a postmortem on everybody who dies less than twenty-four hours after admission or is brought into the Emergency Room D.O.A."

"I guess a lot of hospitals would lose accreditation if it weren't for dead-on-arrival cases," Mark observed.

"You're right," said Pat. "Of course, they make undertakers in the town mad as hell because after a patient has been posted it takes twice as long to embalm the body. But when our reports go in to the American College of Surgeons and the American Hospital Association at the end of the year, our autopsy rate is high enough for us to keep our accreditation without any difficulty."

"Sounds like you solved your problems neatly," Mark commented, signaling the waiter for the wine card.

"Part of them, but I'm also Director of Laboratories for the hospital and Clinic and, incidentally, they're both operated by the same company that administers the Clinic operations."

"Dr. Barrett told me as much."

"Did he tell you that every patient with enough insurance—like Medicare and the Blues—to pay most of his bill has to have twenty-five laboratory tests and often more—not counting X rays, EKGs, and the rest of the lot?"

"No."

"You'll get the message soon enough after you go into private practice—if you fail to order them. Lab tests cost the patient money and money lets hospital operating companies make profits —especially when most of their stockholders are doctors anyway."

"At least the patient gets a good survey."

"He does that—even down to a CAT scan, which most of them don't need—but that's modern medicine, even though it costs like hell. Besides, if you fail to order enough tests and something does show up that you didn't know was there, the patient can demand to see his records. The next day he's in your office with a shyster lawyer yelling about malpractice."

"I've seen enough of that at Lakeview to know how it goes."

"But is that the kind of medicine the doctor who brought you into the world back in North Carolina practiced? The kind that made everybody love him for his dedication?"

"No, but neither is admitting a lot of patients to teaching hospitals when they don't really need it. Or keeping them twice as long as is necessary just to let medical students sharpen their skills in diagnosis and residents learn surgical technique."

"You've made your point," said O'Meara. "Pour the wine and we'll drink to medicine and Aesculapius, even though we know most of us are busy betraying every damned principle we're supposed to hold sacred."

VII

In the air-conditioned coolness of his hotel room, Mark slept soundly and awoke feeling like a million dollars. Pulling on swim trunks, a T-shirt, and running shoes, he threw a towel around his neck and took the elevator to the basement and a tunnel by which bathers could come and go between the hotel building and the beach without being exposed to the constant stream of traffic on Gulf Boulevard. Depositing the towel on a bench near the water's edge, he jogged a few miles along the beach, where only a few bathers had yet come out. Returning to the bench, he pulled off his running shoes and top and waded into the light chop of the Gulf, freshened by the morning's breeze.

The water was warm and he had to wade perhaps a hundred yards out before it became deep enough for him to swim comfortably toward the sandbar located about a quarter of a mile away. His steady crawl ate up the distance, and reaching the sandbar, he waded ashore.

Almost, he could imagine he was alone on an island and that the solid wall of white high-rise hotels and condominiums behind him did not exist. For a few moments he stood there, before the pangs of hunger reminded him that he hadn't eaten breakfast, experiencing a sense of freedom in his mind he hadn't felt in a long time, surrounded as he had been for so many years by the everyday bustle of the great medical center in Baltimore.

The warm salt air, the sun, the salt wash of the Gulf upon the beach around his feet were well worth the drawbacks to private medical practice Pat O'Meara had described last night, he told himself. And though perhaps not yet to the point of full realization, there was always Claire—she of the lovely naked body, the clinging limbs, and the moans of ecstasy as she writhed in his embrace.

The thought reminded him that he had a luncheon date with Claire and, turning, he plunged into the water and swam back until he could stand up and wade ashore. In his room, he showered, dressed in a sport shirt and slacks, and went down to the coffee shop for a huge breakfast of eggs, Southern-style sausage biscuits, and grits—a pleasure he'd almost forgotten after so many years of eating hurried meals in the hospital cafeteria.

When he heard nothing from Claire by lunchtime, he called her office and was told that she was having a consultation at the photographers' about the advertising program for Next-to-Nothing Intimatewear and that it would probably extend through lunch.

An afternoon breeze had sprung up and Mark took a long walk around Gulf City, familiarizing himself with the area where he had already decided he would live and work, at least for the next year. Although he stopped occasionally to call Claire she didn't answer, so around six, he ate a solitary dinner in the hotel restaurant before going back to his room. The telephone was ringing when he opened the door and he hurried to pick up the receiver. It was Claire.

"I owe you an apology, darling," she said. "I've been tied up all day with photographers getting ready to shoot the pictures for the advertising program I went to New York about. What've you been doing?"

"Went for a run and a swim this morning and looked around the city this afternoon."

"I hope you liked what you saw."

"Very much."

"Had your dinner?"

"I just came up from the restaurant."

"Good. I'll have a sandwich here in my condo before dressing for the dance at the Club. It starts at nine, so I'll pick you up about a quarter of."

He was waiting under the marquee when the white Porsche whirled to a stop beneath it, just before nine o'clock. In a pale green short summer evening frock and with bare shoulders, Claire was a picture of sophisticated loveliness.

"Who's liable to be at the dance?" he asked as the car moved into the stream of traffic on Gulf Boulevard.

"Everybody who's anybody in Gulf City—and hasn't gone to the mountains for the Fourth. I like midwinter skiing better than summer in the mountains and try to get to Aspen for a few weeks in midwinter every year. Do you ski?"

"Yes, but Aspen's a little rich for my blood. The Canaan slopes in northern West Virginia are more my style."

"This time next year, you'll be able to afford two weeks in Switzerland at Christmas," she assured him as she brought the Porsche to a stop under the marquee of the Yacht Club. "Even the slopes at Aspen can't compare with those at St. Moritz."

The Gulf City Yacht Club was located on the shore of a broad estuary that formed the harbor. Mediterranean in style, it was like many such structures built along the Gulf Coast during the boom that had spread westward from Florida during the twenties. The clubhouse was an imposing structure and, in addition to a landing for small boats, yachts of all sizes and costs were moored at several slips. Inside, tables were arranged around the dance floor and white-coated waiters moved between them carrying drinks.

As they moved toward the bar, Claire said, "Jerry Thorpe and Alexa McGillivray are over there by themselves. Let's join them."

"It's your party."

As they approached the table she'd indicated, Mark gave Jerry Thorpe a quick appraising glance. What he saw was a tall handsome man who appeared to be in his late thirties. His skin was tanned and, when he arose at their approach, his movements were those of an athlete. It was the girl sitting at the same table who startled Mark, however.

In a white sheath that contrasted sharply with a tan giving her skin the hue of burnished gold, she was, he guessed, probably five feet ten. Her hair was coal black and hung below her shoulders, held back from her face by a hammered silver barrette with some sort of crest at the center that contained a strange pattern, giving it almost the appearance of a coronet. The high cheekbones, the dark eyes, and the almost perfect symmetry of her face and figure, plus her height and a look of quiet self-assurance, gave her, he thought, somewhat the appearance of royalty.

"Dr. Jerry Thorpe, Dr. Mark Harrison." Claire made the introduction casually.

"So you're the wonder boy who's going to turn surgical practice in Gulf City upside down with the microscope." The slur in Thorpe's voice was one of contempt, but Mark ignored it since the man was obviously drunk.

"Operating microscopes are just tools," he said, shaking hands.

"My bailiwick is the female pelvis." Jerry Thorpe's tone took on a belligerent note. "I don't see how you're going to get a microscope in there."

"We don't try very often," Mark agreed.

Claire turned to the girl with the dark hair. "This is Alexa McGillivray," she said briefly before taking Thorpe's arm. "Let's get a drink while I tell you about New York, Jerry. I'll send you a double bourbon from the bar, Mark. Can I order another for you, Alexa?"

"No, thanks," said the golden-skinned girl. "I'll make do with this piña colada."

"How are you, Dr. Harrison?" The tall young woman's handshake was firm and forthright.

"Fine. May I compliment you on your tan?"

"It's not just tan. I'm an eighth-part Creek Indian."

"McGillivray?" Mark frowned. "Could I have heard that name somewhere before?"

"You probably read it in a novel called *Alabama Empire* that was a best seller some years ago. My ancestor, Chief Alexander McGillivray, was one of the major characters in the book."

"I remember the story now."

"Alexander McGillivray was often called the King of the Creeks because he held the nation together during the American

Revolution and for about ten years afterward. Some scholars even called him the 'Talleyrand of Alabama.' "

"That makes you a princess, doesn't it?"

"In the Creek Indian lineage, yes. I was named Alexa after Chief McGillivray because, by some magic jostling of the genes in my chromosomes, the Indian ones seem to have come out on top."

"It made for a very lovely product."

"But still couldn't get me into the Gulf City Yacht Club, except as the guest of a member," she said dryly. "After General Andrew Jackson defeated the Creek Nation at the Battle of Horseshoe Bend, my people were driven like cattle to Oklahoma, along with most of the Eastern tribes."

"Did you come from there?"

"No. I'm a native of what used to be called the Upper Creek Country. A few generations after the Indians were forcibly shipped to Oklahoma, some of my ancestors and relatives returned. They settled in a lovely area with deep canyons, high wooded ridges, and tumbling waterfalls in the extreme northeast corner of Alabama."

"If you love the mountain country so much, why do you live here on the coast?"

"The federal government grudgingly apologized for what they did to the Indians by making special loans and grants to help us get an education. I went to Duke on a scholarship for a B.S. degree in nursing and stayed on two more years to get a master's, most of it by scrubbing for operations."

"How did you get to Gulf City?"

"When I was a little girl, we used to come south for vacations at the beach. I always loved the Gulf, so when I left Duke, I came down here as Operating Room supervisor at Gulfside Hospital. About a year ago, Dr. Barrett decided that since I'd had so much experience in the Operating Room, I could work as first assistant to the Clinic surgeons—"

"But first assistants are usually doctors."

"Not out in what your Baltimore colleagues would no doubt characterize as the boondocks, Dr. Harrison," she said. "The Clinic couldn't afford to have two surgeons tied up during every operation. Besides, I can watch post-op patients through the recovery room and even into the ICU if necessary. By the way, I believe you know a friend of mine at Lakeview; her name is Margaret Fuller."

"She's one of the Operating Room supervisors—" Mark stopped suddenly. "Claire mentioned that someone at the Clinic talked to a nurse she knew at Lakeview about me."

"I plead guilty," said Alexa with a smile. "Meg told me Dr. Ramirez wanted very much to keep you on the Lakeview teaching staff, but he didn't feel like asking you to take the lesser salary you'd earn as an instructor when you could make so much more in private practice."

The music began again just then. "Would you like to dance?" Mark asked.

"I love waltzes." She came up from her chair and into his arms in one fluid graceful movement. Though tall, she was light in his embrace and for a long moment they danced in silence, their bodies responding to every movement in rhythm.

"You're a very graceful dancer, Dr. Harrison," she said. "I can understand why Meg Fuller named you the Casanova of Lakeview."

"That was only a joke," he protested, but she shook her head, her long black hair swinging momentarily against his cheek in an oddly intimate contact.

"I think not. You're an extraordinarily self-confident person, and in a man that quality has a strong attraction for women."

"That's because you're in the same league." They swung in a wide turn that took her away from him momentarily and he noticed the small, thin, black box of a hospital pager attached to the belt of her gown.

"Jerry Thorpe and I are both on call for the Clinic over the weekend," she said. "He's between wives—his second one just divorced him—and lonely. It was his idea for us to kill time together at the Club rather than sitting at home looking at politicians celebrating the Fourth with speeches about patriotism on television."

"You're not perhaps likely to be wife number three, are you?"

She laughed, a full rich sound. "Jerry doesn't look on me as a possible wife—or even a conquest. I'm just the hands that hold retractors, clip sutures he's tied, and occasionally sew up incisions when he's in a hurry to get to the next case."

"I'm afraid I find that hard to believe," said Mark. "You're a very beautiful young woman, with a quality of stability and confidence that goes beyond mere femininity."

"Claire's the same, but in a different way."

"Very different. Did you tell Dr. Barrett everything you learned from Margaret Fuller about me?"

"Not quite. The most important fact was that you were well liked by everybody at Lakeview—both staff and patients—and that you had all the social graces a successful doctor needs. I didn't mention that she said you'd been doing the work of two men for the past six months—"

"I had no choice. Dr. Peters came down with a cancer of the prostate and there wasn't anyone else to run the department."

"Meg said that, too, plus the fact that your friends in Baltimore think you're nearer a breaking point than you're willing to admit."

"Do I look like that now?" he demanded, a little testily.

"No. You've had a few days of relaxation driving down with Claire, but once you join the Barrett Clinic you'll be expected to shift to overdrive and stay there."

"I must say you learned a lot about me in one telephone conversation." Mark's tone was still sharp. "Apparently, you also told Claire about the Casanova bit. Mind telling me why?"

"She happened to hear Dr. Barrett ask me to call Meg and specifically asked me to question her about that aspect of your reputation."

"Why would she do that?"

When the music started once more, they moved back to the dance floor and Alexa McGillivray leaned back in his arms to look in his eyes. For a moment, her body was pressed close to his —disturbingly close—but she drew away quickly without prolonging the contact.

"Either you've created a false reputation in Baltimore or you're trying to con me, Dr. Harrison," she said. "A handsome man who obviously has a lot of sex appeal is a natural challenge to Claire, though a challenge I expect you'll be able to meet easily."

"Thanks," he said. "I don't know whether to take that as a compliment or not."

"In today's world, it is—particularly in medical circles. You're going to be very successful if you decide to stay here in Gulf City."

"What makes you think I might not stay?"

"Because the man I sense behind the easy charm and confidence is a very human and sensible doctor, with an instinct for serving humanity. Financial success—what you think you need most at the moment, I'm sure—isn't the same as being a real doctor, the old-fashioned kind."

"I didn't know they made those anymore."

"I could show you two: one is my uncle, Dr. Homer McGillivray. He runs a small hospital upstate at Peace River in the hill country of eastern Alabama where I grew up. A Lakeview graduate would probably call it a cottage hospital and look down on it, but everybody in town loves Uncle Homer. Besides, he brought many of them into the world and has saved a lot of them from going out of it prematurely."

"And the other?"

"A cousin, John Carr. John's a psychiatrist who took his training at Harvard, but came back home to operate a small institution he calls the Canyonhead Retreat. John has a psychiatric case cure record you won't find equaled anywhere else in the country—or probably in the world."

"I'd like to meet them both."

"I'll take you there someday," she promised. "Jerry and Claire have gone back to the table, so maybe we'd better go back, too."

"Tell me one thing," Mark said as they moved in rhythm toward the table where Claire and Thorpe were sitting. "Jerry Thorpe is obviously half drunk—maybe more—and he's on call. If he had to operate tonight on an emergency—say, a ruptured ovarian follicle that was bleeding severely—how would you get him sober enough to go into the O.R.?"

"If I thought he was over the safety line, I'd pour coffee down him first and then give him an amphetamine. I'm sure you must know from your resident days how those can wake you up; most of the students and residents I knew at Duke fell back on them quite often—plus a lot of the doctors in practice."

VIII

"I'm ready to leave, Mark." Claire made no attempt to hide the irritation in her voice as he and Alexa came back to the table.

"Of course," he said.

"Good night, Dr. Harrison," Alexa moved to take Thorpe's arm, tucking hers under it to support him while giving the illusion that he was being courteous to her.

"Does he get this way very often?" Mark asked Claire as they moved through the foyer of the Yacht Club to the front door.

"More often lately. Did Alexa tell you he was recently divorced?"

"Yes—from his second wife. I'm afraid medicine and marriage don't always mix well."

"It doesn't have to be that way; my father and mother are good examples. He works all the time and she spends her days playing bridge and chairing committees. All in all, it's a very satisfactory arrangement."

"Perhaps that's why you're an only child."

"Neither of them wanted any more after I was born, so maybe you're right."

Under the marquee at the entrance to the Holiday Inn, she brought the Porsche to a stop.

"Sorry I was a lousy partner at the dance," she said, kissing him good night perfunctorily. "Jerry was already maudlin and needed a shoulder to cry on so I got elected."

"Why you?"

"Well, we did have a very torrid affair when he first came to the Clinic a few years ago; were even engaged for a while, until we both realized we were too much alike to make a marriage succeed. But we're still good friends."

"Think you'll ever marry again?"

"Probably—at least long enough to produce a grandson for Fa-

ther to make up to him some of the headaches I've caused him—
by his standards."

"And yours?"

"I don't waste time on regrets," she said with a shrug, then
added, "By the way, Father will love it if you go to the airport
with Alexa in the morning to meet him and Mother. He likes to
be treated as if he were King of the Mountain, so everybody tries
to humor him. Alexa's in the phone book and her apartment is
only a few blocks from where you're staying. Give her a ring in a
half hour or so, after she's had long enough to put Jerry to bed."

"Will I see you tomorrow?"

"I don't know; I've still got several days' work getting this advertising program set up and it's pretty important. Besides, Father
will no doubt be monopolizing you all day. Have you decided yet
to accept his offer to join the Clinic?"

"I'm going to sign the contract for a year anyway, if it's offered
to me."

"Good. I should be through the urgent work by the time you
get back here from Baltimore and we can spend more time together."

"Is that a promise?"

"Cross my heart. When do you think you'll start work?"

"No later than the fifteenth of July, if it suits Dr. Barrett. I
need to get on the payroll as quickly as possible."

"And I want to have you back here as quickly as possible.
Good night—until you come back to stay."

IX

Inside his room, Mark undressed and put on his pajamas, then
took the Gulf City telephone directory from the nightstand. He
found the name he was seeking, "Miss Alexa S. McGillivray,"
without difficulty and dialed it. Alexa answered, sounding a little
breathless.

"This is Mark Harrison," he said. "I'm glad you got home all
right; drunks can sometimes be a bit hard to handle."

"Jerry Thorpe's condominium is on Gulf Boulevard about a
mile beyond your Holiday Inn," she told him. "By the time we

got there, he was almost past navigating, so I had to practically carry him into the living room and stretch him out on a big couch. I heard the telephone ringing as I was opening the door to my apartment."

"How will Thorpe ever be able to see patients tomorrow morning?"

"I'll call and wake him before I leave for the airport to meet Dr. Barrett. With plenty of coffee and amphetamine, he'll make it. He has an operation scheduled for eleven o'clock, but he'll be all right by then."

"Claire suggested that I go with you to meet Dr. and Mrs. Barrett at the airport in the morning. Would that be all right?"

"Certainly. Why don't we leave early and have breakfast at the airport restaurant? I'll take the Clinic station wagon, so there'll be plenty of room for all of us, plus the baggage."

Mark was waiting inside the door of the Holiday Inn when a station wagon with the legend BARRETT CLINIC on the door stopped outside.

"Good morning," Alexa greeted him with a smile when he opened the right front door of the wagon and got in. She was wearing a pale blue pant suit and the long lustrous strands of her jet black hair were plaited and secured around her head with a comb made from a delicate pink shell. Once again, he was struck by the quiet serenity of her beauty.

"You'll get used to the summer heat in a few weeks," she assured him as the station wagon moved down the drive of the hotel. "Summer in Gulf City starts around May first, sometimes even by mid-April. Mrs. Barrett opens her gardens to the public on Sundays in late March. She has a gardener and they're lovely almost up to midsummer."

"The Clinic must be very prosperous."

"Very much so. The staff does twice as much surgery as any other group in Gulf City."

As they sped eastward toward the river on a broad parkway, the occasional elevated overpasses gave Mark a wide view of the western portion of Gulf City. The streets were broad, the vegetation definitely subtropical. Houses were generally white or pastel in color and, along the waterfront, almost uniformly high-rise. With palm trees everywhere and the broad expanse of the Gulf of Mexico stretching to the south in an endless vista, Mark could almost believe he was in Miami or some West Coast Florida city like Sarasota.

Offshore, the blue water of the Gulf sparkled in the sunlight and a line of fishing boats was heading out to open water by way of the river mouth with its jetties protecting the channel, each boat leaving a wide fan of white water in its wake.

"Old Town on the other side of the river goes back to Spanish days before the American Revolution," said Alexa as they approached the high bridge. "You can tell the difference from the top."

A sharp change was indeed apparent the moment they reached the high point of the elevated bridge. East of the river, in what Alexa had called "Old Town," the streets were narrow, the houses small, reminding Mark of old St. Augustine in Florida. Fishing boats with huge nets hanging from outriggers lined much of the waterfront on this side. But when he looked back across the river, Mark could see many luxurious homes with protected mooring slips along the riverfront, most of them with yachts of various sizes tied up. From the highest point of the bridge, he could also see the white sprawl of the Yacht Club with its roof of bright blue tiles and its brood of sailing craft. Farther upstream on the north side of the bridge, he could see a small park replete with weeping willows, shaded paths, and tendrils of Spanish moss hanging from the trees—a haven of retreat from the busy traffic and activities of the city.

"I don't imagine the Clinic gets many patients from this side of town," Mark said as they started to descend from the top of the bridge. "The houses over here don't look very expensive."

"Don't let Old Town's somewhat shabby appearance fool you," said Alexa. "Many retired people have migrated here lately, and besides, it's become something of a colony for artists and musicians. We have our own Mardi Gras like New Orleans and Mobile, and there's even talk of bringing the Spoleto Festival here for a brief stay next year after it finishes the season at Charleston."

"Somebody was certainly smart in locating the airport outside what you call Old Town," Mark observed as the four-lane turnpike approached the surprisingly large facility. "Not many cities have an airport less than half an hour away from the center of business."

"The City Fathers are trying to preserve the natural charms of the older buildings east of the river," she told him. "Did Dr. Barrett tell you we're going to open a satellite Clinic on this side of town soon?"

"He mentioned it."

"The mayor and the Chamber of Commerce are planning a reception for the public when it's dedicated a few weeks from now."

"I suppose the mayor will make a speech."

"Of course." She laughed. "After all, he does own the building."

"I'm going to settle for coffee and toast," said Alexa when they found a table in the restaurant on the second floor of the airport after parking the car in the main airport building.

"Since coming South, I've developed a passion for sausage biscuits," Mark confessed when the waitress appeared. "Bring me two, please—and coffee."

"I hope you and Claire didn't quarrel after you left the Club last night," Alexa said as they waited for their food. "She was obviously tired, and Jerry Thorpe probably bent her ear while we were dancing."

"Did you know they once had an affair?"

"That was before I joined the Clinic staff, but the older nurses say it was pretty hectic."

"Claire told me they didn't marry because both of them realized they were too much alike."

"From what I've seen of medical marriages, it's better if the partners are somewhat plus and minus," she agreed. "That way, enough current will flow between the terminals to keep the marriage alive."

"That's a pretty sage observation," Mark complimented her. "Maybe you should have been a psychiatrist or at least a psychiatric nurse."

"It's not that sage," she demurred. "You've no doubt known

many women, some of them intimately, so you must realize that you're a challenge to Claire."

"But not to you?"

"Not a challenge I intend to accept," she said crisply. "By now I'm sure you know, Dr. Harrison, that almost any woman would have to be made of stone not to feel the effect of your natural charm and your purely physical attributes."

"Now you're being psychiatric again," he warned.

"Did Claire tell you Abner Desmond tried to kill himself about a month after their divorce?"

"No. What happened?"

"Perhaps you should wait for Claire to tell you."

"I think I'd get a clearer picture from an outside observer."

"Claire and Abner Desmond were childhood sweethearts; both families expected them to marry as soon as he finished his professional education."

"I didn't know he was a doctor."

"He wasn't. Abner's college record couldn't get him into medical school, but his family did have enough influence and money to have him admitted to the state dental college. Actually, he did very well there and became a skilled dental surgeon, but he always considered himself a failure."

"Claire implied that, physically at least, he was a failure as a husband."

"Probably that, too; it may even have been one of the major reasons for their divorce, although I think the roots went much deeper than that. Or am I getting psychiatric again?"

"If you are, your viewpoint is a fascinating one."

"Now you come into the picture," she said. "You're very different from Abner Desmond, so naturally Claire would view you as a challenge."

"Go on."

"I've studied doctors—they're a special breed, you know. Unfortunately, so do they."

"The 'God Complex'? It's hard not to develop at least a little of that when you're always giving orders other people must carry out."

"That's not the whole picture, particularly for a surgeon.

Knowing a slip of the scalpel can cause an uncontrollable hemorrhage doesn't exactly breed uncertainty about your own ability."

"I'm not quite sure that particular aspect of the doctor personality isn't overrated, but we won't argue about it. When Desmond attempted suicide, what actually happened?"

"The bullet he tried to put through his brain only left him partially paralyzed. He's working as a dentist in a small town along the coast and loves it."

"Obviously, you've kept in touch. May I ask what's the relationship?"

"Friendship, sympathy, maybe a natural tendency to be a good Samaritan—the doctors here are always accusing me of those kinds of emotions. When he was discharged from the hospital, Abner Desmond moved to a small town just beyond Gulfport and settled there. He married a nurse I knew here and they are very happy with what they have—an excellent practice, plus the respect and admiration of the community. You couldn't find a more happily married couple or a professional man as completely satisfied with what he's doing."

"Perhaps Claire did him a favor by divorcing him," Mark suggested.

"If she did, it was certainly the hard way."

"I still don't think you can put all the blame on Claire," Mark objected. "Throughout the country, the suicide rate for dentists is as high as it is for doctors, and that's three times the average for the general population. Two members of my medical school class killed themselves, one before we finished and the other while a first-year resident."

"I'm familiar with all those statistics, particularly the incidence of what might be called emotional breakdown with the use of alcohol, amphetamines, and other drugs as crutches. It's about a hundred times as frequent in doctors as in the general population."

"I'm curious about one thing," said Mark. "Why did you tell me all this about the relationship between Abner and Claire?"

"Maybe to put you on your guard when the showdown comes with her."

"There doesn't have to be any showdown."

"You know better than that. It's an inevitable part of every man-woman relationship—especially between two strong individuals."

"You're in that class yourself. How can you act as one apart?"

"Perhaps because Indian blood instinctively leads me toward the matriarchal relationship that characterized the Creeks in their heyday." She gave him a sudden wry smile. "Or, then, I could be kidding myself."

X

"Glad to see you got safely to Gulf City, Mark," Dr. Richard Barrett shook hands vigorously with the younger surgeon in the airport after he and his wife had debarked from the plane which had brought them from Atlanta. "You remember Dr. Harrison, I'm sure, dear?" he asked turning to his wife.

"Of course." Mrs. Barrett resembled a somewhat wilted Southern belle. "Nice to see you again, Dr. Harrison. You, too, Alexa, dear."

"You can drop Mark and me at the Clinic, Alexa," said Barrett as they were leaving the parking lot. "Do you have time to take Mother home?"

"Plenty of time, sir. Dr. Thorpe isn't operating until eleven."

"Did you get to visit the Clinic?" Barrett asked, turning to Mark.

"Not yet. I got in late day before yesterday and everything was closed on the Fourth, but I've been looking over the city."

"Have you come to a decision yet?"

"I'll take the year's contract you offered in Baltimore, sir."

"Good! I was certain you would, once you'd seen our city. After we examine the Clinic this morning, Jack Pryor, the administrator at Gulfside Hospital, will take you in hand and show you around. Then this afternoon, we can visit Paul Martenson's office —he's our financial adviser—where you can sign the formal contract."

"I'm ready," said Mark. "Claire was generous enough to take me to the dance at the Yacht Club last night where I met Dr. Thorpe and Miss McGillivray."

"I hope Jerry wasn't obnoxious." Barrett's tone was disapproving. "He's been drinking rather heavily since his second marriage broke up. Besides, as the youngest man in our group, he wasn't very happy about adding another surgeon to it."

"Miss McGillivray tells me you'll soon be opening a satellite Clinic in Old Town," Mark said as they were leaving the parking lot. "I've had some experience with the one Lakeview's been operating for over five years in a small city between Baltimore and Washington."

"So Aldo Ramirez told me. That was another reason—besides your training in microsurgery—why I was interested in adding you to the Clinic staff. The 'short-stay' movement is very progressive. I can see no reason for burdening patients with heavy hospital expense, when hundreds of relatively minor procedures can be performed as outpatients—at the same professional cost to them —allowing them to recuperate in their own homes."

"The whole thing has worked out rather well in our experience in Maryland," Mark agreed. "For the past six months, we've even been repairing hernias and only keeping the patients overnight in one of several rooms that are part of the clinic setup. One nurse was able to take care of them with the help of a first-year resident who covered the Clinic nights and weekends for emergency services."

"That's exactly the sort of thing we hope to do here." Barrett's voice was full of enthusiasm. "I want you to talk to Jack Pryor and tell him what you've been telling me. Jack was against the whole idea at first because he thought it would take patients away from the hospital. I think I've convinced him, though, that by having a crack surgeon like yourself available at the Clinic in Old Town, we can draw patients from all over the county. Besides, Gulfside Hospital's beds are full practically all the time anyway."

"Will Hospitals, Inc., administer the satellite Clinic, too?"

"Of course," said Barrett. "With the buying power of a chain and the efficiency it brings to the everyday business of running a hospital, the average institution can't even compete."

At the Barrett Clinic, located in an impressive-looking building adjacent to the hospital, Mark and Barrett got out of the station wagon and Alexa drove off with Mrs. Barrett.

XI

"Welcome home, Dr. Barrett." The receptionist at a desk in the center of the lobby smiled warmly when they came through the second set of doors into the air-conditioned atmosphere of the Barrett Clinic building. "Hope you had a good trip."

"Excellent, Mrs. Porter—as my golf score proved. This is Dr. Mark Harrison. He's going to join the staff of the Clinic."

"I know you'll like it here, Dr. Harrison; we all do." The voice of the receptionist had a soft Southern accent, quite appropriate to the location.

"Have Dr. Harkness and Dr. Peterson come in yet?" Barrett asked, without waiting for Mark to acknowledge the warm greeting of the receptionist.

"Oh yes! They've been seeing patients since eight o'clock. We're having a very busy day after the long holiday weekend."

"Good! Come along, Mark. You already know Jerry Thorpe but I want you to meet your other associates."

"Glad to have you aboard, Harrison." Dr. Elmer Peterson, the Clinic orthopedist, was a huge bear of a man whose grip almost crushed Mark's fingers. "I don't have much use for an operating microscope in my job, but it's nice to know I can call on an expert in case I happen to cut the femoral artery doing an artificial hip. Ever do any sailing?"

"Not much," Mark confessed. "The ponds where I grew up in the Piedmont section of North Carolina weren't very big."

"I'll take you out sometime and show you what it's like. My boat won the Mobile-to-Nassau ocean race three years ago."

"And he's never stopped talking about it since," said Barrett. "Seen Andy lately, Elmer?"

"I think he's doing an echocardiogram," said Peterson. "I made a diagnosis of Tietze's syndrome on a young woman who complained of severe chest pain after lifting a heavy baby. The diagnosis seemed definite enough, but I thought we'd better rule out a floppy mitral before I try injecting the painful area with hydrocortisone."

What would have been gibberish to the uninitiated was perfectly understandable to Mark. Tietze's syndrome was a very painful condition in which the cartilage—gristle to the lay person —attaching the end of a rib to the breastbone or sternum was partially ruptured, causing intense chest pain that could easily be mistaken for angina. "Floppy mitral" described an anatomical abnormality found in perhaps twenty percent of the general population without causing any symptoms—except in a few. There, it seemed to produce an often bizarre picture of chest pain, irregular heartbeat, and even fainting—all of which could be interpreted as resulting from coronary heart disease that was not actually present.

"Come on, Mark." Barrett led the way down a corridor and knocked on a door. Ignoring the DO NOT ENTER sign on it, he pushed the door open to reveal a dark room.

"What the hell do you mean by barging in here?" a voice with a strong New England twang demanded from the darkness inside the room. Then it added, "Oh, hello, Dick. I might have known it was you sticking your nose into everything."

"Want you to meet Dr. Mark Harrison." Barrett ignored the other man's jibe. "This is Dr. Andrew Harkness, Mark. He graduated from Lakeview about the time you were born, but somehow managed to become a very good cardiologist."

"Glad to know you, Harrison." Mark's pupils had dilated by now to where he was able to see the tall spare man wearing a white laboratory coat, who had been bending over the patient lying on the table. "Aldo Ramirez spoke very highly of you when I talked to him on the phone a few weeks ago about the possibility of your coming here. He and I were classmates at Lakeview."

"You certainly have the New England twang, sir," said Mark.

"Ought to; I grew up in Bangor, Maine. Take a look at this."

Bending over the patient again, Harkness moved the instrument he'd been using to produce sound waves across the patient's chest. Immediately, the waves were bounced back in the form of an electronic picture on a small monitor screen. "Prettiest case of mitral valve prolapse you ever saw," he observed.

"No doubt about that," Mark agreed, as he studied the screen

"Fortunately, it's an accidental finding," said Harkness. "After

Elmer Peterson injects some hydrocortisone a few times into the ruptured cartilage that's causing this young lady's pain, she'll be as good as new." Switching on the lights, he turned to the patient and added, "You'll never have to worry about this little heart condition, young lady, because you were born with it. About one out of every five in the world have what we call a prolapsed mitral valve, but most of them don't even know it."

"Thank you, Doctor," said the patient.

"Get some good pictures of that valve and have them made into slides," Harkness directed the technician who had been sitting beside the patient during the examination. Turning to Mark, he asked, "How about a cup of coffee, Harrison? You, too, Dick?"

"No, thanks," said Barrett. "Got to call Paul Martenson about drawing up Mark's contract and also about a piece of property I saw for sale in West Virginia. I'll leave Dr. Harrison with you for a few minutes, Andy, then I'll finish showing him around and turn him over to Jack Pryor for a visit to the hospital before lunch."

"Come along, Harrison," said Harkness. "I'll introduce you into the only island of sanity we have around here."

A small lounge containing tables, chairs, some vending machines, and a large coffee maker was located at the end of the corridor, with a wide window overlooking the Gulf.

"Prettiest sight in the world when the weather's good, like today—and the worst during a hurricane," said Harkness as he drew two paper cups of coffee and handed one to Mark. "Cream and sugar are on the table, so help yourself. Do you want any of that stuff the vending machines provide—for twice what it's worth?"

"Miss McGillivray and I had breakfast at the airport before Dr. and Mrs. Barrett arrived," Mark explained. "I think I'll forego anything else for a while."

"So you've already met our Alexa. She's a beautiful girl."

"Smart, too, sir."

"Never mind the 'sir' business. I may be old enough to be your father, but you're a highly trained doctor, too, and that makes us equal." The internist took a deep drink from his coffee cup. "So you're going to join the Clinic staff?"

"I'm supposed to sign the final contract this afternoon."

"Think you'll like private practice better than teaching?"

"I don't know," Mark confessed, "but I had to borrow money for most of my education, and it's a quick way to pay it back."

"What did Dick Barrett agree to pay you the first year?"

"Sixty-five thousand."

"Must have some Scotch blood in you, too," the internist commented. "That was the figure we'd set as the highest we would allow Dick to go in hiring a new surgeon."

"I had some good advice beforehand—from Mrs. Desmond. She told me to ask for seventy-five and then haggle."

"Claire's a smart girl; got one of the most profitable advertising and business relations operations in town. Made it on her own hook, too, in a man's world." Harkness gave a deep sigh. "What I wouldn't give to be your age, son, and as handsome as you are. Anything I can tell you about the setup here?"

"I think not. It looks very efficient and I'm sure it's very profitable."

"Too damn efficient, if you ask me."

"I don't exactly understand."

"Take that patient we saw just now," said the internist. "In the old days, I'd've listened to her chest with a stethoscope and told her she had rheumatic heart disease, when I heard a systolic murmur with a click in it. I'd probably have advised her not to play tennis, too, or do any very hard work. Then, if she happened to be the nervous type—which she is—she might have gone through life believing she had a bad heart and visiting me several times a year for reassurance—at the usual fee. Instead, that damn machine in there gave an exact picture of what's going on inside her chest and now I can reassure her—and probably never see her again."

"Which do you prefer? Old-fashioned medicine where you relied on your clinical sense and the physical examination and history to make the diagnosis? Or the new kind where a machine does it for you?"

"Ideally, a good doctor should use as much of both as he needs, but no more," said Harkness. "When you see twenty-five or thirty patients a day, as we do here, though, you can't spend much time dawdling over a stethoscope. More's the pity, too, because sometimes those damn machines turn out to be wrong."

XII

Jack Pryor, administrator of Gulfside Hospital, was in his early forties, plump, brisk, and confident. He spent over an hour giving Mark a guided tour of the hospital facilities. From the gallery of an operating suite, Mark saw Alexa assisting and confirmed for himself what Dr. Richard Barrett had told him—namely, that she was a skilled first assistant. The hospital, too, he saw, was modern and efficient.

"What do you think of our setup?" Pryor asked as he and Mark deposited their lunch trays on a table in a small dining room reserved for the upper-echelon members of the hospital administration, the supervising nursing staff, and courtesy staff doctors who chose to save time by eating there.

"I'm impressed."

Mark chose not to mention some of the things that had troubled him during the tour. Although new, spotlessly clean, and obviously well run, there was a sterile atmosphere about the four-hundred bed structure and its operating personnel. In fact, everything seemed almost as impersonal as the Barrett Clinic echocardiographic machine, with its ability to make a diagnosis in a few minutes that would have required hours of history-taking and physical examination, even by an expert like Dr. Harkness. In such a hospital, Mark suspected, the sick would get sound medical care but little of the sympathy and consideration which, he knew from his own years of experience at Lakeview, were often as important as medication or surgery.

"It's a profitable business, too," said Pryor on a note of vast satisfaction as he vigorously tackled the ample lunch he had chosen for himself. "Gulfside has consistently shown the highest earnings per bed of any facility operated by Hospitals, Inc." He pronounced the last word as if it was spelled "Ink."

"Isn't 'business' a rather strange term to use in describing the running of a hospital?" Mark asked.

"Providing quality medical care is just that, a business," Pryor said firmly. "The reason so many hospitals lost money in the past is because they weren't operated with strictly business methods."

"Obviously, you have superior facilities here," said Mark. "And I'm sure there are equally capable doctors on the staff."

"Every one of them certified specialists—except the Family Practice Section, of course. That's operated largely by FMGs."

"Is your Emergency Department operated by foreign medical graduates, too?" Mark asked.

"I should say not! Two MDs and two DOs handle emergencies on a rotating basis, as well as staffing a primary care station out on I-10. The city Fire Department has the finest emergency equipment and personnel between Pensacola and New Orleans, too." Pryor pushed his empty tray aside. "Ready to visit the Old Town facility?"

"Whenever you are."

Old Town, Mark saw as they drove through the narrow picturesque streets, had much the charm of St. Augustine, Savannah, or Charleston. The building selected for the satellite Clinic proved to be adequate, too. Within easy walking distance for patients coming from almost any part of the town, the somewhat rambling structure afforded ample space for offices and two small surgeries, plus several rooms where patients being kept overnight could be accommodated.

"Once you have this Clinic in operation, I plan to bring a delegation of the brass from Hospitals, Inc., to see it," Pryor confided. "One problem we're having in the company lately is that the new hospitals fill up almost faster than we can complete them."

"How do you explain being able to keep a full house when hospital occupancy rates over the country have been going down lately due to rising costs?"

"Mainly from the growth of the Barrett Clinic, plus the fact that people keep pouring into this area—older people with Medicare and plenty of other insurance to cover health care costs.

Which reminds me—will you need a complete laboratory over here?"

"What we did in Baltimore was take blood for complicated examinations like a CS-18 and send it to the main laboratory at Lakeview," Mark told him. "As for the rest, one technician should be able to handle blood counts, urine examinations, and simple laboratory procedures right here."

"I can see where your know-how is going to be worth a lot to us, Mark, to say nothing of your skill in microsurgery." Pryor looked at his watch. "Sorry I've got to run, but it's after two. I have an appointment at two-thirty, so we'd better get started back."

"If you don't mind, I'll walk," said Mark. "It will give me a chance to see both sides of Gulf City at a little closer range."

"It's a good three miles back to the Holiday Inn and the Clinic," Pryor said doubtfully.

"That won't bother me. I run six miles at least four times a week, but with the temperature in the high eighties here today, I think I'll just walk."

"Okay," said Pryor. "When are you planning to go back to Baltimore?"

"Probably tonight. Now that I've decided, I want to get moved down here as soon as I can."

XIII

The big thermometer atop a Savings and Loan Association building showed ninety-three degrees as Mark started up the pedestrian walkway traversing the high bridge that separated the two sharply different parts of the city. A cooling breeze from the Gulf tended to offset the effects of the heat, however, and at the top, the walkway itself had been widened to form an observation deck on the south side, so he stopped to lean against the rail and rest a few moments after the exertion of the upward climb.

In the center, when he surveyed the vista spread out before him, was the river with stone-walled jetties keeping the channel from silting up extending seaward past the outer islands into the open Gulf. Around the end of the jetties, a half-dozen or so small boats were anchored while the occupants fished, as did many earthbound fishermen scattered along the massive rocks brought in to form jetties. Farther out, a larger fishing boat was moving slowly, trolling lines extended on outriggers while the fishermen lolled in chairs at the stern, ready to seize the rods beside them at the first hint of a prey ready to strike.

Farther south, the outlines of a half dozen commercial fishing boats could be seen. Well beyond them, hardly more than half visible against the horizon, a larger vessel was moving eastward, probably, Mark surmised, heading for the Straits of Florida leading to the broad reaches of the Atlantic. Or, by way of the Yucatan Channel to the Caribbean and the exotic chain of islands that formed its boundaries.

On his left, the smaller area of Old Town could easily be seen because the houses were rarely more than two stories high. Railed balconies at the second level were almost the rule, and many homes had stuccoed walls and roofs of bright-colored ceramic tiles, betraying their origin during the twenties, when that form of construction had been popular all along the coastal areas of Florida and the Gulf of Mexico. To the west, less visible because of the towering framework of the bridge, tall hotels, condominium buildings, and commercial structures clustered in the area near the river and the Gulf, marking the much larger spread of Gulf City itself. Below, the beach was dotted with multicolored umbrellas against the punishing rays of the July sun while antlike figures moved about on the white sands of the beach.

The two cities were as starkly different as the two beautiful women inhabitants to whom he had become attracted, Mark thought suddenly. Alexa McGillivray was much like Old Town: serene, calmly confident, graceful, and beautiful. Claire, on the other hand, was more like the bustling, eager, and strikingly modern newer Gulf City west of the river, aglow with life and exciting promise. And as he began to descend the walkway from the high arch of the bridge, which largely shut out the beauty of Old Town from his vision, just so did the anticipation of being with Claire again in the bustling new Gulf City wipe away the picture of Alexa from his mind.

XIV

The building known as "The Tower," where Paul Martenson had his office, was thirty stories high and for this part of the country exceptionally tall. It was only two blocks from the Holiday Inn and overlooked the river mouth while facing southward toward the Gulf. The lawyer himself was handsome, tall, and very brisk, with only a faint sprinkling of gray at the temples.

"Glad to meet you, Dr. Harrison," he said with a crisp Boston accent. "Dr. Barrett should be here any minute, but meanwhile we can take care of some details, like making applications to the State Licensing Board for you to practice here and applying to the hospitals for surgical privileges. Do you have the certificates Dr. Barrett asked you to bring?"

"They're all in here." Mark handed him a folder.

"Good!" Martenson pressed a buzzer on his desk and a smart-looking secretary appeared immediately.

"Please take these and Xerox them, Agnes," he directed.

"Here's a copy of the contract between you and the Barrett Clinic." The lawyer handed Mark a document from a folder on his desk blotter. "You'll see that it provides for temporary employment for a year, to become permanent at that time if you and the members of the Clinic group agree."

The document was simple enough and Mark saw nothing in it with which to quarrel—until he came to the last clause:

If for any reason either Dr. Harrison or the Clinic staff do not wish to continue his employment after the first year, he hereby agrees not to enter the practice of medicine in this county for a period of five years thereafter.

"What's the idea of this?" Mark asked, pointing to the clause.

"The mere fact of your being associated with the Barrett Clinic for a year will give you a certain—shall we say *éclat?*—in medical circles both in Gulf City and in the surrounding areas," Martenson explained. "If you were free to open an office for yourself at the end of the year, you would have gained a head start, so to speak, in competition with other members of the Clinic. You would then be free to take patients with you, as well as gain others through contacts you may have made with referring physicians in and outside the city. I think you'll agree that giving you such an advantage would be manifestly unfair to your employers."

"It's not the Barrett Clinic I'm concerned about, Mr. Martenson—it's myself. Suppose I put in a year with them and they decide at the end of the year to kick me out—maybe because I'm becoming too popular or something. Where would I be?"

"No worse off financially than you are now. The salary you're being paid during the first year is certainly excellent."

"But no more than the damage to my professional reputation would be from being kicked out of a place like the Barrett Clinic," Mark said bluntly.

"You have a valid point there," the lawyer conceded. "Frankly, I think you could bring action in court and have it thrown out, if you were able to prove that you were not being treated fairly in being discharged from employment by the Clinic."

"What the hell is it doing in the contract, then?"

Martenson hesitated momentarily. "One of the group insisted on its being there."

"Jerry Thorpe!"

"I'm not at liberty to reveal the person's name, but you come so highly recommended and enjoy Dr. Barrett's confidence to such a degree that I'd strongly advise you not to make an issue of that particular clause."

"Would you be willing to represent me, if Thorpe prejudiced the others against me strongly enough for them to push me out?"

"I represent the Barrett Clinic, so ethics wouldn't allow that." Martenson permitted himself a small smile. "I could, however, recommend a colleague—"

Further conversation was interrupted by the arrival of Dr. Richard Barrett. "Sorry to be late, gentlemen. Jack Pryor held me up with some important business," he said. "By the way, Mark, Jack was very favorably impressed by your enthusiasm for the satellite Clinic location in Old Town."

"No more than I was," said Mark. "I think it can be a very valuable asset."

"Are you satisfied with the contract?"

"That last clause troubles me a bit. It seems to imply that I might be willing to work for a year with the Clinic, just to get what Mr. Martenson calls a 'head start' when I open my own office."

"I can understand your feelings, my boy." Barrett's voice had a paternal note. "We put that clause in at the request of one of the group, but I can assure you that no one else has any reservations about you. Besides, my own influence isn't small and I have no more questions about your professional integrity than I do about your surgical ability—which are none."

"In that case, I'm willing to sign."

"Good!" Barrett reached for the contract. "As proof of my own faith, I'll sign first."

The details were quickly wrapped up and Barrett got to his feet. "When are you going back to Baltimore?" he asked.

"Tonight, if I can get a plane out. With luck, I'll be back and on the payroll in a week or less."

"Excellent! Can I give you a lift back to your hotel?"

"Thank you, sir, but Claire advised me to discuss my own finances with Mr. Martenson, so I'll stay a few minutes longer if he can spare me the time."

"I'll be happy to," said Martenson.

"I'd like to schedule a dinner to introduce you to some influential people here," said Barrett. "Would a week from tonight suit you?"

"That's fine with me," said Mark.

"I hope you and Regina can join us, Paul," said Barrett to the lawyer as he was leaving.

"We'll be there," Martenson assured him as he accompanied the surgeon to the door.

Back at his desk after seeing Barrett out, the lawyer reached for a yellow legal tablet.

"Suppose we start by listing your assets, Dr. Harrison," he said.

"That will be easy. Five hundred dollars in cash, a five-year-old Buick Skylark, the clothes I'm wearing, plus a TV, a few pieces of antique furniture, and the medical texts I used in school and during my residency and fellowship."

"Assets in dollars today five hundred, with maybe a thousand more, counting the trade-in value of the car," the lawyer listed in the table he was making upon the yellow tablet. "Plus, the best surgical training in America. We can't set a value on that, of course. But with the tax advantages of being associated with a professional corporation, plus the right to put away a large portion of your income in a retirement fund that's tax-free until you choose to retire, that single asset could easily be worth a million dollars to you over your lifetime."

"The prospects boggle my mind," Mark admitted.

"What about the liabilities?" Martenson asked.

"Three six percent loans of ten thousand each, on paid-up life insurance policies my father bought for me before he died," said Mark. "He was an agent for an insurance company and believed in it—which I'm not entirely sure I do."

"For you now, certainly not," Martenson agreed. "Later, when you have a family, I'll buy you enough term insurance to protect them until your estate is large enough to do the job. You'll save enough in premiums on policies like the whole-life variety the agents will try to sell you to send your children to college."

"Shouldn't I start paying off the loans on the policies I already have?"

"I'd advise against doing it. If you made those loans today, you'd pay around eighteen percent. Meanwhile, the money you might use to pay off the loans now could be earning fifteen percent in the right sort of an investment. Besides, the interest you're paying now is deductible from your income tax, reducing the cost even more when you take into account the IRS bracket you'll be in with your new salary. How much do you figure it will cost you to live per month?"

Mark shrugged. "Maybe a thousand."

"Make it two; a Barrett Clinic surgeon can't live in a garret— even if there were such things anymore. Write me a check for half your salary every month and I'll put it into a tax shelter that will give you enough write-off in depreciation and various other charges to reduce your tax liability close to zero."

"I've heard of 'zero tax,' but I didn't know it was really possible."

"It is, believe me."

"When can I pay off my debts?"

"Leave that to the administrator of your estate; they're only costing you six percent per year, so let your children pay them," Martenson advised. "Neither of us are ever likely to see interest rates as low again as those on your policies, so your debts might as well be earning a profit for you."

"I'm afraid I'm a babe in the woods when it comes to money," Mark confessed.

"Most doctors are—that's why speculators often steal them blind. Come to think of it, though, you'll probably need your first month's salary to catch up on things. First, you'll have to buy a car more suitable for a successful surgeon than an old Buick. Suppose we start with the second month's salary, and I'll take over from there."

"We haven't discussed what *you'll* get out of it."

"Don't worry about my cut; money managers earn commissions from the people they place investments with. Besides, general partners in the kind of limited partnerships I put my clients into don't contribute anything but their know-how, although they have an equal share in the tax write-offs as well as the profits." Martenson rose, terminating the interview. "Come to see me two months from now with a check for half your salary, and I'll take over from there."

"Shake, partner; I'm in your hands," said Mark. "Can I use your phone to call about a reservation?"

"My secretary will make it for you. See you a week from tonight at Dr. Barrett's dinner party. I might as well advise you that it will be indescribably dull, but functions like that can pay off very well indeed."

Two hours later, after leaving a message for Claire with her secretary that he'd be back in less than a week, Mark took the regular limousine to the airport and a night flight to Baltimore— severing his connection with Lakeview, perhaps forever.

Book Two

Gulf City

I

It was after nine o'clock, and raining, six days later when Mark knocked on the door of Alexa McGillivray's apartment in Gulf City. When she opened it, he saw that she was wearing a long nylon robe and carpet slippers, with the dark masses of her hair, loosened from the braids that bound it during the day, falling in a cascade of beauty to her shoulders. Once again, he was startled by her quiet loveliness.

"Hello," she said. "You're a day early."

"My Skylark did better than I expected, even towing a U-Haul with all my worldly possessions. I have a reservation for tomorrow night at the Holiday Inn, but every motel in town appears to be filled tonight."

"They usually are, during the summer tourist season."

"Any idea where I can find a room for the night?"

"I've got a spare and you're welcome to it. Had your dinner?"

"A sandwich at a Howard Johnson's on I-65 about five o'clock. I figured if I came on through tonight, I'd have tomorrow to look for an apartment."

"I was about to make myself a rum collins before I put a TV dinner in the oven and can easily add a second to both," she said. "We'll have our drinks while the dinners are cooking."

"How do you manage to always do everything right?" he asked as he followed her to the small kitchen, where she slid the TV dinners into the oven.

"I don't push." She took a bottle of top-grade rum from a cabinet over the sink. "One jigger or two?"

"Two. I've driven over five hundred miles today."

She poured the drinks, stirred in the collins mixture, and handed him one of the glasses. She had, he noticed, poured only a single jigger for herself.

"Why don't you go back to the living room and have your drink while the dinners are cooking?" she asked. "It will take over thirty minutes and I'll be setting the table and making some coffee."

"I'd rather sit in the kitchen."

It was relaxing to watch the grace and the inherent quality of dignity in her movements, while she set the table and put water on to boil for instant coffee. Every movement she made was as certain as those he'd witnessed when he'd briefly seen her working with Jerry Thorpe in the Operating Room on the day he visited Gulfside Hospital with Jack Pryor.

"Did you know Jerry Thorpe insisted on putting a clause in my contract with the Clinic forbidding me to open an office in Gulf County, if I decided not to stay on here at the end of a year?" he asked.

"No, but I'm not surprised."

"Why?"

"For one thing, you're younger."

"I watched Thorpe doing a hysterectomy when Jack Pryor and I visited one of the O.R. observation galleries. He's very skilled— and so are you."

She smiled. "If you knew how many operations I scrubbed for at Duke, when my feet were killing me and my back was breaking—"

"Ever scrub for microsurgery?"

"Some—enough to be able to recognize what I was looking at in the field of vision."

"That's fine! Jerry Thorpe obviously tried to make me so angry with the terms of the Clinic contract that I'd refuse to sign, but you only mentioned age as the cause."

"That—plus ability."

"I couldn't do a vaginal hysterectomy half as swiftly as he does."

"To Jerry, the mere fact that he is skilled when working in the female pelvis makes him feel inferior to you."

"Why?"

"His expertise is limited, while yours ranges through the whole field of surgery in anatomical situations where Jerry would feel lost."

"You sound like a professor of anatomy," he said with a smile.

She moved swiftly to the oven at the sound of the time indicator. "I paid my way for the Master's Degree in Surgical Nursing at Duke by doubling as an instructor in anatomy for the first-year nursing students."

"I'll bet you were a good teacher."

"They didn't fire me," she said laconically as she slid the TV dinners out of the oven and onto plates at the small table for two in the kitchen. "This isn't anything near as elaborate as the dinner Dr. Barrett is going to stage for you, but it's the best I can do on such short notice."

"You're going to be at the dinner, aren't you?"

"Me? Certainly not. I'm just the hired help, remember?"

"You're a better-trained nurse than a lot of the doctors' wives who'll be there and who graduated from nursing school. I've a mind to make an issue of it when I talk to Barrett in the morning."

"Please don't. It would only be embarrassing for me. After all, I'm perfectly content with my job and everything that goes with it."

"You and I are going to make a fine surgical team," he told her. "As good as the one you already make with Jerry Thorpe."

"If you're implying that Dr. Jeremy Thorpe and I are more than just surgeon and assistant, you're wrong," she said, a little sharply. "I don't mix my profession with my social or emotional life."

"I'll accept that as a basis for our own relationship, but you still haven't given me a real reason why Jerry Thorpe should try to provoke me into going somewhere else," he told her.

"Jerry is a very gifted surgeon in his field, almost an actor you might say. I've never tried to solve his emotional problems or analyze them either."

"What about the relationship between him and Claire Desmond?"

"Why ask me?"

"Because you obviously know both of them very well. And because you're smart enough to know the answer to my question."

"If you're asking whether there was once an emotional involvement between them, you already know the answer—but I'm not sure it's one you would understand."

"Why?"

"Because I'm not entirely certain what it is myself."

"You're a very acute observer when it comes to human beings.

I'd be inclined to accept your evaluation over anyone else's I've met so far."

Alexa shrugged, a movement he couldn't help observing, accompanied by considerable natural grace.

"What's *your* interest in Claire?" she asked. "Besides, of course, the obvious one of sexual attraction?"

"I'm not sure of that either," he admitted wryly. "When I'm with Claire, I'm so infatuated—I guess it's the right word—that I can't be analytical. But I'm certain she and I could never be just good friends, the way I'd like to be with you."

"Is that another way of saying I have no sex appeal?"

"Absolutely not. You're a very beautiful and desirable woman."

"Thanks—for nothing."

"Now you're offended—and I don't want you to be. Would an apology help?"

"For stating a fact? That would be dishonest. Maybe it's just my Creek blood. You see, the Creeks had a reputation for lasciviousness, but they were actually very straitlaced when it came to marriage. Though the husband was allowed several wives, unfaithfulness on the wife's part was punishable by death. It just so happens that I'm more interested in being a loyal, productive woman—possibly even a wife in good time—than I am in being a sexpot."

"Is that all you think Claire is—a sexpot?"

"You've slept with her at least once, I suspect. What's your opinion?"

He chose not to answer and asked instead, "Was the problem between Jerry Thorpe and Claire the same as with the man she married—that he wasn't enough of a man for her?"

They had been sitting in the small kitchen of her tastefully furnished apartment. Now she stood up and started piling their dishes into the sink.

"You're asking me to sit in judgment on other people, and that's against my principles, Dr. Harrison. I've got to work tomorrow and you're going to be busy looking for an apartment until you and Claire go to the dinner tomorrow night, so we'd both better get to bed."

It was a rebuke and he accepted it gracefully. "Thanks for the supper. I'll take you out to dinner the first chance I get—if you'll go."

"I often go out to dinner with friends." A sudden gamine look came into her lovely dark eyes, one he hadn't seen there before. "Some of them are even men."

II

Mark checked into the Holiday Inn the following morning and Claire called him about four o'clock.

"When did you get back?" she asked.

"Last night," he told her, but chose not to mention the fact that he'd spent the night in Alexa McGillivray's apartment. "I was tired from driving and spent most of the morning looking for an apartment but without much luck."

"Leave that to me. I'll be by there about six forty-five to pick you up for the dinner. No, better make it a little earlier."

"You can make it a lot earlier, if you'd like."

Her laugh rang out. "I believe you really are as randy as that nurse Alexa talked to in Baltimore said you were. Come to think of it, though, Father has invited Dr. Anson Drew, president of the County Medical Society, to the dinner with his wife. They're both teetotalers and Evangelicals to boot, so no alcoholic beverages will be served. Do you have any vodka?"

"No, but I can get some downstairs."

"Please do. We'll have a couple of drinks to ease the pain of the evening. Old Anson can't smell vodka on our breaths, so he won't know it. See you around six."

Going down to the package store located on the first floor of the hotel, Mark bought a fifth of vodka and a bottle of tonic for setups, then went back up and showered. He was putting on his necktie when a knock sounded on the door and he opened it to find Claire, looking as beautiful as usual, standing outside. Her kiss was uninhibited, the cavity of her mouth warm and exciting when he explored it. She pushed him away, however, when his hands moved down her body to press it against him.

"No point in getting hot and bothered this early in the evening," she said. "With old fogies like Anson Drew and his wife at this party, it's bound to break up early, so we'll have plenty of time later. Pour me a double vodka and tonic while I watch the local news. Been working all day at the office and barely had time to shower and dress after I got back home."

"You look like a million bucks just the same," he assured her as he busied himself pouring two drinks and handed her one.

"Play your cards right and you'll be worth a million before you're forty-five," she assured him as she settled on the bed to watch the television news. "Did you put your financial affairs in Paul Martenson's hands?"

"Yes. He says I'll start with practically zero tax this year."

"You can depend on Paul. He's been taking care of my finances ever since I incorporated."

"How did you get into public relations anyway?" Mark took his drink over to the bed where Claire was sitting with her back against the headboard, a picture of blond loveliness in a white summer dress as she watched the news.

"A young professor I'd been dating got me a job in New York between my junior and senior years at East Carolina. After I got my degree, I went back to New York for a year to learn Madison Avenue techniques." She had not taken her eyes from the screen where a lissome-looking girl in a wisp of a nightgown was bouncing on a mattress. "That's one of my commercials; we shot it at a studio in Old Town. I bought the place when the people who started it went broke."

"I'm impressed."

"Wait till you see my layouts for Next-to-Nothing Intimate-wear. Compared to what my models will be wearing when we shoot it in a few days, the nightgown on that girl was a Mother Hubbard."

"How are you going to advertise sleepwear, when you don't wear any?"

"I won't be posing for the ads—not that I couldn't."

"You can say that again," Mark said fervently.

"My ad campaign will be directed toward late-night cable television between episodes of R- and X-rated movies."

"The cable companies don't use commercials."

"We'll be sneaking them in," she explained. "When viewers see my girls at that time of night practically naked, they won't know it isn't part of the movie. Actually, it's a new sort of subliminal advertising that's going to revolutionize cable television."

"I suppose the idea originated with you."

"You're damn right. What's more, I'm getting a copyright." She handed him her empty glass. "Be an angel and pour me another. I'll need it to get through this stodgy dinner in your honor."

"Why go, then?"

"Because it's for you, of course. I was the one who convinced Father that you need to make a good impression on the powers that be in medical politics here. With that kind of sponsorship, your applications for a license to practice and hospital privileges will be rubber-stamped immediately, instead of lying around on somebody's desk while he figures a way to keep you from taking some of his patients."

"I know enough about medical politics to appreciate your strategy. And I'm grateful."

"You can't escape medical backstabbing down here. Considering what you've got on the ball, though, nobody is going to be able to hold you back. Give me a moment to go to the john while you put on your jacket and we'll get going to the dinner. Mustn't keep the president of the Medical Society or your new employers waiting."

III

The dinner promised to be boring indeed, until Mark was introduced to Paul Martenson's wife, Regina, who was to be his dinner companion, with Mrs. Barrett on his left. A pert redhead with a distinctly roving eye, Gina—as she told him to call her—was also a pocket Venus. As the group was about to go in to dinner, the remaining members on the guest list arrived. One was a rather striking brunette, whom Mark had the distinct impression of having met before, although she was coldly formal when she and her husband were introduced as Edward and Helene McIntosh. He was a handsome man of about sixty, but his wife was much younger.

"Ed McIntosh's first wife, Louise, died a year ago of breast cancer," Gina Martenson told Mark *sotto voce* as they were going into the dining room. "Helene married Ed about six months afterward, but she'd been sleeping with him for a year while his wife was taking chemotherapy."

"What field is Dr. McIntosh in?"

"Psychiatry. He's chairman of the State Disabled Doctors' Committee and has the most comfortable couch in town."

"Does that mean you've been on it?"

"Only in a social way, darling—not professionally. Ed McIntosh knows more dark secrets about society in Gulf City than anybody else in town. Which reminds me—when you were being introduced to Helene just now, I got the distinct impression that you'd known each other before."

"You're wrong," Mark lied nobly, although the memory of a weekend at a small inn somewhere in northern West Virginia was beginning to take form rather vividly in his mind. "I never saw Mrs. McIntosh before in my life."

"You lie well, darling, but you can't fool little Gina."

"It is an honor to have you as part of the medical fraternity in Gulf City, Dr. Harrison," said McIntosh as members of the group were milling around, seeking their seats. "I'm sure you're going to do well here."

"You must have your wife attend the next meeting of the Auxiliary, Doctor," Helene McIntosh added.

"Sorry, but I'm not married," said Mark.

"He will be, Helene," said Gina Martenson. "Nobody's going to let him go unclaimed for long."

"Don't forget that I saw him first, Gina." Claire was moving toward a chair across the table from Mark and the tiny redhead. "In Baltimore."

"Some people have all the luck, Claire, but be sure to keep a weather watch on the bulwarks—or something." Gina turned to Mark as he took the seat beside her. "Paul tells me he's going to manage your finances."

"What there are of them, yes."

"Is it true that Jerry Thorpe hates you already?"

"I hope not. We're going to be working together for a year, at least."

"All Jerry's women patients love him," Gina confided. "From what some of my menopausal friends tell me, he gives them more of a thrill on the examining table with a speculum and two fingers than most husbands are able to do on Saturday night."

Mark blinked and Claire laughed. "Now you've shocked him again, Gina. That kind of talk is supposed to be restricted to just-between-us-girls sessions."

"Or med students' beer parties," said Mark.

"Say something nice to your hostess, so Dr. Barrett will be pleased and raise your salary," Gina told Mark. "Then Paul will make more money and I can spend it."

Mark dutifully turned to Mrs. Barrett, but she was talking to Dr. Anson Drew, recounting the horrors of the flight they'd had home from The Greenbrier in White Sulphur Springs, West Virginia, so he turned back willingly to his pert dinner companion.

"I hear you took your premed at Duke," said Gina. "I was a cheerleader at U. Ga. and a member of Delta Delta Delta. Down here it's called Tri Delt and *de rigueur* for any girl who plans to make her debut in the Deep South."

"Which in your case, Gina, darling," Claire said sweetly from across the table, where she was sitting between Paul Martenson and Jack Pryor, "was so long ago you must hardly be able to remember it."

"You should know," Gina retorted. "You came out that year, too."

"Did you ever watch two female cats spitting at each other, Mark?" Paul Martenson asked from across the table. "It's really something."

"Just ignore him," said Gina. "My husband's so Back Bay Boston he sleeps with the fly of his pajamas buttoned up. Still, he does have hair on his chest. Do you, Mark?"

"I'm afraid so."

"Oh, good! You must show it to me sometime."

"Any morning at seven. I'm a jogger."

"So is Paul. Be sure and look at Mark's chest tomorrow if you meet him jogging at seven A.M.," she told her husband. "See whether he's got more hair on it than you have; I hate slick-chested men."

Mark turned to Mrs. Barrett again, as much to escape the rapier quality of Gina's wit as to do his duty.

"Miss McGillivray tells me you grow beautiful camellias, Mrs. Barrett," he said.

"It's pronounced cam-*ayl*-ia, Dr. Harrison," said his hostess loftily, "not cam-*eel*-ia."

"I'm sorry. That's the way we always pronounce it in North Carolina."

"I know. But the National Camellia Society, of which I am a regent, insists that '*ayl*' is preferable to '*eel*.' "

"Don't try to put Mark down, Mother." Claire came to his rescue. "He told me in Baltimore that he grew up in North Carolina on a farm that was part of a land grant from the Earl of Granville *before* the American Revolution, while the Barretts were only Scotch-Irish who immigrated to Philadelphia sometime in the late seventeen-hundreds. Fortunately, though, our ancestors had the good sense to settle in this area right after Andrew Jackson stole it from the Creeks because they saw the value of the timber- and the cotton-growing land here."

"Paul owns a farm with the doctors of the Clinic," Gina Martenson confided to Mark. "They raise blooded Arabian horses and lots of tax deductions."

"But no profit, thanks to Paul," said Claire.

"Profit!" Dr. Anson Drew was a little deaf and had heard only the last words. "Practicing medicine for profit is giving the profession a bad name," he said loudly. "People think all doctors are rich, so they sue them for malpractice at the drop of a hat."

"Dr. Drew's insurance company just settled a malpractice suit against him," Gina confided to Mark *sotto voce*. "Don't get him started on that subject unless you want to have your ear talked off."

"I'll remember," he promised. "Tell me something about yourself."

"There isn't much to tell. I was born near Clayton, Georgia, and went to the University at Athens. Paul was there, taking prelaw, and I set my cap for him, as my mother used to say. When he went to Harvard Law, I took a Katherine Gibbs secretarial course in Boston, to make sure he didn't get away. Lots of society girls go to Katy Gibbs to prepare themselves for short careers as secretaries—until they can snag a business executive like my husband."

"I went with a Gibbs girl for a while, but she chose to marry a department head at IBM out in the Research Triangle near Duke, after his wife died."

"That's almost the rule for Katherine Gibbs graduates," Gina agreed. "Paul and I were married after he got his law degree and I worked as a secretary for two years while he was getting his M.B.A. from Harvard."

"Preparing himself to latch onto a lot of gold mines?"

She shrugged. "What good is money if your husband's so busy making it that you have to make an appointment to go to bed with him?"

"I've heard some doctors' wives say it's the same way with the medical profession."

"Maybe, but around a hospital and medical school a girl gets to meet a lot of residents and fellows—like yourself. Fellows, in particular, don't have as busy schedules as successful businessmen and can always get off for a romp in the afternoon." She gave him a probing glance. "Or didn't you already know about that?"

"There was talk at Lakeview."

"Dr. Barrett has obviously chosen you to father the grandson he's always wanted Claire to produce." Gina's eyes surveyed Mark swiftly and he had the absurd impression that he was suddenly unclothed. "He's great on breeding and genes; that's why he likes raising Arabian horses."

"But I'm a peasant," he objected on a jocular note.

"Peasant stock always did beef up royalty. Offhand, I'd say you're a perfect stud."

"Up to your old tricks again, aren't you, Gina?" Mark was startled to hear Claire say from across the table.

"I like to catch 'em after you've broken them in, darling," Gina assured her.

"See here!" said Mark. "Are we talking about people—or horses?"

"With those two it can be either—or both," Paul Martenson told him.

"I'd better talk to my hostess again," Mark said in desperation and turned to Mrs. Barrett, who was avidly devouring a large chocolate mousse. "How did you like The Greenbrier?" he asked.

"It's as good a place to play bridge as anywhere else, I suppose," she said with a shrug. "Richard played golf every day, but it was too hot for me outside."

"I went to a medical convention there once," he volunteered. "Gave a paper on intestinal bypass to control weight."

"I read something about that." To his surprise, she actually sounded interested. "Can you really eat all the sweets you want and not get fat after one of those operations?"

"If you're willing to pay the price, but the side effects are often severe. Besides, you don't need to lose that much weight, do you?"

"I say not, but Andy Harkness keeps warning me that if I gain any more, I'll have to start taking insulin. And I hate being stuck with needles."

"Before I left Lakeview, we had succeeded in transplanting part of the pancreas in several diabetic patients. After the operation, all of them were able to stop taking insulin."

Mrs. Barrett turned to Dr. Anson Drew. "Did you hear that, Anson? Dr. Harrison knows how to cure diabetes with surgery."

"Experiments!" The president of the Medical Society seemed to remain in a state of perpetual indignation. "They're dangerous! Just asking for malpractice suits."

"Looks like you got put in your place again, Mark," said Gina. "Let's talk about something more interesting. I hear you're a specialist in transplanting balls."

"If you mean testicles—"

"All right, testicles, if you want to be technical. Did the guys you transplanted them to become as horny as the ones you took them from? Or does it obey the law of diminishing returns?"

"I don't know; we didn't ask," Mark admitted, laughing. "Two of our cases were able to impregnate their wives, though."

"Big deal! The guy at the filling station around the corner could have done that and saved them the trouble of an operation."

"I'm afraid that would have caused complications. You see, the recipients didn't have any testicles."

"Could they have sex?"

"Oh yes. Even the eunuchs who worked in Arabian harems could do that."

"Weren't they castrated as young boys?"

"Yes, but I expect they had some on-the-job training."

Gina laughed. "I like you, Mark. You'll do well in Gulf City, and with Paul managing your money, you'll soon be rich. Got a girl back home?"

"No, I'm free as a bird."

"Lucky you—and some women down here before long, I'm sure."

"I've already got a particular one in mind." Mark looked across at Claire who was talking to Paul Martenson.

"Claire's a whole lot of woman—more than one man can usually handle." Gina's tone was no longer flippant. "Still, I think she may have met her match in you—at least for the moment."

"Why the short term?"

"Claire and my husband are very much alike in many ways; I guess that's why they're both so good at what they do. If you do marry her, you'll be the one who'll be expected to stay home alone nights, and I've an idea you'll be no more willing to do that than I am."

Dr. Barrett had pushed his chair back and stood up, signaling the end of the dinner. Mark rose, too, and pulled Gina's chair back.

"I enjoyed being your dinner partner tonight, Mark," she told him as they were leaving the dining room. "Paul and I move in the same group with a lot of young marrieds. Since many of them are doctors, we can always use a handsome young man in an emergency. I'll see that you're invited. Good night."

IV

"You and Gina appeared to hit it off," Claire said as they were leaving the Club for her apartment.

"She's fun to talk to—with all that idle chatter about sex."

"Don't be misled by it and try to cuckold Paul. He and Gina are very happily married, in spite of her pretending to be available—"

"For Christ's sake!" he exploded. "I don't make a practice of seducing married women."

"I was just warning you," she said with a shrug. "You wouldn't get to first base with Gina anyway, and Paul was captain of the boxing team at U. Ga. for three years. I'd hate to see that handsome nose flattened."

"Thanks." Mark had regained his good humor. "I'll concentrate on seducing you."

"Now you're talking," she said in that throaty tone he remembered so well from the trip South from Baltimore.

Claire's apartment—one unit of a waterfront condominium about a mile down the beach from the Holiday Inn—was like Claire herself, sleek and very modern. The walls were adorned with Impressionist prints, and a large balcony faced the Gulf. Extended side walls turned it into a private enclosure for sunbathing or an extension of the living room, merely by opening the glass doors facing the Gulf.

"The vodka and fixings are in the kitchen," Claire told him when the door closed behind them. "Pour us some doubles while I'm gone."

Moving toward the bedroom as she spoke, she reached back and expertly unzipped her dress. She was shrugging the garment off her left shoulder as she pushed the door of the bedroom open. And in a large full-length mirror across the room, he was not surprised to see that, beneath the white linen dress she wore only wisps of bra and briefs. Whether or not she had left the door open on purpose, he couldn't know, but he had no difficulty seeing her unhook the bra with a practiced motion before stepping out of the briefs, giving him a tantalizing glimpse of her lovely naked body before she finally shut the door to the bedroom.

Mark busied himself pouring the drinks. When she came back, she had put on a caftanlike garment that enveloped her, although the way it floated about her body showed that it was made of a fabric only a little heavier than air itself.

"That has to be one of your line of Next-to-Nothing garments," Mark said as he handed her one of the drinks and followed her across the room toward the glass doors leading to the balcony.

"I promised to model one for you and here it is." She opened the double doors wide and the moonlight streamed in to reveal that she wore nothing beneath the caftan.

"Beautiful! Beautiful!" He moved to take her in his arms for a long kiss. "I'm sorry I'm not similarly clothed."

"You could easily be," she assured him as she moved out toward the balcony railing.

"In skin?"

"What else?"

Mark wasted no time removing what he was wearing, dropping the pieces on the floor as he moved toward the door and the balcony outside. Nor was he surprised when, as his last garment fell to the floor of the balcony, she lifted the caftan she wore and flipped it over her head, leaving her a naked, but very much alive, statue in the moonlight.

"Out here?" he asked as his arms closed about her and his mouth found hers.

"Why not?" she said against his lips. "The breeze is wonderful. And it *is* private."

"I'll take your word for it," he said, lifting her off her feet and carrying her to a couch on the balcony.

Their coupling was frantic, its culmination explosive. Afterward, he carried her into the bedroom, lowering her to the large bed.

"You're something!" he told her. "Really something!"

"I know. How about pouring us another drink and shutting those glass doors? It was hot out there."

"In more ways than one."

She looked up at him as he handed her the drink she had asked for. "I'll tell you something I've never told a man before, Mark. With you, it's super—and you can believe me when I say I'm really qualified to judge."

He didn't answer—it was something of which he didn't like to be reminded.

"Get in bed and pull up the sheet," Claire directed when she finished her drink and handed him the glass. "I'm going to take a nap."

"If I'm in bed naked with you very long, I certainly won't feel like taking a nap."

She laughed. "I've got a nickname for you—'Old Ready and Able.' I guess that was really the main trouble with Abner."

"Who?"

"My ex-husband. Had you forgotten that I was married once?"

"Maybe I wanted to forget it."

"It wasn't really a marriage; down here in the South, marriages are often arranged between old families, just like they are in Europe. It's a way of preserving what's called the 'Southern way of life.' Abner and I never even made love until our wedding night and then it was a fiasco."

"Don't tell me you were a virgin."

"Me?" She laughed. "Boys were feeling me up in the back seats of cars when I was fourteen. I liked it so I let 'em and my first orgasm came when I was sixteen. The boy was eighteen and the whole thing happened in the back seat of a Cadillac at a drive-in movie.

"It was an Errol Flynn movie and I was already hot and bothered, so I let Tom go all the way. You know by now how explosive my climaxes can be, but that time I wasn't ready for it. I had hysterics and made so much noise that Tom was afraid the management would intervene and drove out of the movie, taking that little loudspeaker they clamp on the front door with us. By the time we'd driven three blocks, I'd quieted down and was ready for another session, but poor Tom had had it for the evening. He drove me straight home and wouldn't come near me for a month. By that time, I was going steady with a college boy who really knew what was what."

V

It was two A.M. and Mark was dressing, donning his clothing piece by piece—*seriatim,* so to speak—in the reverse order from that in which he'd discarded them.

"Sure you don't mind walking home?" Claire asked sleepily from the queen-sized bed. "It's over a mile."

"After the last three hours, I'll float most of the way. Actually, I'm going to jog along the beach to burn up some of that liquor we drank."

"Tomorrow's your first day of work at the Clinic," she reminded him. "I already know you're subject to hangovers, so you'd better look in the medicine closet in the bathroom and take a couple of amphetamines with you."

He had no trouble finding the labeled bottle and poured two of the tablets into his hand, each representing the same stiff dose that appeared to be *de rigueur* with her. Only when he was putting the half-empty bottle back in the medicine cabinet did he notice on the bottom of the label the name of the doctor who'd prescribed the medication.

It was "J. Thorpe, M.D."

Claire was already asleep when Mark came out of the bathroom, so he didn't wake her but pulled the door of the apartment shut, making sure the latch clicked and trying it afterward to be certain it locked. The corridor was empty and so was the elevator in which he descended to the street floor. The security guard nodding in a chair in the vestibule hardly gave him a glance even though he was barefoot with his socks in the pocket of the jacket he carried over his arm and his shoes, the laces tied together, were draped around his neck.

Crossing a largely deserted Gulf Boulevard, he descended a short concrete stairway from the bulkhead to the beach and trotted to the waterline, where the waves, slapping in from a low chop, made a smooth wet surface.

Here and there, couples were in ardent embrace on blankets spread out on the sand and a lone bather was swimming leisurely in the shallow water, a little distance from the shore. The breeze was fresh and, as he ran, he felt his muggy senses begin to clear up a little. In the distance, he could see the looming mass of the Holiday Inn, with floodlights bathing it and the landscaped garden in which it was located.

Covering the mile to the area on the beach in front of the Inn with a steady jogging stride took only about fifteen minutes. Hesitating to cross the lobby at this time of night barefooted and not wanting to put on the shoes hung around his neck, Mark decided to enter through the tunnel leading from the basement of the Inn to the beach for the convenience of bathers. Its mouth was a dark circle, but he found it without difficulty and started inside. Besotted with infatuation and alcohol, he barely heard the rustling movement behind him until it was too late to do anything to protect himself. Even as he realized he was being attacked, a heavy blow on the left temple dropped him in his tracks like a felled ox.

VI

Mark awakened with a splitting headache to find himself in the impersonal atmosphere of a hospital room with the sides of the bed pulled up, obviously to keep him from falling out. The act of opening his eyes caused such a stroke of pain in his head that he closed them at once. Opening them more gingerly a few moments later, he was able to make out the form of a tall man standing beside the bed and holding a finger on the pulse in his left wrist, while a nurse was taking his blood pressure on his right.

"Who—what's happened?" he tried to ask but his tongue and the inside of his mouth were so dry that the words were less than clear.

"That's what we'd like to know," a man's voice told him. "I'm Dr. Charles Minot, a neurosurgeon, Dr. Harrison."

The nurse held a drinking tube to Mark's lips. When he'd taken a swallow of water, his mouth felt clearer and he was able to speak somewhat better.

"Why would I need a neurosurgeon?"

"Somebody zapped you with a blackjack," the tall doctor told him. "You'd have lain all night in that dark tunnel between the hotel basement and the beach, if a couple of youngsters hadn't gone inside looking for a good place to make out. They called the Rescue Squad and the paramedic crew brought you to the Emergency Room of Gulfside Hospital."

Mark looked around him. "This is no E.R."

"Actually," said Dr. Minot, "you might have lain outside the Emergency Room on a stretcher for an hour or two, if Miss McGillivray hadn't been going home about that time after specialing one of Jerry Thorpe's operative patients through a sudden complication of pulmonary atelectasis from a bronchus closed by a mucous plug. There'd been a bad accident out on I-10 about the same time you were mugged and Emergency was crowded with patients. One of the doctors did check you briefly, but you smelled like the effluent of a distillery and had a cut over your temple, so he decided you were only a drunk who'd fallen off the bulkhead and cut his scalp on a shell. They'd have gotten to you eventually, of course, but by that time the slow leak of blood from a tear in your middle meningeal artery could have formed an extradural hematoma large enough to compress the vital centers of your brain and you'd have wound up with a diagnosis of D.O.A."

"Did you say Miss McGillivray found me?"

"She did—on a stretcher outside the Emergency Room where the staff had placed you until they could take care of the other accident cases before sewing up the cut in your scalp. Fortunately, she recognized you and looked at your eyes with a flashlight. When she saw that one pupil was larger than the other, she called me."

"Then I owe her my life?"

"No doubt about it. We hustled you up to the Operating Room and she assisted while I opened the laceration over your left temple and drilled a burr hole in your skull. Blood had already started to clot between the outside of the dura lining of your brain and the inside of your skull, so I enlarged the opening and cleaned out the clot until I could find the laceration of the middle meningeal artery where the hemorrhage was coming from and put ties on either side of it. Except for the fact that your attackers had already made the incision for me, it was a textbook subtemporal decompression for extradural hemorrhage."

"Will that be the diagnosis on my chart?"

Minot nodded. "Miss McGillivray managed to keep the fact that you were already loaded before you got mugged out of the admissions record. And since you hadn't been in an automobile accident, there was no need for a blood alcohol."

Mark was weary and the effort of talking had only made his headache worse. "My head is splitting. Could I have something?"

"Sure. Are you allergic to anything?"

"Nothing but muggers."

"Fifty milligrams of Demerol stat," Minot told the nurse.

"I guess I owe my life to you, too, Dr.—"

"Minot, but don't give me much of the credit. A second-year resident in Neurosurgery could have put a burr hole in your skull and cleaned out the clot. I opened the dura slightly to make sure there wasn't any hemorrhage from the brain itself, but you had a severe concussion, too, and I'm afraid you'll have some pretty severe headaches for a while."

"How long?"

"You never know after these things. It could be weeks, perhaps a month."

"Thanks, Dr. Minot. I'll thank Miss McGillivray later."

The nurse appeared, bringing a hypo, and the surgeon departed with a "See you in the morning." The needle, jabbed expertly into the fleshy part of his buttock, stung, but even before she had removed it, Mark felt a delicious sensation of languor and freedom from pain spreading through his body. Moments later, he was asleep.

VII

When Mark awakened again, Alexa McGillivray was standing beside the bed, in uniform.

"Hello," she said, smiling. "I'm glad you decided to join the ranks of the living."

"Dr. Minot says you're responsible for that."

"In a way, I suppose I am. Six people were deposited into the Emergency Room from an accident at about the same moment you were brought in. In cases like that, the principles of triage say the most urgent cases must be taken first."

"While I appeared to be only a drunk who'd fallen and cut his head," he said with some bitterness.

"When I saw you lying there snoring, I thought the same thing, so don't blame the E.R. surgeon who examined you. After all, you *were* barefoot and there was sand between your toes, so you'd obviously been walking on the beach."

"A stupid thing to do at that time of night."

"Ordinarily, yes. But you haven't been in Gulf City long enough to know that muggers always hang around dark places in the seawall, looking for unsuspecting people who frequent the beach at night."

"I passed some of those."

"About once a month, one—usually two—are killed out there at night. I knew you had been at the dinner earlier and figured you'd gone for a walk."

"A jog—from Claire's apartment to the hotel, when I was drunk as a coot. Please don't try to put the situation into any better light than it really was, but thanks for keeping the drunk diagnosis off the chart."

"There wasn't any point in it being there. You hadn't harmed anybody."

"Except myself. This was going to be my very first morning to work at the Clinic. What will Dr. Barrett think?"

"That you're new in these parts and got mugged. It could have happened in Baltimore or New York, so why not here?"

"At two-fifteen in the morning? How can I explain that?"

"Devoted joggers often get out and run for a while when they can't sleep. It relaxes them."

He managed to smile in spite of the pain. "You know you're pretty wonderful, don't you?"

"Why do you say that?"

"You found me in what was presumably a drunken stupor, but instead of leaving me to sober up overnight in the hospital the way I deserved, you checked me—"

"I was only doing my duty as a nurse—and as a friend."

"Good Samaritan would be the better word. Besides, you were smart enough to see something the Emergency Room doctor who gave me a casual check didn't even look for, a single dilated pupil that could only mean an extradural hemorrhage. If you'd called the attention of the people in the Emergency Room to that, it would have taken probably two or three hours for them to get an X ray, or maybe even do something worse, a spinal puncture. Instead, you called Dr. Minot and maybe in an hour—"

"You were in the Operating Room thirty minutes after I saw that pupil."

"That's what I'm saying. Except for you, there's a good chance I would have woke up dead."

She laughed. "I see you haven't lost your sense of humor."

"How much else have I lost, though?"

"Like what?"

"Jerry Thorpe hates me and Dr. Barrett is bound to have some second thoughts about me. With half the Clinic already against me, what chance will I have of making good down here? In fact, Barrett can toss me out right now if he chooses."

"Not if you insist on your rights. Meg Fuller told me you're an early-morning jogger and there's no reference to alcohol on your chart—"

"But at two-fifteen A.M.?"

"I know a lot of joggers and they sometimes do strange things. The Clinic badly needs your know-how in running the Old Town satellite operation, as well as in microsurgery. Dr. Barrett even tried another young surgeon last year, but he didn't work out." She put her hand over his on the counterpane and gave it a reassuring squeeze. "If you're the kind of doctor all the reports say you are, you'll overcome this setback. Sure you don't need anything else?"

"I could use that P.R.N. order for Demerol. My head still aches like fury and Dr. Minot says that's going to keep up for quite a while."

"I'll tell them at the nursing station," she promised. "See you tomorrow."

VIII

Dr. Richard Barrett came into Mark's room shortly after five, his expression grim. "Dr. Minot called me this morning to say he'd had to do a subtemporal decompression on you early this morning, Dr. Harrison," he said.

"I was unconscious at the time, but so I've been told."

"May I inquire what you were doing out on the beach at that hour, Doctor?"

"I was jogging."

"Jogging! Really? Can you imagine what people will think of that story?"

"If they don't buy it, he can tell them the true one, Father." Claire spoke from the doorway. "That damn dinner you gave last night was so boring that Mark and I went to my apartment for a nightcap. We got absorbed in a late-late movie on TV and didn't realize what time it was."

"But—"

"I imagine you and Mother must have stayed out till two A.M. at least once when you were courting, so what the hell are you criticizing Mark for?"

"The hospital scuttlebutt is that he'd been drinking," Barrett spluttered.

"So what? Jerry Thorpe covers the Clinic lots of nights loaded to the gills. More than once, Alexa has had to carry him home and put him to bed."

"Oh, all right," said Barrett. "Jack Pryor and I are planning to have the dedication of the new Clinic in Old Town in about ten days, Mark, but we can always put it off."

"You won't need to, sir. Dr. Minot wants me up by tomorrow for sure. I'll be in shape to work before the dedication."

"But your head's been shaved."

"Jack Pryor promised yesterday to get temporary privileges for me at the Yacht Club. I'll wear a yachting cap and the lack of hair won't even be noticed."

"All right," said Barrett, the steam of indignation taken out of him by Claire's explanation of Mark's presence on the beach.

"I'm glad you weren't badly hurt, but don't try to come to work too early. The symptoms of concussion sometimes last a long time." Barrett started for the door, then turned back. "Is there anything I can do for you?"

"I had about five hundred dollars' worth of traveler's checks on me that apparently were taken," said Mark. "The numbers are in my hotel room."

"I'll ask Alexa to take care of that," said Claire firmly. "Good-bye, Father."

"Good-bye." Barrett was out the door, obviously glad to get away.

"Thanks for bailing me out," said Mark after she'd leaned over to kiss him. "He obviously came in here ready to fire me."

"It was my duty, darling. After all, you wouldn't have been out there at all if I hadn't seduced you."

Mark managed to smile, although the movement of the muscles caused the pain to shoot through the temple area where the wound was located. *"That,"* he said, "was mutual. Very mutual."

"And all you got for it was a hole in your head." She pulled a chair up beside the bed. "Poor darling. Does it hurt much?"

"Dr. Minot says I'll have headaches for a while."

"You were lucky to get into Charlie Minot's hands. He's the best neurosurgeon in the Southeast."

"I didn't just get into his hands. Alexa found me on a stretcher outside the Emergency Room and made the diagnosis. She called him direct."

"She didn't tell me that when she called me early this morning to tell me what happened," said Claire. "But then, it's like her not to."

"I owe her my life."

"I'll thank her when I see her. I'd've come over this morning, but when I called about nine, they said you were still asleep. I've been on the telephone practically the whole morning with the advertising people in New York."

"If what you modeled for me last night is an example of the line, it's a surefire success."

"Can I use your recommendation in my advertising program?"

"Absolutely."

"By the way," she said, changing the subject, "would you like to rent a condominium in my building for the next six months to a year?"

"It sounds ideal—if I can afford it."

"You can. A couple I've known for years are moving to Chicago temporarily on company business. It's only four floors below me and a duplicate of mine. I managed to haggle them down to six hundred a month with the promise that you'd take care of their furniture. You couldn't do any better, even away from the Gulf, unless you want to live in a slum."

"Your kind of slum is my kind of slum. When can I move in?"

"As soon as you get out of the hospital. Jim had to leave July first and Mary is only staying on to rent the apartment. I paid the first month's rent down for you so you could hold it."

"You're a doll," he told her. "I'll pay you back—"

"Don't bother till you've collected a few months' salary. I won't be here when you move in, though. The Next-to-Nothing people liked the Southern promotion I outlined for them in New York so well that they want me to head up a national campaign, so I'll be spending the next month or so in Los Angeles."

"I'm going to miss you."

"We'll make up for it when I get back." She leaned over to kiss him. "Good-bye for now."

When Claire was gone, Mark tried to read, but his left eye didn't want to work properly—a not unusual sequela from a severe head injury, he knew—so he put away the magazine. His head was throbbing again, too, so he pushed the button on the nurse's call.

"Can I help you?" an impersonal voice asked from the small speaker on the wall beside the bed.

"I'm having a lot of pain. Would you tell the charge nurse I need the P.R.N. Dr. Minot left again?"

"Right, Doctor. She'll be there in a minute."

It was more than a minute before the nurse appeared, carrying the hypodermic. "Turn over," she said cheerfully. "This will send you to dreamland."

"Can I depend on that?" he asked as she jabbed the needle into his backside.

"For a while, at least. If you have to take Demerol very often, though, the dose will start to wear off and it'll have to be increased. Dr. Minot said you could get up this afternoon if you wanted to. How about having your supper out of bed?"

"I'll decide that later."

"Right. Just let me know."

It took longer this time for the familiar floating sensation produced by the narcotic to ease his pain and put him to sleep. When he woke again, Alexa McGillivray was arranging flowers in a vase on the table beside his bed. She was still in uniform, with the dark braids of her hair wound around her head as they'd been when she'd driven him to the airport to meet the Barretts.

"How's the headache?" she asked.

"Pretty bad. It comes and goes—mostly comes."

"With the kind of blow that mugger gave you, I'm not surprised. It had to be a real one to sever a branch of the middle meningeal artery."

"Was it a major branch?"

"Big enough to give you a dangerous hematoma, if it had gone on bleeding; there's not much space between the brain and the inside of the skull in that area." She finished arranging the flowers and stood back to look at them, then shook her head disparagingly. "Flower arrangement isn't my long suit."

"They look fine to me."

"Thanks for being kind. By the way, where's your hotel room key? Claire gave me the key to the condo you've rented, and Dr. Minot says you can be discharged whenever you like. I'll get your stuff and check you out of the Holiday Inn tomorrow on my lunch break. No use paying for a hotel room when you're paying rent on a swanky apartment of your own."

"Have you seen it?"

"No, but they're all pretty much alike; I plan to go by after dinner. You're supposed to have maid service in that condominium, but you know how help is these days."

"Did you know Dr. Barrett came here this morning, ready to fire me?"

"I'm not surprised. He's pretty straitlaced and stubborn when he doesn't get his way."

"I was ready to offer to quit before he fired me and I'm sure he'd've accepted the offer. Fortunately, Claire came in just then and explained that I was with her—and we were both high."

"Dr. Barrett told me you okayed having the satellite Clinic dedication in about ten days," she said, without commenting on his confession. "Think you'll be up to it so soon after a head injury?"

"I'm not going to pamper myself," he said firmly. "By the way, how's Jerry Thorpe?"

"Still drinking too much and feeling sorry for himself, but that will come to a head soon, the way it has before. Jerry will spend a few weeks in a clinic in New Orleans that specializes in drying out high-income businessmen, doctors, and dentists."

"The word for doctors is 'impaired,' but most of the references now are to what's called 'burnout.' Either word covers a multitude of sins and applies to about one doctor in ten, according to the American Medical Association. I've seen a lot of residents and fellows who qualified for the name, too; the suicide rate in that class is about three times the average for the general population."

"I've got to run," she said. "Did the mugger take the key to your room at the Holiday Inn?"

"I wasn't exactly being observant at the time, but the clothes I was wearing are hanging in the closet over there. The key should be in them, if he didn't."

She started looking through the pockets and found the key—along with the amphetamine tablets Claire had given him.

"You'd better not let Dr. Minot know you have these," she said. "He'd be pretty mad if he found out you've been taking this dosage. I'll drop your suit off at the cleaners on my way home and tomorrow I'll check you out of the Inn and move your luggage over to your new quarters."

"Do you always think of everything?"

"Everything I can. Good night."

IX

Dr. Charles Minot arrived about six o'clock, roughly a half hour after Mark had been given a hypodermic for pain—without much relief.

"I'm going to change your P.R.N. for Demerol to a hundred milligrams," the neurosurgeon said. "The nurses tell me fifty doesn't hold you."

"I guess I have a low threshold for pain."

"Most doctors do, but after that blow on the head, you'll have a right to hurt for a while."

"I promised Dr. Barrett this morning that I'd be well enough to go to work in ten days, when they dedicate the satellite Clinic over in Old Town."

"You will be—if you don't mind working with a headache. Can I do anything else for you?"

"No, thanks. Miss McGillivray is moving my things to a condominium I've rented temporarily in a building about a mile away."

"I'd never operated with her assisting before last night," said Minot. "If she ever considers stopping work for the Barrett Clinic, she's got a job with my group any time she wants it."

X

Mark had eaten breakfast and gone back to sleep when Alexa arrived about ten-thirty the next morning.

"It's a shame to wake you up, but I've got to make rounds on our patients in the hospital before I go over to the Clinic after lunch," she said. "Your chart shows that you needed a hypo twice during the night. A hundred milligrams of Demerol is a pretty powerful dose; maybe you ought to stay off your feet for today, at least."

"The kind of headache I had needed something powerful, but I'd still like to try getting out of bed."

"I went by the Holiday Inn and got some pajamas and a robe and slippers out of your luggage. Also, your electric razor and your shaving kit." Placing the robe she was carrying across the foot of the bed, she handed him the pajama bottoms. "Slip these on under the sheet while I roll your bed up a little higher. Then put the jacket on and hang your legs over the side of the bed."

Her movements were skilled as she helped him get into the fresh clothing and slipped on his bedroom shoes. "Ease down on your feet gradually," she warned. "You're liable to have some vertigo when you first stand up."

For an instant after his feet touched the floor, Mark thought he was going to faint when the room swirled around him. He held on to Alexa tightly, however, and the vertigo soon passed. Still holding on to her, he shuffled about six feet to an easy chair and sank into it with a sigh of relief.

"I guess I'm weaker than I wanted to admit," he said. "It's a good thing you're strong."

"I swim in the Bay here about eight months of the year and the Community College has an indoor pool I can use when the weather is bad. I try to do a couple of miles two or three times a week. Is your head clearing now?"

"Yes. What's going on at the Clinic?"

"Dr. Peterson removed a torn cartilage from a boy's knee with the arthroscope this morning. He's very skilled with it."

"By the way, Dr. Minot said yesterday that the reason you were in the hospital after two A.M. when I was brought in yesterday morning was because one of Jerry Thorpe's patients had a lung collapse from a plugged bronchus. How did he treat that?"

"*He* didn't. I thought it wouldn't be wise to get him out after an evening of drinking at the Yacht Club, so I put a bronchoscope down through the patient's nose and suctioned out the mucous plug."

"You what?" he demanded incredulously.

She laughed. "There you go, refusing to admit that a woman can do special procedures like a bronchoscopy as effectively as a man."

"But you're a nurse."

"Technically, yes, but I'm licensed as a nurse-practitioner, so my activities are covered by the Clinic malpractice insurance policy. Bronchoscopy with the new nasal instrument isn't much different from putting down a nasogastric tube for stomach suction post-operatively."

"I guess I've got a lot to learn about how medicine is practiced away from teaching hospitals."

"Nurse-practitioners are a new breed, so new that the medical profession and the hospitals haven't yet learned where to put us. I count myself one of the fortunate ones."

"I'll bet Dr. Barrett didn't give you the responsibilities he's obviously turned over to you until you'd proved you could handle them."

"When a woman seeks a place in what has always heretofore been a man's field, she's got to prove her worth first—but none of us would want it otherwise." She glanced at her watch. "Want me to help you back to bed?"

"I think I'll stay up awhile longer."

"Promise you won't try to stand up again without somebody to catch you. For a moment just now, I thought I was going to have to pick you up off the floor."

"So did I," he told her. "The only thing that kept me from going down was knowing you'd be throwing ice water in my face."

XI

"It looks like the fair-haired boy has lost some hair." Mark looked up from the afternoon paper he was reading to see Jerry Thorpe standing just inside the door of his hospital room.

"Come in," he said. "Glad to see you."

"From what Charlie Minot told me, I doubt that you'll be ready to make surgical history here in the boondocks for a while yet," said the other doctor as he sank into the easy chair. Even at that distance, Mark could smell the bourbon on his breath.

"I'll be back in action before long," said Mark. "When I am, I hope to be able to do as well in my field as everybody tells me you do in yours."

"The female pelvis is a small stage—made for actors with small talents."

"That's not the way I heard it, or the way it looked while I was touring the hospital when I first came down to look over Gulf City. Since we're going to be working together, I'd like for us to be friends."

"I can be hard to get along with—when I'm under tension," Thorpe warned.

"Who isn't? It's part of being a surgeon."

"Alexa says I should apologize to you for the other night at the Club."

"No apology needed."

"Alexa's a pretty rare girl—and the best surgical assistant anyone could want."

"I could see that from the gallery, too."

"Heard from Claire since she left for L.A.?" Thorpe's tone was deliberately casual, but Mark didn't miss the note of tension underneath.

"No, but Alexa is going to move me into an apartment Claire was kind enough to rent for me in her building from someone who's been transferred by his company to Chicago for perhaps a year."

"That was convenient."

"Saved me a lot of trouble, too. I'm indebted to Claire for arranging it."

"That's our Claire." Thorpe tapped a cigarette upon a case he took from his pocket and lighted it. "She's a great arranger and very selective in her choice of men."

"She's not quite like any other woman I've ever gone with," Mark agreed.

"She's one in a million—especially in the sack."

Mark was so startled by the bald statement that he couldn't find words to protest. Before he did, Thorpe continued, "No use beating around the bush. Claire and I had quite a thing going when I first came here, but I wasn't man enough to bat in her league. I hope you can stay on her team longer than I did."

"So far, we're just good friends."

"*Very* good would be my guess, else you haven't lived up to your reputation. Gina Martenson was in to see me today for her annual Pap smear. All she could talk about was how sexy you were."

"She's a lot of fun." Again, Mark was careful in what he said, sensing that anything told to Jerry Thorpe was likely to be broadcast widely. "I enjoyed sitting next to her at the dinner Dr. Barrett gave for me when I first arrived, but I'm afraid I won't be up to much in the way of social activities for a while. Dr. Minot says I have a pretty severe concussion."

"Charlie's a top neurosurgeon." Thorpe stood up and moved close enough to the bed to stub out the cigarette he'd been smoking in the ashtray lying there. "I'm playing tennis tonight with Ted Moran, the pro at the Yacht Club, so I'd better be going. We're paired in a doubles match against the Pensacola Naval Station Officers' Club next week and they're pretty good. Do you play?"

"Haven't since I started my hospital residency. Jogging takes less time."

"And can get you a hole in the head. I'll stick to tennis. Any idea when you'll be able to work?"

"I promised Dr. Barrett I'd be ready to handle the new Clinic in Old Town when it's dedicated next week."

"Dick tells me you've had some experience running one of those in Maryland, so you may turn out to be some use to us after all." The speech, though sarcastic, was obviously intended to be friendly and Mark took it as such.

"I'll certainly try," he said. "Thank you for coming by, Jerry."

XII

The telephone beside Mark's bed rang shortly after nine. It was Claire.

"Hello, lover," she said. "How are you?"

"Lousy! I've got a headache and you're not here—not that I could be much of a lover if you were."

"I called Charlie Minot to ask about you before I left Gulf City. He said you'll have headaches for some time."

"On top of that, I'm getting stir crazy from being shut up in one room."

"The hospital has a lovely rooftop terrace. You could be up there giving some pneumatic young nurse a thrill."

"It's too hot. I've heard of Gulf Coast dog days, and I think we're going into them now. The temperature's hitting a hundred every day and the humidity is ninety-five."

"It's hot out here, in L.A., too; one of those Santa Ana winds the Californians complain so much about. I've been so busy working on the national campaign I haven't had time to be hot."

"Where are you staying?"

"At the Beverly Hills Hotel—it's a divine place. One night I think I'll go down and have a drink in the famous Polo Lounge. Maybe some macho movie star will pick me up."

"Don't you dare. He might introduce you to a producer and the next thing you know they'd be giving you a screen test."

"On a couch at the producer's home in Cold Water Canyon?" Claire laughed. "I'm not exactly a babe in the woods where handsome men are concerned, darling. You ought to know that."

"That blow on my head jarred my memory; I need you back here to remind me again how lovely you are. By the way, when will you be back?"

"It looks like six weeks now."

"You were only going to be gone a month—and it seems like that already."

"Business before pleasure, even the sort of pleasure I had with you," she told him. "You'll be busy getting the new Clinic started and before you know it, I'll be back. Have you ever been to New Orleans?"

"No."

"We'll go there for a weekend, maybe over Labor Day. You'll love it."

"I'll love any place with you."

"I'll have to hang up and dress for dinner—"

"But it's after nine."

"That's only six out here; some friends are going to take me to a lovely place over in the Valley for dinner. They've promised to bring me back across the mountain range by way of that famous Mulholland Drive. It's supposed to be very romantic, and I'll be thinking of you all the way. Good night, lover."

The phone clicked off before Mark could answer. After putting it back on the cradle, he lay there imagining he was watching her dressing for dinner, but the tension generated by the longing the fantasy evoked only made his head hurt worse, until finally he rang for the nurse and the magic hypodermic.

XIII

On the sixth day after Mark's injury, Dr. Minot took the stitches out of his head wound and pronounced it healed. "You'll have to be a little careful what you bump your head against for a while," he warned, "until the periosteum I reflected before I put the burr hole into your skull can generate some new bone."

"You mean you didn't leave a silver dollar in there?"

"With the price of silver these days? Miss McGillivray tells me you've rented a condominium on the waterfront. You can move over there anytime you like."

"How about tonight?"

"No reason why not, but you may need some Demerol occasionally for another few weeks."

"My federal narcotics license should be good down here."

"It is, but druggists don't like to fill prescriptions written by out-of-state doctors for themselves; a lot of so-called 'impaired physicians' get their supply of narcotics that way. I'll give you a prescription for a couple of dozen ampules of Demerol and you can buy sterile plastic syringes at any drugstore. Do you need anything else?"

"Nothing I can think of. Miss McGillivray said she would take me to my apartment when you were ready to discharge me. I'd like to go tonight, so she won't have to take time off duty."

"That's fine if it suits her."

"I'll ask her when she stops by at lunchtime. And thanks, Dr. Minot, for everything."

"Call me Charlie. After all, we'll be on the same hospital staff and in the same medical societies. Check with my office in a few days."

"Will do."

Alexa appeared while Mark was finishing his lunch. "I see that you've been discharged," she said. "Anxious to see your new home?"

"Anything to get out of here."

"I'm teaching an anatomy class for nurses at the Community College this afternoon. Suppose I pick you up at five, when I go off duty?"

"Sounds fine to me."

"I'll tell the floor nurses to have you at the hospital entrance at five."

"Dr. Minot was going to leave me a prescription—"

"It's attached to your chart, but there's no point in your having to go to a drugstore; I'll drop it at the hospital pharmacy. They can fill it and put it and the syringes on your bill."

"You think of everything, don't you?"

"My job is taking care of the sick and you're still sick, as long as you keep having those headaches. See you at five."

Mark was sitting in a wheelchair just inside the hospital entrance where the air conditioning kept the large foyer cool, when Alexa's Volkswagen Rabbit came to a stop at the front door. While the orderly wheeled him out to the driveway, she opened the right front door and pushed the seat up so his few belongings could be deposited in the back.

"I thought you might like a welcoming dinner in your new home," Alexa told him as she guided the small car expertly into the late-afternoon traffic stream on Gulf Boulevard.

"Sounds wonderful! Shall we stop somewhere and pick up a couple of packaged dinners?"

"What sort of a homecoming would that be? I put a fish stew from an old Creek recipe into my crockpot and stopped by your place to start it cooking. That's the big advantage of a crockpot—you can let something cook all day if you like."

"I'd better get one, then. I'm a lousy cook."

"Every fall, Uncle Homer sends me a batch of herbs and spices he grows in a garden back of his hospital at Peace River and dries. You won't believe the bouquet they give to something as ordinary as a fish stew."

"I can hardly wait."

The enticing aroma of the stew assailed their nostrils when Alexa opened the door of his condominium.

"Smells like your dinner is just about ready," she said. "I found a half bottle of bourbon and another of vodka in your hotel room and brought them over with your other things when I checked you out. If you'd like a drink before dinner, you can do the fixing while I check on the stew."

"How about you? Bourbon or vodka?"

"Bourbon—and small. I only drink on social occasions—and then not much."

"A housewarming is certainly a social occasion—even if it's celebrated by only two people."

"Take your drink on a tour of the apartment. I'll join you in a few minutes in the living room."

The condominium was comfortably furnished in a practical sort of way, in stark contrast to the ultramodern decor of Claire's penthouse atop the building. There was even room for the few pieces he'd brought from Baltimore. He could be very comfortable here, Mark decided as he came back into the living room where Alexa had already switched on the TV for the six o'clock news and was sitting on the sofa with her drink.

"How do you like your new home?" she asked.

"Adequate—if not inspired. The view of the Gulf is the main thing."

"It's never the same, no matter when you look at it. Sometimes I sit on a bench along the bulkhead after I've finished work and watch until the moon rises, wondering what my Indian ancestors must have thought when they saw the first Spanish ship anchor offshore more than four hundred years ago."

"Any idea how long your own people had been in this area before then?"

"At least a thousand years, judging from some archaeological excavations of Indian burial mounds by a group from Florida State University. Maybe even longer."

"That makes even the early Spanish explorers Johnny-come-latelies, I guess."

A buzzer sounded from the kitchen and Alexa rose to her feet. "That means the rolls are ready, so I'd better set the table."

"Can I help?"

"Go on and finish your drink. I can see the TV from the dining area while I'm putting our dinner on the table."

The stew was delicious, as the aroma greeting them at the door had promised. The salad was equally so, as were the piping hot french rolls with butter.

"Claire called me a few nights ago," Mark said when they'd finished eating. "Says she's having a ball in California but working very hard."

"The two go hand in hand where she's concerned."

"Jerry Thorpe came by to see me in the hospital, too. He apologized for being rude that first evening at the Club, but I think he still has a little chip on his shoulder where I'm concerned."

"I'm sure of it."

"But why?"

"Envy—for one thing."

"Jerry envying me? That's a switch. From what I hear, he's the darling of the feminine clientele at the Clinic, as well as much of Gulf City."

"You're still a competitor."

"In what way?"

"You're handsome enough and smart enough to attract women, especially someone like Claire who's had an unhappy marriage. Like any other city, this one is full of those."

"You've never had an unhappy marriage that I know of. Do I attract you?"

"Of course, but I know I'm not the kind to attract you."

"What the hell does that mean?"

She laughed. "You were the Don Juan of Lakeview and you can take on that title in Gulf City if you want to. A handsome doctor with lots of sex appeal, plus the potential for making a considerable amount of money with all that means—a house on the riverfront, a Mark IV and a Mercedes in the garage, membership in all the best clubs—is quite a catch."

"Right now, I don't feel like much of a catch. My headache is starting up again."

"Forgive me," she said quickly. "This homecoming was more than I should have put you through."

"I'll be all right. The Demerol you got for me will take care of that."

"There's cereal in the pantry and milk and orange juice in the refrigerator," she told him as she picked up her handbag, preparatory to leaving. "Or if you'd rather go out to breakfast, there's a very nice little coffee shop on the corner next to this building."

"When will I see you again?"

"Whenever you feel like coming to the Clinic; I'm there every afternoon. Good night."

"Good night," he told her. "And thanks for everything."

After Alexa left, Mark undressed and got into pajamas. The familiar throbbing in his temples reminded him once again of the injury and the concussion that had resulted. Opening the package from the hospital pharmacy, he tore the paper covering from a sterile syringe, took out a one-hundred-milligram ampule of Demerol and, breaking off the top, drew the contents into the syringe. Alcohol swabs in small envelopes were also in the package and, wiping an area of skin he could easily reach on his right hip, he injected the potent narcotic deep into the muscle. By the time he finished brushing his teeth, the familiar sensation of floating had erased the pain and he was asleep almost before his head reached the pillow.

XIV

The dedication of the new satellite Clinic in Old Town was set for Saturday, a week after Mark left the hospital. He'd been up and about since coming to his new apartment and several times had driven across the high bridge to inspect the progress of construction in the building, which was leased to Hospitals, Inc. Since the mayor, who owned the building, also happened to be running for re-election, the plans for the dedication included a classic Southern political ploy—a fish fry that was certain to bring a large crowd.

Mark's headache had improved slowly during the week and most of the time now he was able to control it with a few doses of aspirin and codeine during each twenty-four-hour period. A considerable crowd had gathered for the dedication of the still not quite finished building, by the time Mark drove across to Old Town that Saturday afternoon. Workmen were still putting on the final touches inside the building and the whine of a power saw reached his ears through the open back door. Parking his car behind the Clinic in the area reserved for those participating in the dedication, he made his way to where the crowd had gathered before a temporary platform in front of the building. Parked there, too, was one of the city's Rescue Squad ambulances, before which paramedics of the rescue team were giving a demonstration of cardiopulmonary resuscitation. Seeing Alexa at the edge of the crowd, he joined her in the shade of a palm tree that protected them somewhat against the hot afternoon sun of midsummer.

"How's the headache?" she asked.

"Much better. Dr. Barrett wants me to scrub with him on a Whipple operation Monday and reimplantation of the common bile duct can be a little tedious. He thinks we might need to use the microscope."

"That's one operation where I'll willingly yield the position of first assistant to you," she told him. "I haven't seen one since I left Duke."

"They're not very frequent."

"Do you plan to start seeing patients over here Monday afternoon?" she asked.

"We're committed to it, even though the workmen will probably still be here."

The C.P.R. demonstration by the Rescue Squad paramedics was finished. Now, the mayor, a portly man in a white suit and a Panama hat, ascended to the platform, followed by Jack Pryor representing Hospitals, Inc., and Dr. Barrett for the Clinic. The whine of the power saw being used inside the Clinic died away abruptly as the notables took their seats on the platform. Several workmen emerged from the building, but children were still playing in the area behind the Clinic when the mayor rose and approached the podium with the microphone.

"I want to welcome all of you to the dedication of the Old Town branch of the famous Barrett Clinic," he began. "We in

Gulf City are very proud to have a medical center of national renown located here. With a satellite Clinic in Old Town itself, more and more of our citizens will now be able to take advantage of the finest medical facilities available anywhere in the South— or perhaps in the country."

There was a round of applause and Dr. Barrett looked somewhat embarrassed, but Jack Pryor was beaming at the free publicity.

"When I persuaded the County Hospital Authority five years ago to lease the operation of our new Gulfside Hospital to Hospitals, Inc., I knew some of you were doubtful about having a corporation engaged in the business of providing medical care here," the mayor continued, "but we can all be proud of the way our fine hospital is being run. With the same corporation now providing further facilities on the east side of the river in the form of the Old Town Clinic, I'm sure we're going to be as pleased with the new facility as we are with the fine hos—" The word was drowned out by the sudden whine of a power saw cutting through the hot, still afternoon like a scalpel.

"Good God!" Mark heard one of the workmen who had come out of the building for the exercises exclaim. "I must have left that damn thing plugged in."

"Will somebody please cut that off?" the mayor shouted, red-faced with anger.

"I'll get it, sir."

The workman who had spoken was already running toward the open back door of the building. Before he could reach it, a scream of pain from a child topped even the high-pitched whine of the power saw. Instinctively sensing what must have happened, Mark, too, started toward the back door of the Clinic, followed by Alexa. Meanwhile the crowd, the mayor, and those upon the platform were frozen into immobility by the intimation of tragedy.

Before Mark could reach the door, a boy—perhaps about ten, he judged—broke through it. His face was contorted with horror and pain as he watched small geysers of red spurt from the stump of his left arm, which had been severed, obviously by the power saw, at a point several inches above the wrist. Mark caught the boy as he was falling in a faint and closed his right hand firmly around the bleeding stump. The pressure on the severed arteries immediately controlled the flow of blood, but the boy would have fallen to the ground had not Alexa caught his other arm and eased him down.

"He must have slipped inside and switched on the saw." The speaker was the workman who had started for the door. Standing only a few feet away, the blood slowly drained from his face as a look of horror developed in his eyes.

"I've got the bleeding stopped for the time being," Mark told Alexa. "Is there any ice in the Clinic building?"

"When I was there yesterday the workmen had the refrigerator going. It was full of beer cans."

"Find the hand and put it in a pan or bucket with plenty of ice," he directed. "If we get him to the hospital soon enough and keep the hand cold, we can probably save it."

"I'll get it and follow the ambulance." Turning to where the technicians were still standing beside the ambulance, she called, "Over here! Bring a stretcher."

The two Fire Department paramedics, more accustomed to sights such as this than the crowd, went into action immediately. Pulling a portable stretcher from the van, they started moving through the crowd.

"I'm Dr. Mark Harrison," Mark told the first technician to reach him. "I'll go with you to the hospital in the ambulance and Miss McGillivray will follow us with the hand packed in ice."

"Right, Doctor," said the chief technician. "Just tell us what you want us to do."

"Get him in the ambulance and put on a tourniquet," Mark directed. "I don't know how long I'll be able to keep the arteries closed by squeezing the stump."

"We'll handle the boy, Dr. Harrison," the technician told him. "You just keep the bleeding under control until we can get the tourniquet on."

As they were moving through the crowd toward the ambulance, a plump woman rushed forward. "It's Jimmy!" she cried. "He's dead!"

"He only fainted," Mark assured her. "Are you his mother?"

"Yes, but—"

"I'm Dr. Mark Harrison. We're taking him to Gulfside Hospital, but I'll need your permission to operate."

In the excitement attending the accident, Mark hadn't realized that a TV camera with a mobile transmitter was almost at his shoulder, until the bright light above the camera suddenly bathed the gory stump, from which the two bones of the forearm protruded, in its glare.

"Think you can sew it back on, Doctor?" The TV reporter standing beside the cameraman with a portable microphone had thrust it only a few inches from Mark's face.

"I can damn well try, if you'll get that thing out of the way," Mark snapped.

"Ever do one of these before?" the reporter asked unabashed, as he and the cameraman followed Mark while he moved beside the stretcher being handled by the paramedics.

"Of course. Microsurgery is my special field."

"What are you going to do, Doctor?" The mother had recovered a degree of composure when Mark had assured her the boy had only fainted.

"We're taking him to Gulfside Hospital. My assistant has gone to get the hand and put it in ice." Mark slowed the progress of the stretcher through the crowd long enough to answer. "Please go directly to the hospital; we'll need an authorization—"

"But how do I know—?"

"The doctor just said he's a microsurgeon, lady," said the TV reporter. "That's what they do—operate under the microscope to sew blood vessels and nerves back together."

"Thank God you were here, Doctor—?"

"He's Dr. Mark Harrison," the reporter told her. "With the Barrett Clinic."

The technicians were already lifting the stretcher to slide it into place. Still holding the stump in a fist that was rapidly tiring from the strain, Mark climbed in somewhat awkwardly to sit beside the boy.

"Miss McGillivray went inside to find the severed hand and put it in ice," Mark told the TV reporter, who seemed more in control of himself than anyone else in the crowd. "Check on her, please, and see if she's able to follow the ambulance."

"We'll bring her with us in the station control van." The reporter moved away, followed by the cameraman and his equipment. "God, what a picture this is going to make!"

Turning to the ambulance driver, Mark said urgently, *"Let's get this boy to surgery as fast as we can!"*

As the ambulance started to pull away, sirens screaming, Mark saw Alexa emerge from the back door of the Clinic carrying a bucket. When she lifted it in the air, he knew she had obeyed his instructions. Which meant that the tissue of the severed hand and the attached portion of the forearm were being protected in the only way they could be, now that they were no longer connected to the boy's circulatory system—by the power of cold to slow the demand of tissue cells for vital oxygen, until he could start blood flowing to them again by connecting the severed arteries and veins together once more.

XV

Someone—Dr. Barrett himself, Mark learned later—had the presence of mind to telephone the hospital and warn them to start setting up an Operating Room and getting the surgical microscope ready. Thus, Mark was able to bypass Emergency Room procedure and the delay in bringing the vital surgery into action. Less than an hour after the saw, switched on by the curious youngster, had sheared through bone, muscle, tendon, arteries, veins, and nerves in a fraction of a second, he and Alexa were scrubbing in the small room between Operating Rooms One and Two. The patient, already under anesthesia, was being prepared for surgery, the bleeding controlled by the tourniquet a Rescue Squad paramedic had put in place behind Mark's hand as soon as they had put the stretcher in the van.

"How far above the wrist would you say the saw cut through?" Mark asked Alexa as they were scrubbing.

"About two inches, maybe three. The hand was still warm when I put it in the bucket with the ice."

"Good!"

"How about the stump below the tourniquet, since you couldn't cool it?" She voiced the question uppermost in Mark's own mind.

"On the way over in the ambulance, I loosened the tourniquet every few minutes and let it bleed a little," he told her. "We can replace lost blood by transfusion, but we can't prevent the damage to tissues from lack of blood supply for any long period of time. Still, I guess the only way the time could have been shortened was for the accident to have happened right in the O.R. itself. How did you get here so quickly?"

"The TV remote control unit van had a siren. We were right behind the ambulance and the reporter was jabbering all the way about what a scoop they were getting. He called Jack Pryor from the platform by way of the mobile telephone and obtained permission to use the videotapes of the operation."

Mark gave her a startled glance. "What videotapes?"

"Hospitals, Inc., would like nothing better than for Gulfside Hospital to be the main teaching institution when the state opens a new medical school that's been promised to Gulf City. Jack had all the necessary equipment put in while the building was being constructed so it would have television for remote teaching." She gave him a searching glance. "Do you have any ethical qualms about operating in the glare of publicity?"

"Not as long as the equipment doesn't get in my way." Mark dropped the brush he'd been using in the sink and moved to immerse his hands and arms below the elbows in a deep basin of antiseptic. "Let's go. The longer we wait to get the radial and ulnar arteries reconnected, the less chance that kid has of having a usable hand instead of a stump."

XVI

About three hours later, Mark tied the final gossamer-sized 9-0 nylon suture reconnecting cut ends of the ulnar vein and Alexa clipped it a little above the knot.

"You can remove the small clamp from the vein," he told her without taking his eyes from the microscopic field in which they had been operating.

There was no seepage of blood at the suture line when she removed the clamp obstructing blood flow through the vein, so he raised his eyes from the ocular of the surgical microscope to meet hers across the small side table upon which the boy's arm had been stretched during the operation. They'd been sitting on stools facing each other across the arm during the whole first part of the operation.

"That was fantastic!" Her dark eyes were shining. "Imagine connecting together blood vessels not much bigger than matchsticks with sutures you can hardly see."

"The delicate part is over, except for suturing the cut nerve ends and they're usually no problem."

"And the bones?"

"We'll use small Vitallium plates to hold them together. I had to do the vessels first while there wasn't any tension on them."

"His hand is getting pink already and warmer, too. When will he be able to use it again?"

"Part of it tomorrow. The power saw cut across the flexor and extensor tendons well above where they splay out to each of the fingers, and since the muscles receive their nerve supply well above the level of the amputation, they'll be able to move immediately. Return of function in the intrinsic small muscles of the hand will depend on regeneration of the radial and ulnar nerves, of course, but we can stimulate them electrically every day so they won't atrophy."

"It was perfect," she assured him.

He knew it was not, however, and the truth was far more disturbing than the satisfaction he'd achieved by the successful completion of what had been a routine piece of microsurgery in restoring blood flow to and from the severed hand and wrist. Four times in the hour and a half since he'd started dissecting out the cut ends of the radial and ulnar artery and vein, he'd had to stop because of cramps in the fingers of his right hand. It was something he'd never experienced before while operating and even now, his fingers felt slightly numb and their movements heavy, as if they were responding only with reluctance to the stimuli from his brain.

Which could lead to only one conclusion. The daily headaches since the night he'd been mugged had been a sign of at least minor damage to his brain. But the momentary paralysis of the fingers of his right hand, however brief, were proof that the injury was more severe than simply a transient concussion.

XVII

Fixing the bones together with metal plates took longer than Mark had anticipated. Altogether, five hours had passed when he finished molding a heavy plaster splint to hold the boy's forearm in a position with the wrist and the hand cocked up.

"Why not a cast?" the anesthesiologist inquired as Mark was smoothing the strip of plaster of Paris for the splint.

"He needs a support that can be removed and put back on easily, so the physiotherapists can get to the arm and stimulate the intrinsic small muscles of his hand into contraction and prevent atrophy," Mark explained. "Otherwise, he'd end up with a claw hand that wouldn't be of much use to him."

Stimulated by the challenge of the operation and the extra supply of adrenaline it produced, Mark hadn't felt tired. But as he showered in the doctors' dressing room, weariness and the inevitable letdown of the stress produced by five hours of tense surgery began to weigh heavily upon him. Besides, his head had begun to ache—for how long he didn't know, since he'd been too much involved with the surgery to even feel the pain.

The family was waiting outside and he assured them there was every chance for the boy to regain a usable hand. Alexa came out of the Recovery Room as Mark was leaving the small reception area outside the operating section where the boy's parents had been waiting.

"Jimmy's fingers are getting pinker by the minute," she reported. "Did anyone tell you we were on the six o'clock TV news?"

"How could we be? We were operating."

"The station had a portable camera at the dedication to cover the mayor's speech—"

"I remember the reporter pestering me while I was trying to shut off the flow of blood from the stump—"

"The camera caught that and a lot besides. They put together a short tape showing Jimmy coming out of the Clinic building with blood spurting from the severed arteries and you seizing his arm to control the hemorrhage. And they added the first part of the operation as it was videotaped by a fixed television camera inside the Operating Room lamp. The nurses in the Recovery Room saw it on TV and say it was very dramatic. You're a hero."

"A thirsty hero, who could do with a shot of bourbon right now."

She laughed. "I can't offer that, but we do keep a refrigerator with food for snacks in the I.C.U., in case any of us on duty can't get to the cafeteria during serving time. Would you settle for a ham sandwich and a Coke?"

"Sounds better than my cooking. I can always have the bourbon for dessert."

A small table in the nurses' lounge off the Intensive Care Unit was empty. While Alexa made the sandwiches, Mark swallowed three aspirin tablets.

"I guess the strain from five hours of intensive surgery would give anybody a headache," she observed. "Especially when you're just getting over a severe concussion. But you still didn't yell at me once—or throw an instrument."

"That's because you're a perfect assistant."

"Thanks, but it will take me a while to get used to working in a microscopic field."

"I've an idea how to take care of that, too," Mark told her.

"Like what?"

"Did you notice how many times I had to stop the operation and get two fingers of my hand back working properly—the most important two, the thumb and the forefinger?"

"That could happen to anyone who'd been operating for a long time."

"It never happened to me before, when I was doing microsurgery at Lakeview. It's just possible that in addition to the concussion, a few brain cells in the motor area on the left side of my cerebrum may have been damaged beyond recovery."

"Even if they were, others could take over their function, couldn't they?"

"Who knows—when or if?" he said despondently.

"What can you do—except wait?"

"*Wait* is certainly the last thing I'm going to do," he told her. "Before another case of really delicate microsurgery comes along, I've got to determine the extent of brain damage."

"How can you do that?"

"By operating again. What do you do evenings?"

She gave him a startled look. "Nothing in particular. Why?"

"Would you be willing to give up a few evenings while we do some real microsurgery?"

"Of course; the practice would be good for me as an assistant, anyway. But why?"

"Before I left Lakeview, I was working on a project in the Surgical Research Lab that involved some pretty delicate suturing. If I pick up where I left off in Baltimore, I'll soon know just how much the use of my right thumb and forefinger have been damaged by the clot Dr. Minot removed from inside my skull."

"Couldn't an occasional cramp be just a temporary muscle spasm?"

"Those weren't cramps. Each time it happened, my forefinger and thumb seemed for a single instant not to respond to my will. Once I almost dropped the needle holder."

"I noticed that."

"Then you can understand why I have to know the truth. A microsurgeon who never knows whether the motor function of his most important two fingers is going to work properly isn't going to be of much use to anybody."

XVIII

In his apartment, Mark was having his first double bourbon—and still feeling sorry for himself—when the telephone rang shortly after nine-thirty.

"Hello, lover," Claire's voice sounded in his ear when he picked up the receiver. "What're you doing?" The words were slightly slurred, warning him that she, too, had been drinking.

"Getting slowly drunk—and wishing you were here. When are you coming back?"

"Not for several weeks at least, I'm afraid. The boss out here wants me to widen the ad campaign to include the Northeast."

"Even a bride would freeze to death wearing that stuff in winter on her honeymoon."

"Or what *we* usually wear. The brass likes the style of my ads, particularly my idea of using them as subliminal flashes on cable TV."

"Flash is the best description I can think of where those ads are concerned," he agreed.

"I just finished watching you on the six o'clock TV news out here. That picture of you saving the kid's life by shutting off the blood flow was sensational. It was the goriest thing I ever saw."

"I was lucky."

"So was the boy. How did the operation turn out? The last words I heard you say were, *'Let's get this boy to surgery as fast as we can!'*"

"It took Alexa and me five hours to put the severed hand back on, but it was already pink again when we finished."

"Good! I suppose you're getting drunk to celebrate. Wish I could be with you."

"Sounds like you're having a party of your own." Mark had been conscious of voices, laughter, and music in the background while Claire was speaking.

"I'm in the president's apartment—he's throwing *this* party, but there's one out here almost every night. And such bashes you wouldn't believe."

"I would, from what I've read in some of the news magazines. It doesn't help my low spirits to know you're having a good time while I'm sitting here alone missing you and quietly getting loaded."

"Cheer up, darling! You're famous and you're going to be rich! I'll be back in Gulf City before you know it and we'll celebrate with that long weekend in New Orleans I promised you over Labor Day. Sorry, got to run. Don't be depressed. You'll be the talk of Gulf City when tomorrow morning's paper comes out."

The phone clicked in Mark's ear, but as he was pouring himself a second double bourbon, he couldn't help wondering what

Claire's attitude toward him would be when it turned out that the mugging he'd taken on the way back from her condominium that night—it now seemed years ago—might well have finished him as a microsurgeon.

XIX

Sunday morning was bright, clear, and hot when Mark awoke about nine-thirty. He started his morning jog along the beach before breakfast, but soon found the sand cluttered with bathers and sun-worshipers, even that early. Seeking more solitude, he swung back into the city, where the streets were far less crowded, and halfway through his run discovered something he'd only noticed briefly before—an absolute jewel of a park.

Located beneath the towering steel supports for the west ramparts of the high bridge connecting Gulf City proper with Old Town, the park was only a few acres in extent but had obviously been designed with a loving hand that had continued its care in the same vein. Beds of red sage, impatiens, marigolds, and other summer flowers, separated by clumps of flowering hibiscus, lined the curving driveway that took off from the riverfront highway passing under the bridge.

Here and there, small picnic areas had been set out with cast-iron grills for cooking over charcoal. Drinking fountains from the sprinkler system that provided the growing plants with water made a lovely and placid retreat that was still only minutes from the bustling center of the city itself. The whole, too, was shaded for much of the day from the summer heat by the approaches to the high bridge, forming a welcome change from the sun-bright brazen quality of the city itself, yet integrally a part of it.

Panting from the run of several miles, Mark paused to drink from a fountain and found its faint taste of sulfur typical of the water from so many shallow wells in central Florida and along the Gulf Coast. With the rustle of the breeze from the nearby river through the palm trees that gave shade here and there in the park softening the roar of traffic over the approaches to the high bridge, he reveled for a few minutes in the coolness it brought, before starting the run back to his apartment. There, he showered before making coffee and toast for breakfast from the supplies Alexa had left in the cupboard and the refrigerator.

Sunday morning TV in the South, he discovered, was devoted largely to evangelical preachers threatening their hearers with eternal damnation—and that right soon. Unless they repented and joined one of the myriad "partners in prayer" clubs by which the reverend swindlers ensured for themselves a regular income. Nothing they had to say helped Mark get his immediate problem off his mind, however, so he finally called Pat O'Meara at home.

"Well, if it isn't the surgical hero himself," said the pathologist. "Tell me how you managed to have both TV and newspaper photographers on hand when that boy sawed off his arm?"

"The mayor gets the credit—not me."

"Come to think of it, you're right," said Pat. "He not only owns the TV station and the newspaper but the Barrett Clinic building, too—and is running for office to boot. How's the boy you operated on?"

"Fine, when I telephoned the hospital early this morning. The color's good in his fingers and he can even move them a little."

"That makes you a genuine miracle-maker."

"Not quite. I need to talk to you, Pat—privately."

"How soon?"

"The sooner the better."

"Let's see. I'm on call but I'm to meet Lara and the children about twelve-fifteen at the Club for the Sunday buffet. The food's good and Lara hasn't seen you since you came to Gulf City. Why don't you join us for Sunday dinner and we can talk afterward?"

"I need a private session with you, Pat."

"I'll have my own car and we'll ride back to the hospital together."

"Sounds good."

"Meet us in the lobby of the Club at twelve-fifteen, then. Shall I come by and pick you up?"

"No need. I'll walk—and enjoy the bathing beauties."

Pat O'Meara laughed. "The kind of swimsuits they're wearing these days, there's plenty of room for enjoyment—even for an old married man like me. See you about twelve-fifteen."

XX

The Sunday buffet at the Yacht Club was a family affair and Mark enjoyed it. Quite a lot of people recognized him from the television news programs the night before and from the story that had been splashed all over the front pages of the local newspaper that morning—with photographs. Lara had been a nurse at Duke before Mark had gone on to Lakeview, so it was pleasant to see her again. And hard to realize that the happy, plump young woman, who'd been a trim thirty-four at Durham, was now the mother of two school-age kids.

As he and Pat were crossing the parking lot to Pat's car after the meal, Jerry Thorpe and a slender young man with red hair came out of the locker room entrance. They were wearing white tennis shorts, polo shirts, tennis shoes, and carried the inevitable rackets.

"If it isn't the miracle surgeon himself." Jerry's tone sounded friendly. "Nice job, Mark."

"Thank you. None of the publicity was my idea."

"So Alexa told me when I met her making rounds this morning," said the gynecologist.

"She made rounds!" Mark exclaimed, surprised.

"Alexa sees every Barrett Clinic patient first thing in the morning so the surgeons will have an accurate account of their progress for the family, in case any of them catch us before we've seen our patients. She says the boy couldn't be doing better." Thorpe turned to his partner. "Excuse me! You probably haven't met Ted Moran yet. Ted's an Australian and the tennis pro for the Club."

"Glad to know you, Dr. Harrison." The tennis pro had a pronounced English accent. "I learned a lot about you from the morning paper."

"One thing it didn't tell you," said Mark. "I'm a lousy tennis player."

"We can easily remedy that, if you'd like to take up the sport," Moran assured him.

"We'll see," said Mark. "I'm certainly not in the class with

Jerry here. He tells me you and he are going to play next week in a tournament at Pensacola."

"And we're going to win," said Jerry positively. "Ted and I play together like a well-oiled machine. See you tomorrow at the Clinic."

"I don't know what to make of those two," O'Meara observed as he and Mark got into Pat's Mercedes. "Moran is a fruitcake, but a damn good tennis player. He teaches children at the Club and has turned out so many able to get athletic scholarships when they go to college that the club management ignores his personal life."

"Isn't that the best way?"

"I suppose so, as long as he doesn't involve any of his students, and he hasn't so far. He and Jerry Thorpe play in a lot of tournaments all along the coast, and Jerry is certainly not somebody you'd think of as being a homosexual."

"Hardly," Mark agreed.

"The gossip is that he's slept with half the society women in town—married or not. Lara says they even discuss his sexual techniques over the bridge tables."

"That's nothing unusual. Plenty of people, both male and female, are bisexual."

"So I heard, but I don't remember one at Lakeview—and *there* was a sex playground if I ever saw one."

Mark changed the subject. "I want to do some experimental surgery, Pat."

"What the hell for? If ever there was a 'compleat surgeon,' you're it."

"The operation yesterday reminded me that I could grow rusty at real microsurgical technique. I'm not liable to get many such cases—or even more delicate ones—down here as I did at Lakeview."

"You can be sure of that," Pat admitted as he parked the Mercedes at the hospital in a slot bearing his name. "Can I do anything to help?"

"I'd like to set up a surgical laboratory somewhere in the hospital where Miss McGillivray and I can do a few experimental procedures—"

"Is she willing to work nights? No! Don't answer. Any nurse would jump at the chance to get you under some sort of an obligation to her."

"Not Alexa!"

"Maybe not," the pathologist conceded. "Besides, with Dick Barrett grooming you to take his place in the Clinic and also marry his daughter, any woman daring to interfere in your romantic life would be taking a real chance. By the way, where is Claire these days?"

"In L.A.—working on a national advertising campaign for that line of intimate wear she's promoting." Mark changed the subject. "What are the chances of my setting up a small surgical laboratory somewhere in the hospital so I can keep my hand in with delicate microsurgery?"

"No trouble at all, once you get Jack Pryor to agree to the extra cost—which shouldn't amount to much."

"After the publicity I brought to Gulfside Hospital yesterday, Jack ought not to refuse me anything within reason."

"I agree. What do you need? Dogs?"

"Dogs are too much trouble to work with and care for—we'd about stopped using them in the surgical laboratory at Lakeview. Rats are much more adaptive to my sort of research."

"Rats are no problem. We keep a supply of them in the hospital basement for use in special laboratory procedures."

"Is your colony inbred? I need that sort of rat so the tissues of different animals will be so much like those of others they'll almost be like siblings. That way we won't have any trouble worrying about tissue rejection if we do transplants—"

"If I know you, that's what you're going to be doing."

"But no publicity," Mark insisted. "If Jack Pryor knew what I'm going to try, he'd have it all over town before we start."

"He won't learn from me," Pat O'Meara assured him. "In fact, I'd just as soon *not know* what you're doing. That way I don't have to take any of the blame in case something goes wrong."

"What can you give us?"

"A small Operating Room in the Path. Lab—we use it now as a sort of storage room."

"Is it big enough for us to use the microsurgery instruments?"

"Of course."

"I'll speak to Jack Pryor tomorrow, and we ought to be in business before the end of the week."

He didn't tell his friend the main purpose of the elaborate procedure he had in mind, that of either proving the disability of his right forefinger and thumb permanent as far as future microsurgery was concerned—God forbid! Or maybe helping to work out a technique that would let him stay in the field in spite of it.

XXI

Monday's operation with Dr. Barrett went very smoothly. Mark acted as first assistant and Alexa took over the instrument table, which was normally handled by a scrub nurse. When the final step connecting the common duct that delivered bile manufactured in the liver and the secretion produced by the pancreas to the digestive tract was ready to start, Dr. Barrett changed sides of the table and gave Mark the job. Fortunately, the tissues were large enough that he didn't need the surgical microscope and making the connection was a relatively simple one.

Leaving Mark and Alexa to close the operative wound, Dr. Barrett left for the Clinic. It was noon when they finished and Mark joined Alexa in the line at the hospital cafeteria. As they were leaving the cash register, carrying their trays, she said, "There's a special small room across the hall for doctors. You don't have to eat out here with the hired help unless you want to."

"I want to talk to you about something. Remember the difficulty I had the other afternoon when we were connecting Jimmy's hand and wrist back to his arm?"

"Yes, but I still don't think it amounted to anything."

"*You* saw it and *I* felt it—which does make it important. During a really delicate operation, that little break in the connection between my brain and my hand could make the difference between life and death for a patient, so I've got to know what to expect in the future."

"How can you do that?"

"Pat O'Meara's going to let me use a small room in his department as an experimental Operating Room. Would you be willing to help me with some pretty delicate microsurgical operations—after hours?"

"Of course. Where will you find patients?"

"Pat already has them—in cages. We'll use rats."

She frowned. "With organs and tissues that small, you'll really be putting your skills to the ultimate test. What kind of operations do you have in mind?"

"If I had stayed at Lakeview on the teaching staff, I was going to do more rat experiments in pancreas transplants."

"As a possible cure for diabetes?"

"Yes."

"It would be revolutionary."

"We'd already carried out a few successful procedures in animals and one or two in humans, but there are still a lot of bugs to overcome as far as the technique is concerned. If I'm able to work out the operative technique for a microsurgical procedure whereby a complete pancreas can be transplanted from one individual to another and connected to the circulatory system of the recipient without damaging the gland itself, I'll have it made."

"What about rejection in the rats receiving the transplants?"

"Rats breed, on the average, about every three months. Since those used for experiments are usually kept together in colonies, they're inbred from generations of close proximity and develop strains that are isogeneic."

"That's a new word."

"All it means is that those rats are practically twins, so organs can be transplanted from one to another without rejection," he explained. "It's much the same technique we use to transplant kidneys from one twin to another."

"The whole thing sounds fascinating, particularly for children handicapped because of the disease."

"It's worth shooting for, but my main purpose at the moment is to retrain my right thumb and forefinger to where I can always be sure they'll respond."

XXII

The Old Town Clinic opened for patients a week after the dedication. Dr. Julio Montez, one of the foreign medical graduates employed by Hospitals, Inc., as residents at Gulfside, moved into a small apartment over the garage. He was a graduate of a school at Guadalajara in Mexico, and Mark found him willing to work and eager to please if not quite as knowledgeable in the diagnosis and treatment of strictly medical conditions as he would have liked. Dr. Montez was fluent in Spanish, however, and with a large Cuban population now living in Old Town, his services as an interpreter came in handy, on the opening day of the Clinic.

Mark was tired when the first day ended, but he and Dr. Montez had seen two dozen patients, including two who could be scheduled for "short-stay" surgery, as soon as the equipment for the small Operating Room arrived. He was getting ready to leave when Jack Pryor came into his office.

"I was just looking at the books," said the hospital administrator. "You took in two hundred and fifty bucks today, almost enough to cover expenses."

"We'll soon be doing over twice that," Mark told the administrator. "I've scheduled a hemorrhoidectomy and a hernia for two weeks from now, when the O.R. equipment is installed."

"How about stopping by the Club for a drink before dinner?" Pryor asked. "You look as if you could use one."

"I could. Besides, I want to talk to you about something."

"Good. I'll meet you there in fifteen minutes."

"Give me a half hour. My Skylark isn't as fast as your Mercedes and I'm not quite familiar with traffic patterns yet."

Over bourbon and pretzels, Mark introduced the subject of the experimental surgical project.

"You're taking on a lot of work for somebody who was mugged three weeks ago," said Pryor a little doubtfully. "Sure you're up to it?"

"I feel fine, except for an occasional headache. Charlie Minot says that's par for the course."

"Don't push yourself too far. Will Alexa be working with you?"

"Yes, she's anxious to get more experience assisting in micro-surgery. And, since we're using the colony of rats Pat O'Meara already has in his department, there shouldn't be much extra cost."

"I'll find a way to write that off on the books. Can you think of anything else you're liable to need for your project—sterilizing equipment and that sort of thing?"

"We don't use sterile technique with rats and an injection of phenobarbital into the tail vein produces all the anesthesia we need. Miss McGillivray and I can have an early dinner in the hospital cafeteria and be at work a little after six, so we should be out by nine most evenings."

"Don't bother about cleaning up afterward," Pryor told him. "Max Steyer, the diener for the Medical Examiner's Laboratory, doesn't have too much to do. He can easily take care of that part of it."

"Thanks," said Mark. "That will probably save us a half hour of work every evening."

"Just don't make the mistake of burning yourself out, Mark," Pryor advised. "Your future here in Gulf City is much too rosy for you to let that happen."

XXIII

Just how well Alexa McGillivray could anticipate a surgeon's needs, even in such delicate procedures as those involved in transplanting the pancreas of a rat into the abdomen of another, Mark quickly learned. With arteries and veins less than the size of matchsticks to be connected to others of a similar diameter, the magnification afforded by the surgical microscope was absolutely necessary. The sutures of 9-0 nylon he used were actually less than the diameter of a human hair and hardly visible even under the microscope, but after the first few evenings, Alexa became almost as skilled at tying them as Mark was.

In the beginning, Mark wasn't troubled by the vexing lack of communication between the orders of his brain and their execution by his right thumb and forefinger handling needles so small they had to be held with jeweler's forceps. Especially important was achieving an absolutely tight connection between the duct leading from the donor pancreas and the delicate duodenum of the recipient's small intestine. Any slight leak of the highly digestive fluid produced by the pancreas could easily erode around a suture line and send the irritating digestive juice into the peritoneum, causing death very rapidly.

Alexa always seemed as rested when they were leaving the hospital as when Mark made the first incision into the abdomen of the tiny patient each evening. Mark, however, was not so lucky. After a morning spent in performing minor and often frustrating tasks in the Barrett Clinic, where few patients had yet begun to appear who needed microsurgery, followed by a busy afternoon at the Old Town satellite Clinic seeing patients and trying to train Dr. Julio Montez to assume more and more responsibility, he often found himself completely exhausted by five o'clock.

Too, the nagging postconcussion headache which had almost disappeared before he started the research project now appeared again. Fortunately, the jolt or two of potent bourbon he poured for himself as soon as he reached his apartment usually brought relaxation and sleep, although the amount needed to provide that *nirvana* steadily increased.

Often, too, as Mark found himself more and more dependent upon the nightly shots of bourbon to induce sleep, he also found himself jaded and hung over in the morning. On such occasions, one or two amphetamine tablets—for which he had written himself a prescription—taken before breakfast usually counteracted most of the effects of weariness and alcohol the night before, leaving him—at least in his own mind—fresh when he entered the Clinic at eight o'clock.

Mark did not realize that at least one other person suspected to what degree his daily dependence upon alcohol in the evening and amphetamines in the morning was reaching dangerous proportions until he and Alexa had been working together for a week. The surgery that particular evening involved suturing the pancreatic duct of a donor rat to the small intestine of the recipient, an almost daily task in the program of experimental operations he had set for them. For the first time since they had begun the work, however, he experienced once again the brief hiatus of communication between brain and fingers that had been his reason for starting the research project in the first place. As they were washing up after removing gloves, Alexa said casually, "I made a chocolate cake last night. Would you like to stop by my apartment for a slice and a cup of coffee before going home?"

Every fiber of his being yearned at the moment for a double bourbon, but he didn't want to hurt Alexa's feelings. She had been giving up her evenings for what he had termed an experimental project that was actually a device by which he hoped to retrain his own brain and hands to operate without the fear of making an error.

"You don't have to, of course, if you're too tired," she added.

"I'd love it," he lied nobly.

"Would you like a drink before the cake?" Alexa asked as she let them into her apartment, a few blocks back from the waterfront.

"Very much."

"I have a little bourbon. Pour yourself a drink while I get down the cake box and make some coffee."

Going to the cupboard, Mark took down the half bottle of bourbon and a shot glass. With fingers still shaking, he poured three shots and downed them in succession.

"Now I can get to sleep when I get home tonight," he said when she came back from the kitchen carrying a tray with a delicious-looking cake on it and two steaming cups of coffee.

"And need an amphetamine to get you going in the morning?"

"Whatever gave you that idea?"

"I've seen Jerry Thorpe on enough mornings after alcohol and amphetamines to recognize the symptoms."

"Jerry's an alcoholic."

"Not really, although he does go over the edge occasionally. It's only a couple of times a year, though, and he usually goes to New Orleans for a week or two to get dried out."

"I don't know why Jerry drinks so much," said Mark. "Ever since I joined the Clinic staff, he's managed to shove a lot of scutwork like routine pelvic and proctoscopic examinations off on me."

"That's always the case with a new doctor, but it doesn't explain why so many wind up as alcoholics or narcotic addicts. The AMA says it's about ten percent and some articles I've read indicate it may be one in seven."

"Why would you be reading up on that?" His hands had stopped shaking and he was feeling more like himself now, except for the underlying feeling of resentment against her for recognizing his failing and lumping him into a class with Jerry Thorpe.

"Because two people I like very much are close to being in that category—Jerry and you."

"I'm no alcoholic!" Mark exploded angrily. "And certainly not an addict!"

"Maybe not yet, but a lot of doctors are in over their heads before they're ready to admit it. My cousin, John Carr, the psychiatrist I told you about, says part of what he calls the 'Disabled Doctors' Syndrome' is the conspiracy of silence the victims' families and friends join in to keep a secret that would better be made public so something could be done about it before it's too late."

"Every man should have a right to decide how he's going to live," he protested somewhat heatedly.

"Every man, yes. But a doctor has no right to endanger other people's lives."

"Fat chance of my doing that," Mark said bitterly. "The biggest pieces of surgery I've done were attaching the arm on Jimmy and transplanting a pancreas in a rat."

"I saw Jimmy in the rehabilitation clinic today," she said, on a soothing note. "Those electric stimulations you ordered for his muscles are working wonders. His fingers move practically through the whole range of motion already."

"That job really wasn't microsurgery."

"It was still as brilliant a piece of work as I've ever seen anywhere, yet tonight, for the first time since we've been working together, you had to do a suture over twice."

Sudden and, he recognized, unreasonable anger flared in him, part of it due to the bourbon he'd just consumed and part to the nightly weariness that lately had demanded steadily larger doses of sedatives. Even more disturbing was the fact that she had unerringly gone to the heart of his own discovery that control of the movements of the right thumb and forefinger were no nearer normal, in spite of the nightly sessions in the small basement O.R., than on the afternoon when he had successfully reattached Jimmy's severed arm.

"I don't need to be lectured to on surgical technique," he snapped, getting to his feet. "Thanks for everything, but I'll be going now. Your technique of assisting is already perfect, so we won't need to do any more experimental surgery in the evenings."

XXIV

Mark awoke with a grandfather of all hangovers from the two bourbons he'd had after leaving Alexa's apartment in a huff. In spite of two cups of coffee, he still had to swallow two amphetamine tablets before he felt able to go to the Clinic and handle the morning appointments.

At lunchtime in the hospital cafeteria, he was still staring at his empty coffee cup and debating going back for another when Pat O'Meara stopped at his table. "I hate to bring bad news, but I went to the animal room just now to do a rabbit test," said the pathologist. "The last rat you operated on—I think it must have been last night—was lying dead in its cage."

"Dead? Could you tell why?"

"No. I thought you'd want to do a post on it."

"Do you have time to do it with me?"

Pat looked at his watch. "It's Friday and I'm taking Lara and the kids up the river in my cruiser this afternoon to spend the weekend fishing and swimming. If we do the post right away, though, I can still make it."

"I don't want to ruin your weekend, but a postmortem on a rat shouldn't take more than ten minutes."

And it didn't. The evidence was quite clear as soon as Pat O'Meara opened the small abdominal cavity and found it filled with cloudy fluid.

"There's your answer," he said. "One of the sutures where you connected the pancreatic duct to the duodenum must have cut through and leaked enzymes into the peritoneal cavity. The protein-digesting secretion of the pancreas is one of the most powerful digestive juices produced by the body, so it could easily have eroded along a suture line and attacked every organ in the abdominal cavity—as happened here."

"I won't know where the leak occurred until we take down that anastomosis," said Mark.

A quick dissection gave him the answer—at several places along the suture line attaching the pancreatic duct to the small intestine. Instead of picking up only the outer layer of the duct—and thus not penetrating all the way through—the needle he'd used had gone into the duct itself forming a natural pathway for an enzyme as powerful as the trypsin produced by the pancreas.

"The first rule of microsurgery in this sort of an operation," Mark commented, "is not to put the needle entirely through the wall."

Using a hand lens to magnify the area, he took a forcep and picked up the duodenum where the suture had cut through. With the point of a scalpel, he cut two of the gossamer-thin knots on either side of the suture that appeared to have cut through, then took a second forcep and opened the end of the duct. "You can see that at least one of the sutures wasn't placed right."

The pathologist took the lens Mark handed him and examined the area. "It cut through, all right," he agreed.

"If that stitch had been placed properly, the connection would have been tissue to tissue, with nothing intervening to form a pathway for the trypsin to escape."

"Could just one suture have caused the rat's death?"

"Yes, though more than one cut through. If I were joining small arteries together, a tiny wound like this one wouldn't have made much difference. A little blood would have leaked around where the suture cut through, then the clotting tendency would have sealed off the opening and nothing would have happened. But when you're dealing with a powerful enzyme like trypsin, the situation is much different."

Mark dropped the forceps into a basin and looked up to meet his friend's concerned eyes. "I spent nearly two years learning microsurgery, Pat—"

"You've been out of practice for a while—"

"The situation is more serious than that. Once or twice when I was putting that boy's hand and wrist back in place the other day, I noticed an aphasia involving the forefinger and thumb of my right hand, the two most important instruments a microsurgeon uses. What happened to this rat proves that the aphasia is probably permanent."

"You're jumping to conclusions," O'Meara protested. "One of the first things we were told in medical school was never to base any decision on a series of one case—and that's what this is."

"I did three perfect anastomoses on the first rats we operated on, Pat. This one was the fourth, which means I can never be exactly certain the line of communication between my brain and fingers isn't going to break, even momentarily. In this particular case, that instant was enough to kill this rat."

"Nobody's perfect—"

"Nobody who has to drink two to four jiggers of bourbon every night so he can go to sleep. Then wakes up in the morning with such a hangover that he has to take a couple of amphetamine tablets to clear his head enough to get to work."

"You've been working too hard. Why don't you take the weekend off and go upriver with us in the cruiser? There's plenty of room."

"I'm covering for the Clinic. Jerry Thorpe is playing tennis in Pensacola tomorrow—"

"Is Ted Moran going to be his partner?"

"Yes. Why?"

"There's beginning to be talk that Moran is Jerry's partner in more than just tennis." The pathologist picked up the dead rat by the tail and tossed it into a waste container. "The diener in the morgue will get rid of this carcass. Have you told anybody else about your aphasia?"

"Only Alexa McGillivray."

"You can count on her not to blab it and you can certainly count on me. That way, any disability you may have—and I don't think it's nearly as serious as you do—is a secret between the three of us."

"That's something I'll have to decide for myself, but there's no escaping the fact that if the patient in this particular operation had been a human being instead of rat, I'd be responsible for a death."

"People who've had head injuries get over aphasias all the time, and the last person you'd want to get stirred up over this is Dick Barrett. He's as quick as the next society surgeon to operate on patients who can pay—with little justification for the surgery —but he's pretty rigorous where the Clinic and the mortality of its patients are concerned. Every time someone loses a case or there's an unexpected complication, he launches a Grand Inquisition. Demands a clinical pathological conference and raises holy hell if I can't find some other cause besides the mistake the surgeon made."

XXV

Dr. Julio Montez, the FMG who handled the medical part of the work at the Old Town Clinic, had left early—with Mark's permission—so he was busy in the Clinic until after six o'clock that evening. His head had started aching shortly after Pat O'Meara demonstrated the searing chemical inflammation of the dead rat's peritoneal cavity produced by the leaking suture line. It had grown steadily worse during the afternoon until, as Mark drove across the high bridge to the newer portion of Gulf City, his brain felt like a throbbing ball of intense pain.

Eager to get home and prepare an injection of Demerol, he stopped only for a sandwich before driving on to his apartment. By that time, he was shaking so badly that he had trouble putting the key into his lock. And in his hurry to get to the refrigerator where he kept an ample supply of the Demerol prescribed for his concussion, he left the keys hanging in the outer lock.

For a moment, Mark considered injecting two ampules at once, since the relief afforded by one had steadily diminished over the past several weeks. He put that aside, however, having no way of knowing what effect doubling the already heavy hundred-milligram dose would have. His hands were trembling badly and he held the syringe tightly in one hand while he drew up the contents of an ampule of Demerol with the other. When he noticed a vein standing out on his clenched left hand, the answer to obtaining the maximum effect of the powerful narcotic suddenly struck him. Without stopping to think how much greater the effect of the drug would be when given intravenously, he jabbed the needle through the skin over the distended vein on the back of his hand. When a spurt of blood into the barrel of the syringe containing the narcotic told him the needle was inside the vein, he injected the contents of the syringe into his bloodstream in a single bolus of the powerful narcotic.

Never having taken the drug before by the intravenous route, Mark had no criteria by which to judge how quickly it would take effect—or to what degree. He was startled, however, by a surge of intense pleasure—almost as high as that he'd experienced with Claire on the balcony of her apartment the night of the introductory banquet.

His head started reeling, too, as the single dose struck his brain *en masse,* and he staggered toward the bed without trying to undress. The room was already beginning to spin around him, when he pulled the needle from the vein. Trembling fingers dropped it on the floor but, before he could stoop down to pick it up, the impact of the powerful drug upon his brain swept him into oblivion.

Book Three

Canyonhead

I

Mark awakened to find sunlight pouring through the open glass doors to the balcony and the sound of someone moving about in the kitchen, from which came the savory aroma of frying bacon. He felt no pain and his head was clear, a fact easily explainable when he glanced at the bedside clock and saw that it was half past seven, about twelve hours since he'd injected the Demerol last night.

Remembering how he had fallen across the bed in the final seconds of consciousness before the drug had taken its rapid effect, he was surprised to find that his shoes had been removed, as had his jacket and tie, although he was still wearing the slacks and light short-sleeved shirt that was the summer uniform of business and professional men in this climate.

"Who's there?" he called and was startled to see Alexa McGillivray appear in the doorway to the kitchen, holding a spatula in her hand.

"Decided to wake up?" She was in her customary uniform of white slacks and jacket, but both were rumpled.

"What are *you* doing here?"

"It's a long story; you have just enough time before breakfast to brush your teeth before hearing it. How do you like your eggs?"

"Over light."

By the time Mark came out of the bathroom, Alexa had set a card table for two on the open balcony.

"Drink your orange juice while I cook your eggs," she told him.

He obeyed without question, sinking into one of the chairs and picking up the glass. Minutes later, she appeared from the kitchen with a plate of bacon and eggs in one hand and a cup of steaming coffee in the other.

"You look more like a human being now," she told him. "When I found you last night about seven-thirty, flopped across the bed and breathing eight times a minute, you looked like the proverbial wrath of God—"

"How did you get in?"

"Your key was hanging in the lock outside the door." Returning to the kitchen for her own plate and cup of coffee, she put them down in front of her chair. "That Gulf breeze feels good. If my apartment faced the water, I'd eat out here every morning."

"You haven't explained how you happened to come by."

"I was at the hospital late, specialing an acute gall bladder. As I was passing through the basement heading for the parking lot, Max, the night diener in the morgue, told me the rat we'd operated on last night was dead. I stopped to see why and Max showed me where one of the stitches—"

"Had cut through."

"How do you suppose it happened?"

"I *know* how," he said bitterly. "For an instant while we were operating, the connection between my fingers and my brain was broken, just long enough for me to put the needle in too deep, wrecking my surgical career."

"You've just had a setback. That's no reason to go off the deep end."

"I wish I had your optimism, but I still can't figure out how you knew I was in trouble after you found the dead rat."

"Maybe it's ESP. When I rang your phone here, nobody answered, so I drove by on my way home and found your car parked diagonally across a couple of parking spaces, as if maybe you'd become ill and rushed home. Your keys were hanging outside the door to your apartment, too, so I came in."

Picking up the coffeepot from the small table, she filled his cup once again. "An empty ampule of Demerol and the syringe were lying on the floor, with a blood-stained handkerchief beside them. I put the evidence together and concluded that you had injected it into a vein—what regular addicts call 'mainlining.'"

"Did you think I'd tried to kill myself?"

"Hardly. It would have taken more than one ampule of Demerol, even given intravenously, to do that. I figured that you'd been depressed after finding the dead rat and tried to drown your sorrows with Demerol."

"It's a damn sight better than alcohol," he said. "If I'd gotten drunk, I'd've had a granddaddy of a headache this morning, but as it is I feel fine."

"So the Demerol O.D.s Dr. Hirschberg treats in the Emergency Room say," she told him dryly. "Under the circumstances, all I did was take off your shoes and jacket and stretch you out on the bed, figuring you wouldn't wake up until morning."

"Why did you stay, once you were sure I wasn't going to die from an overdose?"

"You're on call for the Clinic—remember? If the phone had rung or the night operator had tried to raise you on your beeper, you probably wouldn't have heard either one. Then you'd have had to answer to Dr. Barrett Monday morning and he would have discovered what you'd been doing."

"Suppose I *had* gotten a call—how would you have managed to wake me up enough to see a patient?"

"I've had some experience in such situations with Jerry Thorpe, so I carry syringes and ampules of adrenaline, coramine, methylphenidate, and Narcan in my medical bag. One of them would have brought you out rapidly."

"I still owe you a considerable debt of gratitude. How can I ever repay you?"

"I can't think of a *quid pro quo* at the moment, but I'll let you know when I do," she said. "For starters, though, you can promise not to go overboard with alcohol and Demerol every time you get slugged by circumstance."

II

Mark was reading a medical journal early Saturday afternoon when the telephone rang. It was Gina Martenson.

"Hi, stranger!" she said. "What've you been doing while Claire's cavorting with Hollywood machos?"

"Working. I'm in charge of the new Clinic over in Old Town."

"Which is booming, from what I hear—and all because you're a superefficient doctor."

"I do my best. How's Paul?"

"Fine, I'm sure. He's in one of his favorite places, Boston, attending one of those Harvard M.B.A. seminars. His partner was supposed to take me dancing with a party of friends at the Club tonight, but the poor guy called just now to say he's down with a case of the 'Green Death.' How'd you like to take his place?"

"I'd love to, but I'm on call to cover the Clinic."

"That doesn't make any difference. They can always reach you on the beeper."

"I can't have more than one drink, either."

"This isn't a binge, just some good clean fun. All the men who'll be there will have to go to work Monday morning, just like you."

"When shall I pick you up?"

"We live at the edge of town on the river, but there's no need for you to come all that way. I'll catch a ride in with some of the others who live close by. Meet us at the Yacht Club around nine. We'll have some drinks, dancing, and whatever—in that order."

"I don't know exactly what you mean by 'whatever.'"

"Whatever we want to do. I'll see you at the Club about nine," she added blithely before the telephone clicked in his ear.

After Gina hung up, Mark decided to take his usual five-mile run to sweat the rest of the Demerol out of his system. When he came out of the shower after returning, he heard the telephone ringing and picked up the receiver. It was Alexa.

"I was about to hang up and have the operator call you on the pager," she said.

"I went for a run and was taking a shower, so I didn't hear the phone. What's up?"

"I'm worried about a patient Jerry Thorpe did a Wertheim operation on yesterday. Could you see her with me?"

"Sure. Where are you now?"

"At the hospital. I usually make rounds Saturday and Sunday mornings unless I'm on vacation, but was late this time. Had to go home and shower and dress before going to the hospital."

"I'll meet you there in fifteen minutes."

III

Alexa was waiting at the nursing station of the floor reserved for gynecologic patients, looking cool and comfortable in a sleeveless summer dress. The patient—a Mrs. Thomas—appeared to be in her early sixties. She was complaining of pain in the right flank, which was odd, for Wertheim operations involved radical removal of the uterus, ovaries, and tubes for cancer, literally a cleaning out of the pelvis. The patient's blood pressure had been falling steadily, too, for about twelve hours, in spite of continuous intravenous injections started in the Operating Room.

When Mark examined her, he found the abdomen soft except for the discomfort of pressure over the incision. But when he pressed in the right flank, the patient cried out in pain, although he couldn't be certain whether he distinguished a mass in that area because of intense muscular rigidity.

"How's the urinary output?" he asked Alexa.

"Less than it should be thirty-odd hours after surgery."

"Looks like the right kidney might be kicking up for some reason," said Mark when they were out of the room where the patient could not hear. "Did Jerry have any trouble with the operation?"

"Some. He couldn't be sure the growth hadn't extended beyond the uterus itself, so he went as wide of it as he could. Besides that, he had some trouble with an aberrant artery."

"On the right?" Mark was suddenly doubly alert.

"Yes. It was apparently a branch of the ovarian or the uterine artery, but it was larger than you'd normally expect to find in that area."

"I don't see a typed description of the operative procedure on the chart."

"Jerry was running late for a tennis match somewhere out of town that afternoon. He said he would dictate the operative account on Monday when he gets back."

"Is that his usual custom?"

"He's no different from a lot of surgeons when he's in a hurry; some wait a day or two before dictating operation reports."

"It's a good thing you were there or we'd be working entirely in the dark," Mark commented.

"What do you think?"

"It could be several things. A hematoma dissecting along the wall of the pelvis—possibly from that artery Jerry had trouble with—would cause the pain she has in the right flank and also the rigidity I felt. Another possibility is a beginning infection of the right kidney."

"Her temperature is only slightly above normal."

"That tends to rule out an infection, and a severed ureter between the right kidney and the bladder should have caused trouble earlier than this. Was she matched for transfusion?"

"Yes. She had one unit of blood during the operation."

"Order another then and step up the Demerol to a hundred milligrams q4h P.R.N. If her pain continues, we might have to take a look inside her tomorrow. By the way," he added, "I've been invited to the Saturday night dance at the Yacht Club later on this evening, but you can always raise me on the pager if you get worried."

IV

The dance at the Yacht Club was just beginning when Mark walked into the lobby. He had no trouble finding Gina Martenson, however; she was in the midst of a noisy group occupying a table near the dance floor.

"Mark!" Gina hurried across the floor to take his arm and lead him to the table. "Having your head shaved makes you look like that divine Kojak."

"Not much longer, I hope. Am I late?"

"Not at all. The McIntoshes haven't arrived yet; they always manage to be last so Helene can make an entrance."

The group of something over a dozen people to whom Gina introduced Mark was composed of four doctors, the others divided equally between lawyers and bankers. The women were smartly groomed, sleek, and dressed to the nines, the men prosperous-looking and self-confident. They'd already had several drinks around but Mark accepted only a bottle of beer, with the excuse that he was on call and one hospital patient wasn't doing too well.

"Yours?" a doctor asked.

"No," said Mark. "Whoever's on call nights and weekends takes care of all Clinic patients."

"That probably keeps you pretty busy sometimes," a second doctor commented. "When I try to get a patient into Gulfside, it always looks to me as if most of those already there belong to the Barrett Clinic."

"That's no more than right," said the first doctor. "If Dick Barrett hadn't gone to bat with political ex-patients of his in Washington, the city could never have gotten enough Hill-Burton money to build the hospital."

"Particularly if the federal authorities had known it would be leased immediately to a corporation-for-profit like Hospitals, Inc.," another doctor commented.

The McIntoshes arrived just then, with the statuesque Helene indeed making an entrance, as Gina had predicted. Edward McIntosh greeted Mark warmly, but his wife was reserved—until Mark asked her to dance.

"Thanks for not letting on that you remembered me," she said when they were on the dance floor, safely out of earshot of the others. "I hope you really haven't forgotten that charming rustic inn at Berkeley Springs, West Virginia."

Memory came flooding back and Mark had no need to pretend when he said, "How could I?"

"I left Baltimore about a month after our visit to Berkeley Springs."

"I missed you."

"Maybe, but I'm sure you had plenty of other opportunities. I might as well admit that I could have fallen in love with you then without half trying."

"The feeling was mutual," he lied gallantly.

"Thanks—even though it wasn't. You were about to finish medical school, but I had no wish to marry a hospital resident and support him through another five years by working as a nurse."

"It turned out to be seven years—all told."

"That would have been even worse; I saw too many of my classmates in nursing school go that route. They had a kid or two in the later years of their husband's residency, when salaries got to the point where they could manage to live without her working.

Then the husband went out into private practice and divorced her a few years later, leaving her with the kids to look after on what she could get for child support—after the lawyer took his cut."

"It doesn't always have to be that way."

"That's still the trend. When you've been here longer, you'll get so you can recognize the victims of that syndrome who have to work in the hospital to keep themselves and the kids alive. Besides looking a lot older than others their age, they have to leave work the minute they're off duty to pick up little Jack or Jill at a nursery school. They always look a little sloppy, too, from wearing wash-and-wear uniforms that don't need ironing and they're too worn out after feeding the children and putting them to bed to worry about going out socially."

"Good God! You're painting a dreary picture of medical marriages."

"Ex-medical marriages—and nurses who fall in love after several weekends at secluded country inns and marry young doctors. A few more trysts at places like Berkeley Springs and I might have taken the same route, but I'd already decided it wasn't for me."

"I'd say you've done very well for yourself."

"Why not?" She shrugged. "I came to Gulfside Hospital as a supervisor on the surgical floor about a year before Edward's wife died from breast cancer. He's twenty years older than I am, but he's still surprisingly vigorous, especially in the sack. Not like you, of course, but there are perks—like my Cadillac Cimarron, a fine home on the riverfront, a full-time maid, and a discreet fling sometimes when my husband goes to a convention." She gave him a sidewise glance. "Like a couple of weeks from now when the American Psychiatric Association holds its annual meeting in Chicago. Edward will be there delivering a paper on 'The Impaired Physician.' He's chairman of the state committee, you know."

"I'd heard—but I hope I'm never impaired."

"You certainly weren't at Berkeley Springs. Edward wanted me to go with him to Chicago, but I have a sorority meeting the day he leaves that I've got to attend. I'm up for first vice-president."

"Couldn't you catch him later in Chicago?"

"He's going to be gone almost a week," she continued. "While he's away, we can have another weekend in a place just as lovely as the one at Berkeley Springs, but we'll have to be careful. You've no idea how jealous Edward can be—even of people I knew before I married him."

Before Mark could react to the bald invitation for a brief but discreet affair, Gina came up and tapped Helene on the arm.

"Mark's mine, darling. Go take care of your own. That's what you married Edward for, wasn't it? To love, honor, and obey in sickness and in health—while hoping the sickness will be short—and terminal?"

"You're a real bitch, Gina." Helene McIntosh showed no resentment as she stepped away, allowing Gina to take her place. "I enjoyed our dance, Dr. Harrison. Ask me again sometime."

"I'm still dying to know what was between you two at Lakeview," said Gina as they moved in rhythm to the music.

"Nothing, I swear it. I never saw her before Dr. Barrett's dinner."

"You're a lousy liar, but I'm glad you can be discreet; a lot of men who attract women like to brag about their affairs—to other men. If Edward McIntosh knew you and Helene had once been intimate, he'd manage to slip cyanide into your tranquilizer."

Mark laughed. "I'll be careful not to need a psychiatrist—especially Dr. McIntosh."

"You won't—and neither will I," she assured him.

"How do you know that?"

"Because we're much alike in many ways. You're a North Carolina farm boy, while I'm an old-fashioned girl who's all for the old-fashioned virtues: a lovely house, all the money I need to spend, a full-time maid, and a lover who can perform satisfactorily in the 'missionary position'—which Paul does to perfection."

A high-pitched electronic squeal suddenly startled them both.

"What the hell is that?" Gina exclaimed.

"My pager. Where's the nearest telephone?"

"In the manager's office, just inside the front door."

When Mark called the answering service for the Clinic, he was told that Alexa McGillivray wanted him to call her immediately at Gulfside Hospital.

"Miss McGillivray, please," he said when the hospital operator answered. "This is Dr. Harrison."

Alexa's voice sounded in his ear almost immediately. "Mrs. Thomas is having more pain and the flow of urine has almost stopped. I think she's going into shock rapidly."

"Call Dr. Barrett and ask him to meet us at the hospital right away," Mark ordered. "She's going to need more surgery and it would be better if he backs me up."

"Right!" Alexa broke the connection.

"I'm sorry, Gina," said Mark. "One of Jerry Thorpe's patients is in trouble. I'll have to operate. Can you get home safely?"

"Sure," she said. "It's times like this that make me glad I didn't marry a doctor."

V

Alexa met Mark at the nurses' station of the Intensive Care Unit and handed him the chart—which spoke for itself. The temperature curve was still normal, almost certainly indicating that the complication he'd suspected when he examined the patient earlier that afternoon was not an infection. Other parameters, however, were far more alarming.

The patient's heart rate had been rising steadily, he saw, and was now nearly a hundred-twenty. In spite of the transfusion he had ordered, blood pressure was down to ninety over sixty and the blood chemistry reports were diagnostic of an impending state of surgical shock. A state which, if it continued, could rapidly undermine the stability of the patient's circulation and lead to heart failure with all it represented.

Urine production, too, had almost stopped and, when coupled with a rising level of blood urea nitrogen, was diagnostic of a gradual poisoning to a grave degree by an accumulation of the patient's own body wastes.

Mark's examination was thorough. He was finishing it when Dr. Richard Barrett came into the I.C.U. cubicle where Mrs. Thomas lay, carrying the latest laboratory reports in his hand and frowning.

"Glad you were available, sir," Mark greeted him. "I believe we should open her up immediately."

"With what diagnosis?" Barrett was feeling the patient's pulse while he studied the chart.

"Maybe we'd better discuss that in a somewhat more private place." Mark had seen the anxious face of the husband peering around the open glass door separating the cubicle from the main part of the surgical I.C.U.

Barrett nodded and moved toward the door, stopping to speak to Mr. Thomas. "Dr. Harrison and I have to go over your wife's record," he told the distraught husband. "We'll be able to talk to you in a few minutes."

"She's going to die, isn't she, Doctor."

"She's had a serious setback," said Barrett patiently. "We may have to operate again."

"Is the cancer spreading already? Dr. Thorpe told us he thought he'd gotten all of it."

"This complication appears to involve the right kidney and it's almost certainly not a spread of the cancer," Barrett assured the family. "I'll talk to you as soon as Dr. Harrison and I can agree on what should be done."

In the small office that provided privacy for doctors while writing up patient records, Richard Barrett's manner changed abruptly. "I don't see any operative record here, Alexa," he said. "Where is it?"

"Dr. Thorpe didn't get to dictate one before he left—"

"He knows better than that! Was he drunk again?"

"No, sir. He *was* in a hurry to leave early because he's playing in a tennis tournament this weekend."

"Thank God you were there," said Barrett resignedly. "You can probably describe the operation as well as Jerry could anyway—or even better. What went wrong?"

"It was a routine Wertheim procedure, except for some difficulty with an aberrant artery I told Dr. Harrison about."

"What aberrant artery?" Barrett demanded.

"Dr. Thorpe couldn't identify just where it came from—"

"Or where it went, which is more important," Mark interjected. "If my hunch is correct—and I'll admit it's mainly a gut reaction —Jerry tied off the blood supply of maybe half the right kidney."

"A surgeon can't always depend on gut reactions," Barrett objected. "Where's the evidence to support it?"

"Mainly in the clinical course," said Mark. "There's pain and marked tenderness over the lower pole of the right kidney—exactly the portion that probably lost its arterial supply when Dr. Thorpe tied off what he thought must have simply been an aberrant artery near the pelvic brim, according to the way Alexa— Miss McGillivray—described it to me."

"Was the artery very large, Alexa?" Barrett asked.

"About the size of a hospital drinking straw, sir," she said. "Large enough for me to question Dr. Thorpe about tying it off, but he'd already cut it, so he didn't have any choice."

"Too bad you weren't there, Mark," said Barrett. "You could have reconnected the cut ends under the microscope."

"I still may be able to do just that," said Mark pointedly.

Barrett's eyebrows lifted doubtfully. "With the kidney already badly damaged? If your diagnosis is correct, wouldn't it be simpler just to remove it?"

"Simpler perhaps, but far more costly when your insurance company settles out of court," said Mark bluntly.

"You have a point there," Barrett admitted. "But if the blood supply to the lower part of the right kidney has been shut off, as you suspect, why didn't the symptoms of shock start earlier?"

"I suspected what might have happened when she started having severe right-sided pain and showed some signs of shock," said Mark. "At that time I was depending almost entirely on instinct and, as you say, that's not always a sound enough reason to reoperate."

"Are you certain it is now?"

"I'd stake my reputation on it," said Mark without hesitation.

"That's good enough for me," said Barrett. "Start getting an Operating Room ready, Alexa, and call Dr. Porter for the anesthetic."

"Yes, Doctor," she said and left the room to obey the order.

"I'll check the surgical microscope and start getting ready to operate," Mark told the older doctor. "Will you explain to the family what we're going to do and why? I think they might like to hear it from the head of the Clinic."

"I'll tell them *what,* but not *why,*" said Barrett. "A stone blocking the kidney pelvis could produce this picture in a patient whose general condition has been severely weakened by a serious pelvic operation like a Wertheim."

"But—"

"One thing a surgeon needs to learn early, Mark, is not to alarm a patient's family unduly—especially when you don't know what you're dealing with anyway."

"You'll scrub with us, won't you?" Mark asked.

"You and Alexa are accustomed to working together under the surgical microscope," Barrett told him. "Another pair of hands would just be in the way when you start to reconnect the damaged arterial supply to the portion of the kidney which seems to be lacking it now. She's in your hands, Mark."

Fortunately, Mark had taken the precaution on Friday afternoon of having the surgical microscope brought up from the temporary basement experimental surgery to the regular Operating Room, in case it was needed on Saturday or Sunday. What he hadn't counted on was the sudden headache that assailed him as he was undressing in the doctors' lounge adjacent to the scrub room—or hands that started shaking so badly he could hardly tie the strings of his mask behind his head.

Fortunately, he recognized what was happening, and, knowing Mrs. Thomas's life could easily hang on his being able to control those hands, reached into the medical bag he now carried everywhere he went. Taking out a one-hundred-milligram ampule of Demerol and a sterile plastic syringe in its small container, he removed the syringe and pulled off the rubber sleeve that protected the needle from contamination. Snapping off the top of the ampule with an alcohol sponge, he sucked up its contents into the syringe.

The prick of the needle was barely noticeable but the sharp sting, as he injected the powerful narcotic deep into the muscles of his left upper arm just below the shoulder, was. He'd had to inject high, though, where the mark of the needle prick would not be visible beneath the short sleeve of the operating pajamas he wore. Dropping the syringe and needle with the ampule into a wastebasket, he carefully rearranged the papers in the bottom of it so they would not be easily seen.

By the time he entered the scrub room where Alexa—her hair covered by a gauze hood that Operating Room nurses often wore—was already scrubbing, he could feel the tension in his head and his hands easing.

"Everything's ready," she told him. "I'm glad you thought to have the surgical microscope brought up to the O.R. from the basement."

"So am I," he told her as he started to scrub. "We'll go in through Jerry's midline incision and hope to do whatever needs to be done without having to make another one to expose the kidney."

By the time Mark finished scrubbing, a rigidly maintained period of ten minutes, the trembling of his hands had ceased. Moreover, as he accepted the sterile gown and rubber gloves from the scrub nurse he no longer felt unsure at all but, with the support of the narcotic, was now certain of his actions and completely in control.

Alexa had already clipped the black silk sutures holding the edges of the lower midline abdominal skin incision together. The wound itself was bloodless when Mark used the flat handle of a scalpel to separate the fatty layer beneath the skin, whose edges had already begun to adhere in the process of healing. Only a few moments were required for Mark and Alexa, working together like a well-oiled machine, to reopen the abdominal incision, including the deepest layer of the peritoneum lining the cavity itself. When Alexa lifted the edge of the abdominal wound on her side with her left hand, he lifted the corresponding edge with his and slid the blunt jaws of a self-retaining retractor between them, separating them to open a wide space giving access to the abdominal and pelvic cavities.

"A little more Trendelenburg, please," Mark ordered.

"Right!"

The anesthesiologist pressed buttons on the electrically controlled operating table, smoothly raising the lower half of the table while depressing the upper. With the sick woman's body now elevated at a sharp angle, the contents of the abdominal cavity, mainly the small and large intestines, slid out of the much smaller pelvic cavity into a space in the upper abdomen beneath the diaphragm where Mark carefully packed them away out of danger with moist gauze pads. While he was doing that, Alexa was using suction to remove a small amount of blood-tinged fluid that had accumulated in the depths of the pelvic cavity.

"See anything?" Richard Barrett asked from the elevation of a two-foot-high stool upon which he was standing where he could look over Mark's right shoulder directly into the pelvic cavity.

"Looks good so far." Mark picked up a large Kelly clamp to point out the suture line where Jerry Thorpe had brought together the layers of the peritoneum he had reflected before removing the organs of the reproductive system, along with the cancer the uterus had contained.

"Any sign of cancer?" Richard Barrett asked.

"None at all. Jerry does a beautiful hysterectomy."

"That's good. It will help a lot if I can assure the family that no cancer has been left."

"If you'll show me where Dr. Thorpe ran into the trouble with that aberrant artery," Mark told Alexa, "I may be able to expose it without tearing down much of the peritoneal covering of the area where he removed the tubes, ovaries, and uterus."

"There," she said pointing with a blunt hemostat to a slight bulge beneath the peritoneal sutures near the pelvic brim.

Gingerly, Mark slit the peritoneum where Jerry Thorpe had carefully sutured it over the lump of tissue containing the cut ends of the offending artery, after it had been tied off by means of a suture with a needle thrust through the tissues around it.

"Jerry did a good job of hiding his tracks," Mark told Dr. Barrett, who was watching closely.

"His error was in not recognizing what he had cut and sending for help," said Barrett harshly. "Good surgeons don't operate in a hurry to get out of town for the weekend. What are you going to do now, Mark?"

"First, I'll identify the artery Jerry cut and had to ligate. Then I'll see where it goes to."

"Not where it comes from?"

"That, too. But in this instance, where it goes to is more important because it was carrying blood that might have been vital to the existence of an organ. Once we determine where it went to, we can worry about finding either where it came from or see if we can't dissect out another artery and make a connection to supply the blood the first one originally carried."

"What if you can't?" Barrett asked.

"Then we'll find one we can count on to supply the blood that's needed," said Mark. "If my hunch is correct, the eventual life of this patient's right kidney will depend on what we can connect to the distal portion of the artery that supplies it."

"Any idea what artery you'll use?"

Mark shrugged. "We'll have to see."

For the next half hour, Mark was busy with a careful dissection of the area where the uterus, tubes, and ovaries—now removed—had obtained their blood supply. When he finished, the course of the accessory artery upward and outward toward the right kidney could be plainly seen, with the ligature the gynecologist had used to close the cut end plainly visible.

"Your diagnosis of what happened was right on the nose, Mark," Barrett complimented him. "Are you going to pick up the ovarian artery now to make the connection?"

"First, I'd like to test my theory that some collateral circulation inside the kidney itself has probably kept the lower pole from dying for lack of oxygen," said Mark. "If I'm wrong, the logical thing could still be to remove the portion of the kidney that has lost its circulation."

"How can you test that?" Alexa asked.

"By removing the ligature Dr. Thorpe used to close the end of the damaged artery," Mark explained. "If the lower pole of the kidney has received enough blood through collateral circulation inside the organ itself to keep it alive, we should get a back flow of blood from the artery."

Using a fresh scalpel blade so as to make the cleanest possible wound, Mark cut directly across the artery just back of the ligature closing it. For a moment nothing happened, then a clot perhaps an inch long that had obviously developed inside the artery beyond the ligature suddenly popped from it and was followed by a spurt of bright red blood.

"That means the kidney can be saved," said Barrett. "But I can't say as much for Jerry Thorpe's hide."

"What happened here could have happened to almost any surgeon," said Mark.

"Any surgeon who didn't remember his *Gray's Anatomy* and the fact that accessory renal arteries occur very frequently," said Barrett.

Discovering a vessel that could be used to direct blood to the partially damaged kidney took another thirty minutes. It turned out to be the ovarian, which the patient needed no longer, with both ovaries removed during the first operation. Mark felt considerable satisfaction when he discovered that the cut end of the now freely movable ovarian artery could easily be brought to reach the damaged kidney artery he'd already exposed.

"Do you expect to have any trouble making the connection?" Barrett asked.

"None at all." Mark spoke to the circulating nurse: "Please wheel the surgical microscope into position and switch on the laser for illumination."

"How is she?" Barrett asked the anesthesiologist.

"Fine, Dick. I gave her some mannitol to decrease the blood viscosity and alleviate the shock condition."

"Thank you for coming over, sir," Mark told the older doctor.

"I'm going to call a special meeting of the Clinic staff Monday afternoon at five to discuss this patient, and I want you and Alexa there," said Barrett. "Jerry is due back tomorrow night or early Monday morning, so he can be there, too. We can't afford to have this sort of thing happening just because he brings in a lot of society patients. Meanwhile, I'll tell the family we found that an artery supplying part of the right kidney was blocked by a blood clot and removed it, restoring the blood supply to that portion of the kidney. It's all true, isn't it?"

"As far as it goes, yes," Mark conceded.

"Why tell them more? She should be all right now, shouldn't she?"

"I don't expect any more trouble."

"How much longer will it take?"

"Not more than thirty or forty-five minutes," said Mark. "Once I've connected the ovarian artery to this accessory renal, plenty of blood should flow to the lower pole of the right kidney."

"They won't ask any more questions, I'm sure," said Barrett. "I'll send them on down to I.C.U. to wait for her. Incidentally, Mark," he added as he was leaving, "you're living up to everything I expected of you."

Working under the forty-power magnification afforded by the surgical microscope, Mark swiftly started to secure the open end of the ovarian artery to the similar opening in the vessel whose closing had almost cost Mrs. Thomas her life. He placed the first three sutures about one hundred twenty degrees apart, using them to bring the cut ends of the vessels into close contact—mouth to mouth, so to speak. By placing additional sutures between two of the first ones, whose ends he had left long so the arteries could be manipulated by them, he achieved a blood-tight closure of two thirds of the circumference of the vessels being connected. Finally, he used the long ends of the sutures forming the third one-hundred-twenty-degree section to rotate both arteries so he could place the vital remaining sutures at the back side—the most difficult part of the entire operation—but making sure of a smooth connection.

When Alexa removed the rubber-shod clamps that had prevented blood from flowing while he secured the connection between the cut end of the ovarian artery and that going to the lower part of the kidney, Mark watched closely. He felt a surge of satisfaction when the vessel carrying the brunt of the makeshift circulation began to pulsate synchronously with the beat of the patient's heart.

"You can add the heparin to the I.V.," he told the circulating nurse. "It looks like we're home safe, but it's just as well to prevent a clot at the point where the two vessels are connected."

"Congratulations!" said Alexa. "It was a beautiful job."

"We've done as well with rats' tails," he reminded her.

The operation was completed swiftly, once the flow of blood through the damaged artery was restored. As Mark came out of the doctors' dressing room, after showering and changing to civilian clothes, he saw Mr. Thomas and his daughter standing beside the doors leading to the surgical Intensive Care Unit.

"Did Dr. Barrett talk to you about Mrs. Thomas?" he asked.

"He described what was done so even we could understand," said the daughter happily. "I guess Dr. Barrett is one of the finest surgeons in this part of the world."

"I'll second that." Mark chose to go along with whatever Barrett had told them.

"You must feel very good at being allowed to work with such a fine surgeon," the husband added.

As the Thomases moved away, Mark heard a sound that appeared to be stifled laughter and looked up to see Alexa standing in the open door leading to the Intensive Care suite. He didn't doubt she had heard most, if not all, of the conversation. Angered a moment ago by Barrett's having left at least the impression with the family that he had performed the delicate operation, the smile on Alexa's face suddenly reminded him how absurd it was to allow his resentment to show.

"Wipe that silly smile off your beautiful puss," he told her, a little shortly, as he passed her.

"If I hadn't happened to come out, would you have told them the truth?" she asked.

"Maybe. I was certainly tempted. If you're driving home tonight, I'll follow you and see that you get to your apartment safely."

"Thanks, but I think I'll stay on and special Mrs. Thomas until the morning shift comes on. I.C.U. is one nurse short tonight."

He was halfway to the elevator when he turned back and saw her still standing in the open doorway. "Will you see Jerry early Monday morning?" he asked.

"Yes. He's doing a laparoscopy at ten. Why?"

"Maybe you'd better bring him up to date on what happened

here tonight and what's going to happen when the staff meets in the afternoon. It wouldn't be fair for Dr. Barrett to spring it on him at the Clinic staff meeting without his knowing all the details."

"Why not tell him yourself?" she asked.

"I would, but he might think I was gloating."

"I'll warn him," she promised, "but he isn't going to like it."

VI

Mark was five minutes late for the Monday afternoon staff meeting. The entire staff, including Alexa, were present in the Clinic lounge and Dr. Barrett was looking particularly stern.

"Sorry to be late," Mark apologized. "As I was finishing the day's work, a patient came in with a thrombosed external hemorrhoid. I didn't have the heart to make him suffer through the night with it."

"I hope he wasn't on Medicaid," said Barrett.

"I doubt it," said Mark. "His name is Parks and he's a banker. Said you and he are good friends, Dr. Barrett."

"Sam Parks!" Barrett's manner thawed perceptibly. "We play golf together."

"He was grateful."

"Let's get on with the staff meeting," said Jerry Thorpe. "I'm playing tennis with Ted Moran at seven-thirty."

"Moran—and tennis—can wait," said Barrett icily. "In fact, that's part of what this meeting's all about."

"What the hell does that mean?" Thorpe demanded.

"Let's get on with it, Dick," said Elmer Peterson. "I'd like to get in a few hours of sailing before dark."

"All right," said Barrett. "Do any of you have questions about the duty roster this week?"

"I've got another tournament next weekend," said Thorpe. "In Tallahassee."

"We'll take that up later," said Barrett. "How are things at the Old Town Clinic, Mark?"

"Fine, sir. Dr. Montez is settling in nicely and his speaking

Spanish is a great asset. We'll probably get a lot of the Cuban clientele because of it."

"Many of them are very stable people with good middle-class incomes," said Barrett. "The way you're going, you can develop a large practice over there with the Spanish-speaking group."

"But don't try to take it with you if you don't stay on the staff," Jerry Thorpe warned. "It's *verboten*—"

"I know," said Mark.

"Let's get to the main business of the meeting," said Barrett. "For the benefit of the others, Mark, I'd like for you to report on some complications that developed in a Clinic patient operated on by Jerry last Friday morning before he left the city."

Mark had been dreading the request, but he didn't try to back out. "Jerry did a Wertheim for cancer of the uterus on the patient under discussion—"

"And cleaned out the pelvis, leaving no sign of any spread of the malignancy beyond the uterus," Thorpe interposed.

"I certainly found none," Mark agreed.

"Unfortunately," said Barrett, "you also tied off a major aberrant artery supplying the lower pole of the right kidney, Jerry. When Mark called me Saturday evening, urinary excretion had practically ceased and the patient was in incipient shock from a gradual shutdown of kidney function because of it."

"Miss McGillivray deserves the credit for realizing that the patient was getting into deep trouble," said Mark. "She called me and I saw Mrs. Thomas around five Saturday afternoon. The picture was somewhat confusing, until Miss McGillivray remembered that Dr. Thorpe had encountered some difficulty with an unusually large artery branch in the adnexae."

"It was a branch of the ovarian or the uterine artery," said Jerry.

"You're right about the origin of the artery," Mark conceded. "Unfortunately, the other end furnished a large part of the right kidney with most of its blood supply."

"How in hell could you have failed to recognize that an artery of that size probably wasn't just a branch, Jerry?" Elmer Peterson demanded.

"Since when are you an authority on the female pelvis, Elmer?" Jerry Thorpe asked acidly.

"Let's not start bickering," Richard Barrett interposed before Peterson could answer. "The important thing is that Mark and Alexa recognized the danger and called me."

"From the findings," said Mark, "we were able to make a presumptive diagnosis that about half of the right kidney was in serious danger. Actually, if some arterial blood supply hadn't been available through collateral channels inside the kidney itself, the lower half of the organ could have become necrotic."

"With the shock from kidney shutdown probably causing the death of the patient even before she would have gone into uremia," Barrett added.

"You could have waited until I got back," said Thorpe. "After all, she was my patient."

"Clinic patients are not the private property of the operating surgeon, Jerry," said Barrett sharply. "Besides, what would you have done if we had waited?"

"Taken out the right kidney this morning, of course," said the gynecologist.

"And left the Clinic open for a large malpractice suit," Andrew Harkness said dryly. "It seems to me that instead of being angry with Mark and Alexa for realizing what happened and doing something about it, you should be grateful, Jerry."

"Just what did you do anyway, Harrison?" Jerry Thorpe demanded.

"I picked up a fairly large branch of the ovarian artery and connected it to the proximal end of the artery going to the kidney just beyond where you tied it off," said Mark.

"Under the microscope, I suppose?"

"Of course. The lumen of either vessel wasn't much more than two millimeters in size. That kind of surgery is practically impossible without a microscope."

"I didn't see any description of the operation on the chart this morning."

"I dictated it to the stenographic pool before I left the hospital last night," said Mark. "They probably hadn't typed it when you made rounds this morning."

"Incidentally," Richard Barrett added, "there was no record of what you did on the chart either, Jerry, and none in the steno-graphic pool when I checked. If Alexa hadn't remembered the trouble you had with one artery during the Wertheim, Mark would have been working practically in the dark."

"Any surgeon knows what's included in a Wertheim," Thorpe protested.

"This wasn't just a simple Wertheim. Anyway, we can all be thankful that Alexa looks after our patients in the hospital and that Mark was able to restore the circulation to the lower pole of that kidney. The question is, what are we going to do about you?"

"What the hell do you mean, Dick?"

"You're a fine gynecologist, Jerry, we all know that," said Barrett. "Lately, though, you've been drinking too much and playing too much tennis when you should be looking after your patients. Last night, Mark saved the Clinic and also your reputation, but we can't take chances on something like this happening again. If you hadn't been drunk the night before—plus being in such a hurry to go to New Orleans for a tennis tournament—you'd have traced that artery to the kidney as soon as you discovered it and realized it shouldn't be ligated. Or if you had ligated it and cut it, you could have called Mark here to sew it back together again."

Jerry Thorpe shrugged, but did not comment.

"To me, it looks like you need a little vacation, Jerry," said Elmer Peterson. "It's been two years since you took the last one, and everyone on the staff of Gulfside Hospital knows you've been heavy on the sauce for more than six months now."

"So what are you going to do?" Thorpe was starting to lose his belligerent attitude. "Fire me?"

"Of course not," said Richard Barrett. "When you're function-ing properly, you're a great asset to the Clinic. But if you keep on drinking and shortchanging your patients until you become really impaired, Ed McIntosh and the Disabled Doctors' Committee of the State Medical Association will bring you up on charges. If they went so far as to take away your license the way they've done to quite a number of doctors during the past year on similar charges, both you and the Clinic would be in a hell of a fix."

"Not all of them justified either," Andrew Harkness interposed.

"All in all," said Barrett, "it will be a lot better for the Clinic and for you, if you voluntarily go somewhere—perhaps that place in New Orleans you went to once before—and get dried out."

"Who's going to do vaginal hysterectomies while I'm gone?" Thorpe demanded. "They bring in half the income received by the Clinic."

"Not half, but admittedly a considerable part—that we don't want to lose," Richard Barrett admitted.

"I couldn't do a hysterectomy if I had to," said Elmer Peterson. "You'll have to take this over, Dick."

"I haven't done a hysterectomy since Jerry joined the Clinic," said Barrett, "but we'll make out somehow."

"I had a year on GYN when I was surgical resident at Lakeview," Mark volunteered.

"I suppose the residents up there do vaginal hysterectomies every day," Jerry Thorpe said scathingly.

"Not quite, but Dr. Spofford's wife was dying of cancer that year, so I did get to do a few hundred operations."

"That settles it," said Andrew Harkness. "But will you have time to handle the GYN service until Jerry gets back and also your own work?"

"Looks like I'll have to. Fortunately, the work at the Old Town Clinic is just getting started and there's very little microsurgery to be done over here at Gulfside yet."

"What do you say, Jerry?" Barrett asked.

"All right. I'll go to New Orleans," said Thorpe with a shrug. "They'll load me up with Antabuse, so I'll puke if I even smell alcohol, which ought to make all of you—particularly Harrison here—happy."

"If you ask me," said Elmer Peterson, "that's a hell of an attitude to take toward somebody who's just gotten you out of a bad hole, Jerry."

Thorpe only shrugged. "If the Inquisition is over, I'll head for the Club and my tennis match."

"When do you propose to go to New Orleans?" Barrett asked.

"This weekend, if the clinic there can take me. The sooner I get this over with, the better I'll like it." Thorpe turned to Mark. "I leave my practice in your hands, Harrison, but don't forget to turn it over to me when I get back."

"You can have it and welcome," Mark assured him. "Good luck."

"Thanks to Mark, we got out of that without too much trouble," said Elmer Peterson after Jerry Thorpe had stalked out of the room. "I think we ought to give Mark an official vote of thanks."

"I'll second that," said Andrew Harkness, and the vote was unanimous.

"If Mr. Thomas doesn't go to a smart malpractice lawyer, we're home free," said Andrew Harkness as the meeting was breaking up. "By the way, how is she doing, Mark?"

"I was operating at the Old Town Clinic early this morning and didn't get to make rounds," said Mark, "but I'm sure Miss McGillivray did."

"Mrs. Thomas is improving rapidly and the urine output is back to a normal level," Alexa reported.

"There's no reason why she shouldn't come through without any more complications," Barrett added. "The family is very grateful that we were able to save her after the unexpected setback."

The departure of Jerry Thorpe for New Orleans Friday afternoon of that week went largely unnoticed, except for an item in the weekly staff bulletin of Gulfside Hospital to the effect that Dr. Jeremy Thorpe, Chief of Gynecology, was spending a month in New Orleans taking a special course in the treatment of gynecologic malignancies. Busy at the Old Town Clinic, Mark didn't see Jerry Thorpe the last day. But when his telephone rang late that night, he immediately recognized the voice mouthing curses into the phone.

"Harrison?" the slurred voice said.

"Yes. Who is this?"

"Ne'm—mind. Jus' wanted you to know I'll get even—"

"For what?"

"Stealing my patients and my practice, you son of a bitch. I'll ruin you if it takes the rest of m'life."

"Listen, Jerry—" Mark said no more, for the circuit had already clicked off and he was no longer connected, but as he hung up the phone, he couldn't help shivering a little. Although the speaker had obviously been drunk, the venom in the tone and in his actual words was far more disturbing than the sight of Jerry Thorpe's face would have been.

Unable to get to sleep again or control the throbbing pain that had developed in his brain, Mark finally took a syringe and an ampule of Demerol from his medical bag. Minutes after he injected the contents into his right buttock, the headache had disappeared and he was asleep.

VII

Jerry Thorpe's drunken threat was quickly pushed into the background of Mark's mind in the weeks that followed by the flood of work that threatened to engulf him. Thorpe's gynecology patients were an added burden upon his schedule, already becoming steadily more demanding as the Old Town Clinic expanded its activities rapidly. Still, by concentrating the GYN appointments and posting the operative cases which soon began to flow his way early in the morning at Gulfside Hospital and also the work in the Barrett Clinic, Mark was able to devote most of his afternoons to work in the satellite operation across the river.

Busy as he was, Mark hardly had time to notice how exhausted he was at the end of the day. Even more troublesome was the return of the headaches, which until then had almost disappeared. At first, he endured them, gulping aspirin tablets several times a day. But when the aspirin no longer controlled the pain, he found himself falling back on Demerol hypodermically, and steadily increasing the dose needed to bring relief. Soon he was injecting two hundred and sometimes three hundred milligrams as soon as he reached home and, occasionally, an additional dose if he were called to the hospital for an emergency during the night and returned to find sleep impossible.

On the mornings after such emergencies, he usually awoke with a jaded headache that required the use of a heavy dose of amphetamine to clear his brain. And when this, too, ceased to be sufficient, he found that another injection of Demerol was needed to quiet his jangled nerves so he could begin the work of the day.

In the beginning, he comforted himself with the assurance that he could easily stop using the narcotic once Jerry Thorpe returned and took over his share of the Clinic work. After a while, however, two and even three hypodermic injections a day were the only things that kept him going, and he soon ceased to feel any qualms about resorting to them. A siren mistress, Demerol not only proved capable of quieting his nerves by day, allowing him to perform surgery, but brought *nirvana* at night.

Mark didn't realize anyone was conscious of his increasing resort to the use of the narcotics, until he was leaving the hospital late one night. He and Alexa had just operated upon a ruptured ovarian follicle, an emergency resulting from a continued hemorrhage from the ovary after the normal monthly sex cell called an ovum had broken through the surface. The operation itself was not difficult, only requiring an incision into the abdominal cavity to remove a small wedge-shaped piece of the ovary, including the bleeding nest from which the ovum had come, closing it, and stopping the bleeding with a few sutures. But the emergency had caught him at the end of his usual long day when both body and emotions were drained.

Alexa came out of the Recovery Room to which the patient had been wheeled after the operation, just as Mark was pressing the elevator button.

"Mind if I cross the parking lot with you?" she asked. "It's not always safe out there this time of night."

"Why don't I follow you home and make sure you get safely to your apartment?"

"I'd appreciate that," she said, "but you must be very tired."

"It was a very simple operation."

"You're exhausted by five o'clock every afternoon now. Anyone who sees you, when you stop by the hospital in the early evening to visit a particularly sick patient before going home, could easily realize that—"

"I promised to keep Jerry Thorpe's practice going," he protested. "If I neglect his patients after operation, they could drift to other doctors and he'd lose them."

"They wouldn't have to if you'd stop allowing the others to dump all the work they can on your shoulders."

"Who'd do it if I didn't?"

"Dr. Barrett could easily take over much of the GYN load. I've worked with him in operations involving malignancies that had spread to the pelvis, and he's quite at home there. But then, of course, it might interfere with his golf."

There was truth in what she said, Mark conceded, but he was proud of having been given the responsibility for the extra load and didn't want to admit it was more than he could handle without danger to himself.

"Besides," Alexa added, "Jerry's being away is a product of his conflicts. There's no reason you should burn yourself out because of it."

"I'm not burning myself out," he protested as they came out of the emergency entrance to the hospital and started across the not always brightly lit parking lot to where she left her car each morning in an assigned space in a section marked DOCTORS ONLY. "I've been here less than three months."

"You were well on the way to what's now called 'burnout' before you came here from handling the Microsurgery Department at Lakeview."

"How could you know that?" he demanded.

"Meg Fuller told me, when Dr. Barrett asked me to call her about you, that your friends at Lakeview were worried about you then. And, since Jerry Thorpe left to get dried out, you've been driving yourself harder than anyone ought to do."

"You seem to be the only one who has noticed."

"The nurses who work with you noticed the change the first week, but the Clinic doctors don't want to see it, for fear they'll have to take over some of the work you've been doing. All that work, coming on top of the concussion, would be enough to burn out an even stronger doctor than you."

What she had said was true, he conceded, but didn't answer because to do so implied a weakness he didn't want to admit, even to himself.

"The headaches have returned, too, haven't they?" she asked.

"Yes, but I can take care of that."

"Demerol is only a stopgap."

"What makes you think I'm taking narcotics?"

"When you came to the hospital to operate on the case we just finished, your pupils were contracted and your words were a little slurred."

"Are you saying I wasn't competent to operate?" he demanded in sudden anger, as much at the acuity of her perception and his knowledge of its truth as at the idea of anyone else realizing how rapidly he'd come to be dependent on the powerful narcotic during the past month or more.

"You could have done that operation in your sleep," she said, with a shrug. "And almost did."

"That's none of your business!"

"True—at least not at the moment." The calm note in her voice only infuriated him more as she continued, "I've had to give Jerry Thorpe methylphenidate more than once to wake him out of an alcoholic stupor, I don't want to have to start giving you naloxone to wake you up from a narcotic so you can operate."

"What are you?" he sneered. "Little Miss Fixit?"

"I'm certainly not little." She laughed, then sobered. "And I'm not enough of a rabid feminist to take pride in occasionally having to remind doctors of their duty to patients under the Hippocratic Oath. Good night, Dr. Harrison."

She got in the Volkswagen and slammed the door, but rolled down the window immediately. "You don't have to follow me home either," she added. "On my own home ground, I don't need any help in taking care of myself—especially from a man who's half out of touch from a narcotic and would hardly be much protection anyway. See you in the morning, Dr. Harrison."

VIII

Mark had another shock a few days later when he stopped by the hospital pharmacy to get twenty-five additional ampules of Demerol on the prescription Dr. Charles Minot had left him when he was discharged from the hospital. This would have been the fourth time he'd had the prescription refilled, but when he appeared at the window, the clerk asked him to wait. Shortly, the director of the department—one of the new bright young men who'd taken the additional training required to receive the degree of Doctor of Clinical Pharmacy—opened the door near the window. The identification tag he wore said DR. CHARLES PINKERTON.

"Would you step into my office a minute, Dr. Harrison?" Pinkerton asked.

"I'm in a hurry," said Mark. "Is there a hitch?"

"I'd rather talk to you in here, Doctor," Pinkerton insisted.

The office was small but private, once the pharmacist closed the door. "Dr. Minot notified us the last time we called him about refilling your prescription that it was not to be refilled again," he said.

"For what reason?" Mark felt a surge of anger against the neurosurgeon, although he'd liked him earlier.

"He didn't say, Doctor."

"Why didn't you tell me then?"

"I—" The younger man hesitated, "I guess I thought you might not need any more Demerol and didn't want to upset you. Perhaps if you call Dr. Minot—"

"I intend to do just that. Meanwhile, I'm out of Demerol and my head is about to split from a postconcussion headache. So what do I do, Dr. Pinkerton?"

"You have a narcotic license of your own, don't you?"

"Of course."

"The Federal Drug Administration frowns on doctors writing many narcotics' prescriptions for themselves, but they certainly wouldn't be suspicious of an occasional one in an emergency."

"Suspicious!" Mark demanded. "Suspicious of what?"

The pharmacist looked embarrassed. "Surely you must know that narcotic addiction is about three times as frequent in the medical profession as in the general population."

"Are you accusing me of being addicted to narcotics, Dr. Pinkerton?" Again Mark felt a surge of anger which, at any other time, he would have recognized as unreasonable.

"Certainly not, Dr. Harrison. But if a narcotics' inspector came around and found many prescriptions written by you for yourself in our files, he'd insist on cracking down."

"Get me a prescription blank, then, and I'll write my own. Do you want to see my federal license?"

"Of course not, Dr. Harrison. I was only trying to help you—and myself—avoid any unpleasantness with the Drug Enforcement Administration." He stepped out and came back moments later with a prescription blank and twenty-five units of Demerol in the one-hundred-milligram ampule size.

"By the way," Pinkerton added, as Mark was signing the charge ticket for the narcotic, "if you'd be willing to use cartridge-type ampules—the kind with the sterile needle attached that you just slip into a special injector like dentists use for blocking nerves with local anesthesia—I could probably put you in the way of obtaining all the medication you would need for your headaches—without the FDA sticking its nose into your business."

"What the hell are you talking about, Pinkerton? I'm breaking no law by having to take an occasional injection of Demerol to relieve the pain of a postconcussion headache."

"Nobody's saying you are, Doctor, but the DEA still frowns on self-injection of narcotics, especially by doctors. And if your headaches require long treatment, you're going to need a source other than your own prescriptions."

"Go on," said Mark.

"Well, when I first came here the hospital was using cartridge-type ampules for many medications. I pointed out the extra cost to Mr. Pryor and he agreed that we should stop using cartridge-type ampules and go back to old-fashioned ones and to plastic syringes as a substitute—"

"While still charging the patient the same?"

Pinkerton laughed. "I wouldn't know about that. All we do is send the invoices for the drugs we receive into stock to the hospital corporation management. When Mr. Pryor decided to make a change to a cheaper type of ampule, the wholesaler who supplied us then was left with a pretty large stock of the old type the hospital had been using."

"So what?"

"As it happens, the wholesaler also owns the pharmacy right down the street from your Old Town Clinic."

"You know we can't tell patients to take their prescriptions to a particular pharmacy, Pinkerton. It's against ethics and probably against the law, too."

"Nobody wants you to do that, Doctor. But if Old Town Pharmacy sends you prescription blanks, there's no law that says you can't accept them as a convenience."

"And for that I get a supply of medication for my postconcussion headaches at a bargain and no questions asked—on either side?"

"I can't promise anything, of course." Pinkerton was hedging as a matter of form, but Mark understood fully that a deal could be struck whereby he would be able to get all the Demerol he needed in the future.

"Tell your friend to have his prescription blanks printed up, Pinkerton," he said. "I suppose he also knows how to place them where Dr. Montez and I can hardly reach for any others."

"No problem," Pinkerton assured him. "As a matter of fact, Dr. Montez already gets a ten percent discount on anything he and his family buy at the Old Town Pharmacy."

Mark was not at all surprised when all prescription blanks in the Old Town Clinic were mysteriously replaced by those bearing the imprint of the Old Town Pharmacy. Or that neither Dr. Montez nor any of the nurses involved objected. He was less satisfied with a telephone call the next afternoon.

"This is Charlie Minot, Dr. Harrison," the caller identified himself. "Dr. Pinkerton tells me you were somewhat disturbed because I didn't okay a refill for your Demerol prescription."

"It didn't make any difference," Mark temporized.

"Meaning you found another source?"

"I don't know as that's any of your business, Doctor."

"You're right, of course," said Minot on a soothing note. "I just wanted to be sure you understood my motives."

"They were of the best, I'm sure."

"You can be sure of that," said the neurosurgeon.

"Then there's really nothing to discuss, is there?"

"If you'd prefer not to discuss it, but I do feel it's my duty as a friend and fellow physician"—Minot ignored Mark's attempt to cut him off—"to point out several things. One: postconcussion headache falls into somewhat the same category as whiplash injuries to the neck. We can't always demonstrate that the symptoms actually account for the disability."

"Are you implying that I'm a malingerer, Doctor?"

"Of course not, but it's no secret in Gulf City that Dick Barrett has been letting you carry the burden of Jerry Thorpe's practice, plus the job of getting the Old Town Clinic going. Either of those are heavy loads, certainly as much as one doctor should try to carry alone."

"I'm handling it, Dr. Minot—"

"But at what cost to yourself, if you're having to rely on Demerol to keep yourself going? Everything I hear about you tells me you're a very promising surgeon with extraordinary ability, not only in your field of microsurgery but in general surgery as well."

"Thank you for the compliment," said Mark. "I hope I'm doing my work well."

"Everything I hear says you are, but I'd still hate to see you go down a road with which I am—to put it bluntly—quite familiar. Nowadays, about one in every seven doctors and probably as many dentists, lawyers, and even ministers wind up in trouble eventually because of narcotic addiction, alcohol, or both. I'm not saying you're going to be among the one-in-seven, but the parallels are so much like what's happened to other promising young doctors I've known that I can't help believing they're there. Moreover, I'm concerned by the fact that I may have had something to do with the whole thing because I was in charge of your case when you had a real bona fide concussion."

"Aren't you still implying that I'm a malingerer?" Mark asked.

"I wish I knew, Mark," said the neurosurgeon. "Just as I wish I knew where you're going to end. You've got a wonderful future before you, in a field of medicine that's rapidly eclipsing the fields in which those of us among what might be called the 'older statesman' place ourselves. I'd hate very much to see an ability such as you have developed over many years of study devoted to microsurgery destroyed by addiction to drugs, alcohol, or both. Goodbye, Mark, and please accept my apology for any interference I've made in your life."

IX

The telephone call that came Friday evening didn't help Mark's increasing difficulties either. The phone rang just after he'd finished the leisurely consumption of a double measure of bourbon and was settling down to enjoy another while he watched the evening news on the television screen.

"Mark?" He recognized the feminine voice on the other end; it was Helene McIntosh.

"Yes. How are you, Hel—"

"Please, no names. I just called to tell you my husband's gone to a weekend convention meeting—"

"Very commendable of him," Mark broke in. "The AMA looks with favor on doctors who keep up their continuing medical education programs—"

"Come off it, darling. This is no time for jokes." The soft voice at the other end of the line had suddenly become a little sharp. "Are you off call for the weekend?"

"Yes."

"Good! I was thinking of driving over to a small hotel overlooking Mobile Bay at a town called Daphne, just beyond Mobile on U.S. 98. It's only a couple of hours' drive, so why don't you join me there for dinner about eight-thirty? The stone crabs are out of this world."

"I'm sorry, Hel—ma'am, but I've already had two drinks of bourbon and my blood alcohol must be up sharply. If I were caught driving on the highway, they'd certainly take a breathalyzer test and I'd wind up in jail for D.W.I."

"I'm sober and I can be there in ten minutes to pick you up. Just pack a toothbrush and a razor. You won't need pajamas."

"Sorry, dear." Mark had no intention of getting into a romantic situation with another doctor's wife—even an old flame whose amatory ability he remembered very well. "I don't think that's wise."

"Why the hell not? You weren't nearly so reluctant one weekend at Berkeley Springs."

"That was a long time ago. You're married now—"

"It wouldn't have made any difference to you at Berkeley Springs a few years ago, so why should it make any difference now?"

Grabbing desperately for a straw, Mark found what he knew was a weak one—and considerably far from the truth. "I'm practically engaged," he said.

"To Claire Desmond? Don't make me laugh! She's slept all over Gulf City, with any man who could get it up. If you read the West Coast gossip columns, you know they say she's sleeping all over Hollywood right now, too, wherever it will help sell that line of lingerie she's promoting. Claire will never marry anybody as long as she can twist men around her fingers the way she already does."

"I've got a virus," he improvised on a sudden inspiration. "I think I've got herpes—"

"Down there?"

"I wouldn't want to give it to you, Hel—"

"Where the hell did you get it?"

"Who knows—with herpes? But it's ruining my love life."

"You're a son of a bitch, Mark Harrison." The voice at the other end of the line was suddenly filled with venom. "Good night."

X

Jerry Thorpe came back to duty at the Clinic the first day of October—obviously in high spirits.

"Thanks for keeping the feminine part of the Clinic practice happy, Mark." Jerry had apparently forgotten the drunken curses he'd mouthed into Mark's home telephone the night he'd left for New Orleans.

"Forget it," said Mark. "The sight of so many females in stirrups has long since removed any temptation I might have had to become a gynecologist. How can you stand it every morning anyway, Jerry?"

"Each *fourchette*—that's French for the *frenulum labiorum pudendi,* in case you've forgotten your anatomy—has a dollar sign stenciled on it, my friend. Once the dear creatures finish birthing their husband's or lover's get—it's usually only two now, where a few years ago it was three or even more—they decide their days as brood sows are over and opt for a vaginal hysterectomy—my speciality."

"And one you can have," Mark assured him.

"Alexa says you've polished your skills to the point where you can snake out the uterus, ovaries, and tubes in forty-five minutes," Jerry added. "Just don't forget that the local record is held by yours truly."

"You're welcome to it."

"Come to think of it, you're looking a lot more peaked than you were when I left." Jerry's tone was one of exaggerated concern. "Alexa reports that you've been working your tail off, but now that I'm back to take over the GYN load, you can start to relax."

"I've got an ovarian cyst posted for tomorrow morning, but it shouldn't take long," Mark told him. "That can be my swan song as far as gynecology is concerned."

"Dick Barrett won't let you rest long. You wouldn't believe how that bastard can drum up business, once he gets somebody capable of doing it without his having to bother himself."

"I like to work."

"Take care, friend, and don't burn yourself out the way I almost did. In New Orleans these past weeks, I've learned that other things in life are even more important than money."

The ovarian cyst operation Mark had posted for early Monday morning following Jerry Thorpe's return to work was expected to be simple. He planned to be finished and out of the way well before ten, when the gynecologist had posted another Wertheim on a victim of uterine cancer. But when Mark finished making the incision and spread the jaws of the self-retaining retractor that allowed exposure of the pelvic cavity, he saw a dark looking sac almost filling it and groaned in disappointment.

"Just my luck for my last GYN operation to be the worst—a chocolate cyst," he said.

"Endometriosis?" Dr. Eric Porter, the anesthesiologist, asked from the head of the table.

"Yes."

"Nothing else messes up a woman's insides more, so you're going to have your hands full this morning, Mark," said Porter. "Did she have pain every month?"

"Excruciating." Mark held out his hand for Mandelbaum scissors and the instrument nurse slapped them against the palm of his glove. "If I hadn't been rusty on my GYN symptomology, I'd have made the preoperative diagnosis from the clinical symptoms. This should be Jerry's case, not mine."

"Are you going to call him in?" Alexa was working across the table from him in the usual position of a first assistant.

"This is my gynecological swan song, so I might as well end my career in a cloud of glory."

"More like a flood of dark menstrual blood that couldn't get out," Dr. Porter commented. "I'll lay you two to one you nick that sac trying to dissect the cyst loose from the surrounding structures."

"No bet!"

Chocolate cysts, Mark knew, differed from the most common ovarian tumor in that the lining of the liquid-filled sac contained tissue resembling closely that forming the inner wall of the uterus called the endometrium. Regularly every twenty-eight days, the lining of the uterus itself was discharged in normal menstruation. But with endometriosis, the presence of a similar tissue inside an ovary, as well as almost any surface in the abdomen, created a considerable difference. Every menstrual cycle, the aberrant—out of place—tissue simply swelled and then attempted to extrude itself. If it happened to be inside an ovary, the result was a cyst that enlarged each month as it filled with blood which could not escape and became darker the longer it remained—hence, the term "chocolate cyst."

I should have taken two hundred milligrams of Demerol this morning instead of a hundred, Mark thought as he began to dissect the large cyst from its attachments to surrounding structures, a characteristic of menstruating tumors that caused much of the symptoms they produced. He didn't allow his fears concerning the waning of his surgical efficiency because of the prolonged operating time to hinder him in the job before him, however. Rather, the knowledge that during the latter part of a long operation he might well find himself impaired in his surgical skill only drove him to move faster, in the hope of achieving the most difficult part before the letdown occurred. The dissection was tedious and it was nearly ten-thirty, time for Jerry Thorpe to start the Wertheim operation in the adjoining Operating Room Two, when the gynecologist appeared, dressed for scrubbing.

"You told me yesterday you'd be out of here a half hour ago, Mark," said Thorpe. "Having trouble?"

"*Your* kind of trouble," Mark said as he finished tying the ends of the catgut suture with which he'd closed the incision in the peritoneum lining the abdominal cavity. "A chocolate cyst."

"And a big one." Thorpe had moved over to the table where the tumor was placed, ready to be sent downstairs to the pathological laboratory. "You were lucky to get that one out without puncturing it."

"Lucky is right."

Mark's hands were already beginning to tremble and the warning throb was starting inside his head, sure sign that the smaller dose of Demerol he'd given himself that morning because he hadn't expected to face a difficult operation was wearing off.

If only I'd taken the two hundred milligram dose, I'd have been spared these symptoms, he thought again, but couldn't do anything about that until he finished the operation and reached the doctors' dressing room.

"Are you ready to close the fascia?" Jerry Thorpe asked.

"As soon as Alexa clips this last knot of the peritoneal closure."

"Then you can spare her to help me," said Thorpe. "Eric's starting the anesthetic on my Wertheim now."

For the first time—so intent had he been on his own rapidly increasing need of another narcotic injection—Mark noticed that the regular anesthesiologist had been replaced at the head of the table by one of Dr. Porter's highly trained nurse-anesthetists.

"Sure," he said, hoping neither Alexa nor Jerry noted the quaver in his voice. "Thanks for the backstopping," he added as

Alexa stepped away from the table and the instrument nurse took her place across from it. "This was a tough one."

The scrub nurse was experienced, though she didn't possess Alexa's unusual skill. Mark completed the closure of the muscular and fascial structures of the patient's abdominal wall without incident, working rapidly in order to reach the doctors' dressing room between the two main theaters as soon as possible. There he could get a hypodermic syringe and the Demerol he needed from the small medical bag he now carried everywhere.

When he finished strapping the gauze dressing over the incision after placing the skin sutures and stepped away from the table, the nurse-anesthetist, who had taken over when Dr. Porter had gone to the adjoining O.R., handed him the chart and a fountain pen.

"Dr. Porter said you would write the post-op orders, Dr. Harrison," she said. "He expects to be tied up for another hour, and this patient is already coming out of anesthesia."

"Of course." Taking the clipboard Mark wrote rapidly, hoping the trembling in his fingers didn't make the normally near illegible scrawl of doctors writing in hospital order books completely unreadable.

"*N.P.O.* [nothing by mouth]. *Five percent glucose I.V. in normal saline,*" he scribbled and handed the clipboard back to the anesthetist. She glanced at it an instant, then frowned and looked up.

"Did I forget anything?" Mark asked. "I usually leave the post-op order to Dr. Porter."

"She's already beginning to wake up, so she'll probably need something for pain pretty soon," said the graying anesthetist—veteran of thousands of operating procedures.

Pain! The word rang in Mark's mind like a bell. *How could a patient who was asleep feel half the need of something for pain his already throbbing head did—two hundred milligrams of the magic drug that brought immediate relief.*

"Of course," he said and, taking the clipboard, scribbled: "200 mg. Demerol q4h, P.R.N."

Handing the clipboard to the anesthetist, who was busy at the moment coping with a sudden attack of nausea as the patient started to waken from the anesthetic, Mark rushed to the adjoining dressing room. There he quickly prepared the two hundred milligrams of Demerol that had been in the front of his mind for the last half hour and, jamming the needle into his right buttock, pumped the magic pain remover into the muscles before dropping the empty syringe and needle into the wastebasket and stepping into the shower.

By the time Mark emerged from the shower stall and started drying himself, before dressing to cross the river to the waiting lines of patients at the Old Town Clinic, the familiar feeling of relaxation and complete self assurance brought by the daytime hypos was flooding his body with the knowledge that he could carry on the work of the afternoon without difficulty. Pausing only for a brief word to the anxious family of the patient and a quick dictation of the operative procedure for the hospital stenographic pool, he drove toward the high bridge. By the time he reached the topmost point, he was so high that he could almost believe the shabby old Skylark could easily have taken wing and negotiated the rest of the distance by air.

An hour later, while Mark was examining a patient, the Old Town Clinic chief nurse, Mrs. Doggett, poked her head inside the door of the examining room.

"Dr. Porter wants you on the telephone stat, Dr. Harrison," she said. "Says it's important."

"What's wrong, Eric?" Mark asked, when he picked up the telephone.

"I was called away from Jerry Thorpe's operation a few minutes ago to see your endometriosis case," said the older physician. "She was in a state of marked respiratory depression, breathing four times a minute."

"What the hell could cause that?"

"Two hundred milligrams of Demerol a damn fool nurse gave her intramuscularly right after the operation."

"Two hundred!" Mark exclaimed. "How could that have happened?"

"I'm afraid that was the order you wrote on her chart, but the nurse still should have checked with me when she saw an order that was double the regular protocol for post-ops. Fortunately, they called me in time to give the patient an injection of a narcotic antagonist and a respiratory stimulant."

"Is she all right now?"

"Yes. The respiratory rate has risen to ten and her blood pressure is normal. What I don't understand is how you ever made the mistake of writing an order for two hundred milligrams of Demerol q4h P.R.N.—"

"But I didn—"

"It's on the chart, Mark. Initialed by you, too. The thing I can't understand—"

"Don't try, Eric," said Mark resignedly. "I wrote two hundred because at the moment that was what I was thinking about—for myself."

There was silence on the phone for a long moment, then Mark spoke again, "You understand what I'm saying, don't you, Eric?"

"Yes," said Dr. Porter. "Everyone around here knows Dick Barrett has had you working your ass off while Jerry Thorpe was away. I'd been hearing rumors, too, but—"

"They're true, Eric. When I finished the operation this morning, I was so busy thinking of what I was going to give myself when I got to the doctors' lounge, that I just wrote down the same dose for the patient. How many people know what happened?"

"Practically nobody but me and the nurse who gave the injection. She's so scared of getting canned because she didn't question the dosage before she gave it that she won't say anything, and you can be damned sure I won't either. I've already changed your order from two hundred to one hundred, so there's no evidence on the chart anymore."

"Thanks, Eric. I won't forget it."

"Christ, man! What are friends for? The order's changed and the patient's okay, so forget it ever happened. You were tired from overwork and this was a tough case, so a mistake like that could happen to anybody. I'd better get back to Jerry's Wertheim, though, before he starts asking questions."

When he hung up the phone, Mark sat looking at it for a long moment—a moment during which the exhilarating feeling he'd experienced just now at the top of the bridge suddenly evaporated, to be replaced by a plummeting sense of depression and despair.

With Jerry Thorpe back, Mark was able to devote practically full time to his duties at the rapidly growing satellite Clinic—particularly short-stay surgery. He didn't realize just how neatly Jerry Thorpe had slid back into his former routine, though, until he dropped into the hospital cafeteria for dinner one evening before going home. He'd had little opportunity to talk to Alexa beyond the monosyllabic communications across the operating table when the occasional case requiring microsurgery was turned over to him by Dr. Barrett or one of the others. Seeing her eating alone in a secluded corner when he stopped in the cafeteria after making evening rounds, he took his tray to her table.

"Mind if I join you?" he asked.

"Not at all," she said. "You don't have very much on that tray for a hard-working doctor, though. Can I get you anything else?"

"No, thanks. My appetite seems to have deserted me—along with my usual good spirits."

"I'm not surprised. Everybody knows you were doing the work of two men while Jerry was gone—and then some."

"The number of short-stay operations in the Old Town Clinic has doubled in the past two weeks," he volunteered. "I understand that Jack Pryor is ecstatic."

"Can you blame him?"

"Only late in the afternoon when I'm so tired I can hardly drive myself back to my apartment."

"Doctors always work too hard. It's an occupational hazard that sometimes destroys them—the way it's destroying you."

"So what? How else can a doctor earn sixty-five thousand a year right out of hospital training? That's the most important thing."

"Is it—when you're burning yourself out and may wind up a cripple?"

"Let's not make the mistake of quarreling about that again; coming from so many people, it's beginning to be irritating. And since you seem to know everything that goes on in our small world, you must have heard that Charlie Minot stopped my Demerol prescription."

"Everybody also seems to know you've found another one," she told him, "and that Dr. Porter saved you from having to explain an overdose ordered for a post-op patient that almost killed her."

"How in the hell did that get around?"

"By now you should know that the hospital grapevine has everything almost before it happens."

"If so many people know about my problems, why don't they turn me in to the Federal Drug Administration?"

"A conspiracy of silence protects a doctor who's on drugs or drinking too much—you know that as well as I do," she said. "It's fed by nurses who see him mornings with his pupils contracted from an injection taken just before beginning surgery. And by family and friends who realize something has happened to him."

"Why do they protect him?"

She shrugged. "Nobody wants to finger somebody else who's obviously decided to destroy himself."

"Jerry seems to have found the answer to stress as far as he's concerned," Mark protested. "Have you ever seen him happier than he is now?"

"No, but that's not just because he's conquered drink."

"Why else did he go so heavy on the sauce, if it wasn't from normal doctor stress? To me he always seemed to have the world by the tail otherwise."

"As far as it went."

"Now you're being profound and I'm too tired to cope," he told her. "The night Jerry left for New Orleans, he telephoned and threatened to get even with me for precipitating the crisis that sent him there by operating on Mrs. Thomas."

"I'm not surprised."

"Fortunately, Jerry seems to have forgotten about all that since he came back."

"I wouldn't take his apparent forgiveness as the last word there either," she advised. "Jerry can be pretty devious when he wants to be."

He stared at her in amazement. "Do you know that's the first time I ever heard you say something bad about anyone? Why this time?"

"Maybe because I don't want to see you—or anyone else for that matter—suffer for a sin you didn't commit."

"I'll remember to be wary," he promised. "But if I could get the pieces of my life back together as simply as Jerry seems to have done with his, I'd be tempted to try the cure he took."

"It wouldn't work for you."

"Why not?"

"For one thing, you're much nearer the breaking point than Jerry ever was. The amount of Demerol you're obviously taking, plus the dosage error you made, proves that. For another, what's troubling you goes far deeper than what was troubling Jerry."

"You're practicing psychiatry again," he warned.

"Forgive me. I know you never like me to do it."

"This time I'm intrigued, though. Please give me the full analysis."

"We'll start with Jerry Thorpe. Did you know Ted Moran, the tennis pro at the Yacht Club, took his vacation the last two weeks while Jerry was at the clinic in New Orleans?"

"So what?"

"Jerry was an outpatient there and stayed in a nearby motel—with Ted. They played tennis together nearly every day, and now Ted has moved into Jerry's condominium—on a permanent basis."

"But Jerry—" The realization of what she was telling him suddenly burst in his weary brain. "I guess you think I'm either pretty naïve or pretty dumb," he admitted sheepishly.

"Or too tired most of the time to notice what's happening around you."

"That, too," he agreed. "It all does seem to fit in neatly, doesn't it?"

"You don't have to be a psychiatrist to see that."

"Touché," he said. "But with homosexuality so much an accepted part of life these days, I don't see why Jerry experienced any difficulty. Some of the best-known doctors in the country are homos, and it's pretty well known in the field of sex psychology that handsome fellows like Jerry are often bisexual and have sex with both men and women. The word, I think, is satyriasis."

"Maybe admitting an open relationship with his lover was the best way of life for Jerry. It does seem to have cleared up a lot of his conflicts, and I'll be surprised to see him start drinking again any time soon. But you're a much deeper person and far more intelligent than Jerry could ever be, so what fits his situation certainly wouldn't fit yours."

"If you know that already, why can't you put your finger on my particular conflicts?"

"I've an idea they're related to a feeling deep inside you that you're not fulfilling your own particular purpose in life."

"I'm twenty-eight years old, making sixty-five thousand dollars a year, and well on the way to a career Paul Martenson says will make me a millionaire by the time I'm fifty. Why would I be dissatisfied with what I'm doing?"

"You'll have to discover that for yourself, I'm afraid." She picked up her tray preparatory to leaving. "Good night."

"Good night," he told her. "And thanks for the analysis."

XI

Claire returned in mid-October, six weeks after she'd promised Mark the weekend together in New Orleans over Labor Day. He met her at the airport when she arrived, looking svelte and, as usual, completely self-assured. Her kiss, however, was perfunctory.

"You look like the wrath of God," she told him. "What have you been doing?"

"Working—and pining for you."

"Fat chance of that," she said as they took the escalator down to Baggage Claim. "If I know the women of Gulf City, you've been chased from the moment I left."

"Chased but not caught; my headaches have taken care of that."

"What does Charlie Minot say about them?"

"That they'll eventually go away—if I live long enough. Besides, with Jerry away for close to six weeks, I was swamped with work."

"Gina wrote me that her friends say you're almost as good a gynecologist as Jerry. Are you going to stay in the field?"

"I'm not competing. He can have it."

"From what you wrote me, you've made a real success of the Old Town Clinic, too." She handed her baggage checks to a skycap. "Where are you parked?"

"Across the lot. I'll bring the car around by the time the porter gets your baggage."

She was standing at the curb beside the porter and a pile of luggage when he drove up to the loading zone.

"This car looks like hell," she said. "If I'd known you weren't going to get a new one, I'd have left you the key to my Porsche."

"The old Skylark gets me back and forth between my condominium, the hospital, and the Old Town Clinic, and that's all the traveling I do anyway. Meanwhile, Paul's socking away most of my salary in high-interest money-market certificates while the rates are climbing." Mark tipped the skycap and got into the car. "Obviously, California agreed with you. I never saw you looking more healthy and beautiful before."

"L.A.'s where the action is. Next-to-Nothing Intimatewear is making me vice-president in charge of advertising, so I'll be moving to California next month."

"Moving! What about me?"

"You're the only thing I regret about leaving Gulf City, darling —maybe because I feel partly responsible for your coming here."

"Partly, hell! You were the bait."

"I guess it did work out that way, but don't blame Dad. He didn't even know I was going to come down to join you at breakfast that morning. Besides, you gained a lot, too."

"A recurring headache that won't go away and a job that keeps me hopping twenty-four hours a day," he said with some bitterness.

"Plus," she added, "a salary of sixty-five thousand a year, the opportunity to sock away a million after taxes before you're fifty, and a few sessions in the sack with me. A lot of men would set a high value on the latter perk alone."

"I do, but I think I've fallen in love with you."

"Don't, Mark. I never intimated that I considered you anything more than a superb male to go to bed with. You must have realized from the start that I'm not the marrying kind—"

"You did try once," he reminded her.

"And failed miserably enough to make me decide not to ever try again. The fact that I enjoy sex is a byproduct for which I'm grateful, but I don't kid anybody about the whole scene and I didn't kid you either. Considering your reputation at Lakeview, I was sure you'd be sophisticated enough to understand."

"What about that weekend you promised me in New Orleans?" he demanded with some anger. "Is that off, too?"

"Not at all. In fact, I expect that to be the *pièce de résistance,* so to speak, of our relationship. Shall we make it the Columbus Day weekend that's coming up on Friday?"

"That'll be fine; it's my turn to be off duty."

"I'll be busy until Friday afternoon getting my records packed for shipment to L.A. and subletting my apartment," she told him. "How about our spending this Columbus Day weekend together at a lovely place I know of on Mobile Bay—"

"Don't tell me it's a country inn at a town called Daphne."

"So you know about that one already." Claire laughed. "Who did you go there with?"

"Nobody. I turned down the invitation."

"More the fool you, if the woman was attractive."

"She was—and married."

"Really, Mark! Could you possibly be that naïve after some four months in practice here—and among the Upper Crust at that?"

"I still have a few scruples," he said. "One of them is against making cuckolds of other men."

"You're one of the few of that breed left in Gulf City. Then it's settled; we'll take my car and drive to Point Blue Friday afternoon for the weekend. It's a marvelous place, with a big swimming pool, a golf course, and tennis courts, in case you feel athletic."

"How about dinner tonight?"

"Sorry, but I'm selling my advertising agency to a man from

Pensacola and am meeting him for dinner. We'll probably be dickering until midnight, so be a good boy and let me have the rest of the week for business. Once we start for Point Blue, I promise you my undivided attention."

XII

Point Blue was everything Claire had said it would be—a sprawling hotel surrounded by tennis courts, an olympic-sized swimming pool, and a championship golf course. They arrived shortly after seven Friday night and were shown to a suite with connecting rooms.

"I made the reservations in your name," Claire explained. "This place is very popular and we're liable to run into some people I know, so I asked for adjoining rooms."

"I hope we don't see any of those people this time," he said. "It's been bad enough having you in Gulf City and not even being able to see you."

Mark felt the tension of expectation building within him and with it, the beginning of a familiar headache. They entered the suite through his room, and when the door shut behind him, he turned the latch so the DO NOT DISTURB sign showed on the outside. When Claire came into his arms her kiss was as fervent as he remembered from the night—ages ago it seemed now—when they'd come back to her apartment after the dinner Dr. Barrett had given to introduce him to the medical élite of Gulf City. But when his hands moved to loosen the zipper at the back of her dress, she pushed him away.

"Not so fast, lover," she said. "We've got the whole night before us and two days to boot."

"If I last that long," he said, as she moved across the room toward the door leading to her own. "Want another drink?"

"Not yet. I don't want to take the edge off the high you've just given me with that kiss. Back in a few minutes."

"Don't make it long. I've got a lot of time to make up."

"So have I," she said. "Just give me time to slip into something more appropriate."

"Why not nothing?"

"That's a possibility; just stay in suspense," she said as she stepped through the door.

Mark started undressing, but the headache was developing rapidly, now that he was faced with measuring up to Claire's extremely high standards when it came to making love. Too, his whole body was starting to crave the familiar boost he always got from an injection of Demerol. Opening the medical bag he carried with him everywhere, he quickly prepared an ampule of the narcotic for injection. He was swabbing his upper arm with an alcohol sponge while holding the syringe between his fingers, when Claire's voice startled him from the doorway.

"What the hell are you doing?" He turned to see her, gloriously naked, tying a blue ribbon around her hair.

"The headache came back, but it will be gone in a minute."

"So Gina wasn't lying when she wrote me you were addicted to drugs. How long has this been going on?"

"Since I was mugged after leaving your apartment—"

"Don't try to blame me for your weakness," she snapped.

"You once boasted of sniffing cocaine," he said equally sharply. "What's the dif—"

"Getting a high while you're on a binge is one thing, but shooting narcotics every day is another. I'm not making love with a junkie." Turning, she was gone before he could try to explain.

The click of the lock on the connecting door was so final that he didn't even bother to plead with her. Picking up the syringe, he wrapped a handkerchief around his wrist to make a tourniquet and distend the veins on the back of his hand. Shoving the needle through blood vessel and skin in one thrust, he injected the powerful narcotic directly into his circulation.

As on the previous occasion with an intravenous injection, the effect came quickly and his fingers obeyed his rapidly failing brain barely long enough to remove the ampule from the injector. Dropping both on the bedside table, he fell across the bed naked and dived into the depths of complete languor.

Mark awoke to find the lights still on in his room, his body shivering, and his teeth chattering from the coldness of the air conditioning. The bedside clock said three A.M. and, staggering to where he'd opened his suitcase, he got pajamas and a robe from it and put them on, fumbling at the buttons in a half stupor from the narcotic. Crawling back into bed, he pulled up the covers and slept until nine o'clock.

Holding on to the bed to steady himself, he went to the connecting door leading to Claire's room and pounded on it. But when it was finally opened from the other side, he was startled to see the face of a plump black maid.

"Where's the lady who has this room?" he demanded, the words barely recognizable because his tongue was still twisted from the effect of the drug.

"What you sayin', mister?" The maid looked scared.

"The lady who was in this room last night. Where is she?"

"You mean a pretty blonde?"

"Yes."

"She done checked out, mister. The housekeeper told me to clean the room."

"Did you see her leave?"

"Yes, sir. She come out of the room with her luggage as I was pushin' my cart down the hall. Through the glass doors of another room, I saw her get into a white car parked outside and drive off."

"What kind of a car was it?"

"One of them foreign ones, small and with a top you could let down."

It had to be Claire's Porsche—which meant she'd left him stranded without any transportation back to Gulf City.

"You sick or something, mister?" the maid asked as he stumbled back into his room. "The manager can call a doctor for you."

"I *am* a doctor and I'm all right. I'll order some breakfast from room service."

"Want me to straighten up your room?"

"No. I'll be okay."

"The lady was sure pretty, but she looked awful mad, too," said the maid. "You must have had a spat or something."

"Just shut the door and lock it, please," he told her.

Back in his room, Mark ordered breakfast from room service

but, when it came, was too nauseated to do anything except drink some orange juice. Leaving the tray in the hall outside the door, he went back to his suitcase, took out two ampules of Demerol, and injected them in rapid succession before crawling back into bed.

Six ampules of Demerol and thirty-six hours later on a bright Sunday afternoon, Mark signed an American Express card for the two rooms—Claire hadn't bothered to pay for hers—and the few meals he'd been able to eat. At a car rental booth in the lobby, he signed another to rent an automobile and drove back to Gulf City, arriving about eight o'clock. Leaving the rental car at the airport, he took a taxi to his apartment and crawled into bed once again.

XIII

Still furious at Claire for calling him a junkie and giving him no opportunity to explain, Mark didn't even bother to try to call her. On Tuesday morning when he came down to the condominium garage to get his own car, the white Porsche had disappeared from her parking space, and he assumed that she was driving back to Los Angeles.

Gina Martenson called him Thursday night about nine o'clock. "I just talked to Claire in Dallas on the way to L.A.," she said. "What happened between you two?"

"We went to Point Blue for the weekend but quarreled, and Claire walked out, leaving me stranded."

"Why didn't you call me? Paul and I'd've come to your rescue. That's what friends are for."

"I'm through with Claire," he said with finality.

"Fine!" said Gina. "You're much too good for her anyway."

Mark awoke at five-thirty in a sweat. Rather than turn on the air conditioning and go back to bed, however, probably to toss and turn until morning, he decided to take an early morning run. Although it was October, the air outside was still warm so, pulling on running shorts, a light Windbreaker, shoes, and socks, he shoved his wallet into the back pocket of his shorts, in case he

decided to eat at a nearby fast-food restaurant he often visited at
the end of his morning run.

The sun was just beginning to appear above the horizon of the
broad expanse of the Gulf of Mexico when he came out of the
condominium and headed down to the beach. He saw that at least
one person, a swimmer, was ahead of him when he looked across
the water toward the sandspits separating the Bay from the open
Gulf.

A terry cloth robe, a large towel, and a pair of women's sandals
were lying on one of the concrete benches placed at intervals
along the beach near the bulkhead. When he looked seaward for
the owner, he saw the swimmer moving toward the jetties with a
powerful stroke that indicated a trained athlete. She turned back
before he finished his run, and when he came back to where he'd
left his Windbreaker, he saw to his surprise that the lone swimmer
was Alexa McGillivray. She was wearing a light blue maillot, setting off the golden hue of her skin beautifully.

"Haven't seen you running very often in the mornings lately,"
she called when he came nearer.

"I've been backsliding, but it feels good again. Isn't the water
rather cold this time of year?"

"Cold enough to be stimulating." Putting on the terry cloth
robe, which barely covered the maillot, she peeled off her swimming cap and began to towel her long hair that had been curled
about inside it. "You probably noticed that I was swimming
pretty fast."

"Faster than I could," he said as he pulled on his Windbreaker.
"Had breakfast?"

"Not yet."

"The McDonald's near the pier opens at five-thirty. What they
call their 'Big Breakfast' is delicious, and they don't mind people
in shorts or swimsuits."

"I use it often when I'm on the way to the hospital for an early
morning operation," she said. "This robe is so short, though, that
if I go inside I'll feel like every man there is ogling my legs."

"I don't blame them, but I can solve that problem. I'll pick up
some Egg McMuffins and coffee and we can have breakfast in the

little park under the ramp of the high bridge. I often take mine there after a run."

"That would be fine," she said. "I love the park."

Carrying their food, they jogged the two blocks to the small park and found it completely deserted. By now the sun was shining through the steel supports of the bridge to make a dappled pattern of sheer beauty with the flower beds of the park.

"I love this place," said Mark as they were eating under the bridge in a protective niche where the sun shone brightly. "When I'm finishing my work late in Old Town, I often pick up a sandwich at McDonald's and eat here where I can enjoy watching the sun go down."

"Melga Doggett, your chief Clinic nurse over there, is an old friend of mine," Alexa told him. "She tells me you're working very hard."

"Not as much as when I had to handle Jerry Thorpe's patients, too, but Dr. Barrett has started referring most of the short-stay work from the regular Clinic across the river to me."

"That's because he knows you can handle practically any problem that arises. It's no secret either that you're as good a gynecologist as Jerry Thorpe."

"Don't tell him that."

"He already knows it—and *that* should worry you."

"Worry? Why?"

"Jerry doesn't take defeat easily. When he tries to bring you down—as I'm sure he will one day—it won't be by fair means."

"Actually, Jerry's been very friendly since he came back from New Orleans."

"Timeo danaos et dona ferentes," she said cryptically.

"Fear the Greeks, especially when bearing gifts," he translated. "Fortunately, I remember enough Latin to know what you're saying, but I still hope you're wrong."

"So do I, but keep your guard up just the same."

"Thanks, I will. I suppose the hospital grapevine has been buzzing lately with the news that Claire Desmond tossed me out of her life—for good."

Alexa smiled. "I got it from the horse's mouth instead, when she called me and asked me to forward any mail to her new address in Los Angeles."

"Don't you ever get tired of picking up after the staff of the Barrett Clinic and their families?"

"That's what I'm paid for."

"Only the medical part. Pulling me out of a narcotic stupor or looking after Claire's mail doesn't exactly belong in that category."

"You're part of the Clinic, and that makes you part of my duty. To be perfectly frank, right now I'm troubled that you're pushing yourself too far toward a possible burnout."

"Coming from anybody else, I'd resent that as interference in my affairs," he said. "Why don't I resent it from you?"

"Probably because you know it's the truth and because you also know I don't have an ax to grind."

"A lot of times I get pretty frustrated doing small surgical jobs in the Old Town Clinic when I should be doing major surgery at Gulfside," he confided. "It isn't exactly what I expected when I joined the Barrett Clinic staff but, as you say, it's part of my job."

"Dr. Barrett didn't expect the satellite Clinic to build a practice in twice the time you've taken to make it possible. Your patients are grateful, too, and to me that must be the greatest reward a doctor has."

"*Used* to have," he corrected her. "My grandfather had a horse-and-buggy practice in North Carolina before the roads were paved. More than once, I heard my father tell how as a teenager he rode with Grandfather to deliver a sharecropper's baby. Or used a water glass with a sock doused with chloroform stuffed in it to give an anesthetic to a young mother who'd miscarried, while Grandfather took a curette out of a handkerchief and cleaned out the remains of the placenta. They didn't have either penicillin or sulfa in those days, yet patients hardly ever got infected, but in these times, more infections are acquired inside hospitals than anywhere else."

"Over all, the balance is more in favor of modern medicine than against it," she insisted.

"Sometimes I wonder—"

"Only when you're depressed and working too hard, the way you are now."

"Who's going to build up a reputation for the Old Town Clinic if I don't?"

"They could always hire a good FMG. How many other places do you know where a young doctor could be trained by a teacher of your caliber?"

"Now you're buttering me up," he said, with a smile.

"No." She was quite serious. "I've worked with enough doctors to know quality when I see it."

"Even though I failed with that rat we worked on together?"

"That was due to a temporary physical disturbance," she said. "It doesn't have to be repeated any more than you need crutches like alcohol and Demerol to keep going, so why drive yourself the way you've been doing lately?"

"You should have been a trial lawyer," he said wryly.

"Forgive me. I have no right."

"You said once we could be friends. And friends do have the right to interfere."

He realized he had used the wrong word when he saw her suddenly stiffen.

"Thanks for the breakfast, Doctor," she said, rising to stuff the paper cup from which she'd been drinking coffee into a trash can. "I won't make the mistake of *interfering* in your life again."

"Hey!" he called to her. "I didn't mean any—"

But she was already a dozen paces away and he saw from the rigid set of her shoulders—still as beautiful as any he remembered seeing—that nothing was to be gained by following her and trying to apologize.

XIV

By Thanksgiving Mark was so busy in Old Town that he rarely had time to visit the hospital or the main Barrett Clinic building, except for the Monday afternoon staff meetings. His mornings were now devoted largely to short-stay surgery, so the patients could have the whole day to recover from the immediate effects of the operation before going home in the evening. More and more often, he found himself uncertain about being able to finish even such short operations without the crutch of a morning Demerol injection before going to the Clinic.

He'd largely given up drinking. However, dropping a cartridge of the powerful narcotic into the metal injector, twisting off the rubber sleeve that kept the needle sterile until ready, and pumping the contents deep into a muscle of his upper arm, thigh, or buttock gave him far more control of himself than even two drinks of bourbon or vodka.

The conspicuous success of the new venture would have been a tonic for Mark's now almost always depressed spirits, had the challenge of the operations he carried out at the Old Town Clinic been anything but miniscule. For the most part, they were limited to removal of skin lesions like sebaceous cysts and small potential skin cancers, acute hemorrhoids, and uncomplicated hernias.

He'd heard nothing from Claire, which didn't surprise him. Her anger the night she'd discovered him trying to give himself a quick injection of the narcotic as a preliminary to making love had been explosive enough to rule out any possibility of a reconciliation. As for social life, he still received many invitations, including an occasional one from Gina Martenson and her friends. But at the end of the day, he was too tired and depressed for anything except a quick snack at a fast-food restaurant on the way home from the Clinic or a TV dinner put in the oven while he was skimming through a medical journal.

Since his return from New Orleans, Jerry Thorpe was usually quite affable at the Clinic staff meetings. He went out of his way to be friendly, now that Mark was no longer a competitor in his particular field of gynecology. And he even relinquished to Mark his own opportunity to attend the annual Southern Medical Association meeting in November—which Clinic doctors were allowed to attend in rotation.

Since the convention was being held in Birmingham, only about an hour's flight away, Mark took advantage of the opportunity, hoping the change would do him good. Jim Hall was the first Lakeview friend he ran into in the teeming lobby of the hotel that was convention headquarters. Jim looked tanned and fit some six months after joining his father's group in Tampa, but seeing him again only made Mark the more depressed because of the changes that he knew had occurred in his own appearance, as well as his life.

"Mark, my boy!" Jim exclaimed as they shook hands. "How are things in Gulf City?"

"I'm not setting the world afire with microsurgery. Actually, I spend most of my time running a satellite Clinic in Old Town."

"You sound depressed and that's not like you, particularly since you struck gold with Dick Barrett and his group."

"I was mugged while running on the beach at night shortly after I got to Gulf City," Mark explained. "It left me with a post-concussion headache that doesn't want to clear up."

"As I remember it, you were pretty much fagged out after having to take over Dr. Peters' work in microsurgery those last six months at Lakeview," said Jim. "Weren't you planning an extended vacation?"

Mark smiled wryly. "As extended as my pocketbook would have stood, which wouldn't have been very long. Fortunately, several days before my fellowship ended, Dr. Barrett offered me the job I have now."

"So you missed out on the vacation?"

"Yes, Barrett wanted me to start in right away."

"I wonder if that was wise?"

"Why would you say that?"

"It looked to me like you were getting pretty well burned out before we left Baltimore. Even an athlete like yourself can stand only so much."

"I'm all right," said Mark, a little shortly. "The headaches following the mugging still bother me a lot, but Charlie Minot says they'll eventually go away."

"Five months is a long time for them to hold on." Jim looked at his watch. "I'd better run; a lecture I want to hear should be starting soon in the Pediatric Section."

"See you around," said Mark, but he knew it wouldn't happen again—except by chance.

Seeing Jim so obviously happy had done nothing to improve Mark's spirits; in fact, the obvious difference in their lives had only set his head to aching more. Not wanting to go back to his hotel room for a hypo of Demerol, however, he made his way through the crowd to one of several hospitality rooms set up by leading pharmaceutical manufacturers. Free drinks were being served to doctors massed three deep around the table, and a double bourbon lightened Mark's spirits somewhat. Leaving the Hospitality Room, Mark went back to the exhibition hall located on the main floor of the giant hotel. Most of the expositions were devoted to sales of medicines, instruments, equipment, and other appurtenances to medical practice, but since he was not responsible for buying equipment for the hospital, he passed those up in order to visit the much smaller area devoted strictly to scientific exhibits.

One booth in particular seemed to be shunned by most of the attending doctors, and when Mark came closer to it, he understood why. Across the front on a large banner was written THE IMPAIRED PHYSICIAN PROGRAM and below it the information: HELP FOR DISABLED DOCTORS. The back and sides of the booth were covered with large placards displaying charts and other information on alcoholism and narcotic addiction.

The only occupant was a tall dark-skinned man with a lean, nevertheless attractive, face, a shock of iron-gray hair, and a pair of warm blue eyes. His face seemed somehow familiar to Mark, although he couldn't ever remember having seen him before. Obeying an impulse he could not have identified, he stepped inside and started reading some of the charts and tables of information that made up the walls of the booth.

"Dr. Harrison!" When Mark turned toward the lone occupant who had spoken his name, the man's face was warmed by a smile that softened its angles and planes, giving them a warmth Mark found very infectious.

"We've never met, but we do have a mutual acquaintance," the booth's occupant said. "I might even say a friend."

JOHN CARR, M.D., Mark read on the other man's nameplate as they shook hands. Beneath it the words CANYONHEAD RETREAT registered in his memory.

"I'm Alexa McGillivray's cousin," Carr told him, and memory suddenly took form in Mark's mind.

"You must be the psychiatrist she told me about."

"Alexa and I grew up together about eighty miles north of Birmingham. We're cousins, but actually we've always been more like older brother and younger sister."

"You're the one who lives on the rim of the canyon she talks so much about, aren't you?" said Mark. "It must be a very lovely place."

"It is. Here, take a look." Carr handed him a printed brochure whose front page featured a long rambling building with the appearance of a rustic motel, located at the head of a canyon in whose depths flowed a small river. The picture was in color, and the vista afforded by the deep cleft in the earth where the stream flowed was breathtaking.

"It's as lovely as Alexa said it was."

"Keep it," said Carr. "Alexa hasn't seen this new booklet, so you can show it to her when you get back."

"I'm afraid I'm not in very great favor with her at the moment," Mark confessed.

"So?" Carr's somewhat bushy eyebrows lifted. "She usually gets along very well with everybody. I'm surprised."

"It's all my fault. She gave me some advice when I was very depressed. And, like the dolt I am, I accused her of interfering."

"If the Samaritan in the Bible had ignored the man who fell among thieves, like the priest and the Levite did, that man would have died," Carr reminded him.

"She was justified in taking umbrage."

"Then tell her you were wrong. Alexa is a very understanding person."

"I will, but I've been so depressed lately that I didn't feel like making the effort."

"Depression is an illness, Dr. Harrison; I'm sure you know that."

Mark glanced around the booth. "You don't seem to be doing much business."

"None that you can see," John Carr admitted with a smile. "What I'm doing here is delivering a subliminal message—one too slight to be consciously perceived—but still capable of registering."

"A friend of mine is using that principle in advertising," said Mark. "She says it works."

"Psychologists discovered that fact long ago. It's true that very few doctors passing this booth read the caption above it or even stop—largely because they're repelled by the statistic that one out of every seven practicing physicians already suffers some impairment of his faculties and his professional ability because of alcohol or drugs."

"My guess would be that it's more the thought: *'There but for the grace of God go I.'*"

"Exactly," said Carr. "Nevertheless, they do learn, even from the glance that repels them, how good Samaritans in the medical profession are trying to help others avoid the pitfalls of burnout, alcoholism, or addiction. Then, if one day they find themselves on the brink of disaster or even over the rim, they'll remember where they can obtain help and, hopefully, seek it."

"Do you work directly with the State Disabled Doctors' Committee?"

"Quite often, with several states," said John Carr. "Canyonhead Retreat was selected for the treatment of those whom the local committees refer to the state organizations."

"May I ask why you were chosen?"

"Since I finished my fellowship in psychiatry at Harvard, I've been working with victims of alcoholism and drug addiction," Carr explained. "On the basis of our experience at Canyonhead, the Retreat was selected by several state committees as the institution of choice in this area because we are already treating disabled physicians from several other states, much the same way the Georgia plan does at an institution near Atlanta."

Mark wondered just how much Alexa had told the psychiatrist about his own problems but decided not to inquire.

"When the scope of what the AMA called the 'Impaired Physician' problem was first realized five years ago, it was hoped that doctors whose abilities—their whole lives in fact—are crippled by alcoholism or drug addiction would seek aid of their own accord," John Carr continued. "Unfortunately, that rarely occurs, and they usually don't come to the attention of the committees until the drinking or drug problem is severe enough to cause their licenses to be in danger of being revoked by the Medical Licensing Board."

"Which is where you come in?"

"Not quite at that point. The local and state committees inside the medical societies are supposed to act as buffers, so to speak, in persuading the patient to accept treatment. If he agrees, they refer him to me."

"But if he doesn't agree?"

"The committee involved has no choice except to turn the case over to the Medical Licensing Board," said Carr, "and even then, most victims are given a second chance to seek help voluntarily. Failing that, of course, the Licensing Board has no option except to bring charges against the doctor and revoke his license—temporarily at first, but permanently if he doesn't cooperate. Or, as happens far too often, he or she commits suicide rather than face the reality and the consequences of addiction."

"How long does the treatment at your institute last?" Mark asked.

"At Canyonhead, we don't like to accept a patient who doesn't voluntarily agree to remain with us for a period of about three months of active treatment. Even after he leaves us, though, the Disabled Doctors' Committees usually insist upon a probation period of two years, with regular reports upon his status."

Mark's head was already aching and he felt his hands start to tremble, a dramatic warning that he needed an immediate injection of Demerol very badly. When he stood up, he swayed suddenly and had to catch a corner of the table covered with stacks of literature to avoid falling.

"Are you all right, Dr. Harrison?" John Carr rose quickly and took Mark's arm.

Mark shook the steadying hand off his elbow. "I suffered a severe concussion about five months ago from a mugging. Still have some headaches and dizziness, but it goes away if I lie down for a while. I'll be all right now."

"Please give my love to Alexa when you see her again," John Carr said in parting. "I'm very fond of her."

In the safety of his hotel room, Mark quickly gave himself the injection his body and his mind were craving and shortly found oblivion in sleep.

XV

From the Gulf City airport early Sunday evening, Mark took a taxi to his condominium. Dropping his suitcase at the foot of the bed, he started to the kitchen to pour himself a double bourbon, but stopped short at the door of the closet where he kept his supply of Demerol and the kit for injecting the cartridge-ampules. One glance at the shelf warned him that someone had been in the apartment during his absence. Someone who was not merely a junkie seeking a fix—for not even one cartridge-ampule had been taken—but who was obviously interested only in obtaining evidence of Mark's addiction, though for what reason he could not at the moment fathom.

Pouring the drink in the kitchen, Mark came back to the living room and sank into an easy chair. The first swallow warmed his stomach and eased somewhat the feeling of dark fear that had assailed him at the tangible proof that the secret of his addiction was no longer a secret. Calmed somewhat by the drink, he dialed Alexa McGillivray's telephone number. She answered almost immediately.

"Do you have time to talk to me about something important?" he asked.

"Certainly. I was going to call you tomorrow evening to apologize for leaving in such a huff after we had breakfast in the riverfront park."

"Is it too late for me to come over there?"

"Of course not."

The short walk in the brisk evening air of early November helped Mark get a grip on himself and his emotions. When she opened the door, Alexa's eyes were grave with concern.

"I met John Carr in Birmingham," Mark told her. "We talked for quite a while."

"John called me last night to say he was very much impressed with you, but also concerned about your obvious depression and particularly your preoccupation with how the Disabled Doctors' Committee operates."

"He must have recognized that I'm already addicted to narcotics."

She gave him a quick glance. "You've never admitted it before."

"Because I've been telling myself I could stop any time I wanted to," he admitted.

"Can you?"

"I'm not sure any longer, but I'm certainly going to try—starting tomorrow."

"Why not tonight?"

"Tonight, then, but it may already be too late."

"What makes you think that?"

"Someone entered my apartment while I was in Birmingham and searched it thoroughly. They found the kit where I keep my supply of Demerol cartridge-ampules and even photographed it. I found a used flash bulb on the floor where it was dropped by the prowler."

"He still could have been only a junkie." Mark winced at the word, reminding him as it did of that night with Claire at Point Blue. "Addicts looking for narcotics break into doctors' houses and offices all the time."

"This one didn't take my supply of Demerol cartridges or even the money that was in the drawer of the bedside table. Obviously, the only thing he was looking for was evidence that I've been using narcotics."

"Why would anyone do that?"

"To use it against me. What else?"

"If you're thinking of the Disabled Doctors' Committee program, it doesn't operate that way," she protested. "They can't even take any action until someone—a member of the family or another doctor—brings evidence of addiction."

"It's another doctor I'm thinking of. The night Jerry Thorpe left for New Orleans, he called me and promised to get even for what he called stealing his patients. He was drunk that night, but since he came back he's so friendly that I forgot all about the threat."

"You were right to be concerned, though." Alexa's voice was taut. "Jerry's a very complex personality, and I wouldn't put it past him to break into your apartment hoping to cause trouble for you."

"But the door hadn't even been tampered with."

"If yours is like most, he could have gotten in by using a credit card, a nail file, or even the blade of a pocket knife pressing against the bolt and moving it. Do you lock it with a key when you leave?"

"No. I guess I should but I never bothered."

"Most people don't, which is the reason why almost anyone can get in whenever they want to. Still, I don't see how whoever did break in would be able to use the evidence of some snapshots of narcotic cartridge-ampules, when you're a doctor and have a perfect right to have them there. Do you have any idea how many cartridges were in the kit?"

"About forty, I guess."

"No doctor needs to carry that much in his medical bag, unless he's using them on himself."

"That's what I figured."

"So what are you going to do?"

"Stop using the stuff—for one thing. Then, even if I'm brought up before the State Disabled Doctors' Committee, I can always swear that I've stopped and they could hardly do anything more than put me on probation without actually lifting my license."

Mark got to his feet. "Thanks for letting me talk the problem out with you."

"This time I didn't interfere," she reminded him with a smile as she opened the apartment door. "You made the decision to stop using Demerol of your own accord."

"I'll still need help at times," he told her. "And I hope you won't mind giving it."

"Just say the word. That's what friends are for."

"See you at the staff meeting tomorrow afternoon," Mark said. "And thanks again for letting me tell you my troubles."

"Now that you've stopped using Demerol, maybe you won't have many."

But there, as it happened, she was wrong.

XVI

During a whole week of torture—thanks to heavy doses of diazepam and other tranquilizers—Mark managed to stagger through his workdays without either alcohol or Demerol. Then, when he was beginning to congratulate himself that, in spite of the severe headaches which plagued him even more than before, he had the situation under control, the roof fell in.

It began on Monday of the second week, when he looked at the morning paper while having breakfast at the nearby McDonald's restaurant before going across the river to the Old Town Clinic for a morning of surgery.

A two-column article bore the headline:

DRUG SALESMAN INDICTED IN NARCOTICS SALE

The lead on the article below the headline said:

Yesterday afternoon federal narcotics agents arrested Donald McCumber, salesman for a local wholesale pharmaceutical firm, on a charge of selling narcotics illegally to a large number of customers. Details concerning the purchases were not given at the time of McCumber's arrest, but it is rumored that several Gulf City doctors and a number of other prominent names will be on the list when it is published at the time McCumber is arraigned before a federal magistrate this afternoon or tomorrow.

Mark's hands were trembling so much when he put down the paper that he knocked over his cup of coffee. Conscious that practically every eye in the busy restaurant was suddenly on him, he rose quickly from the booth and fled. Nor did he stop until he reached his apartment. Rushing inside, he opened the closet where he kept the Demerol. His hands shook so badly that he had trouble giving himself the injection but, when he sank into a chair and buried his head between his hands, he could feel the powerful sedative action of the narcotic beginning to take effect, calming him so he could begin to think intelligently.

That a connection existed between the search of his apartment a little over a week ago and the arrest of the man from whom he'd been buying his supply of narcotics for months, he could no longer doubt. Nor the fact that when the list of customers to whom Donald McCumber had sold drugs illegally was published, his own name would be on it.

A second injection was required before he could get himself under enough control to drive to Old Town. When he entered through the back door, his worst fears were confirmed.

"A Mr. Connors is waiting in your office to see you, Dr. Harrison," said the Chief Nurse, who was waiting for him just inside.

"A patient?"

"The only thing I could get out of him was that he wanted to see you on business."

"Thank you, Mrs. Doggett." Mark resisted the instinctive urge to leave. "I'll let you know when I'm ready to start the first operation."

The man in Mark's office was quietly dressed and wore horn-rimmed glasses. Nor did he waste any time in coming to the point.

"My name is Roger Connors, Dr. Harrison," he said and opened a small leather folder to display the emblem identifying him as an agent of the U. S. Department of Justice. "I'm assigned to the Drug Enforcement Administration."

"I renewed my license to prescribe narcotic drugs only last month," Mark said, as he took the chair behind his desk.

"I'm not concerned with that, Doctor," said the narcotics agent. "Did you see the article in the newspapers this morning concerning the arrest of Donald McCumber?"

"Yes, but I don't see how it concerns me."

"We think it concerns you very much, Dr. Harrison." Connors' voice had taken on a steely note. "The department has reason to believe you're one of McCumber's customers, perhaps one of the best."

"Did he tell you that?"

"McCumber chooses to remain silent at the moment, which is his right. When we searched his office at the time of his arrest, however, we found a receipt from you—"

"Surely not for narcotics, Mr. Connors."

"It was marked 'medicines,'" the agent admitted. "May I ask what they were?"

"I don't remember, Mr. Connors. You see, I've had a severe postconcussion headache for the past four or five months, and I often buy analgesic drugs like sodium zomepirac, as well as some others."

"From a wholesaler? Come now, Doc—"

"They're much cheaper that way, Mr. Connors. Surely you know doctors are allowed to buy medicines at wholesale prices."

"Both sodium zomepirac and Demerol are cheaper by the dozen, I'm sure. The point is that Mr. McCumbers had no prescriptions on file for narcotic sales to you."

"Then you're seeking evidence against him?"

"We have enough for an indictment already, but as a physician I'm sure you would want to cooperate with us in halting the illegal sale of narcotic drugs."

"Naturally." Mark was beginning to hope that somehow his luck would be better than he'd thought when he saw the newspaper article that morning. Moreover, he could now dare to hope his name would not appear on the list the newspaper article had said would shortly be made public. "What can I do?" he asked.

"Tell us whether you bought narcotics from Donald McCumbers," said the agent.

"Are you implying that I'm a—I believe the term is 'pusher,' Mr. Connors?"

"Of course not. We know you've been using meperidine hydrochloride—probably as Demerol—for some time—"

"How do you know that?"

"We have ways of finding out such things, Doctor."

"I'd be interested to hear about them, Mr. Connors."

"I imagine you would, but let's stop beating around the bush,

Dr. Harrison. Are you willing to testify that Donald McCumbers sold you a quantity of meperidine for your own use?"

"Wouldn't that be tantamount to naming myself an accomplice in the illegal drug traffic?"

"Not necessarily. If you choose to cooperate, the department would not report to the State Disabled Doctors' Committee the evidence we've accumulated that you are addicted."

Mark recognized that Connors was playing his trump card and was strongly tempted to cooperate. After a week without narcotics, except when he'd panicked that morning, he could be fairly certain he could continue without them. And since the federal narcotics agent was obviously fishing because he didn't have enough evidence from Mark's own purchases from McCumbers to publish his name on any list, he might get off scot-free—though he could no longer take narcotics like Demerol. But to do that would be to betray a man who'd supplied him with medication when his pain had been almost unbearable.

"I think we're both wasting time, Mr. Connors," Mark said firmly. "Besides, I have a patient waiting for surgery."

"Very well, Doctor." Connors rose from his seat. "Since you choose not to help, we have no choice except to turn the information we have about your addiction over to the State Disabled Doctors' Committee and also to the State Licensing Board."

"Good day, Mr. Connors," Mark said as he picked up the telephone. "Get the patient ready for surgery, Mrs. Doggett," he directed the nurse who answered. "I'll start scrubbing as soon as I can change clothes."

XVII

Mark's hope that he had successfully evaded the question of his addiction to narcotics was shattered before the week was over. The proof came in the form of a letter under the heading of the State Medical Society's Disabled Doctors' Committee. The message was terse:

"On November 30 you will be examined by a delegation of fellow physicians from the Disabled Doctors' Committee," it read. "Please meet with the delegation at the headquarters of the Gulf County Medical Society at three P.M. You may bring counsel, if you wish." It was signed by the state chairman, Edward C. McIntosh, M.D.

Mark considered asking Paul Martenson to accompany him to the committee meeting as counsel but decided against it, hoping he could convince the doctors making up the committee that he had indeed won the battle against dependence on the drug. But deep inside himself he knew, and was further depressed by the knowledge, that in a crisis situation such as he'd found himself when he read of Donald McCumber's arrest, he was still liable to panic and fall back upon the chemical support of the narcotic syringe.

At three o'clock on the afternoon of November 30, Mark entered the headquarters of the County Medical Society and was directed to a conference room. Edward McIntosh was sitting at the head of the long table, flanked by two doctors, neither of whom Mark knew.

"Thank you for coming, Dr. Harrison." McIntosh didn't shake hands, and when one of the other doctors started to rise, a chill glance from the psychiatrist stopped him. "Do you know Dr. Ponder and Dr. Hayes?"

"I'm afraid not," said Mark. "Good afternoon, gentlemen."

"Dr. Ponder is from Choctaw and Dr. Hayes from Surfside." McIntosh's tone was still as cold as his manner. "Both are members of the State Disabled Doctors' Committee. I presume that you know the reason why we have asked you to appear before us as a delegation representing the full committee, Dr. Harrison."

"I haven't been informed of the reason, Dr. McIntosh," said Mark.

"Don't quibble, Doctor!" McIntosh snapped. "It will only make things—"

"Wait a minute, Ed," said Dr. Ponder, a plump jolly-looking man who appeared to be in his early fifties. "The protocol for action by the committee explicitly states that the first confrontation shall be in a friendly situation. We're trying to help another doctor, not sitting in judgment on him after having convicted him in advance."

"There's some merit in what Jack says, Ed," Dr. Hayes added, but on a less positive note. "Dr. Harrison certainly has a right to know exactly what he is being accused of."

"All right, if you want to quibble," said McIntosh, in a tone of much irritation. "Here are the facts: Dr. Harrison has been a known user of narcotics over a period of roughly five months. He is also an alcoholic—"

"Do you have any proof of those charges, Doctor?" Mark demanded.

"I do."

"Then present it, please."

McIntosh shrugged and picked up a sheet of paper lying on several prints of snapshots which Mark couldn't see clearly enough to recognize.

"On November third," he read, "a search of Dr. Harrison's apartment revealed the presence of over a gross of Demerol cartridge-ampules with injectors, alcohol sponges, and other paraphernalia used for such injections—"

"Who made that search, Dr. McIntosh?" Mark demanded.

"I am not at liberty to reveal—"

Mark suddenly wished he'd risked further exposure by bringing Paul Martenson to represent him. But he had no intention of letting McIntosh pillory him for what he was beginning to suspect, judging by the psychiatrist's manner from the start, could be personal reasons.

"Was this search made by a representative of the committee, Dr. McIntosh?" he demanded.

"Wel—ll—, no—" McIntosh stammered, obviously caught by surprise that Mark would even seek to defend himself.

"Or a police officer?" Mark insisted.

"Who *did* make the search, Ed?" Dr. Ponder demanded.

"I am not at liberty to reveal the source," McIntosh said stiffly.

"Then you cannot use what was found as evidence," said Mark. "Since this is called the Disabled Doctors' Committee, I presume you have evidence that my professional judgment and ability have been seriously impaired during the five months I've been in Gulf City and on the staff of the Barrett Clin—"

"I can promise that you will not have that position much longer," McIntosh snapped. "Richard Barrett already knows—"

"Are you saying that as chairman of the Disabled Doctors' Committee, you have already discussed Dr. Harrison's case with someone who is not a member of the committee?" Dr. Ponder demanded sharply.

"Well, I—"

"Yes or no, Ed?" Ponder insisted.

"I naturally inquired whether Dr. Barrett was satisfied with Dr. Harrison's work as a physician," McIntosh said angrily.

"Did you tell him why you were asking?"

"Of course not. It was just a friendly question."

"Dr. Barrett knows you are chairman of the committee, Dr. McIntosh," Mark interposed. "I doubt that he took such an inquiry as simply a friendly question."

"You can consider whatever you damn please!" McIntosh snapped. "We didn't come here to be questioned by you, Dr. Harrison."

Before Mark could answer, Dr. Ponder intervened.

"I'm not going to be a party to this meeting as long as you conduct it in this manner, Ed," the other doctor said firmly. "You're obviously prejudiced against Dr. Harrison for some reason, and if this hearing is to continue, I insist that you step down and let one of us chair the hearing."

"I won't have my impartiality questioned by—" McIntosh said heatedly, but Ponder cut him off.

"I know you've been taping the proceedings, and I'll not be a party to having them on a record either, considering the way you're handling it. Either step down, or we'll call it quits right now."

McIntosh started to rise, then sank back. "All right, if that's the way you want it."

Ponder turned to Hayes. "Are you with me, Jack?"

"It does seem that the whole thing could have been handled

differently." Hayes was obviously reluctant to go against McIntosh.

"I'll take over then." Ponder turned to Mark. "I'm going to ask you direct questions, Dr. Harrison. You are not required to answer, although you could expedite this hearing considerably if you would be completely frank with us."

"I have no objection to that, Dr. Ponder, even though it appears that the committee has a great deal of information about me, most of which was obtained illegally—"

McIntosh started to intervene but yielded to a warning glance from Ponder, and before he could be questioned, Mark began his statement:

"Let the record show that I sustained a severe head injury in July, shortly after coming to Gulf City to join the staff of the Barrett Clinic, with an extradural hemorrhage requiring surgery by Dr. Charles Minot. Since then, I have been subject to severe headaches, such as frequently happen in what is sometimes called the 'postconcussion syndrome.'

"In order to ease the pain, I have occasionally had to resort to injections of Demerol," Mark continued, "and frequently have a drink or two in the evening to relax after a hard day's work at the satellite Clinic I head in what is known as Old Town. I deny strongly, however, that either alcohol or Demerol have in any way impaired my ability to function in my capacity as a physician. Nor do I believe the question of how I obtained the medication necessary to relieve my headaches is within the province of this committee."

"Is that the extent of what you have to say to us, Dr. Harrison?" Ponder asked.

"Yes, sir."

"Do you have any questions, Jack?" Ponder asked Dr. Hayes.

"No."

"What about you, Ed?"

"What's the use? He's obviously lying."

"I'm going to ask you to wait outside, Dr. Harrison," said Ponder. "We will deliberate, and I will let you know what we decide with regard to the charges against you."

Effective December 20, your employment by the Barrett Clinic is permanently terminated by vote of the Clinic staff. Please remove any possessions you have from Clinic property and do not appear there after the day you receive this letter.

> Richard Barrett, M.D.,
> President

Depressed and defeated, Mark drove to the riverfront park he'd grown to love during his morning jogging, the same one where he and Alexa had shared breakfast a little over a month ago. There he methodically inserted a butterfly needle into a hand vein, strapped the needle down by means of the flanges attached for that purpose, and began to pump Demerol ampules, each containing a hundred milligrams of the powerful—and possibly lethal—narcotic into his circulation.

Halfway through the fourth ampule, he slumped on the seat of the car unconscious, not caring that, when the syringe he was using fell from his hand, it became disconnected from the needle, allowing blood to flow back through it and drip to the floor of the car.

XVIII

Mark awakened to the pain of a sore throat in which a tube had been inserted and the rhythmic click of a respirator. The hospital bed on which he lay was festooned with racks bearing intravenous-solution bottles and tubing through which whole blood was pouring into his circulation by way of a needle in an ankle vein and another in the antecubital fossa in front of his left elbow. Reflected in the mirror of the dresser at the foot of the bed, he could vaguely distinguish the small glass window of a monitor across which an electrographic tracing was moving rapidly.

"Decided to join the living?" The voice was familiar but, when he turned his head, he was barely able to make out the face of Alexa McGillivray.

"Wha—?" The sound was only a croak because of the tube in his throat.

"Don't try to talk," she told him. "You were in respiratory arrest and practically exsanguinated when the Rescue Squad brought you to the Emergency Room of Gulfside. Dr. Hirschberg had to put a tube in your trachea and connect it to a respirator."

Mark managed to lift his right hand high enough to point to his throat and she understood the meaning of the gesture.

"I'll get Dr. Hirschberg," she told him. "You'll have a sore throat after he takes the tube out, but you should be a lot more comfortable without the respirator and the soreness will clear up very quickly."

Dr. Hirschberg was tall, bearded, and very capable. He removed the intratracheal tube in Mark's windpipe deftly and swiftly. When he finished, Mark could talk, although his voice reminded him of a bullfrog he'd heard the morning he and Alexa had eaten breakfast in the small park under the ramparts of the high bridge across the river where he had tried to kill himself with a narcotic injection.

"Somebody up there must like you, Dr. Harrison," said the bearded Emergency physician. "If your Chief Nurse at the Old Town Clinic hadn't recognized your car in the riverfront park when she was driving home, I'm afraid you'd be in a local funeral home right now instead of here in Gulfside."

"How long have I been here?" Mark managed to ask.

"About four hours," Dr. Hirschberg told him. "You were in both respiratory and cardiac arrest when the Rescue Squad Mrs. Doggett called got to you. Recognizing that you had tried to kill yourself with Demerol, they started the respirator and put EKG sensors on you. When the EKG picture was transmitted to me here at Gulfside, I told them to zap you with the defibrillator before bringing you to the hospital. It took two zaps before they had your heart beating again and were able to start fluids and give you a drug to combat the depressing effects of the Demerol on your circulation and respiration. Mind telling me why somebody with your ability and future potential went to such great lengths to destroy yourself?"

"It's a long story," said Mark wearily. "I guess I owe you a considerable debt, Doctor, but right now I'm not sure I appreciate your efforts."

"Most attempted suicides don't at first," Hirschberg assured him cheerfully. "Once they get their thinking straightened out, though, they usually come to us and thank us."

"I'll take a raincheck on that. Right now I'd rather go to sleep."

"Be my guest." Hirschberg moved swiftly and skillfully; moments later Mark felt the prick of a hypodermic needle and soon sank into the delicious *nirvana* of sleep.

XIX

It was midafternoon when Mark awoke again and he felt considerably better. Only one intravenous needle now dripped fluid into his veins and his throat felt ten times less sore. Not so his mood, for the depression in which he'd been sinking steadily, it seemed now for months, was as deep as ever. It was lightened somewhat by the appearance of Alexa McGillivray shortly after four.

"Feeling better?" she asked.

"Physically, yes; mentally, no. I wish Mrs. Doggett hadn't gotten there in time."

"She almost didn't. Fortunately, she was trained in advanced C.P.R. techniques, like most of the nurses in Gulf City and recognized that you were both in respiratory and cardiac arrest."

"How did she happen to find me anyway?"

"She had just finished a day's work at the Old Town Clinic and the road to her house passes the riverfront park. You hadn't been at the Clinic all afternoon, so when she saw your car parked there, she stopped to ask you about the next day's surgical schedule. Fortunately, her husband travels and has a CB radio in his car, so she knew how to call Channel Nine on yours and have the police send the Rescue Squad immediately."

"How did you learn what I had done?"

"Caroline Doggett called me as soon as she got home. I was at the Clinic staff meeting, but she had the operator ring through."

"Did you go back to the staff meeting afterward?"

"Only long enough to give Dr. Barrett my resignation and let them all have a tongue-lashing for doing what they'd done to you."

"You shouldn't have done that. I'm not worth losing your job over."

"We can talk about that later," she said. "Right now, I want you to promise me something."

"Without knowing what it is?"

"At the moment, yes. You should know you can trust me to see that whatever I ask is in your best interests."

"I promise," he said. "You knew Dr. Barrett fired me, didn't you?"

"I didn't until the staff meeting, when Jerry Thorpe started boasting about how he had broken into your apartment and found the evidence he turned over to Dr. McIntosh so charges could be brought against you before the Disabled Doctors' Committee. I saw red then, and I saw even redder when Dr. Barrett told the others he'd dismissed you without giving you a chance to defend yourself."

"I don't suppose any of them was inclined to be lenient," said Mark bitterly.

"Dr. Harkness was but the rest were obviously afraid any publicity about your having been involved in the arrest of that drug salesman, plus the fact that you had been using narcotics, would backfire against the Clinic and they might lose some of their rich clientele."

"Did they know Dr. McIntosh convinced the state committee that I should go away for four months without giving me a full hearing?"

"Yes, but Dr. Barrett was more concerned with firing you before there was any publicity. He'd already called Paul Martenson about the clause in your contract forbidding you to practice in Gulf City if you were no longer connected with the Barrett Clinic. What was worrying him was whether firing you for cause put the clause into effect."

"Even if it didn't, what chance would I have, here or anywhere else?"

"Disabled doctors are returning to practice every day," she insisted. "Besides, you've done a magnificent job with the satellite Clinic, in spite of your impairment."

"You don't have to be kind. Claire gave me the right title before she left for California when she called me a junkie."

"After a period of rest and rehabilitation, you could always go back to Lakeview if you wanted to. I remember you once told me Dr. Ramirez has a job waiting for you."

"That was nearly six months ago. Lakeview would hardly employ me again, now that I've been branded a narcotics addict by my fellow doctors. Incidentally, what happened in the McCumber case?"

"He's out on bail, according to the newspaper. Apparently, no one who bought narcotics from him would testify against him, so the federal authorities don't have much of a case. Chances are, the whole thing will be dropped unless there are other developments or somebody is willing to testify against him."

"It looks like I'm the only one who's going to suffer in this whole mess, particularly when I could have avoided the whole thing by telling them what they wanted," said Mark bitterly.

"I'm trying to tell you that you don't have to be a permanent victim," she insisted.

"I don't buy that," he said. "But at least I can make some amends by forcing you to take your job back."

"I'll go back—if you agree to a *quid pro quo.*"

"Let me have the bad news. I can't feel any more depressed than I am already."

"I want you to agree to put yourself in John Carr's hands for as long as it takes to cure you of depression and addiction to Demerol."

Mark started to laugh, but the effort brought on a spasm of coughing from the irritation in his trachea and ended in a croak.

"What's so funny?" Alexa demanded.

"I've already had that prescription—from Dr. McIntosh and the Disabled Doctors' Committee."

"All the more reason you should do it then."

"I guess that's what I was running away from when I started killing myself methodically that afternoon in Riverside Park," he admitted. "When the truth is told, though, I seem to have been trying to do the same thing for the past year. First, it was with overwork at Lakeview before I came to Gulf City. And then it was getting the Old Town Clinic going here—plus that blow on the head and the aftereffects from concussion."

"I'm going to hold you to that promise to go to Canyonhead," she warned.

"I'll go," he told her. "With all my faults, and their name is legion, I do have a habit of keeping my promises."

XX

Mark had another visitor that evening. It was Andy Harkness, the internist and cardiologist of the Barrett Clinic.

"You came damn near to destroying the best young surgeon I've seen in many a day, Mark," Harkness scolded him.

"I wasn't thinking very clearly," Mark confessed. "But from where I was sitting, the view was pretty bleak."

"It's never too bleak as long as you've got friends, my boy. When I talked to Aldo Ramirez about you before Dick Barrett offered you a position on the Clinic staff, he said you'd been working too hard and should take a rest. But knowing the fine opportunity in the job Dick was going to offer you as a young surgeon, Aldo didn't have the heart to tell you not to take it."

"I probably wouldn't have listened anyway. You never know when you're burned out until the fire's beyond control."

"I knew you were working very hard getting the Old Town Clinic started, especially when you pulled us out of the hole left when Jerry had to go to New Orleans to get himself dried out. But I figured you had things under control."

"So did I," Mark admitted. "It was about then that the headaches really started getting worse and I began shooting more narcotics."

"It's never too late to start up the ladder again." The internist lit a small cheroot and puffed vigorously. "Especially when you've got someone like Alexa McGillivray pulling for you."

Light burst suddenly in Mark's brain. "She asked you to come to see me, didn't she?"

"I was coming anyway, after I heard that son-of-a-bitch Jerry

Thorpe boasting about breaking into your apartment. You should bring charges against him."

"It would only make matters worse," said Mark. "Besides, I can't really blame anybody but myself for what happened. The Demerol was there, and I'd already let myself become dependent on it. If I'd kept on the way I was going, the whole thing would have come to light eventually, so it's just as well that it did now."

"Maybe you're right, especially when another time you might have succeeded in putting yourself out of the way for good. If you ask me, though, the whole impairment program has gotten out of hand, the way Ed McIntosh has been handling it as chairman of the state committee. You know he's actually using it as a stepping-stone toward the presidency of the State Medical Association, don't you?"

"I didn't," said Mark. "But with all the furor nowadays over doctor impairment, I suppose that's one of the best ways for a politically minded doctor to get ahead."

"It was different in the old days," said the internist. "If a doctor was so far gone on narcotics that he was a danger to his patients—as many of them became—he went to that federal institution in Lexington, Kentucky, I think it was. There he was treated as if he'd contracted a disease, which is what both alcoholism and addiction really are. If he had enough guts to come through the treatment, he came back home and started work again with nobody looking over his shoulder to see whether he was going to slip, the way they insist on doing nowadays. Even if he did backslide, he was given a second chance before the Board of Medical Examiners told him to find something else to do that didn't involve having narcotics at hand all the time."

"But if doctors don't police each other—"

"You're using the wrong word, Mark; doctors are supposed to *help* each other. Instead, some of them use the 'impaired' label to get rid of a physician they don't like—usually because he's been stealing patients away from them—by reporting him to the Disabled Doctors' Committee. And if the chairman, as in your case, has got it in for you into the bargain, what chance have you got of being able to organize any sort of defense and save yourself? About as much as a snowball in hell."

"The committees still need authority, even if it gives them the power to destroy a doctor's professional reputation, as they did in my case," Mark insisted.

"The committees—or people like Ed McIntosh?"

"In this case, they're both the same thing, but I doubt if it happens that way too often."

Harkness gave him a quick, probing glance. "What I don't understand about all this, is why Ed McIntosh hated you enough to risk losing the chairmanship of the committee in order to destroy you. I had a talk with Ponder afterward, and he told me he had to take over before Ed practically turned the whole thing into an inquisition."

"It already was," said Mark. "But I do owe a lot to Dr. Ponder."

"I still can't understand the reason for Ed's being so much against you, unless of course you made the mistake of shacking up with the lovely Helene."

"Not shacking up expresses it much better."

"So you spurned the invitation, and to get even she put the finger on you? I thought that might be it."

"I guess I was a sitting duck," Mark admitted. "But I didn't think she would go that far."

"All she had to do was reverse the roles by telling Ed you tried to seduce her," said Harkness. "As jealous as he is, the fuse was lit."

"That's evidently what happened," Mark agreed. "After the committee hearing, Dr. McIntosh met me in the parking lot at the Medical Society building and accused me of trying to seduce Helene. He said he'd get even—and he certainly did."

"Maybe not quite so easily as he thinks," said Harkness grimly. "I'm on the local Disabled Doctors' Committee, and if I leak what you told me to a few people at the state level, who dislike Ed McIntosh as much as I do, we might just get your case reopened."

"Please don't," said Mark. "The best thing I can do now is leave here and get myself off both the sauce and the needle. Then maybe I'll be able to find a spot where an ex-alcoholic and ex-addict can do useful work."

"You can always have a recommendation from me, my boy." Harkness got to his feet. "And whether you want it or not, I'm still going to take some of the wind out of Ed McIntosh's sails by dropping a word here and there in State Medical circles about the way he handled your case. You can bet he won't be successful in gaining the presidency of the Association by playing God through the Disabled Doctors' Committee. When are you going to Canyonhead?"

"As soon as Dr. Hirschberg discharges me. I'll talk to him tomorrow when he makes rounds."

Pleased by Mark's decision to seek psychiatric help, Dr. Hirschberg discharged him at the end of the week. Meanwhile, Alexa had packed what clothes he would need and had wired the owners of the condominium he was renting, notifying them that Mark was leaving Gulf City. On Friday afternoon, she drove him in his car to Canyonhead Retreat.

"I'm going down to Peace River in the valley to stay with Uncle Homer McGillivray," she told Mark when he'd been registered in and assigned to a room in the central part of the private psychiatric hospital. "He's having some circulatory trouble in one of his legs and I want to make sure he's not in real danger. The head nurse tells me John Carr will be back sometime late tonight, so you'll probably see him in the morning."

"How will you get back to Gulf City?"

"John will have someone drive me to Gadsden Sunday afternoon. I can catch a night plane from there."

"Will I see you again before you go back?"

"Sure. I promised John and Elsa to have lunch with them here before I go to Gadsden."

XXI

With a liberal dose of flurazepam—a Valiumlike drug useful in insomnia—Mark slept soundly and was awakened at seven-fifteen the next morning by a knock on the door of his room.

"This is Henry, the attendant assigned to you, Doctor," a voice with a soft drawl told him. "Dr. Carr would like for you to have breakfast with him at eight in the staff dining room at the end of the corridor. I put a hottle of coffee outside your door, in case you'd like an eye-opener."

"Thank you," said Mark.

When he opened the door, the small flask—known as a hottle because it would keep the contents warm for some time—was standing on a small tray, along with a cup and saucer, a packet of artificial cream, two small packets of sugar, and a plastic spoon. Mark poured a cup and sipped it while he shaved, showered, and dressed. Afterward he drew the draperies aside and stepped out on the balcony.

Canyonhead Retreat was true to its name. Located at the head of a deep cleft in the hill country of northeastern Alabama, the canyon itself extended as far south as Mark could see. About a quarter of a mile to the east, a stream tumbled over a granite ledge to disappear in the depths of the deep gorge.

The gorge itself was about a mile across and perhaps a thousand feet deep. The awesome magnificence of the canyon and the rustic simplicity of the room to which he had been assigned combined to lift some of the weight of depression that still gripped him.

Glancing at his watch, Mark saw that it was almost eight, so he stepped out into the corridor and turned toward the center of the rambling building. He had no trouble finding the staff dining room where many of the night-shift personnel were still at breakfast.

"Select what you want to eat from the steam tables, Mark," John Carr called from where he was sitting at a table in the corner. "Then come over here and join me, if you will."

With an appetite he hadn't remembered feeling for a long time, Mark ordered a large breakfast. When he carried his tray over to the table where the director was sitting, John Carr rose to shake hands.

"Welcome to Canyonhead," he said warmly. "I'm pleased that you decided to visit with us."

"The state committee made it rather plain that this is where I should come—if I want to continue as a doctor," Mark said somewhat wryly as he took his seat. "Alexa pinned me down, too, with a promise that if I would come, she would withdraw her resignation from the staff of the Barrett Clinic."

"She's very convincing and usually gets her way. We're flattered here that several neighboring states have selected Canyonhead Retreat as the best available institution in the area to carry on a rehabilitation program for disabled doctors," the psychiatrist continued. "So far, I'm proud to say, our success record has been very high."

"If the view from the balcony outside my room is an example, I can understand why just being here would help convince anyone he was lucky to be alive."

"The Upper Creeks and the Choctaws loved it," said Carr. "When Andrew Jackson had them deported to Oklahoma, they were angry and depressed. A few came back to die, but soon found a will to live in a land they'd thought was lost to the greed of white men. With that fresh drive, they began to build a new homeland in the old one, by adopting many of the white men's ways. As a result, there's been a thriving community, centered around the town of Peace River farther down the canyon, ever since the Civil War."

"That's where Alexa grew up, isn't it?"

"Yes. She lettered on every girl's athletic team at Peace River High School and could easily have been a professional woman athlete if she hadn't chosen to study nursing instead."

"I've never had a surgical assistant who could equal her," Mark commented. "But getting back to my case, when do I start treatment?"

"It's already begun. The maid who's cleaning your room has been instructed to remove all alcoholic drinks or drugs of any kind she finds and place them in safekeeping."

"Isn't 'cold turkey' rather drastic? I thought these institutions used a tapering off program."

"Not here, and I should warn you that you'll have a pretty rough week or ten days in the beginning," said John Carr firmly. "Because you really need to be hospitalized during that period, you'll be housed in the main building. Afterward you can move to one of a half dozen cottages. That part of our treatment routine amounts to group therapy in which the occupants of the cottages draw upon each other for support. You will discover for yourself very quickly, I hope, that it will be the most important part of your recovery."

"Suppose I elect to stop treatment?"

"The next step would then be up to the Disabled Doctors' Committee of your state. Unless you convince them otherwise, your license to practice will be refused until you either elect to come back here or carry out the prescribed period of treatment. We lose a few during 'cold turkey' and occasionally one afterward, but only a few ever leave. And most of those come back later on."

"I couldn't go back to Gulf City to practice, even if I wanted to, so I certainly have no reason to stop treatment."

"I'd think the Barrett Clinic would be happy to take you back," said Carr. "From what Alexa told me on the phone, you've done an exceptional job of organizing the new satellite Clinic for them."

"The Old Town Clinic made a profit during the second month of operation, but the Barrett Clinic doesn't coddle misfits. I was fired the minute Dick Barrett received the report of the state committee."

"That sort of reaction has hampered our work with impaired physicians from the outset—even after they complete the prescribed period of treatment," said Carr. "Of thirty doctors we treated last year from one state, five weren't able to return to practice in their home cities because of prejudice. One even fled to Canada because no doctor would monitor his work."

"Why?"

"I suppose they were afraid patients would think the monitoring physician was also an addict. Another doctor had completed his treatment and was back doing fine work, but when the hospital board that employed him learned he'd been labeled as impaired or disabled, they fired him. Still another's partner refused to take him back under any circumstances."

"Not everybody who sins is cast into the outer darkness, as I well know," said Mark on a strongly resentful note. "The Barrett Clinic, for example, didn't boggle at sending Jerry Thorpe, with his big practice in vaginal hysterectomies on society women, away for a month to be dried out. But they dropped me like a hot potato the minute they heard the Federal Narcotics Administration had been investigating me."

"If you'd been with your group long enough to have developed a really lucrative practice, the outlook may have well been different," Carr agreed.

"I suppose you received a report on my case from the State Disabled Doctors' Committee?"

"Yes. Didn't they give you a copy?"

"No. Ed McIntosh was so eager to get me out of Gulf City he didn't bother. And I was too depressed to ask for it."

"You're entitled to see this." John Carr opened a letter file he'd been reading when Mark entered the dining room and handed him a sheet. "It's pretty brief, though."

The report over the signature of Dr. Edward McIntosh as chairman of the State's Disabled Doctors' Committee was almost as brief as the letter Mark had received from the committee notifying him of its action in his case.

History of addiction to Demerol for a period of five months, the report read. *The effectiveness of this physician in the further practice of medicine is definitely impaired beyond any treatment other than the four-month period prescribed for such conditions by the committee. Following discharge after treatment, this case will be evaluated further by the committee with regard to bringing it to the attention of the Board of Medical Examiners.*

"So I lose, even if I win over being a junkie," said Mark. "Ed McIntosh is obviously determined to have his pound of flesh."

"For what?" John Carr asked.

"What's the use? He has the right to destroy me."

"He may not always have it," said John Carr grimly. "If you're being railroaded out of medicine, as I believe you are, I know a lot of highly ethical doctors who are going to ask why."

"Please don't go out on a limb on my behalf," said Mark. "The way this 'impaired physician' problem is developing, you could lose a lot if any of the state committees that send patients here decide you're too lenient on M.D. addicts."

"I'll be the one to decide that," said Carr. "I've assigned a young associate, Dr. Hal Morton, to study your case. When he's finished and I've made my own study, we'll decide whether you were treated fairly by the state committee. If you weren't, you can be sure I'll report it to them and suggest less drastic action than the usual four months of treatment."

"McIntosh has a majority of the committee members in his pocket, so you'd still probably be wasting time," Mark warned. "Besides, he's right on all but one charge, and that's not even in the report. I'm addicted to Demerol, and the sooner you get me off the stuff the sooner I can start hunting for a job. I can always work for the government; they're crying for doctors all the time."

"They don't get surgeons of your caliber very often, and with my recommendations, they'd jump at the chance to employ you, but I'm not going to see you buried in some VA hospital." Carr looked at his watch. "It's almost ten; I'll show you the way to Dr. Morton's office. He's a Tarheel like you and was trained at Duke, so I think you'll like him."

Dr. Morton was very thorough. It was after noontime before he finished taking Mark's history and giving him a complete physical examination.

"I'll do a spinal puncture this afternoon and also order a skull X ray," Morton told him when they broke for lunch. "Offhand, though, I'd say your headaches are not due to concussion."

"Why else would I have them?"

"Everything you've told me, and what was in Dr. Harkness' letter about his telephone conversation with Dr. Ramirez at Lakeview Hospital, suggests that you must have been on the border of what used to be called 'impairment' when you were employed by the Barrett Clinic. Nowadays, the condition is more often called 'burnout,' and after those six months of hard work at Lakeview when your superior became unable to function, you were certainly a candidate for it. Like anyone starting a new job, too, you wanted to be successful in Gulf City, so you were under even more stress from the start."

"Who wouldn't be, coming into a new job as I was?"

"Granted," said Morton. "My hunch is that after you discovered the relief Demerol brought, a mechanism to justify the use of a pleasant device for alleviating physical symptoms of depression and near exhaustion developed in your unconscious mind. We see this psychosomatic mechanism all the time here at Canyonhead—in professional people, in business executives, and even in so-called 'blue collar' patients who are suddenly thrown into stress situations. It's one of the hazards—the greatest in my opinion—of today's rather hectic life-style."

"And the treatment?"

Morton smiled. "At Canyonhead we help victims of burnout rest and find themselves again. More important, though, we let them learn to like themselves and their fellowmen once more."

XXII

The next week—what Mark remembered of it—was pure hell. Between periods of semicoma induced by heavy doses of tranquilizers and diazepam, in which he existed in a phantasmorgia of consciousness alternating with delirium, his head throbbed and every bone in his body ached as if he were being stretched on a rack like those who came into the hands of the Spanish Inquisition. Vaguely, he remembered telling Alexa good-bye when she came by on Sunday afternoon, but everything else was hazy. On the morning of the seventh day, however, he awoke to hear birds singing outside his window and the rush of the wind in the canyon below. When he threw open the door to the balcony, the crisp December air filled his lungs.

"Here's your hottle of coffee and some toast, Doctor," said a soft voice with a Southern accent, and he turned to see the smiling face of a black attendant in a short white coat standing in the open doorway. Vaguely, he remembered the name as Henry, the man who had brought his belongings to his room when he enrolled at Canyonhead.

"How did you know I'd be able to eat this morning?" Mark asked.

"Most patients feel alive again at the end of the first week, Doctor." The attendant laughed. "Before that, it's like seasickness; most of the time you're afraid you're going to die, and the rest of the time that you won't. Dr. Carr and Dr. Morton will be making rounds pretty soon. So your coffee won't get cold, why don't you eat while I make your bed."

"Where were they all last week when I needed them?" Mark demanded.

"They've been in to see you regularly several times a day, but most of the time you were out of your head."

"Did I confess my sins?"

The attendant laughed heartily. "Only the ones a fine-looking doctor like yourself has a right to commit."

Dr. John Carr and Dr. Hal Morton arrived as Mark was finishing his second cup of coffee. Carr was carrying a typed history attached to a clipboard.

"Hal and I were making bets on how long it would take you to come out of the cold-turkey stage," said Carr. "He won."

"The most important question is, will I want any more narcotics?"

"Once you discover the pleasure of feeling practically every cell in your body relax from a powerful narcotic, you never quite get rid of it," Carr told him. "But now that you know you can do without it and are even better off, you'll be able to put temptation behind you—except perhaps in a time of great stress, which I hope you won't be subjected to again."

"I'm already under the stress of wondering how I'll pay the cost of my stay here," Mark told him. "And where I'll get another job when I get out."

"Don't fret about either one," said Carr. "You can always give me a note for what you owe me."

"But I don't even have any idea what the cost runs?"

"The rate here is about a thousand a week, but the hospitalization insurance you have will probably cover at least part of that. I don't think you'll have any trouble getting another job either, after the way you're coming along here."

"Didn't I read somewhere that some state and local committees recommend loans to help impaired physicians with rehabilitation?" Mark asked.

"That's been done occasionally, but under the circumstances—" Carr didn't finish but Mark knew the statement was an admission that he could expect little from a group dominated by Dr. Edward McIntosh.

"What about the maxim I've heard that 'Once addicted, always addicted'?"

"That is sometimes true," said Carr, "but neither Hal nor I think it is in your case. You certainly got a raw deal from the State Disabled Doctors' Committee, largely because of Dr. McIntosh's determination to railroad you out of Gulf City. On the other hand, judging by the strain you were working under when you were already near burnout, you would undoubtedly have soon become addicted anyway. Our job here would then have been considerably more difficult."

"So in a way, I should be thankful to Dr. McIntosh?" Mark asked on a sarcastic note.

"That would be going more than the second mile," Hal Morton assured him.

"So what do I do next?"

"You and I are going to have a long talk and it might as well be now."

Carr turned to the other doctor. "Suppose you finish rounds, Hal, while I stay here and have a chat with Mark.

"Why don't we sit out on the balcony," Carr added as Morton was leaving. "The view from here is conducive to relaxation, one of the first things you're going to have to learn to do."

"Will I stay in this room?"

"No. We use this building for treating acute cases during our preliminary evaluations and the drying out process. In your case, that seems to be finished, so this afternoon you'll be transferred to one of the eight cottages where you'll be living with from four to ten other patients."

"All doctors?"

"Burnout isn't restricted to the medical profession, by any means," Carr assured him. "Our patient population includes dentists, lawyers, businessmen—practically every sphere of activity."

"That sounds like there's a mold that fits those of us who crack up under stress."

"That is true to a considerable extent," said Carr. "All of you are intelligent, hard-driving, ambitious—"

"Too ambitious for our own good?"

"Yes—if the ambition is unharnessed. Take your own case. When Dr. Peters became unable to carry the microsurgery department at Lakeview, you stepped into the breach and took the whole burden on your shoulders. That wasn't the first time you'd done a similar thing, either; Hal thinks you've been doing it all your life."

"Everything I've gotten I've had to gain pretty much by my own efforts," Mark admitted.

"You've done a magnificent job, too. Phi Beta Kappa at Duke, in spite of playing varsity football and basketball. Getting elected to AOA—the Phi Beta Kappa of medicine—at Lakeview, and graduating at the top of your class. Plus, a residency in surgery and a two-year fellowship in a special field. Those accomplishments aren't exactly hallmarks identifying a run-of-the-mill individual."

"Then topping it all off by becoming a junkie," said Mark bitterly. "Nobody would consider that an accomplishment."

"Maybe not, but let's look at it as being a case of a man who one day bites off a little more than he can chew at the moment."

"I handled tough problems all the way through college and medical school without cracking up until I came to Gulf City and got mugged," Mark reminded him.

"Speaking of Gulf City and the Barrett Clinic, were you happy with what you were doing there?"

"Why wouldn't I have been? I was making sixty-five thousand dollars a year, plus being given a chance to marry the boss's daughter—which, incidentally, didn't work out."

"Did that have anything to do with your crackup?"

Mark shook his head. "Claire and I would never have made a go of it anyway—I guess we're too much alike."

"I doubt that," said Carr.

Mark gave him a startled look. "Do you know Claire—professionally, I mean?"

"She was a patient of mine briefly a few years ago," said the psychiatrist. "When Abner Desmond tried to kill himself and failed, Dr. Barrett sent Claire to me because he was afraid she'd become morbid about having caused Desmond to try suicide."

"I'd lay you ten to one she didn't—and that you got nowhere with her."

"No bet. She stayed a week and left—with my permission. I told Dick Barrett his daughter was one of the most beautiful examples I ever saw of a completely self-centered and amoral individual, supremely confident of her own ability to do anything she wanted to do with her life and quite able to do it."

"That sums her up," Mark agreed. "Not that you'll ever get Dick Barrett to agree because it would mean admitting he's cast from the same mold."

"The mold you were supposed to fit into in Gulf City?"

"Fat chance," said Mark vehemently. "I'm not cut out to be that kind of a doctor, thank God."

"God maybe," said Carr dryly, "but from what Hal tells me and my own observations, your grandfather fits the role of *deus ex machina* a lot better."

"But I can hardly remember him except from what my father told me."

"Yet that was enough to make you want to be just like him?"

"I suppose so, yes."

"Did your grandfather ever have another opportunity in medicine except to be a horse-and-buggy doctor?"

Mark frowned, then his face suddenly cleared. "Come to think of it, he did. He had an opportunity to practice in Richmond."

"Why didn't he?"

"Dad said Grandfather would have no part of a city practice. All he wanted to do was be a country doctor and live on the farm one of our ancestors got as a land grant from the Earl of Granville somewhere around the time of the American Revolution. We've been there ever since."

"Are you the first one to enter medicine since your grandfather?"

"Yes."

"Didn't you pattern yourself after him unconsciously and maybe even consciously, then?"

"What's wrong with that?" Mark demanded.

"Nothing, of course."

"Are you trying to tell me I cracked up in Gulf City because I wasn't doing what I really wanted to do, deep inside?"

"Didn't you?"

"One thing I hate about psychiatrists," said Mark, "is the way they keep answering a question with a question. But if it's going to make you happy I'll admit that Gulf City wasn't my first choice. A year ago I was scheduled to join a group of young doctors from UNC, Duke, and Lakeview in a Health Maintenance Organization in the sandhills of North Carolina."

"What happened?"

"The government bureau that was going to finance a grant to renovate a veterans' hospital that was about to be abandoned down there because of VA cutbacks ran into budget trouble and the project was deferred, maybe permanently. Even if we'd been able to get the HMO started in an existing hospital, it would have been six months at least after I finished my fellowship before I would have been able to start work with them."

"What were you planning to do with those six months?" Carr asked.

"For starters, I was going to go to Myrtle Beach and just relax in the sun and surf while I got myself unwound after those last six months in Lakeview."

"And also get over the fact that you were disappointed at not being chosen to head the microsurgery section at Lakeview when a doctor from another part of the country was brought in instead?" Carr asked.

"Why do you have to get inside a man and tear the guts out of his own soul?" Mark demanded indignantly.

"Because it's the best way I know to get those guts back to functioning properly again."

"All right," said Mark. "I *was* sore because I didn't get to succeed Dr. Peters in microsurgery and because the HMO project fell through. So when Dick Barrett came to Baltimore and offered me sixty-five thousand a year, I naturally accepted it."

"Wasn't the shine on your ideals tarnished a little at some time though?" Carr asked.

"Maybe. But that couldn't be the whole problem."

"Nobody suggested that it was," John Carr told him. "Let me give you sort of a scenario of what may have happened, not necessarily because I'm right. First, you resented not being made chief of microsurgery when you'd filled the position very effectively for six months but lost out to someone else. Second, you came to Gulf City expecting, maybe unconsciously, to be the fair-haired boy but were plunged immediately into another difficult task—and a mundane one at that—of getting the Old Town Clinic off the ground as fast as possible. Third, you got into an unsettling romantic situation, and fourth, you suffered a head injury that was not only painful but also pretty embarrassing."

"I still think you could place that mugging as Number One."

"We won't argue about it. The fact is, that even before you got to Gulf City you were on the verge of burnout. And when the final factor occurred, it pushed you over the edge."

"What final factor?" Mark demanded. "I don't understand."

"Perhaps you don't understand because you really don't want to. Once you joined the staff of the Barrett Clinic, you couldn't help observing that although the staff members were all highly competent in their fields, more attention was paid to income from surgery than to the reasons for the operations."

"I don't think you could say that about Dr. Harkness."

"Neither do I. Harkness is an excellent doctor, but Jerry Thorpe is a surgical shyster."

"But a skilled operator."

"In his field, yes. But what happened in that case where you had to bail him out by reconnecting the vital artery he had severed in his hurry to get away is proof that he's dangerous outside his field and sometimes even in it. That's particularly true when he resented your bailing him out so much that he turned you in to Dr. McIntosh for action by the Disabled Doctors' Committee."

"Don't forget that Ed McIntosh was quite ready to hear what Jerry had to say."

"I don't doubt that either. There have been some questions about the way McIntosh has been handling the program in your adopted state."

"I'd just as soon not go into that," said Mark.

"Very well. I remember a note on your chart by Hal Morton that you like to run. A circular trail winds along the rim of the canyon at its head. The trail's about six miles long and ends up back of the Retreat. Why don't you try it as a part of your therapy program?"

"Is that all?"

"No. This afternoon we'll be moving you to one of the cottages. Two thirds of the men there are doctors, and I'm sure they'll be eager to pick the medical brain of a hotshot from Lakeview."

XXIII

Rockspring Cottage was a rustic building located several hundred yards away from the main headquarters of Canyonhead Retreat on a rocky knoll from beneath which burst a large spring that provided water for the entire establishment. The other cottages all had much the same view of the vast chasm, a part, he was sure, of the therapeutic value of the institution.

At the cottage, Mark was welcomed by a gray-haired man in slacks, a polo shirt, sweater, and leather sandals.

"My name is Sven," he introduced himself, when Mark approached the desk in the large living room of the cottage.

"I'm Mark Har——"

"No last names, please," said Sven. "Most of us don't want to be singled out by the rest for whatever sins we committed or neglected to commit in the past. You're just in time for tonight's meeting of Canyonhead Anonymous, a combination of AA, Al-Anon, and your own particular need to unburden yourself."

"Is that expected the first night?"

"Only when the spirit moves you," Sven assured him. "I'll show you to your quarters, although you're going to find them a bit Spartan for a thousand a week. These buildings used to be officers' quarters for an encampment the Army had here during World War II, probably for something like the Green Berets."

"Do you like the Spartan simplicity and the lack of privacy?" Mark asked.

"I didn't at first, but when you consider that we're all at Canyonhead for the same reason—whether obligatory or voluntarily as the case may be—it seems to make sense for all to be as close as possible so we can help each other."

"That's the second time today I've heard the phrase 'help each other.' Isn't it carrying things a bit far for a group of people who come from different cultures and social backgrounds and never knew each other before to feel that they can actually help each other solve their problems?"

"Three months ago, I would have said the same thing," Sven admitted. "But you'd be surprised how being in the same boat generates a feeling of comradeship and concern for one another. You'll see how it works when you attend the weekly rap session tonight after dinner."

"Is attendance required?"

"No, but you'll be making a mistake not to go. Keeping your troubles bottled up only generates more emotional pressure—"

"You talk like a psychiatrist."

"That's because I am one. We shrinks get disabled even more often than other doctors."

"I'd heard that. Do you have any idea why?"

"I didn't until John Carr showed me what might be the mechanism. I don't have to tell you that the human misery of emotional turmoil is worse than physical pain. Psychiatrists enter the field hoping to cure people of their emotional ills overnight but soon discover that patients tend to hang on to their neuroses. They even coddle their psychoses because they can live in a world where they don't have to bother much about other people. So when psychiatrists discover they can't really cure anybody, unless the patients are willing to put firm hands on their own bootstraps and lift themselves out of the morass of depression and anxiety in which they're drowning, they develop a sense of futility. The next step is to dull our disappointment with whatever crutches are most easily available."

"Like what?"

"The three most available crutches for a doctor who's personal image is getting considerably tarnished in his own mind are women, alcohol, and drugs. Unfortunately, casual affairs are a poor treatment for emotional disturbances. And once you start depending on the other two, the sex drive gets dulled—"

"Or the other alternative's more attractive," Mark commented.

"You'd have trouble convincing a young male of that, but it's true just the same," said Sven, with a smile.

They had been walking through the barracks-like building, carrying Mark's luggage, and now the older man stopped before one of the rooms. Mark thought they looked remarkably like a monk's cell from the Middle Ages, except that the walls, the floors, and the ceilings were made of rough pine lumber instead of stone or bricks, and the partitions were made of what was once called "beaver board."

"Here's your niche," Sven assured him. "The latrine's at the end of the building."

"What's the routine here?"

"Pretty much what you want to make it. Nobody blows a bugle at dawn, but you'll soon discover that it's pleasant to have breakfast about seven-thirty in the morning with your fellow sufferers. The mess hall—or dining room if you object to the military ancestry of the building—is in the center of the quadrangle where the various cottages are located. Fortunately, snow and sleet are rare in this clime and the paths are usually open, though you'll need a raincoat and galoshes at times."

"I like to run a few miles before breakfast."

"There's a special table for us runners where we can be fed after we finish our morning jogs and showers."

"I take it that you're an *aficionado?*"

"I wasn't until I came to Canyonhead, but the view of Peace River Canyon from the running path is something out of this world that nobody should miss early in the morning. It may be hard to locate anything like that in Birmingham, once I leave here, but I'm going to try my damndest to find a route that circles the mountain there and gives me a view of the valley."

"Does that mean you're going back to your old practice?"

"Possibly. Most of my patients have enough emotional troubles of their own to know—and maybe even sympathize with—the doctor in his, so they won't hold having to seek help against me. How about you?"

"My contract with my former employers forbids me to practice in the same area for five years after I severed my connection with them."

"Severed—or be severed?"

"The latter, I'm afraid."

"I thought so," said Sven. "We doctors are a lot of self-righteous bastards who are content to tell ourselves it can't happen to us. Yet, the fact that one in seven actually winds up disabled to the point where he chooses—or is compelled to choose—help proves that we're as vulnerable as anyone. Getting back to your question about the schedule; here in the cottages we practically make our own rules, except that no alcohol or narcotics are allowed."

"I can subscribe to that," said Mark.

"Right now, yes. Are you married?"

"No."

"You're lucky. The rest of us usually have wives and families at home that have to be considered, and sometimes our concern interferes very seriously with our rehabilitation. Take me, for example. Would you say I'm pretty well adjusted to my problem?"

"From where I sit, yes."

"That's where you're wrong. In Birmingham, I was a society psychiatrist, which meant that a lot of women with well-to-do and busy husbands—typical doctors' wives, although the syndrome is not limited to them by any means—constituted most of my clientele. They brought their problems to me and I listened to their stories, clucked sympathetically at the right places, and prescribed tranquilizers or antidepressants—without once realizing what that kind of practice was doing to my own soul. Now that I do realize it, I'm about ready to go back, but not at all sure I want to."

"Did John Carr accomplish that for you?"

"Not John alone, though I'm sure he understood it all. The discussion of your emotional problems with a psychiatrist during a therapy session—even with the built-in secrecy that accompanies it—is quite different from standing up before a jury of your peers and telling what happened without sparing yourself, as we do here."

"Am I supposed to do *that?*"

"Not supposed to, but until you do, you won't really be getting anywhere toward curing yourself—"

"At a thousand a week, I should have the privilege of curing myself?"

"You'll come to learn that the price is really cheap," Sven assured him. "Jesus knew what he was talking about when he said, *'Physician, heal thyself.'* Nor is it surprising that this particular statement was recorded by Luke, himself a physician. What John Carr does at Canyonhead is show us the way to help ourselves; the rest of the job, as you'll discover before long, is up to us. Don't let me bend your ear any longer. Shall I stop by just before six and take you to dinner?"

"I'd like that," said Mark, then added wryly, "right now, I feel a bit like the gladiators of old must have felt before they faced the lions."

"Friends, not lions," Sven corrected him. "I'll see you at a quarter to six."

Mark lay down but couldn't sleep, so at about four he pulled on running shorts and shoes, plus a lightweight jersey against the early winter chill. He had no trouble finding the circular path Sven and John Carr had referred to, but quickly discovered that the six-mile course was considerably more tiring than his usual route along the beach at Gulf City. Parts of it ascended several hundred feet above Canyonhead Retreat itself for an ever-changing view of the chasm far below and the almost toylike appearance of the town of Peace River near the bank of the stream in the depths of the valley.

The last time Mark could remember jogging was nearly two months earlier, when he'd found Alexa swimming in the tidal river that separated the beach at Gulf City from the islands offshore and they'd gone to McDonald's and Riverside Park for breakfast. He hadn't heard from her since they'd said goodbye at Canyonhead about a week earlier but he could imagine her now, slim and lovely, running as effortlessly as a doe along just such a woodland trail.

Deep in reverie and in the beauty of the chasm as he trotted along the trail, Mark found himself losing some of his first flush of apprehension at meeting his confrères that evening. By the time Sven knocked on his door promptly at a quarter to six, he had showered and dressed.

XXIV

Dinner was delicious and not at all as Spartan as the living quarters. The patient population of Canyonhead Retreat appeared to be made up of people of practically all ages and all walks of life. It was after seven and the dishes had been cleared away, when Sven rose and tapped on a glass for attention.

"I don't need to remind you who have been here for some time that at Canyonhead we remain anonymous, except for first names. Furthermore, none of us is obligated to confess his sins—if you want to consider them that. Like Quakers, whenever the spirit moves any of us to speak—not only for the cleansing of his own soul but also for the help of others—each of us is free to speak his piece or remain silent."

A tall man, who appeared to be about forty-five, stood up. "I guess you old-timers are already fed up with listening to me confess my sins," he said. "But since we have new people here from time to time and I have already admitted my errors—from which I hope they can learn something of help to themselves—I don't think it's going to hurt anyone for me to repeat them. Moreover, by admitting my sins once again, I can further cleanse my soul of ever deeper layers of emotional debris.

"I came here to Canyonhead like so many of you," the speaker continued, "when the Disabled Doctors' Committee of my state told me I had to come or get booted out of medicine. Like most of you, too, I considered the committee at first to be a lot of self-righteous bastards. Now that I've been here long enough to be classified as perhaps the oldest resident, I can tell you that you'll soon discover they were, and will be, the best friends you ever had. So now that we've got the hypocrisy behind us, let's get down to the nitty-gritty.

"For three years, before a committee of my peers forced me to admit the truth that unless I got myself straightened out, I'd either wind up one of these days by making a surgical error that would cause someone's death or lay myself open to a serious malpractice suit, I resisted admitting that I was living in a fool's paradise—the sort of paradise, that's familiar to many of you, in which I usually wound up at the end of the day, sometimes even before, with a consuming desire to drink myself into oblivion at the country club bar. More often than not, my wife would have to drive out to the club and bring me home for dinner, drunk as an owl. The rest of the time, since I was a generous contributor to the Police Benevolent Association, the bartender would call a friendly cop who would drive me home. In other words, I was a hopeless alcoholic."

"Not hopeless, Dan," Sven interposed. "When your state committee finally told you to come here for treatment, or else, you didn't fight them—which is much more than a lot of us lacked the good sense not to do."

"I guess something inside me, perhaps my medical conscience, was still functioning," the man called Dan agreed. "If it hadn't been, I'd never have been able to boast of two Mercedes in my garage, like so many of you here today. As for emergencies arising among the patients I'd operated on the day before, I was forced to rely on hospital residents, or some friendly surgeon would come in to take over if the crisis seemed to be too much for the residents to handle.

"Every morning, I'd pump myself full of methylphenidate hydrochloride or amphetamine, so I could stagger to the hospital in order to make rounds. Once there, I could be sure the nurses would protect me, and I'd somehow manage to see the patients I'd operated on the day before. Thanks to the conspiracy of silence among my family, fellow staff members, hospital nurses, and others to protect me, I was able to keep on operating. Sometimes I even had to be fed a horse-sized dose of amphetamine through a straw by one of the nurses in the middle of an operation in order to keep me awake long enough to finish. At other times, I would have to leave the Operating Room and mainline a shot of Demerol into my veins so I could keep going."

"How did you get here?" one of the listeners asked.

"The same way most of you did, by being reported to the Disabled Doctors' Committee."

"Who reported you?"

"My wife—the day she filed for divorce. I was drunk the night I learned what she had done and tried to kill her. Fortunately, while I was chasing her I fell over some furniture and knocked myself out, winding up in the Emergency Room of the hospital and beginning the process that brought me here."

"Are you going back together when you return to practice?" Sven asked.

"If she'll have me," said Dan. "For a while I hated her for exposing me, but when John showed me how she'd probably saved my life—as well as the lives of one or more patients—I saw that she'd done me a favor. And if a lot of you were honest enough to admit it, you'd say the same thing now."

The speaker sat down and the moment Mark had been dreading materialized when Sven stood up and tapped on a water glass for attention.

"We have a new member of our group with us tonight," he announced. "Let me introduce to you, Mark, a brother sufferer." He turned to Mark. "The floor is yours, but you don't have to speak. These rap sessions are always voluntary."

"I think I'll forego the opportunity tonight, then," said Mark. "What happened to me is still too painful for me to say very much about it."

"We hold these sessions every week and you can talk whenever you're ready," Sven assured him. "Unless there's further discussion, we will adjourn."

"I guess I'm a disappointment to you and John Carr and Hal Morton," Mark admitted as he and Sven were walking back to their cottage.

"Not at all," said the psychiatrist. "It was almost a month after John and Hal dried me out before I summoned up enough courage to talk to other people about my own case. When I finally found the courage to speak, though, I felt as if a great burden had been lifted from my mind. It was only then that my real recovery began."

"I'll try to make it next time," Mark promised. "Good night, Sven, and thanks for looking after me."

"Think nothing of it. When you've been here a while, you'll understand that the most important part of our own treatment and rehabilitation is the opportunity to help our fellows."

XXV

Mark was raking the yard in front of the cottage several mornings later—all of the residents had prescribed duties—when John Carr stopped on the way from his own house at the end of the long row of buildings to the central hospital section.

"Good morning," he said. "Are you comfortable in the cottage?"

"Very much. Sven has been very kind."

"Sven's a rare individual," said Carr. "I've offered him a position on the professional staff, and he's considering it."

"He'd be a valuable addition, I'm sure."

"I'm convinced of that, but he had a large practice in Birmingham before he tried to carry the burdens of the world on his shoulders and found it was too much."

"Could he go back and pick up where he left off?"

"If he wanted to; his patients had so much confidence in him that I'm sure he wouldn't lose many. What really brought him down, though, was losing his wife from breast cancer about six months ago. They were very close, and when it happened, Sven just sort of fell apart."

"From what I hear in talking to the others, most of them cracked up when some personal crisis arose."

"Quite often that's true," Carr agreed, "but no one thing actually brings a doctor—or anyone else—to the point of dangerous impairment. It's always a combination of factors."

"One thing does trouble me," Mark confessed. "Even though medicine has always been a highly competitive profession, why the sudden rash of impaired doctors lately?"

"It isn't a sudden rash, just that the number involved is now being discovered. The doctor-patient ratio in the country has increased steadily now to a point where we've already reached the saturation point—or maybe gone beyond it—especially in highly lucrative fields like surgery and psychiatry."

"Beyond what the Disabled Doctors' Committees can handle?"

"I doubt that the programs, even though new ones are being organized in practically every state, can do much more than handle the increase from year to year."

"From what Alexa told me, Canyonhead must have one of the most successful rehabilitation programs in the country."

"Possibly second only to Georgia," Carr conceded. "They, of course, were the pioneers."

"Why don't you enlarge your own facilities, then?"

"I've resisted temptation so far. You see, an important feature of our work is the fact that we're relatively isolated here. The physical surroundings, too, are conducive to letting our patients get far enough from their problems to develop a perspective in looking at them."

"I agree with that, even though I haven't confessed my sins at one of the rap conferences."

"I'd much rather you didn't force yourself into any early unburdening," said Carr. "By all means, wait until it is definitely going to help you—as I'm sure it will."

"Has Alexa told you anything about what's happening in Gulf City? Or at the Clinic?"

"If it's any comfort to you, Dick Barrett hasn't found anyone to take over your work at the Old Town Clinic yet. A considerable shakeup is going on in the State Disabled Doctors' Committee, too. I rather think Dr. Ponder will take over the chairmanship because so many people are dissatisfied with the way Ed McIntosh has been handling, not only your case, but a number of others."

"Maybe I'm getting cured," said Mark wryly. "I can't really wish Ed McIntosh much harm anymore."

"You're getting there," Carr assured him. "Your lack of rancor is one of the signs that indicate your progress."

"That six-mile circle with the canyon in view most of the way is an experience every runner should have," said Mark. "In a way, I suppose it's a form of psychotherapy, though I doubt if you intended it that way."

"I *did* intend it that way, but not too many realize the fact as quickly as you do." The psychiatrist turned to go. "I'd better get about my duties, although I'd much rather stay here and talk to you. Alexa writes that she's coming up in a week or so to see Uncle Homer. Both of us are worried about some circulation difficulties he's having with his right leg."

XXVI

Three weeks after his arrival at Canyonhead, Mark felt sure enough of his own degree of rehabilitation to speak at one of the rap sessions. The daily runs had furnished a period of introspection and self-analysis buttressing him against the occasional bouts of depression and hopelessness that still assailed him when he thought of the future and the wreckage of his own career. The chasm in which the small but potent river had etched its way during millions of years was proof in itself that time could indeed accomplish miracles, whether measured in eons, days, hours, or even in minutes.

Sven opened the rap session after dinner that night as usual and Mark was the first one to rise to speak.

"Most of you already know me by name as Mark," he began. "I grew up in the Piedmont section of North Carolina, and working in the corn and tobacco fields in summer, plus football and basketball in the fall and winter, gave me a physique that paid my way through college on a football scholarship. In medical school, I found, like many of you, that my Phi Beta Kappa Key meant nothing, since practically everybody there also boasted one."

A murmur of laughter and nods of agreement swept over the audience.

"I graduated with honors from medical school and entered the hospital residency system, as many of you have, so I won't go into details. After thirty-six hours on duty you fall into bed, only to be aroused by the alarm clock for rounds almost before you're asleep. Under such circumstances, it is well recognized now that hospital residents and fellows maintain their energy largely with the use of alcohol, amphetamines, and, too often, narcotic drugs which are easily available.

"The *nirvana* furnished by a hundred or two hundred milligrams of Demerol can be very tempting indeed, and it is hardly surprising that so many of us yield to it. Also, the high rate of suicide among hospital residents attest to the drain such a regime puts upon one's emotional system, to say nothing of the physiological mechanisms that sustain it.

"I can't tell you just when my own reliance upon the crutches afforded by chemicals began, although I never resorted to narcotics until after I had entered practice about six months ago. In the second year of my fellowship in microsurgery, the head of the department, who was my teacher, was felled by carcinoma of the prostate. As a result, most of the work done in that particular department of the surgical service during the rest of the year fell upon my shoulders. This was work I was eager to assume in order to prove myself to my fellow members of the house staff, the faculty, and even more important, to myself.

"In the course of the final six months, I must have done two hundred delicate microsurgical operations, but by the time I finished my fellowship, I was practically living on alcohol and amphetamines—uppers and downers—the typical program of a young doctor finishing a grueling period in a fellowship or residency.

"It is perhaps understandable and I don't know that I should make any particular apology for the near-burnout state in which I found myself in July of this year. I must confess, however, that, like many of you, I didn't realize the condition I was in when I undertook an important and very lucrative staff position with a clinic of which many of you already know, but which I will not name.

"The rest of my own story is really not particularly different from yours, except that I was mugged and sustained a small extradural hematoma resulting in a postconcussion syndrome characterized by headaches. These I relieved with injections of Demerol, in a steadily increasing dosage as time passed until I was taking four hundred milligrams a day and sometimes more.

"What happened after I reached the point of dependence on narcotics occurred so rapidly that I hardly realized it was taking place," Mark continued. "First, my source of narcotics dried up very suddenly when the federal authorities arrested the man who was supplying me. Second, someone I thought I had helped conquer his own difficulties used what he knew about me to attack me because of my own failings. The results in rapid succession were: one, an appearance before the Disabled Doctors' Committee in my home state; and two, the decision of the committee to recommend—no, I must say, demand, as was their right—that I come to Canyonhead for treatment."

"And since you've been here?" Sven asked.

"What happened here is so logical, so simple, and so familiar to all of you that I have difficulty analyzing how it all came about. At Canyonhead I found a release from tension and from the urge to drive my body and my mind beyond its capabilities. Plus, I might add, an ability to detach myself from myself as a person mired in a morass of problems that seemed insoluble; a detachment, I must say, that arose through the knowledge that all of us here are in much the same boat, largely a product of our own failure to realize what was happening within our bodies and our own minds. Needless to say, my experience at Canyonhead has meant more to me than anything else that has happened in my life."

Back in his quarters in the cottage after the painful catharsis, Mark slept like a baby and awakened to hear the birds singing in the trees outside. When he looked down the gorge, none of the fog which so often hung over the river itself was visible. Instead, the tiny stream, so powerful through the ages, was flowing peacefully in its bed along the winding course. Well below the elevation upon which Canyonhead stood, the picturesque town of Peace River was clearly visible, too.

Book Four

Peace River

I

On Thursday evening, Mark was surprised to receive a long-distance call from Alexa McGillivray. "I'm flying up to Gadsden tomorrow afternoon and renting a car," she told him. "It's only about thirty-five miles to Canyonhead from there. Could you go with me down to the town of Peace River that evening?"

"Sure. What's up?"

"I'm worried about Uncle Homer. I think he's in danger of losing his leg because of decreased arterial supply."

"That could be serious. I'll do anything I can."

"My plane gets to Gadsden at four-thirty and I should be at Canyonhead by six. It's only a half hour's drive down to Peace River, and we can have a late dinner with Uncle Homer and Aunt Sehoy. I might as well tell you now that I want to sort of sneak up on him with another opinion about the artery in his leg."

"Sounds fine to me. I'll be waiting."

After Alexa rang off, Mark telephoned John Carr's office on the intramural line. "Alexa's flying up to Gadsden tomorrow afternoon and renting a car," he said. "She wants me to see Dr. Homer McGillivray."

"I'm glad she's coming and that Uncle Homer can be examined by an expert," said Carr. "One of the top vascular surgeons in Birmingham told him some time ago that his right popliteal artery is slowly closing, but Uncle Homer is as stubborn as a mule. Refuses to have that section of the artery replaced until he's got a doctor to take his place in Peace River. Alexa is the only one in the family who can make him listen; with your help, maybe she can convince him that he can't afford to wait."

"She wants me to have dinner with her uncle and his wife down in the valley," said Mark. "Do I need a pass or anything like that to go down there with her?"

"I'll leave an order at the gate that you're free to go and come as you choose."

Alexa arrived at five-thirty looking weary and depressed, the first time Mark remembered seeing her other than calm and serene in the months he had known her. Nevertheless, the surge of pleasure he felt at seeing her again was greater than any he'd experienced since coming to Canyonhead Retreat.

"You look bushed," he said, as he got in the car. "Hard trip?"

"Not particularly, but things in Gulf City are pretty hectic. Dr. Barrett has been in a pet most of the time lately."

"Couldn't happen to a nicer guy. What's bugging him?"

"*You!* Or rather your not being there. The Old Town Clinic's fallen apart since you left, and Dr. Barrett had to send a wealthy patient with an arteriovenous aneurysm you could have handled easily to Birmingham."

"Losing a professional fee of at least five grand," Mark commented.

"On top of that, Dr. Harkness lit into Jerry Thorpe at the first staff meeting after you left for picking the lock to your condominium and turning over the evidence he found there to Dr. McIntosh."

"I don't resent what Jerry did anymore," Mark told her as she skillfully negotiated the winding road leading from the crest of the chasm at Canyonhead to the valley below, where the town of Peace River was located. "If I'd gone on shooting Demerol much longer, I'd've been a confirmed addict and it would have been a lot harder to get off the stuff than it has been."

"Then you *are* off it?"

"Completely."

"You'd never know to see you now that you were ever on it."

"The credit goes to John Carr and Canyonhead."

"If Dr. Barrett could see you, I'm sure he would take you back."

"It's too late for that. If the Clinic had merely given me a leave of absence, the way cases like mine are supposed to be handled under the Disabled Doctors' Committee rulings, it might have been possible. But not anymore."

"May I ask why?"

"I'm not sure I quite understand why myself," Mark admitted. "John thinks my breakdown—to be charitable and call it that—was due to two factors: one was overwork before I came to Gulf City; the other was a rebellion of my professional conscience against the moneygrubbing that goes with a society practice like that of the Barrett Clinic."

"Do you have any idea what you're going to do after you leave Canyonhead?"

"Not yet."

"How about the HMO in North Carolina?"

"A surgeon from the University of North Carolina Medical School took the job—when it comes alive again, which may be never."

"Something else is bound to come along," she said confidently.

"By the way, how is Mrs. Thomas doing?"

"Fine. I saw her in the Clinic last week."

"I suppose she still thinks Dr. Barrett saved her life?"

"I'm afraid so." She gave him a probing look. "Does that still make you angry?"

"Not anymore. That six-mile circular path I've been running around the head of the chasm and across the falls at Canyonhead has a strange effect on me. In fact, I'm not sure it isn't the most important part of the treatment at Canyonhead."

"I've started jogging, now that the weather is too cool for swimming," she told him. "I love it, so I'll probably keep it up and maybe not even start swimming again next spring."

The car topped a rise near the canyon floor and Mark saw the town of Peace River spread out below them. Though it was close to the riverbank, the elevation was high enough to avoid any danger of flooding. Lights were already on along the streets and in most of the houses, giving the village an almost storybook character. Actually, the wide tree-shaded streets, the large lots, and the white-framed houses could have been lifted bodily from the New England countryside—along with the general air of peace that seemed to pervade the town.

"I never realized, when I looked down at Peace River from Canyonhead, how much it's like a New England village set down here in the Deep South," Mark exclaimed.

"That's because it originally *was* a New England village back in the eighteen-seventies and -eighties," said Alexa.

"How did that happen?"

"After the Civil War, a group of smart Yankees migrated here from the North and bought up thousands of acres of fine timberland from freed Negroes who had homesteaded it during the Reconstruction. They also dammed the river about ten miles south of here at Fort Jackson to operate a sawmill.

"You'd hardly believe it now but the Peace River valley experienced quite a boom for twenty years or so after eighteen-seventy. Eventually, though, the forests were cut over and a hurricane came through, flooding the valley and damaging many of the homes, when the dam was broken and the sawmill was wrecked. By that time there wasn't much timber left anyway, so most of the New England owners sold out to Creek and Choctaw Indians who'd come back from Oklahoma. The Indians—my kinspeople—renovated the houses in Peace River and settled down here."

"The town has a lot of charm, but what about industry?"

"There's plenty of that, farther down the valley at Fort Jackson near where the dam was. One of the reasons why so many of my people love Peace River is because they can live here without bumping into each other. They grow a lot of their food in gardens on these large lots and still make whatever money they need by driving five days a week to the industrial plants at Fort Jackson."

"With no crowding, no crime, and no pollution—"

"Plus room to stretch; something that appeals to Indian blood."

"Do you expect to come back here to retire?"

"Maybe *before* I'm that old," she said. "The town fathers of both Peace River and Fort Jackson have been trying to get a Hill-Burton grant from the federal government to build a new hospital about halfway between the two towns. There's a cottage hospital like Uncle Homer's at Fort Jackson, and by combining that one with his, they could take care of patients from a considerable area." She gave him a quick, appraising glance. "Actually, the whole project is somewhat similar to that regional one in the sandhills of North Carolina you told me about."

"Wouldn't a project like that put your uncle out of business?"

"Nothing could suit Uncle Homer better; actually, he's one of the leaders in the movement to build the new hospital. When it's ready, a year or so from now—if they get the grant—he'll be happy to retire and spend most of his time fishing. Peace River and the streams that flow into it are full of trout."

"Sounds like paradise."

"If Uncle Homer has two legs to stand on then," she said soberly as she pulled the car to a stop before a white frame house standing about three hundred feet from a considerably larger building.

"That's Uncle Homer's hospital," she explained. "He and Aunt Sehoy live in the cottage. They're expecting us."

Dr. Homer McGillivray was a stocky man in his sixties with craggy features and a ready smile.

"I've been looking forward to meeting you, Dr. Harrison," he said. "Alexa has told me a lot about you."

"The good things, I hope," said Mark. "The rest I'd just as soon forget."

"Then we will," said Alexa. "This is Aunt Sehoy."

Sehoy McGillivray was a small woman whose wrinkled face still showed signs of considerable beauty. Supper—as it was called here in the Deep South—was waiting in the oven: fried chicken, string beans canned from the McGillivray garden, mashed potatoes with gravy, and hot biscuits.

"Alexa has told me about the work you do in microsurgery, Dr. Harrison," said McGillivray as he and Mark were relaxing in the living room of the cottage after the meal while Alexa helped her aunt with the dishes. "It must give you a tremendous satisfaction to be able to connect vessels no larger than matchsticks and see blood flow through them again to bring life to endangered organs."

"It was, when I could do it," said Mark. "I'm a patient of John Carr's now because I came to rely on two frail crutches—alcohol and drugs."

"In my day, there were far more laudanum-drinking doctors than we cared to admit, and all too often they caused the deaths of their patients," said the old doctor. "Nowadays, the system of locating and treating disabled doctors early and returning them to practice is far better."

"John Carr is doing fine work. I certainly owe him a lot."

"We're proud of John. He could have been a great success as a teacher at Harvard, but he chose to come back to the homeland of his people instead."

"You Creeks have a proud heritage," Mark told him. "Alexa has told me something about it."

"What was I telling you?" Alexa asked from the dining room, where she was putting away the silver.

"We were talking about Creek history," Mark told her.

"I practically bent Mark's ear the first time we met, Uncle Homer," she said, "boasting about how I'm a princess in what's left of the Creek Nation."

"My father graduated from the Carlisle Indian School the federal government maintained in Pennsylvania," said Homer McGillivray.

"As a poor atonement for the sins of Andrew Jackson in transporting the Southern Indians to Oklahoma around eighteen thirty-nine," Alexa interposed hotly.

"Now, Alexa," her uncle admonished mildly. "Old Andy may have even done our people a favor in letting them escape being massacred by land-hungry Georgians. Don't be too hard on him."

"That's enough genealogy for tonight," Alexa told him firmly. "I brought Dr. Harrison down here to check the circulation in your legs, so don't give me any more backtalk about not having any trouble with them. The nurses at the hospital tell me you often have to stop while making rounds because of cramps in your right leg."

"That's only because I've been loafing lately and not getting enough exercise," McGillivray protested.

"No excuses," she insisted. "Dr. Harrison's an expert, and I want his opinion tonight."

"All right," said McGillivray. "You'd worm it out of me anyway, so I might as well tell you the whole story. I've known the arterial circulation in my right leg has slowly been decreasing for several years but put it down to old age and too much cholesterol buildup inside my arteries."

"You're not that old," said Alexa. "And Aunt Sehoy never has fed you much saturated fat. Indians didn't eat that kind of diet anyway."

"When I was in Birmingham in November for the meeting of the Southern Medical Association," the old doctor told Mark, "I stopped by the Peripheral Vascular Clinic at the medical school there—"

"Incidentally, it's one of the best in the country," Mark interposed.

"Been sending patients to them for years," said McGillivray, "but I hesitated to go this time because I didn't want them threading a catheter down through my femoral artery. Instead, they used what they called a Doppler velocity meter with ultrasound in a test I think was called the Echo Flow System. I guess you know all about that, Dr. Harrison."

"I've used the Echo Flow tests at least a thousand times," said Mark. "They depend on the Doppler principle that the frequency of sound reflected from an object in motion varies with the speed of the object. A good example of that is the lonesome sound a train used to make when it passed near our farm back in Carolina. From what you told me, sir, I would guess that they found a narrowing of the popliteal artery behind the knee."

"Go to the head of the class," said McGillivray.

"Removing that section and replacing it with something like a Dacron tube isn't difficult or painful," Mark told him. "I'm surprised that they didn't want to do it in Birmingham while you were there."

"They're ready when I am," said McGillivray. "The trouble is I'll be out of action for maybe a month, and I can't leave—"

"You mean *won't* leave," said Alexa.

"Either way. I'm not going to leave my patients here without a doctor in the middle of the winter when so many of them get sick. Unless I find somebody to take over my practice for the time I'll be gone, I'll just have to limp around as best I can."

"Any prospects?" Mark asked, but McGillivray shook his head.

"None so far, but I'm looking all the time. Anyway, I can always have the operation in the spring when there's less sickness."

"And maybe wind up on crutches or in a wheelchair with no right leg, if that narrowed artery gets blocked some night," said Alexa.

"I told you, I'll have the operation in the spring," said McGillivray a little irritatedly. "Meanwhile, I'll try to get someone to take over for a *locum tenens.*"

"That's a promise," she insisted. "As soon as I get back to Gulf City, I'll try to find an FMG who's looking for a place. If the Old Town Clinic folds—the way things look like it might—Dr. Montez might be looking for a position."

"Montez is very good," said Mark. "Bringing him to Peace River could be the answer to Dr. McGillivray's problems."

Alexa glanced at her watch. "It's after ten, so we'd better be getting back up to Canyonhead. John and Elsa invited me to stay with them tonight, but I'll come by tomorrow before I start back to Gadsden to catch the plane and see how things are with you," she told her uncle.

"Are you going back to Gulf City so soon?" Mark asked. "I was hoping we could have a picnic tomorrow afternoon somewhere up near the falls."

"Sounds wonderful," she said. "My return flight doesn't leave Gadsden until late tomorrow afternoon."

In the car driving up the curving road to the Retreat on the crest of the chasm, Alexa asked, "How much danger is there that Uncle Homer might suddenly have a block of that popliteal artery?"

"It could happen anytime—or he could go on for months, perhaps a year," said Mark. "I couldn't even make an educated guess without giving him a full peripheral vascular examination, and the tools for that are nowhere around here."

"What time do you run in the mornings?" she asked.

"About seven. Why don't you join me?"

"I would like to see the Canyonhead trail and the falls again," she admitted.

"They're well worth the effort," he told her. "I usually wear shorts and a light Windbreaker. Can I lend you anything?"

"I came prepared," she assured him. "Good night."

II

Alexa came out the front door of John Carr's cottage exactly at seven. In brief white running shorts and a snug white sweater, she was fully as beautiful as when he'd seen her that first evening in a white sheath of an evening gown at the Gulf City Yacht Club. Her long black hair was plaited and wrapped around her head the way she wore it beneath a surgical operating helmet. Her eyes were bright and her cheeks flushed from the brisk morning air, giving her an entirely new appearance from the somewhat dejected one he'd noted when she'd arrived last night. John Carr came out behind her and stood leaning against the porch railing, holding a cup of coffee in one hand and a pipe in the other.

"You two could pose for one of those *National Geographic* paintings of our Creek ancestors," said the psychiatrist. "Are you sure you don't have some Indian blood in you, Mark?"

"I'm afraid not. Can I talk to you about something after breakfast, John?"

"Sure. Why don't we all have breakfast together in the staff dining room after you finish your run? Elsa will be happy to get out of having to fix it."

Mark glanced at Alexa who nodded agreement. "That would be fine," he said. "We'll see you in maybe an hour and a quarter."

"I'll let you set the pace," he told Alexa as they started off along the trail in an easy run. "But if I know you, I'll be hard put to keep up."

When the way began to ascend toward the crest of rock at the head of the chasm, where Peace River Falls burst through a narrow gate of stone to start its downward plunge, Alexa began to slow down.

"I'm not used to climbs," she confessed a little breathlessly. "On the beach, it's all level."

"The view from the head of the gorge is beyond description. I usually stop there to rest for at least a few minutes."

When they came out on the broad crest of the cliff beside the river, where they could watch it begin a series of cascades to the new channel far below them, Alexa cried out with pleasure.

"No wonder John loves it so much up here that he bought the old buildings of an army camp and established Canyonhead Retreat," she said. "It's the most beautiful sight I've ever seen."

"You'll get no argument on that from me." Mark spread the Windbreaker he'd been carrying on an outthrust of rock beside the stream. From that vantage point, they could watch the falls and see the plumes of spray rising when the tumbling stream struck outcroppings on the way down the cliff that formed the head of the chasm. "Some days, when the humidity is right, a cloud seems to swell upward from the gorge."

"I remember now that the Upper Creeks called this area the Cauldron of Fire," said Alexa. "They thought steam from underground fires escaped through cracks in the face of the cliff."

"I can understand their mistake. Since I came to Canyonhead, I've grown to love this spot. Both John and I think the surroundings have done more to cure me than his psychotherapy—plus, of course, the rap sessions where the patients confess their sins to each other."

"Have you confessed yours yet?"

"A few nights before you came. Sven had told me I'd feel a burden lifted from my soul when I did, but I could hardly believe it—until it happened."

"Then you must be cured."

"Not quite. I still have to prove I can resume surgery without needing the crutch of alcohol, Demerol, or some other narcotic to support me."

"When does John think you'll be able to do that?" She shivered a moment as a light breeze whipped some of the vapor from the falls against their bodies.

"You were hot from running and that vapor is cool, even if it does look like steam," Mark said quickly. "We'd better go back."

"No, please; it's been such a long time since I've been as content as I am now. Just put your arm around my shoulders and I'll be all right with your warmth."

It was pleasant to obey, especially when she leaned close to him and he felt the warmth of her body and the softness of her breast against his shoulder and arm.

"That better?" he asked.

"Much better. You didn't tell me how you plan to complete your cure by proving you can operate on serious cases without a crutch—as you call it."

"I had no idea how—until we went down to Peace River last night," he admitted. "After we came back, I lay awake for about an hour while I figured out the solution. If John will let me and your uncle will have me, I'd like very much to drive down to the hospital every morning and do what I can to help Dr. McGillivray in his work there."

"If Uncle Homer would want you!" she exclaimed, her eyes suddenly bright. "It's his chance to keep the hospital running until the new regional center can be finished. Oh, Mark!" She turned suddenly and her face was only inches from his own. "I could kiss you for offering to help."

"That's the best—" he started to say but her lips had already touched his and, when his arm tightened about her shoulder, they softened under the sudden demanding pressure of his own.

What had started out as a casual kiss suddenly turned into a tiny cauldron of passion. And when her right arm went around his neck, their bodies strained against each other in a fervent embrace that startled both of them with its intensity. His hands were moving instinctively to the hem of the white sweater, rolling the fabric up to expose the lovely breasts it was hiding, when she pushed him away.

"None of that!" she exclaimed breathlessly, but there was no anger in her tone, only a sense of wonder. "What happened?"

"I guess we both got carried away," he admitted a little sheepishly, still astounded by the depth of feeling the impetuous embrace had loosened in both of them. "Do you forgive me?"

"There's nothing to forgive. Creek maidens were reported in the old days to be forward when it came to passion, but I never before knew just how forward they could be." She stood up and started brushing off some leaves the upward swell of air from the chasm below had deposited on her shorts and sweater. "What will you think of me?"

"That you're very desirable, as well as lovely. I wonder how I ever failed to realize just how desirable you really are."

"I guess because almost the only times you ever saw me out of uniform were at the Club and when we had breakfast at McDonald's," she said as they started running down the path from the crest. "That first night you were so infatuated with Claire you couldn't have seen anyone else." Then she changed the subject. "How soon can you start helping Uncle Homer?"

"Monday, if John Carr approves. Of course, I'll still have to be carried on John's records as an in-patient in order to fulfill the order of the Disabled Doctors' Committee. My license will still be suspended for a few more months, too, so I'll have to work on your uncle's staff in the capacity of an assistant physician or something similar."

"Uncle Homer won't care, and it will be a great comfort to Aunt Sehoy and me to know you'll be there to take the load off him and also to watch and see that he doesn't get into trouble."

"If that happens, it might be fast," he warned. "Can you send me a high-powered loupe, some Dacron tubes, and sutures in case I should need them?"

"The first thing Monday morning," she promised. "But would a loupe give you the magnification of a surgical microscope?"

"The popliteal artery in a human is roughly the size of a pencil," he told her. "The standard surgical binocular loupe gives two and a half times magnification at ten inches and works perfectly well in suturing vessels even smaller than the popliteal."

Back at Canyonhead they showered, dressed, and joined John Carr at his private table in the staff dining room, where he was reading some typed sheets that were spread out on the table before him.

"Sorry we're late, John," said Alexa as she put down her tray across the table from him. "The falls were so beautiful this morning that I made Mark let me stay longer than we should have, admiring them."

"Anybody as radiant as you are has to be forgiven," said Carr, adding as Mark approached the other side of the table bearing his own loaded tray, "how can you two eat a breakfast like that?"

"Running makes you ravenous," Mark told him. "You should

take it up, John. Sven runs my legs off whenever we go out together, and he's a lot older than either of us."

"Sven's a superman," said the psychiatrist. "By the way, I'm in the process of sending the D-D Committee a report on your first month of rehabilitation. If they take my recommendations, you can start doing surgery again anytime."

"Under the eyes of a monitor?"

"That's the required setup, but it's sometimes hard to manage."

"I may have an even better answer," said Mark. "Dr. McGillivray needs help badly because of that narrowed popliteal artery he has, and I still need the support of you, Sven, and the others here at the cottage, with the rap sessions. I can easily drive down to Peace River every day to help your uncle, though, and still get back here in the evenings."

"Sounds good to me," said Carr. "When do you want to start?"

"Monday—if you approve."

"Fine. I'll include in my report to the Disabled Doctors' Committee for your state that you are now working with Dr. Homer McGillivray, who will act as the monitor they require."

"That will do, for the time being, at least," Mark agreed. "I still haven't decided what I want to do in the future except that, if you had a surgical department here, I'd certainly be looking for that."

Carr laughed. "I have enough trouble with emotional illnesses without taking on those caused by the scalpel. Anyway, you're going to find enough opportunity to use your surgical skills with Uncle Homer."

"Only when I'm able to handle a scalpel safely. I still get the shakes at the idea of what might happen if my disability should hit me in the middle of a really serious operation."

"You'll come through with flying colors," John Carr assured him.

"I can almost believe you," said Mark. "A month ago, I couldn't even see the sun shining through a crack in the wall of despair that hemmed me in. Yet now I feel as though Monday morning will be the start of a new period in my life. And I owe it all to you two."

"For the most part, you can thank the fact that here at

Canyonhead you've had a chance to back off and take a look at your life—as it was and as it can be," John Carr told him.

"Miss McGillivray," the cashier of the dining room called to Alexa. "There's a phone call for you at the front desk."

"I'll be back in a few minutes," Alexa promised. "It may be something about my flight back to Gulf City this afternoon."

She was gone a full fifteen minutes but when she returned she looked happy.

"That was Uncle Homer's chief nurse, Mrs. Allen," she said. "She's been waiting for a vacancy in the hospital at Birmingham to have a triple bypass, and they just notified her that they have a bed. She wanted to know if I could take over for her in the hospital at Peace River for a few weeks."

"Can you?" Mark asked.

"I called Gulf City and told Dr. Barrett I *have* to. I'll fly down this afternoon and drive back as soon as I can get some uniforms and extra clothing. I should be back here in two or three days at most."

"Don't forget those Dacron tubes and the loupe I mentioned," said Mark. "Dr. McGillivray can go to Birmingham as soon as he breaks me in at the hospital, but I want them ready anyway."

"I'll bring them myself," she promised.

III

During the next two weeks, Mark was happier than he remembered being since leaving Lakeview. Mornings, he rose at seven for breakfast and then drove down the winding road leading to Peace River valley. There Alexa, who had returned from Gulf City on Wednesday, seemed to be as happy with her work in the small hospital as she had been at Gulfside. As the old doctor had told Mark, because of the difficulties with his right leg, he'd been forced to give up practically all elective surgery at the hospital, but Mark did not undertake to expand this part of Dr. McGillivray's practice immediately.

There were, however, emergencies, and these he had to cope with. A youngster playing shortstop broke his arm when he collided with the second baseman while catching a pop fly. The inevitable case of colic in a fat baby made him remember some of the pediatric lessons he'd learned years and years ago. And a young mother who chose to have her baby, while Dr. McGillivray was at Fort Jackson one afternoon, got into trouble, facing him suddenly with the use of an instrument he hadn't had in his hands for years.

At least seven years had elapsed since Mark had performed the almost plebian tasks assigned to medical school students and first-year residents of obstetrics and gynecology, that of delivering babies in the slum tenements surrounding the hospital in Baltimore. But when the first cry of protest against being plucked from the ultimate haven of its mother's uterus into an alien world came, Mark was as thrilled as he remembered being by his first successful operation in microsurgery.

"Uncle Homer couldn't have put on forceps more expertly than you did just now," Alexa told him as they were having a late lunch in the small hospital dining room following the successful delivery.

"The last time I put on a pair of forceps was in a slum tenement in Baltimore when I was the extern on the OB service for six months," Mark told her. "If the director of the service had even suspected that the patient would get into trouble, he would never have signed for her to be delivered at home."

"I had very much the same sensation the first time I was first assistant at a major operation," she said. "The feeling that I was adding something to the procedure gave me a sense of purpose when I chose to work for the Barrett Clinic at a fantastic salary instead of staying on at Duke and teaching."

"You don't need to worry about purpose," he told her. "You're something special—very special to a lot of people, and particularly to me."

"Come off it!" Her voice was suddenly husky with emotion. "Whenever I start boasting about being a descendant of Alexander McGillivray, John Carr reminds me that I'm still 'the poor Indian,' and that my being able to do what I do now was only because the federal government happened to feel a sense of guilt over what Andrew Jackson did to the Southern Indians in the eighteen-thirties and tried to make up for it in the form of scholarships."

"That's a pragmatic view and a justifiable one, considering what the government did to your people."

"It still doesn't give me much of a feeling of dedication."

"That's where you're wrong. You're a legitimate—and also a very lovely—descendant of one of the great men of your nation. And, incidentally, I'm going to ask you to marry me one of these days."

"When will that be?" Alexa asked softly.

"When I can pick up a scalpel and know I'm competent to use it without needing the backup of a hypodermic needle before the operation."

IV

A major reward for working in Peace River with Dr. Homer McGillivray, Mark quickly discovered, came from the daily contact with the people of the town. Through attending to their minor illnesses, he came to know many of them well and was surprised again and again by their calm approach to the conflicts of day-to-day living.

Because so many of the men worked in the mills about ten miles downstream at Fort Jackson, Homer McGillivray had adopted the custom of opening his office for two hours on Tuesday and Thursday evenings to accommodate those who worked during the day. Alexa helped with the nightly clinics, and afterward Mark would often sit with her, Dr. McGillivray, and his wife over coffee and cake in the old doctor's bungalow for an hour of talk.

These were very pleasant relaxed hours at a time when Mark forgot any worries about what he would do when his sixteen-week stay at Canyonhead Retreat was finished. As the weeks passed, he found working in the valley so pleasant that he would have considered continuing it indefinitely, as Dr. McGillivray offered, had it not involved giving up most of the work for which he had spent so many special years of training.

Like so many Southern towns, Peace River shut down at noon on Wednesdays. The hospital was closed for all except extreme emergencies, and even the drugstores were not open.

"Got any plans for this afternoon?" Alexa asked as they were having a cup of coffee before starting office hours on the morning of the second Wednesday of his daily visits to Peace River.

"I was sort of hoping you'd be able to drive down to Fort Jackson with me and let me get a chance to see some more of the country."

"I'd love it."

"We could have dinner somewhere down there—"

"Do you like to roast wieners?"

"Of course. Who doesn't?"

"Why don't I take some? There's a lovely spot downriver, the place where Uncle Homer and Dr. Feldon hope the regional hospital will be built. We could build a fire and roast wieners. I'll pick up some slaw and potato salad, too, and with the fire, it might be very pleasant indeed."

As they were leaving the hospital dining room after lunch, Alexa picked up a picnic basket prepared by the staff. She was wearing woolen slacks and a sweater, and for the first time since he'd come to the hospital, she'd let her hair down to fall in lustrous dark masses almost to her waist. She was using a hammered silver barrette to hold it back from her face and he recognized it as the same she had worn the first time he'd seen her at the Gulf City Yacht Club dance.

"There's a spring I want you to see," she told him as they went out to the car. "Or at least I'd like to show you where it was before the rock slide covered it."

"You're the guide. Everything about Peace River fascinates me."

The spring had obviously burst from a cliff at the head of a steep-sided ravine a short distance away from the highway. Although the spot was almost within the town limits, only a pile of rubble, which had obviously fallen from the face of the cliff sometime before, now covered the area. And that was permeated by evergreen shrubs which had picked their way among the boulders. As they climbed over the rocks at the face of the cliff from which the stones had fallen, Mark saw a trickle of water creeping through between some of the boulders to dribble down the face of the cliff. And when he wet a finger and touched it to his tongue, the mineral taste was very pronounced.

"Has anyone ever noticed this trickle of water from the rocks before?" he asked Alexa.

"Uncle Homer did years ago. He owns the land where the spring was located."

"This mineral taste could come from lithium."

"It does come from lithium, along with a number of other things. Uncle Homer sent some of it away and had it analyzed years ago."

"Then it might be possible to blast open the face of the cliff and start the old spring flowing again." Mark felt a sudden rising sense of excitement. "Did your uncle consider doing that?"

"Yes. He and John Carr discussed the possibility at great length."

"Is there enough lithium in the water to make it valuable as a spa?"

"John says it is, along with a high concentration of minerals like those found in the famous springs of West Virginia and many of the spas in Europe."

"Considering what's known now about the value of lithium in the treatment of mental illness, a spring like this could be tremendously valuable. Your uncle and a lot of other people could make a fortune."

"Can you imagine Peace River with a great hotel, golf, and tennis courts, and all the rest of what goes with a famous resort?" she asked.

"Why not? It would be progress."

"Fort Jackson has progress; Peace River has charm. The people are contented and everyone who wants to work is employed. Even you found peace and happiness here, in spite of all your troubles. What else does Peace River need or want?"

"Money. Everybody wants money."

"You were making sixty-five thousand a year with the Barrett Clinic. What good did it do you?"

"But—"

"Lithium chloride is widely used now in carefully measured doses for treating some forms of mental illness. John and Uncle Homer decided that water containing a high concentration of lithium, such as comes from this spring, shouldn't be made available, even though it could turn Peace River into a spa and make a lot of money for everybody. Besides, this area is already a panacea for emotional sufferers. Look what being here for less than two months has done for you."

"Why do you always have to be so infernally right on everything?" Mark asked in a tone of mock despair.

"I'm not. The first time I saw you, I said to myself: 'There goes a great surgeon—and the man I'm going to marry.' "

He gave her a startled look. "What changed your mind? Claire?"

"No. I realized from the start that you and Claire would never make it to the altar and that she was something you had to get over—like an attack of shingles."

"What else, then? I'm still a surgeon."

"A surgeon who's afraid to use his scalpel where it could do the most good—in major surgery."

"Suppose I find my surgical skills once again. Would you still marry me?"

She smiled. "Is this a proposal?"

"A conditional one, I suppose. I didn't realize how much I want you until that day on the Loop Trail at Canyonhead when you kissed me. Stay on at Peace River and I'll do everything I can to regain my surgical skills—if you'll marry me."

"I fell in love with the man I saw coming across the dance floor at the Yacht Club that first night, but you're only half a man without the skill to operate successfully. The day you do a major surgical operation without a shot of Demerol to fortify yourself—I'll come if you want me, wherever you are and wherever I am. But not before."

"You drive a hard bargain."

"So did my several-times Great-Grandfather McGillivray when he was King of the Creeks," she said, with a smile. "It goes with the territory."

"If I'm ever going to claim that territory, I need to start building up my strength. Where do we cook the wieners?"

"We'll picnic where the new hospital will be built," she promised. "It's only about five miles downriver and almost as beautiful as Canyonhead and Peace River itself."

She was right, Mark decided when he saw the spot. A fairly high knoll, it was located at a bend of the river that allowed the valley to be seen almost as far north as the town of Peace River and south to Fort Jackson.

"Has the land for the hospital already been purchased?" he asked as they were gathering wood for the fire.

"Uncle Homer and Dr. Feldon in Fort Jackson founded a nonprofit corporation a few years ago and bought fifty acres, including the high land here. They paid for it out of their own pockets, but since then a lot of contributions have come in—"

"Have they chosen a name?"

"Peace River Valley Clinic. The doctors will be employees of the corporation and draw salaries."

"That's an HMO, very much like the one I was thinking of joining in the sandhills of North Carolina."

"I thought the idea would appeal to you," she said. "They've already got a Certificate of Need from the proper authorities, and the owners of a dozen factories in Fort Jackson have agreed to collect the health insurance premiums from their employees and pay them into the corporation, once it gets going. That way the clinic can not only get a Hill-Burton grant from the government to build the hospital but also a subsidy for starting up. The Peace River Valley Clinic will be a brand-new structure with all modern equipment."

Mark gave her a probing look. "You talk like you plan to be a part of it."

"I've already agreed to be the chief nurse, once the whole operation gets into gear."

"No wonder you're so enthusiastic."

"Wouldn't you be?" she asked, handing him a steaming frankfurter on a spit made from an unbent coat hanger.

"It sounds like what I've been wanting since before I entered medical school, but my ever being a part of such a scheme depends on my being able to pull myself up by my bootstraps, particularly after that promise you just made me."

"Here's a small sample of your reward." She leaned over to kiss him and this time there was nothing perfunctory about it. When they broke, both of them were breathing quickly and Alexa's eyes were bright, her cheeks rich with color.

"Wow!" Mark said, when she pushed him away. "If that's a sample, I can't wait for the main course."

"Nevertheless, you will," she said firmly as she speared another wiener and held it over the coals. "Uncle Homer and I had a long talk about you last night. You're settling so well into the work here at the hospital that he has agreed to go with me to Birmingham, when I leave in about another week for Gulf City, so he can have that obstructed artery replaced."

"When he comes back, he won't need me anymore, so it looks like I'll have to start looking for something to do."

"We'll look together," she said. "After all, our whole future depends on it."

V

Mark had about decided to leave Canyonhead and Peace River when Homer McGillivray was able to return to work after the operation in Birmingham and the rest of the period of rehabilitation required for him to regain his license was completed. Then suddenly, his whole outlook changed when, on Thursday of that week, Homer McGillivray said, "Dr. Feldon from Fort Jackson will be the speaker at the Lion's Club meeting tomorrow night, Mark; he's going to talk about the new hospital we're planning to build. I'd like you to come as my guest if you don't need to get back to Canyonhead early Friday evening."

"I'd only watch 'Wall Street Week' on TV. And when I'm paying John Carr a thousand a week, I don't have anything to invest."

"You will, in time," McGillivray assured him. "I've been watching you since you came to help me, and you're a born surgeon—"

"Who's lost the power to operate."

"Every surgeon loses confidence occasionally, but it's like being thrown from a horse. If you don't get back in the saddle soon, you'll never ride again. If you do, though, things work themselves out and, right now, you're doing everything here except major surgery."

On Friday night at the Lion's Club meeting, Mark found that he knew many of the members from his work at the hospital during the past several weeks. It was the usual civic club crowd, a little more boisterous than Rotary but with the same format of singing, announcements, roast beef with mashed potatoes and gravy, and apple pie for dessert.

Dr. Harry Feldon was a tall man who appeared to be in his early sixties but was quite vigorous. His subject, as Homer McGillivray had said, was the planned clinic and Health Maintenance Organization of which it would be a part.

Although Feldon spoke briskly and was in full possession of the facts, there was nothing new to Mark in his presentation—except that the Hill-Burton grant had finally come through from the federal government and construction on the new hospital was scheduled to begin in a few weeks.

"I've invited Dr. Feldon to stop by the house for a little while after the meeting, Mark," said Homer McGillivray as they were leaving. "He graduated from Lakeview years ago, but you could still have a great deal in common."

Feldon proved to be intelligent and gracious, very much the same sort of man—and doctor—that Homer McGillivray was. The talk was pleasant and noncommittal until he said, "I talked to Andrew Harkness in Gulf City about you last night, Dr. Harrison. He and I were classmates at Lakeview."

"I became very fond of Dr. Harkness while I was with the Clinic," said Mark.

"I know," said Feldon, "that's why I called him to ask about you."

"Did he tell you about the trouble I'm in?"

"And the railroading you got from McIntosh," said Feldon.

"I don't blame McIntosh or the committee anymore for what happened to me," Mark said quickly. "John Carr has helped me see that I was headed for trouble before I left Lakeview, so I can hardly blame them."

"I also talked to Dr. Aldo Ramirez in Baltimore, and he confirmed that you were already in danger of burnout," said Feldon.

This time, it was Mark's turn to be startled. "Why would you be interested in me, Doctor?" he asked.

"Now that the government grant will let us start construction on the new hospital, we're looking for highly trained young men to staff it," Feldon explained. "Homer and I have a lot of fishing to do, and we're anxious to get started on it, just as soon as he gets that popliteal artery of his fixed up so he can climb over the rocks in a trout stream."

"I know several young men at Lakeview who would jump at the chance to join a venture like the one you described in your speech tonight," said Mark.

"No doubt," said Feldon. "Actually, though, we've already picked a man for the job of Chief Surgeon."

"He'll be lucky."

"You should know, because you're the one we've picked."

"Me! You must be mistaken, Doctor."

"No, Dr. Harrison. John, Homer, and I all agree that you'll make an excellent choice."

"A surgeon who can't operate because he's disabled?" Mark asked bitterly. "If this is a joke—"

"None of us believes your disability is permanent," Homer McGillivray said quickly.

"With your training and ability, Dr. Harrison," Feldon added, "you can certainly ask, and no doubt get, a position that pays much more than we could offer, at least in the begin—"

"I've already had a taste of that kind of job and look what happened."

"Aren't you a wiser man than you were then?" Homer McGillivray asked.

"Wiser, yes, thanks to John Carr, Alexa, and you, sir," said Mark. "But certainly still badly impaired."

"John Carr tells me most of your recovery is due to your own determination and your having unburdened yourself, so to speak, to others at the Retreat in the same situation," said Feldon. "Don't make up your mind until you've had a chance to think over our proposition, though. You need to consider a lot of things, one of the most important being the fact that living in Peace River won't be as exciting as in Baltimore or Gulf City."

"And considerably less dangerous," said Mark. "It isn't living here that bothers me, Dr. Feldon; I'd be happy to spend the rest of my days in the Peace River valley. The setup you described tonight would be ideal, too, but it wouldn't be fair to you or to the people of the valley who join the HMO to have it headed by a crippled surgeon."

"At least you can start the planning, with the understanding that when you're able to operate again, you'll become head of the Surgical Service at the new hospital."

"When—or if?"

"None of us believes it will be *if*, Doctor," said Feldon. "But if that's the only way we can get things started so we'll have the staff ready for the new clinic when the hospital is finished, we're ready to take you on that basis."

"Don't turn it down out of hand, Mark," said Homer McGillivray. "In the past several weeks, I've come to know you well—as a doctor and, even more important, as a compassionate human being. More than anything else here in the valley, we need that sort of person to sparkplug the entire venture."

"I'll accept on that basis then," Mark agreed.

"Fine," said Feldon. "I'll have our lawyer draw up the contracts for you to sign."

"Anytime," said Mark. "I'm looking forward to helping plan the new hospital and clinic."

"With that worry off my shoulders, I can run over to Birmingham as soon as the Vascular Clinic there can take me and get my game leg fixed," said McGillivray. "Sure taking care of things here, plus the new project, won't be too much for you Mark?"

"I can handle them both while you're gone, sir," said Mark with more confidence than he'd felt in a long time. "As soon as John Carr discharges me from Canyonhead and you're back at work, I'll run up to Duke and Lakeview to survey the possibility of talking a number of young doctors into coming down here for the Peace River Valley Clinic. While I'm at it, I'll try to find a young man who can be Chief Surgeon—"

"When you move up to become administrator of the hospital," Feldon assured him. "But I've got an idea you're going to end up by being both."

"Thanks for the vote of confidence," said Mark. "I wish I was as certain as you are that it's justified."

VI

"The Vascular Clinic at University Hospital in Birmingham called this morning," Alexa told Mark when he came into the hospital the next day for their morning cup of coffee before starting office hours. "They want Uncle Homer there Sunday afternoon so they can operate on Tuesday."

"That's about ten days early, isn't it?"

"Yes. They had a cancellation."

"How does he feel about it?"

"He's anxious to go and get it over with, especially now that you're definitely committed to go with the clinic project."

"How about you?" he asked, trying to hide the disappointment he felt at the prospect of her not being there anymore.

"I can hardly wait for the new hospital to open and start my own duties there as Director of Nursing Services. It's all working out fine."

"Except for one thing. The Chief Surgeon is still a surgeon in name only."

"That's only temporary."

"I wish I was as certain as you are," he told her. "Fortunately, Dr. Feldon and your uncle both want me to be administrator, if not the surgeon, so I can always settle for that. If I'd gone with the Veteran's Administration or even an insurance company, when my period at Canyonhead and the probation is ended, my duties would still have been mainly administrative."

"Do you think you'd be happy here in Peace River simply as the head of the new hospital?"

He shrugged. "Probably as much as I could be anywhere else under the circumstances. Besides, I'll be near you."

"That's going to create a somewhat awkward situation, don't you think? Suppose I decide to marry someone else?"

He smiled bleakly. "Then I'll wish you well, and fold my tent like the proverbial Arab and steal away. Let's get to work."

Shortly before five that afternoon, they had an unexpected patient. Homer McGillivray had formed the habit of chopping wood for the cottage fireplace since he'd had to give up any walking exercises because of the pain in his right leg. He came into the hospital Emergency Room a little after five, as Mark was getting ready to drive back to Canyonhead, holding a towel against the back of his right leg above the knee.

"Glad you're still here, Mark," he said. "My ax struck a spike somebody must have driven in the tree a long time ago and glanced off. It hit the back of my leg a pretty hard glancing blow and hurt like hell at the time but apparently only scraped the skin enough to start it bleeding. Sehoy wasn't at home, so I just picked up a towel and stuck it against the wound before coming over here."

"That ax more than scraped the skin," Mark reported when he removed the temporary bandage. "You've got a shallow laceration close to six inches long. I'll infiltrate with Novocain so I can clean up the wound and suture it. Have you had a tetanus toxoid shot lately?"

"About a year ago, when the hook of a trout fly stuck in my scalp," said the old doctor.

"All you'll need then is a booster shot. Alexa can give it to you while I'm closing the wound."

The whole procedure took less than half an hour. At the end, Mark put a dressing in place over the wound and Alexa taped it securely.

"Better lay off chopping wood again until you come back from Birmingham," he advised, "or else the surgeon who operates on that leg won't be able to find a clear place to put his incision."

"I still wish you were doing the surgery, my boy," said McGillivray. "Alexa told me how you connected those tiny little arteries together and saved that woman's kidney."

"That was in another life, one I never want to go back to. Try to make him stay quiet tonight, Alexa. We don't want anything to interfere with that engagement he has at the Vascular Clinic in Birmingham."

Sven was just coming in from his afternoon run when Mark parked his old Buick before the cottage. "You were late, so I figured you'd been held up down in the valley and went on and ran," the psychiatrist told him.

"I had an emergency. Dr. McGillivray was cutting wood and the ax glanced off a spike and hit his leg."

"Couldn't that be serious with his circulatory condition as poor as it is?"

"It was only a superficial wound, and besides, he's going to the Vascular Clinic in Birmingham next week to have a new Dacron artery put in to replace the pipestem he's got behind his right knee now. Alexa is going to try to keep him quiet."

"They have a fine group there—one of the best in the country," said Sven. "John was telling me the good news that you're going to be the Chief Surgeon of the Valley Clinic when the new hospital is built."

"Chief Surgeon or Chief Administrator. Either way, I guess I'm lucky to have a job to go to once I've finished my term of penal servitude here."

"You'll be back in harness and using the scalpel like Lancelot handled his sword long before then," Sven assured him. "Emotional blocks like yours are nearly always temporary."

"Nearly?"

"There are no one-hundred-percent cures in medicine, Mark; you know that as well as I do. Your psyche has only been wounded a little by overwork and hard luck; when it decides to come back, things will start to happen in a rush. Coming to the rap session tonight?"

"I guess so. Right now, I'm feeling pretty low."

"That's the very time you need to share your troubles with others the most," the psychiatrist assured him. "I'll see you at dinner."

As it happened, however, there was to be no rap session for

Mark that night. He was finishing a dinner for which he felt no appetite when John Carr came into the dining room and sought him out at the table where he was eating with several other patients.

"Alexa just called, Mark," he said. "Uncle Homer is in trouble."

"The wound in his leg must be bleeding—"

"I don't know. She was almost hysterical and that isn't like Alexa, so I didn't waste any time in questioning her. She wants to talk to you right away."

Mark reached Alexa at the hospital in the valley a few minutes later. By that time, she wasn't hysterical, but she was obviously still distraught.

"Get here as fast as you can, Mark," she said the moment the connection was made. "I think Uncle Homer has had an embolus."

"Where?"

"In the right leg, the one you sewed up this afternoon. I can't get a pulse in the anterior tibial artery or the dorsalis pedis. He's in great pain, too, and the leg is as pale as marble."

"He needs to get to the Vascular Clinic in Birmingham right away," Mark told her. "I'm coming down, but you'd better start getting an ambulance from Fort Jackson."

"His leg looks like it might start developing gangrene any minute," she said on a note of desperation. "I don't think there'll be time to take him to Birmingham."

"Pack it in ice to decrease the need of the tissues for oxygen, then," Mark directed. "I'll be there in twenty minutes."

He was there in fifteen and one look at Homer McGillivray's right leg told him Alexa had been correct in her evaluation of the old doctor's circulation. From just above the knee, the leg was obviously receiving almost no arterial supply and therefore less vital oxygen than the tissues needed, a condition that could rapidly result in gangrene and make an emergency amputation necessary. Although conscious, McGillivray was in considerable pain.

"I gave him two hundred milligrams of Demerol, but it hasn't helped much," Alexa volunteered.

"What happened?" Mark asked the old doctor.

"I'd just gone to bed when the pain suddenly started in my calf," said McGillivray. "What do you suppose it is?"

"The blow from the ax that broke the skin on the back of your lower thigh must have damaged the intimal layer of the femoral artery just where it becomes the popliteal," said Mark. "The artery is so superficial there that it's easily injured and a clot probably formed, stopping the flow of blood. With your popliteal artery as narrow as it is just below that area, the clot only had to move a few inches before it blocked the entire circulation to the rest of your leg."

"Does that mean an amputation?" McGillivray asked.

"Amputation is one answer; opening the artery and removing the clot is another."

"Wouldn't that leave the popliteal still as narrow as it was before?" Alexa asked.

Mark took a deep breath before giving the answer, the only one he could in good conscience. "It could be in *worse* condition. You see, getting the embolus out would almost certainly damage the intimal lining of the popliteal artery, too, with the probability that a thrombus would then block it again."

"So the logical treatment is to resect the popliteal artery along with the embolus and replace it with a Dacron implant, isn't it?"

"Yes, but we don't have the equip—"

Alexa interrupted before he could finish what he was saying. "You asked me to bring a loupe and some Dacron tubes from Gulf City," she said. "Before I left, I went by the supply room and picked up everything a skilled vascular surgeon would need to take care of Uncle Homer's leg—just in case something like this happened."

Her emphasis on the words "skilled vascular surgeon" left no doubt of her meaning.

"What I brought includes a large loupe to provide magnification and Dacron replacements for the arteries with the sutures necessary to put them in place," she continued. "With all that equipment, wouldn't you have everything you need to resect the popliteal artery and replace it with the implant?"

"Why—yes," he admitted.

"You're a highly skilled vascular surgeon; I've seen you work and I know you're capable of doing what has to be done. Will you do it?"

Mark hesitated no longer. The moment he'd seen the marble pallor from lack of blood supply in Homer McGillivray's leg and realized that gangrene was impending, he'd known he would be faced with the ultimate challenge to operate.

"I'll try, if you aren't afraid to trust me, Dr. McGillivray," he said.

McGillivray managed to smile even through his pain. "Of course I'd trust you to operate, Mark. It's the only chance I have of keeping my leg, and I'm counting on you to save it for me."

"I've sent for a nurse-anesthetist from Fort Jackson, and we're already setting up the O.R.," said Alexa. "She should be here by the time we're ready for the surgery."

Mark had changed into operating pajamas and was tying the strings of his mask before starting to scrub, when doubt of his own ability to operate—the thing he'd been fighting since before he left Gulf City—struck him once again. Cold sweat broke out on his body and the fingers tying the mask were suddenly unable to handle the simple knots.

He couldn't possibly succeed in operating on Homer McGillivray's leg in such a state, he realized, and in the same instant knew the answer. He'd seen it waiting on a medicine cart in the hall just outside the door to the scrub room when he'd come in to change—a rack of Demerol ampules and, beside them, a packet of sterile hypodermic syringes with needles attached, held together by a rubber band.

Only seconds were required to step out into the corridor and make sure no one was watching. Alexa, he knew, was directing the final preparations in the O.R. before she came in to scrub with him as his assistant, giving him a few minutes to spare. With fingers that still trembled, he seized a syringe in its sealed paper container and plucked an ampule of the powerful narcotic from the medicines on the cart. Hurrying back to the scrub room, he quickly stripped away the covering that kept syringe and needle sterile and broke off the top of the ampule containing the drug.

The pronounced tremor of his hands and the hurry of getting the injection ready before Alexa came into the scrub room made it difficult for him to get the needle into the ampule. When he finally plunged it through the rubber cap and sucked up two hundred milligrams of Demerol, the ampule dropped from nerveless fingers and, in scrambling to get it, he also dropped the syringe. Fumbling on the floor for it, he was acutely conscious that he had been in almost exactly a similar situation once before, the night when he and Claire had gone to the hotel on Mobile Bay for the weekend she had promised him after returning from Los Angeles. This time, too, he heard a woman's voice and looked up to see Alexa standing in the doorway between the scrub room and the O.R. looking at him.

"I—I couldn't—" His tongue wouldn't function, unwilling to confess to her that his hands refused to obey his will.

She didn't answer but disappeared immediately through the door leading out into the corridor. Moments later, she came back, carrying an ampule filled with a clear solution and a syringe in a paper cartridge.

"What were you taking?" she asked.

"Demerol," he said. "Two cc.'s."

"Two hundred milligrams, right?"

"Yes."

"I've two cc.'s in this syringe. Pull up your sleeve." When he obeyed, she swabbed the skin briefly with an alcohol sponge, then jammed the needle deep into the muscles, pulling the plunger back to ensure that it had not entered a vein before injecting the contents deep into the deltoid muscle in the upper part of his left arm.

"There," she said, "that should take care of you."

Almost before she removed the needle, he experienced the familiar flooding of warmth and assurance into his brain and into the muscles of his arms, stopping the tremor.

"Thanks," he said, and started scrubbing. She didn't answer, however, but picked up a brush beside him and, pulling up the strings of her mask, began to scrub, too.

VII

Thirty minutes later, Mark sponged away the small amount of bleeding caused by an eight-inch incision into Homer McGillivray's leg back of the right knee. Since the injection, his movements had been swift and certain, with no hesitation. Now, the lower end of the femoral artery and the first portion of its popliteal extension behind the knee were easily visible, a firm cord running through the depths of the incision and, normally, bringing almost the entire blood supply of the lower leg.

Above the place where the femoral artery became the popliteal, the thick-walled vessel was pulsating steadily with the old doctor's heartbeat. Just below the junction with the popliteal, however, the pulsation suddenly stopped, leaving the artery below inert and pale, obviously with no blood passing through it to the rest of the leg.

"The embolus apparently struck almost exactly at the junction of the femoral and the popliteal artery." Mark answered the unspoken question in Alexa's eyes above her mask. "It's blocking the popliteal in its narrowest portion."

"Are you going to remove the embolus?"

"With the artery as narrow as the studies in Birmingham showed it to be, that would be a waste of time," he said. "The simplest thing to do is to remove the popliteal with the embolus inside it and implant a Dacron tube to furnish a continuation of the circulation to the leg. Did you bring a tube about the size of the artery there?"

"I brought several—just in case. They're all sterilized, and you'll only have to choose the right one."

"Good," he said. "Rubber-shod clamp, please."

The powerful instrument, with each of its metal jaws covered by sections of rubber tubing to prevent danger to the blood vessel whose flow it was designed to shut off, came into his hand with an audible snap that any instrument nurse would have been proud of. Clamping the femoral artery at the upper angle of the incision, he left room below it for a cuff to which he would attach the

Dacron substitute vessel, once the blocked artery below it was removed.

"We'll clamp the lower end of the popliteal just above where the anterior tibial comes off," he said.

"What if there's a clot below it?" Alexa asked, as she handed him another rubber-shod clamp.

"Then we'll use a small catheter and suction out the clot before we complete the anastomosis."

With the second rubber-shod clamp, Mark closed its jaws about the lower end of the obstructed artery, and a few swift strokes of the scalpel separated the popliteal from its smaller branches. These were quickly clamped off, and when he lifted the resected portion of the artery damaged by the ax blow from the space behind the knee, the glistening white sheath of the posterior ligaments of the knee joint itself were easily visible.

"Give me a tube about the same size as the femoral artery," he told Alexa.

She handed him a section of Dacron tubing, and placing the implant in the space left by the removal of the popliteal, he prepared to suture the cut upper end to the mouth of the femoral artery just below the rubber-shod clamp that closed its terminus.

"Loupe," he told the circulating nurse, who quickly adjusted the magnifying lens about his forehead. Held in place by a fibrous band, the lens would enlarge the area in which he was going to work about two and a half times.

"Sorry you didn't bring a loupe for yourself," he told Alexa, "but Indians are supposed to have keen sight anyway, aren't they?"

She smiled, the first time since she'd come into the scrub room and had seen him fumbling on the floor for the hypodermic of Demerol. "I can see well enough to catch needles and pull them through."

"Good! I'll tie them, so if anything goes wrong, I'll be the one to blame."

"Nothing's going to go wrong," she said in a tone that was firm with confidence. "I've never seen a better job than this one has been."

Working swiftly and with no hesitation in his movements, Mark completed the anastomosis of the living artery to the artificial one. Some fifteen minutes were required to connect the femoral to the substitute popliteal artery using fine nylon sutures, but when he was finished, the connection appeared to be tight.

"We'll do the one below before we remove the clamp from the femoral and test the anastomoses," he told her.

Moving down to the lower angle of the incision, Mark began to place the delicate but tough nylon sutures there, now connecting the artificial artery to the living one below. With both connections completed, he drew a deep breath before reaching for the upper rubber-shod clamp to remove it. When he loosened its jaws, the fabric tube that now lay in the depths of the surgical wound began to pulsate in rhythm with the beat of Homer McGillivray's heart.

"You've done it!" Alexa cried, her eyes shining.

"Not so fast," said Mark. "We still don't know about the vessels below the implant."

"The anastomoses are holding," she said. "There's no leakage, even though the full pressure of the blood flow is against the suture lines now."

"We'll know the rest in a moment." Mark reached for the second clamp, the removal of which would allow blood to flow into the arterial branches below where the injury had been and, hopefully, bring life-giving oxygen to tissues deprived dangerously of it during the period of almost three hours since the embolus had blocked the normal popliteal artery behind the knee.

Loosening the clamp, he watched while the artery below the suture lines began to pulsate, faintly at first, then more strongly when the full force of the pressure in the circulatory system forced it open again after the prolonged state of collapse. When there was no diminution in the pulsation that would have indicated a further block farther away from the heart beyond the new connection, he felt a sense of elation flood through him.

"We can close now," he said.

As he started to place the closing sutures, Mark experienced a sudden emptiness. The sense of elation he'd felt at almost certainly saving Homer McGillivray's leg was now almost nullified by the reminder of the price he'd paid for being allowed to do it. Nothing less than the loss of everything he'd gained in the past few months with the help of John Carr, Sven, and the many friends—fellow victims of burnout—who had cured themselves at Canyonhead. For since he'd needed a hypodermic injection before regaining his surgical skill for a period long enough to save a life, everything he had accomplished in the past few months now appeared to have been lost.

Sensing the letdown he was feeling, Alexa said quietly, "You must be exhausted. I'll close the skin if you'd like me to."

"Please do." Mark stepped back from the table and peeled off the rubber gloves that covered his hands. "Better start him on I.V. heparin, just in case any of the distal arteries might have small clots inside them."

"Right," she said. "I'll take care of it."

VIII

Mark was sitting in the scrub room with his head between his hands when Alexa came in. He felt no doubt that the sacrifice of the strength he'd developed against the temptation to use a narcotic as a crutch was worth what he'd accomplished, but wondered whether he'd ever have the courage to pull himself up from the depths again.

"I felt the dorsalis pedis and posterior tibial pulses after I put on the dressing," Alexa said as she began to pull off the operating gown she'd been wearing during the surgery. "They're fully as strong as they are in the other leg."

"I'm not surprised. The flow through the implant appeared to be adequate."

"Are you regretting the price you paid for being granted the skills you once thought you'd lost so you could save Uncle Homer's leg?" she asked.

"A little, I suppose," he admitted. "But I'd do it again for him and for the friends I've made here. What I'm wondering now is whether I'll ever have the strength to come off drugs again."

"You're still off."

"But you injected—"

"Not Demerol." Reaching into the wastebasket where she'd dropped the ampule from which he'd seen her fill the syringe before injecting its contents into his arm, she took up the small glass container and handed it to him.

"Look at this," she said.

Even though he could hardly believe the evidence of his own eyes, he could not fail to see the words written on the ampule: STERILE DISTILLED WATER, PYROGEN FREE.

"But—" He stopped, then went on, "How could you take that chance?"

"I had to, if you were ever again to be the whole man I love."

He came up from the stool where he'd been sitting and took her in his arms. "I still don't understand how you had the courage to take the risk."

"Indians, especially princesses, are very special people—as you once told me." Her eyes were shining now. "But if you ever call me your squaw, I'll scalp you."

Frank G. Slaughter, one of the most popular and prolific authors of our time, has written more than fifty novels, many drawn from his successful medical practice, including the bestselling *Doctors' Wives* and *Plague Ship*. Dr. Slaughter received his M.D. from Johns Hopkins University at the age of twenty-two and was later commanding officer of a hospital ship during World War II. He lives in Jacksonville, Florida.